Murder
at
Bridge

By Anne Austin

Originally published in 1931

Murder at Bridge

© 2012 Resurrected Press
www.ResurrectedPress.com

Published by Intrepid Ink, LLC

Intrepid Ink, LLC provides full publishing services to authors of fiction and non-fiction books, eBooks and websites. From editing to formatting, to publishing, to marketing, Intrepid Ink gets your creative works into the hands of the people who want to read them.
Find out more at www.IntrepidInk.com.

ISBN 13: 978-1-937022-55-6

Printed in the United States of America

RESURRECTED PRESS CLASSIC MYSTERY CATALOGUE

Journeys into Mystery
Travel and Mystery in a More Elegant Time

The Edwardian Detectives
Literary Sleuths of the Edwardian Era

Gems of Mystery
Lost Jewels from a More Elegant Age

Anne Austin
One Drop of Blood
The Black Pigeon
Murder at Bridge

E. C. Bentley
Trent's Last Case: The Woman in Black

Ernest Bramah
Max Carrados Resurrected:
The Detective Stories of Max Carrados

Agatha Christie
The Secret Adversary
The Mysterious Affair at Styles

Octavus Roy Cohen
Midnight

Freeman Wills Croft
The Ponson Case
The Pit Prop Syndicate

J. S. Fletcher
The Herapath Property
The Rayner-Slade Amalgamation
The Chestermarke Instinct
The Paradise Mystery
Dead Men's Money
The Middle of Things
Ravensdene Court
Scarhaven Keep
The Orange-Yellow Diamond
The Middle Temple Murder
The Tallyrand Maxim
The Borough Treasurer
In the Mayor's Parlour
The Saftey Pin

R. Austin Freeman
The Mystery of 31 New Inn from the Dr. Thorndyke
Series
John Thorndyke's Cases from the Dr. Thorndyke
Series
The Red Thumb Mark from The Dr. Thorndyke Series
The Eye of Osiris from The Dr. Thorndyke Series
A Silent Witness from the Dr. John Thorndyke Series
The Cat's Eye from the Dr. John Thorndyke Series
Helen Vardon's Confession: A Dr. John Thorndyke
Story
As a Thief in the Night: A Dr. John Thorndyke Story
Mr. Pottermack's Oversight: A Dr. John Thorndyke
Story
Dr. Thorndyke Intervenes: A Dr. John Thorndyke
Story
The Singing Bone: The Adventures of Dr. Thorndyke
The Stoneware Monkey: A Dr. John Thorndyke Story
The Great Portrait Mystery, and Other Stories: A
Collection of Dr. John Thorndyke and Other Stories
The Penrose Mystery: A Dr. John Thorndyke Story
The Uttermost Farthing: A Savant's Vendetta

Sir William Magnay
The Hunt Ball Mystery

Mabel and Paul Thorne
The Sheridan Road Mystery

Louis Tracy
The Strange Case of Mortimer Fenley
The Albert Gate Mystery
The Bartlett Mystery
The Postmaster's Daughter
The House of Peril
The Sandling Case: What Would You Have Done?

Charles Edmonds Walk
The Paternoster Ruby

John R. Watson
The Mystery of the Downs
The Hampstead Mystery

Edgar Wallace
The Daffodil Mystery
The Crimson Circle

Carolyn Wells
Vicky Van
The Man Who Fell Through the Earth
In the Onyx Lobby
Raspberry Jam
The Clue
The Room with the Tassels
The Vanishing of Betty Varian
The Mystery Girl
The White Alley
The Curved Blades
Anybody but Anne
The Bride of a Moment

Faulkner's Folly
The Diamond Pin
The Gold Bag
The Mystery of the Sycamore
The Come Back

Raoul Whitfield
Death in a Bowl

And much more!
Visit ResurrectedPress.com
for our complete catalogue

FOREWORD

Anne Austin started out her literary career writing romance novels about young women overcoming adversity and finding true love, but within a few years turned to the mystery genre as more rewarding or at least more marketable. Her first mystery was *The Black Pigeon*. She then began writing a series of novels featuring James "Bonnie" Dundee that spanned the decade of the 30's. Dundee was a Special Investigator for the Office of the District Attorney in the town of Hamilton.

The series began with *The Avenging Parrot* in 1930, continued on with *Murder Backstairs, Murder at Bridge, One Drop of Blood* before ending with *Murdered But Not Dead* in 1939. Several of the early novels also appeared in serial format in various newspapers.

The exact location of Hamilton is never specified. It is identified only as a small midwestern city. However, certain clues such as the fact that it is within a six hour train ride of Chicago would most likely place it in Indiana, Illinois, Ohio or possibly Michigan. It has many of the trappings of similar sized municipalities, a country club, several mivie theaters, a sanitarium.

Whereever Hamilton is located it would seem that, like St. Mary Mead, the home of Agatha Christie's Jane Marple, it is, as one critic phrased it "the murder capitol of the nation." Not only do corpses appear with regularity in the books of the series, but the crime is so common that the police department of Hamilton, despite its small size, has a dedicated Homicide department headed by a police captain.

Like the mysteries of other early American women mystery writers such as Mary Roberts Rinehart and the later works of Carolyn Wells, the Hamilton stories take place among the upper middle class, not the world of extreme wealth that so often figured in mysteries around the turn of the century. There are no fabulous gems or great inheritances. It is a world of the cream of society of a small city. A world of country club lunches, bridge parties, local theater groups, followed by cocktails in the parlor, where everybody knows and is known by everyone else.

It was a different America than what had gone before and that is reflected in the stories' tone. The novels were written during the depression and the first few were written before the repeal of prohibition. Gangsters, while a product of the not so distance big cities might not be in evidence, but they were on everyone's mind. While life was still good for those who had money, the possibility of failure was ever present. An example of this is the failed real estate development where the murder takes place, a development with only one house and the short length of sidewalk in front of it.

It is also a world that is somewhat grittier and more realistic than that of Austin's predecessors. Despite the fact that the early books in the series appeared as serials in family newspapers, the pasts of at least some of the characters are a bit sordid. Petty jealousies and small time greed come into play as motives rather than grand schemes and thefts of millions. It should be noted that these novels were published in exactly the same timeframe as those of Dashiell Hammett.

Anne Austin is not well known today, a product of a decade eighty years in the past. Yet her mysteries are not without their charm and interest. It is therefore with pleasure that Resurrected Press brings you this new edition of *Murder at Bridge*.

About the Author

Born in 1895, Anne Austin began by writing romance novels about young women in the mid 1920's but soon turned her talents to producing a string of mysteries through the 1930's, some of which appeared as serials in newspapers.. Many of these mysteries feature as the detective "Bonnie" Dundee, Special Investigator for the District Attorney, including *Murder Backstairs*, *The Avenging Parrot*, *Murder at Bridge*, and *One Drop of Blood*. Several of her mysteries were translated into French, including *Le Pigeon Noir* and *Le Crime Parfume*. Despite her success as a novelist, Anne Austin disappears from the public record after the 1930's.

Greg Fowlkes
Editor-In-Chief
Resurrected Press
www.ResurrectedPress.com

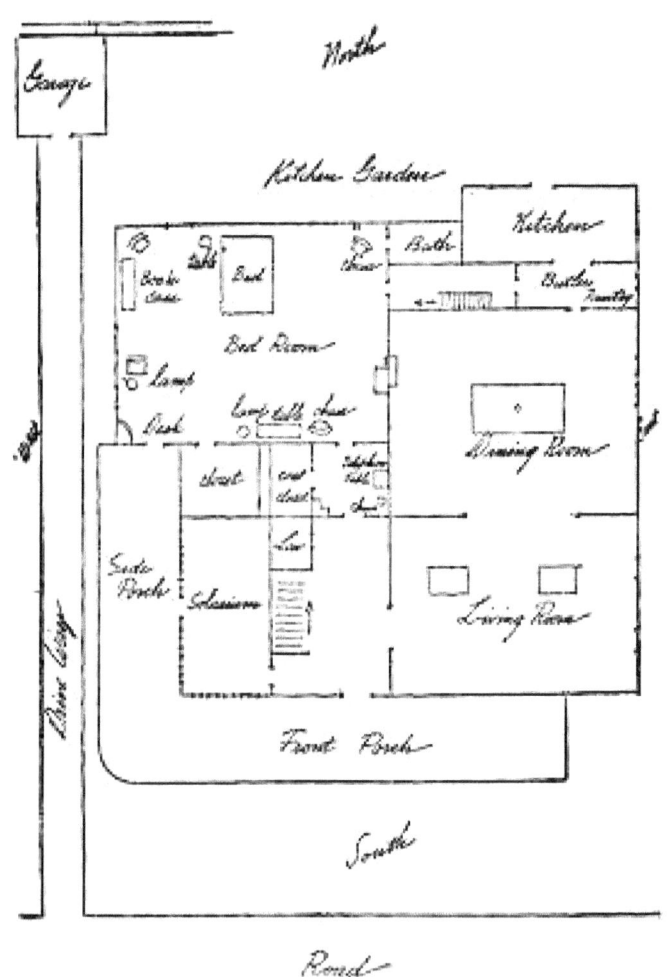

Ground-floor plan of Nita Selim's house in Primrose Meadows, showing the bedroom in which the murder was committed.

CHAPTER ONE

Bonnie Dundee stretched out a long and rather fine pair of legs, regarding the pattern of his dark-blue socks with distinct satisfaction; then he rested his black head against the rich upholstery of an armchair not at all intended for his use.

His cheerful blue eyes turned at last—but not too long a last—to the small, upright figure seated at a typewriter desk in the corner of the office.

"Good morning, Penny," he called out lazily, and good-humoredly waited for the storm to break.

"Miss Crain—to *you*!" The flying fingers did not stop an instant, but Dundee noticed with glee that the slim back stiffened even more rigidly and that there was a decided toss of the brown bobbed head.

"But Penny is so much more like you," Dundee protested, unruffled. "And why should I be forced always to think of you as a long-legged bird, when even our mutual boss, District Attorney William S. Sanderson, has the privilege of calling you what you are—a bright and shining new penny?"

"I've known Bill Sanderson since I was born," the unseen lips informed him truculently, even as the unseen fingers continued their fiercely staccato typing.

"Ah! That explains a lot!" Dundee conceded handsomely. "I just wondered, amidst all this bonhommie of 'Bill' and 'Penny,' why I—"

"I only call Mr. Sanderson 'Bill' when I forget!" the small creature defended herself sharply. "Goodness knows I *try* to be an efficient private secretary! And I could be a lot more efficient if lazy strangers didn't plump themselves down in our best visitors' chair, and try to flirt with me. I don't flirt! Do you hear?—*I don't flirt with anybody!*"

"Flirt with you, you funny little Penny?" Dundee's voice was a little sad, the voice of a man who finds himself grievously misunderstood. "I only want you to like me, if you can, and be a little nice to me, for after all I—"

"Oh, I know!" Penny Crain jerked the finished letter from her typewriter and spun about on her narrow-backed swivel chair to face him. "I know you are 'Mr. James F. Dundee, Special Investigator attached to the office of the District Attorney,' and that you have a right to drive me crazy if you want to."

"*Crazy?*" Dundee was genuinely amazed, contrite. "I beg your pardon most humbly, Miss Crain. I'll go back to my cell—"

"Your office is almost as big and nice as this one," Penny retorted, but her sharp, bright brown eyes—really almost the color of a new penny—softened until they took on a velvety depth.

Dundee did not fail to notice the softening, nor did the little heart-shaped face, with its low widow's-peak, its straight, short nose, and its pointed little chin, made almost childish by the deep cleft which cut through its obvious effort to look mature and determined, fail to please him any more acutely than on the other days of the one short week he had been privileged at intervals to gaze upon it.

"But the files, and—other things—are in this office," he told her, his blue eyes twinkling happily once more.

"Don't you *dare* touch my files again!" Penny cried, springing to her feet and running toward the wall which was completely concealed by drawers, cabinets and shelves, filled with the records of which she was the proud custodian. "That's why I said just now that you were driving me crazy. Thursday you took a whole folder of correspondence out of the letter files and put it back under the wrong initial. I had to hunt for it for two hours, with Bill—I mean, Mr. Sanderson—gnawing his nails with impatience. He thought I had filed it wrong, and you might have made me lose my job."

Unconsciously her slightly husky contralto voice had sunk lower and trembled audibly.

"I'm awfully sorry. I shan't touch your files again, Miss Crain."

"Oh—go on and call me Penny," she conceded impatiently. "What do you want now?... And you can get anything you need out of the files if you'll just put the folder in the bottom drawer of my desk, so that I can file it myself—correctly!"

"Thank you, Penny," Bonnie Dundee said gravely. "I'd like awfully to have the complete transcript of 'The State versus Maginty.' Mr. Sanderson is determined to get a conviction where our former district attorney most ingloriously failed. The new trial comes up in two weeks, and he wants me to try to uncover a missing link of evidence."

"I know," she nodded, and stretched her short, slender body to pull down the two heavy volumes he required.

Without a by-your-leave, Special Investigator Dundee resumed his comfortable seat, and laid the first of the volumes open upon his knees. But he did not seem to take a great deal of interest in the impanelling of jurors in the case of one Rufus Maginty, who had won the temporary triumph of a "hung jury" under the handling of the state's case by District Attorney Sherwood, deposed in November's election.

Rather, his eyes followed the small, brisk figure of Miss Penelope Crain, as it moved about the room, and his ears listened to the somehow charming though emphatic tapping of her French heels.... French heels! Hadn't she been wearing sensible, Cuban-heeled Oxfords all other days of this first week of his "attachment" to the district attorney's office?... Cunning little thing, for all her thorniness and her sharpness with him, which he now saw that he had deserved.... Pretty, too.... Damned pretty!... What color was that dress of hers?... Ummm, let's see ... Chartreuse, didn't they call it? Chartreuse with big brown dots in it. Bet it was sleeveless under that short little jacket of golden-brown chiffon velvet.... By Jove—and Dundee lapsed into one of the Englishisms he had picked up during his six months' work in England as a tyro in the records department of Scotland Yard, before he had come to Hamilton to make a humble beginning as a cub detective on the Homicide Squad—yes, by Jove, she was all dressed up, for some reason or other.

"Of course! Because it's Saturday and you have the afternoon off!" Dundee finished his reverie aloud, to the astonishment of the small person trying to reach a file drawer just a little too high for her. "I mean," he hastened to explain, "that I've just noticed how beautiful your costume is, and found a reason for it."

There was sudden color in the creamy face. The French heels tapped an angry progress across the big office, and Penny sat down abruptly in her swivel chair, reached across the immaculate desk, snatched up a morning paper and tossed it, without a glance, in the general direction of her tormentor.

"Page three, column two, first item," she informed him ungraciously, and then began to search with a funny sort of desperation for more work to consume her extraordinary energy.

Bonnie Dundee grinned indulgently as he opened *The Hamilton Morning News* and turned to the specified page and column.

"Ah! My old friend, the 'society editress,' in her very best style," he commented as he began to read aloud:

"'Mrs. Juanita Selim, new and charming member, is entertaining the Forsyte Alumnae Bridge Club this afternoon, luncheon to be served at the exclusive new Breakaway Inn on Sheridan Road—'"

"I've read it—and I'm busy, so shut up!" Penny commanded, as she gathered up pencils to sharpen.

Quite meekly, Bonnie Dundee subsided into silent perusal of an item he was sure could have no possible interest for himself, in either a personal or professional capacity, unless Penny's name was in it somewhere:

"—after which the jolly party of young matrons and maids will adjourn to Mrs. Selim's delightful home in the Primrose Meadows Addition." He chuckled, and dared to interrupt the high importance of pointing-up pencils. "I say, that's funny, isn't it?... 'Primrose Meadows Addition'!"

"I don't think it's funny," Penny retorted coldly. "It so happens that my mother named it, that my father went into bankruptcy trying to make a go of it, and that 'Mrs. Selim's delightful home' was built to be our home, and in which we were fortunate enough to live only two months before the crash came."

"Oh!" Dundee groaned. "Penny, Penny! I'm dreadfully sorry."

"Shut up!" she ordered, but her voice was huskier than ever with tears.

Dundee's now thoroughly interested eyes raced down the absurdly written paragraphs:

"Although not an alumna of that famous and select school for girls, Forsyte-on-the-Hudson, graduation from which places any Hamilton girl in the very inner circle of Hamilton society, Mrs. Selim has been closely identified with the school, having for the past two years directed and staged Forsyte's annual play which ushers in the Easter vacation.

"Indeed it was Mrs. Selim's remarkable success with this year's play which caused Mrs. Peter Dunlap, long interested in a Little Theater for Hamilton, to induce the beautiful and charming young directress to come to Hamilton with her. Plans for the Little Theater are growing apace, and it is safe to conjecture that not all the conversation flying thick and fast about 'Nita's' bridge tables this afternoon will be concerned with contract 'conventions,' scores, and finesses which failed.

"Lovely 'Nita' was elected to membership a fortnight ago, when a vacancy occurred, due to the resignation of Miss Alice Humphrey, who has gone abroad for a year's study in the Sorbonne. The two-table club now includes: Mesdames Hugo Marshall, Tracey A. Miles, Peter Dunlap, John C. Drake, Juanita Selim, and Misses Polly Beale, Janet Raymond, and Penelope Crain."

Dundee lowered the paper and stared at the profile of District Attorney Sanderson's private secretary. So she was a "society girl," a "Forsyte" girl! Was that the reason, perhaps, why she had been so thorny with him, a mere "dick"? Well, he wasn't just a dick any longer. He was a Special Investigator ... A society girl, playing at work....

But there was more, and he read on: "As is well known, the 'girls' have their 'hen-fight' bridge-luncheon every Saturday afternoon from the first of October to the first of June, and a bridge-dinner, in which mere men are graciously included, every other Wednesday evening during the season. Mr. and Mrs. Tracey A. Miles are scheduled as next Wednesday's host and hostess."

"I take off my hat to your 'society editress'," Dundee commented with false cheerfulness, when he had laid the paper back upon Penny's desk. "She makes half a column of this one item in what must be a meager Saturday bunch of 'Society Notes,' then writes it all over again, in the past tense, for an equally meager Monday column.... Like bridge, Miss Crain?"

Penny snatched up the paper and crushed it into her wastebasket. "I do! And I like my old friends, even if I am not able, financially, to keep up with them.... If that's why you've suddenly decided to stop being—comrades—"

"Please forgive me again, Penny," he begged gently.

"I was born into that crowd, and I still belong to it, because all of them are my real friends, but get this into your thick Scotch-Irish head, Mr. Dundee—I'm working because I have to, and—and because I love it, too, and because I want to earn enough before I'm many years older to give Mother some of the things she's missing so dreadfully since—since my father failed and—and ran away."

"Ran away?" Dundee echoed incredulously. How could any man desert a daughter like this!

"Yes! Ran away!" she repeated fiercely. "I might as well tell you myself. Plenty of others will be willing to, as soon as they know you are—my friend.... As I told you, my father"—her voice broke—"my father went bankrupt, but before the courts knew it he had sent some securities to a—to a *woman* in New York, and when he—left us, he went to her, because he left Mother a note saying so. His defrauded creditors here have tried to—to catch him, but they haven't—yet—"

Very gently Bonnie Dundee took the small hand that was distractedly rumpling the brown waves which swept back from the widow's-peak. It lay fluttering in his bigger palm for a moment, then snatched itself away.

"I won't have you feeling sorry for me!" she cried angrily.

"Who owns your—the Primrose Meadows house now?—Mrs. Selim?" he asked.

"The 'lovely Nita'?" Her voice was scornful. "No. She rents it from Judge Hugo Marshall—or is supposed to pay him rent," she added with a trace of malice. "Hugo is an old darling, but he is fearfully weak where pretty women are concerned. Nita Selim had known Hugo in New York—somehow—and as soon as Lois—Mrs. Dunlap, I mean—had got Nita off the train, the stranger in our midst hied herself to Hugo's office and he's been tagging after her ever since.... Though most of the men in our crowd are as bad as or worse than poor old Hugo. How Karen keeps on looking so blissfully happy—"

"Karen?" Dundee interrupted.

"Mrs. Hugo Marshall," she explained impatiently. "Karen Plummer made her debut a year ago this last winter—a darling of a girl. Judge Marshall—retired

judge, you know—had been proposing to the prettiest girl
in each season's crop of debs for the last twenty years,
and Hugo must have been the most nonplussed 'perennial
bachelor' who ever led a grand march when Karen
snapped him up.... Loved him—actually! And it seems to
have worked out marvelously.... A baby boy three months
old," she concluded in her laconic style. Then, ashamed; "I
don't know why I'm gossiping like this!"

"Because you can't find another blessed scrap of work
to do, you little efficiency fiend," Dundee laughed, "Come
on! Gossip some more. My Maginty case will wait till
afternoon, to be mulled over while you're losing your
hard-earned salary at bridge with rich women."

"We don't play for high stakes," she corrected him.
"Just a twentieth of a cent a point, though contract can
run into money even at that. The winnings all go to the
Forsyte Scholarship Fund. On Wednesday evenings the
crowd plays for higher stakes—a tenth—and winners
keepers. Therefore I can't afford to go, unless I sink so
low as to let my escort pay my losses—which I sometimes
do," she confessed, her brown head low for a moment.

"Is this Mrs. Peter Dunlap a deep-bosomed club
woman, who starts Movements?" he asked, more to bring
her out of her depression than anything else. "Bigger and
Better Babies Movements, and Homes for Fallen Girls,
and Little Theater Movements?"

The brown head flung itself up sharply, and the
brown eyes hardened into bright pennies again. "Lois
Dunlap is the sweetest, finest, most *comfortable* woman
in Hamilton, and I adore her—as does everyone else,
Peter Dunlap hardly more than the rest of us. She *is*
interested in a Little Theater for Hamilton, but she won't
manage it. That's why she got hold of Nita Selim. Lois
will simply put up barrels of money, without missing
them, and give a grand job to a little Broadway gold-
digger. Funny thing is, she really delights in Nita. Thinks
she's sweet and has never had a real chance."

"And what do you think?" Dundee asked softly.

"Oh—I suppose I'm a cat, but I can see through her so clearly. Not that she's bad; she's simply an opportunist. She's awfully sweet and deferential and 'frank' with women, but with men—well, she simply tucks her head so that her shoulder-length black curls fall forward enchantingly, gives them one wistful smile out of her big eyes that are like black pansies and—the clink of slave chains!... Now go on and think I'm catty, which I suppose I am!"

Bonnie Dundee grinned at her reassuringly. Not for him to explain that practically all women and many men found themselves "gossiping" when he led them on adroitly, for reasons of his own. Which of course helped make him the excellent detective he was.

"So all the men in your crowd have fallen for Nita Selim, have they?"

"Practically all, in varying degrees, except Peter Dunlap, who has never looked at another woman since he was lucky enough to get Lois, and Clive Hammond, who's engaged to Polly Beale," Penny answered reluctantly, her color high.

"Including *your* young man?"

"I haven't a 'young man,' in the sense of being engaged," Penny retorted, then added honestly: "I *have* been letting Ralph Hammond—that's Clive's brother, you know—take me about a good deal.... Ralph and Clive have plenty of money," she defended herself hastily. "They are architects, Clive being the head of the firm and Ralph, who hasn't been out of college so very long, a junior partner. It was the Hammond firm that drew up the plans for Dad's—I mean, my father's—Primrose Meadows Addition houses. He had our house built as a sort of show-place, you know, so that prospective builders out there could see how artistic a home could be put up for a moderate sum of money. But he didn't quite finish even that—left half the gabled top story unfinished, and Nita has been teasing Hugo to finish it up for her. It looks," she added with a shrug, "as if Nita will get what she wants—as usual."

"And Ralph has acquired a set of slave chains?" Dundee suggested, with just the slightest note of sympathy.

"*And how!*" Penny assured him, grimly. "A simile as out-of-date as my clothes are going to be if I don't get some new ones soon. Not that the crowd minds what I wear," she added loyally. "I could dress up in a window drape—"

"And be just as charming as you are in that grand new party dress you have on now," Dundee finished for her gallantly.

"*New!*" Penny snorted and turned back to her desk in a futile effort to find something left undone.

Dundee ignored the rebuff. "How many suckers—I mean, how many gentlemen with moderate incomes actually built in Primrose Meadows?"

"You are inquisitive, aren't you?... None! Our house, or rather the one Nita Selim is living in now, is the only house on what used to be a big farm.... Why?"

"I was just wondering," Dundee said softly, almost absent-mindedly, "why the 'lovely Nita' chose so isolated a place in which to live, when Hamilton has rather a large number of 'For Rent' signs out just now.... By the way, know what time it is now?... Twenty to one! Get your hat on, young woman. I'm going to drive you out to Breakaway Inn."

"You're not! I'm going to take a bus. One runs from the Square right past the Inn," she told him firmly.

And just as firmly Dundee escorted her out of the almost deserted, rather dirty old courthouse to where his brand-new sports roadster—bought "on time"—was awaiting them in the parking space devoted to the motors of those who officially served Hamilton County.

"I know why you want to drive me out to the Inn," Penny told him suddenly, as the proud owner maneuvered his car through Saturday noon traffic. "You want to see Nita Selim. Clank! Clank! I can hear the padlocks snapping on the slave chains right now."

"Meow!" Dundee retorted, then grinned down at her with as much comradely affection as if they had been friends for years instead of for a couple of hours. "Is Nita very small?" he added.

"Little enough to tuck herself under the arm of a man a lot shorter than you," Penny assured him with curious vehemence. "And if Penelope Crain is no mean prophet, that's exactly what she'll do within five minutes after she meets you—just as she is wistfully inviting you to join the other men for the cocktail party which is scheduled to break up the bridge game at 5:30. Then, of course, you'll be urged to join us all at the dinner-dance at the Country Club tonight."

"Will she?" Dundee pretended to be vastly intrigued, which caused the remainder of the drive to be a rather silent one, due to Penny's unresponsiveness.

Breakaway Inn was intensely Spanish in architecture and transplanted shrubbery, but its stucco walls were of a rather more violent raspberry color than is considered quite esthetic in Spain or Mexico.

"There's Lois Dunlap's car just driving up," Penny cried, her face softening with the adoration she had freely professed for her friend. But it clouded again almost instantly. "And Nita Selim. I suppose Nita was a little ashamed to drive up in her own Ford coupe."

As Dundee helped his new friend to alight his eyes were upon the two women being assisted by a uniformed chauffeur from Lois Dunlap's limousine.

In a moment the four were a laughing, exclamatory group.

"Oh, what a tall, grand man you've got yourself, Penny darling!" the tiny, beautiful creature who could only be Mrs. Selim cried out happily. "*May* I meet him?"

"I shouldn't let you," Penny answered frankly, "but I will.... Mrs. Selim, Mr. Dundee.... And Mrs. Dunlap, Mr. Dundee.... How are you, Lois? And Peter and the brats?"

"All well, Penny. Petey's off on a week-end fishing trip, and not one of the brats has measles, scarlet fever or hay fever, thank God," Dundee heard Mrs. Dunlap say in the comfortable, affectionate voice that went with her comfortable, pleasant face and body.... Nice woman!

But his eyes were of necessity upon Nita Selim, for that miniature Venus was, as Penny had predicted, almost tucked under his arm by this time, her black-pansy eyes wide and wistful, her soft black curls falling forward as she coaxed:

"You'll come to the cocktail party at my house at 5:30, won't you, Mr. Dundee?"

"Afraid I can't make it," Dundee smiled down at her. "I'm a busy man, Mrs. Selim.... You see, I'm Special Investigator attached to the District Attorney's office," he explained very deliberately.

"O-o-oh!" Nita Selim breathed. Than, step by step, she withdrew, so that he was no longer submitted to the temptation to put his arm about her too intriguing little body. And as she retreated, Dundee's keen eyes noted a hardening of the black-pansy eyes, the sudden throbbing of a pulse in her very white neck....

"No, don't mind about calling for me," Penny protested a moment later. "Ralph has already volunteered.... Thanks awfully!"

As Dundee backed out of the driveway his last glance was for a very small figure in a brown silk summer coat and palest yellow chiffon frock, slowly rejoining Penelope Crain and Lois Dunlap. What the devil had frightened her so? For she had been almost terrified.... Of course she might be one of those silly women who shudder at the sight of a detective, because they've smuggled in a diamond from Paris or a bottle of Bacardi from Havana....

But long before his car made the distance back to the city Dundee had shrugged off the riddle and was concentrating on all the facts he knew regarding the Maginty case. It was his first real assignment from Sanderson, and he was determined to make good.

Four hours later he was interrupted in his careful reading of the trial of Rufus Maginty by the ringing of the telephone bell. That made four times he had had to snap out the fact that District Attorney Sanderson was playing some well-earned golf on the Country Club links, Dundee reflected angrily, as he picked up the receiver.

But the call was for Dundee himself, and the voice on the other end of the wire was Penny Crain's, although almost unrecognizable.

"Speak more slowly, Penny!" Dundee urged. "What's that again.... Good Lord! You say that Nita Selim...."

After a minute of listening, and a promise of instant obedience, Dundee hung up the receiver.

"My God!" he said slowly, blankly. "Of all things— *murder at bridge!*"

CHAPTER TWO

As Special Investigator Dundee drove through the city of Hamilton at a speed of sixty miles an hour, his way being cleared by traffic policemen warned by the shrill official siren which served him as a horn, he had little time to think connectedly of the fact that Nita Selim had been murdered during a bridge game in her rented home in Primrose Meadows.

Even after the broad sleekness of Sheridan Road stretched before him he could do little more than try to realize the shock which had numbed him.... "Lovely Nita," as the society editor of *The Morning News* had called her, was—*dead*! How, why, he did not know. He had asked no details of Penny Crain.... Funny, thorny little Penny! Loyal little Penny!

"Judge Marshall has telephoned Police Headquarters," she had told him breathlessly over the telephone, "but I made him let me call you as soon as he had hung up. I wanted *our* office to be in on this right from the first."

Beautiful, seductive Nita Selim, almost cuddling under his arm within three minutes of meeting him—*dead*! A vision of her black-pansy eyes, so wide and luminous and wistful as they had looked sideways and upward to his, pleading for him to join her after-bridge cocktail party, nearly made him crash into a lumbering furniture van. Those eyes were luminous no longer, could never again snap the padlocks of slave chains upon any man—as Penny had expressed it.... Dead! And she had been so warmly alive, even as she had retreated from him at his mention of the fact that he was attached to the office of the district attorney as a special investigator. What had she feared then? Was her death a payment for

some recent or long-standing crime? Or had she simply
been withdrawing from contamination with a "flat-
foot"?... No! She had been *afraid*—horribly afraid of some
ulterior purpose behind his innocent courtesy in driving
Penelope Crain to Breakaway Inn.

Well, speculation now was idle, he told himself, as he
noted that his speedometer had dropped from sixty to
thirty in his preoccupation. He speeded again, but was
soon forced to stop and ask his way into Primrose
Meadows. The vague directions of a farmer's son lost him
nearly eight precious minutes, during which his friend,
Captain Strawn of the Homicide Squad, might be
bungling things rather badly. But at last he found the
ornate pair of pillars spanned by the painted legend,
"Primrose Meadows," and drove through them into what
soon became a rutted lane. Almost a quarter of a mile
from the entrance he found the isolated house,
unmistakable because of the line-up of private cars
parked before the short stretch of paved sidewalk, and
the added presence of police cars and motorcycles.

Dundee turned his own car into the driveway leading
from the street along the right side of the house toward
the two-car garage in the rear. Ahead of his roadster were
two other cars, and a glance toward the open garage
showed that a Ford coupe was housed there.

As he was descending Captain Strawn's voice hailed
him from an open window of the room nearest the garage.

"Hello, Bonnie! Been expecting you.... Damnedest
business you ever saw.... There's a door from this room
onto the porch. Hop up and come on in."

Dundee obeyed. Driving in he had noted that a wide
porch, upheld by round white pillars, stretched across the
front of the gabled brick house and extended halfway
along its right side, past a room which was obviously a
solarium, with its continuous windows, gay awnings,
and—visible through the glittering panes—orange-and-
black wicker furniture.

It was easy to swing himself up to the floor of the porch. Strawn flung open the door which led into the back room, remarking with a grin:

"Don't be afraid I'm gumming up any fingerprints. Carraway has already been over the room.... The Selim woman's bedroom," he explained. "The room she was killed in."

"You *have* been on the job," Dundee complimented his former chief.

"Sure!" Strawn acknowledged proudly. "Can't be too quick on our stumps when it's one of these 'high sassiety' murders. Dr. Price will be here any minute now, and my men have been all over the premises, basement to attic. Of course it was an outside job—plain as the nose on your face—and we haven't found a trace of the murderer."

Although Mrs. Selim had taken the house furnished, it was obvious that this big bedroom of hers was not exactly as the Crain family had left it. A little too pretty, a little too aggressively feminine, with its chaise longue heaped with silk and lace pillows, its superfluity of big and little lamps, its bed draped with golden-yellow taffeta, its dressing table—

But he could not let critical eyes linger on the triple-mirrored vanity dresser. For on the bench before it sat a tiny figure, the head bowed so low that some of the black curls had fallen into a large open bowl of powder. She was no longer wearing the brown silk summer coat whose open front had given him a glimpse of pale yellow chiffon.

He saw the dress now, a low-cut, sleeveless, fluffy affair, but he really had eyes only for the brownish-red hole on the left side of the back of the bodice, about halfway between shoulder and waist—a waist so small he could have spanned it with his two hands, including its band of fuchsia velvet ribbon. There also had been a bow of fuchsia velvet ribbon on the lace and straw hat she had swung so charmingly less than five hours ago.

"Shot through the heart, I guess," Strawn commented. "Took a good marksman to find her heart, shooting her through the back.... Funny thing, too. Nobody heard the shot—leastways none of that crowd penned up in the living room will admit they did. They'll all hang together, and lie like sixty to keep us from finding out anything that might point to one of *their* precious bunch! But if a gun with a Maxim silencer *was* used, as it must have been if that whole crew ain't lying, the gunman musta been *good*, because you can't sight with a Maxim screwed onto a rod, you know."

"Have your men found the gun?" Dundee asked.

"Of course not, or I'd know whether it had a Maxim on it or not," Strawn retorted. "My theory is," he added impressively, "that somebody with a grudge against this dame hired a gunman to hang around till he got her dead to rights, then—plop!" and he imitated the soft, thudding sound made by the discharge of a bullet from a gun equipped with a silencer.

"Doesn't it seem rather strange that a professional gunman should have chosen such a time—with men arriving in cars, and the house full of women who might wander into this room at any minute—to bump off his victim?" Dundee asked.

"Well, there ain't no other explanation," Captain Strawn contended. "Outside of the fact that my men have gone over the whole house and grounds without finding the gun, I've got other evidence it was an outside job.... Look!"

Dundee followed the Chief of the Homicide Squad to one of the two windows that looked out upon the driveway. Both were open, since the May day was exceptionally warm, even for the Middle West. The unscreened window from which he obediently leaned was almost directly in line with the vanity dressing-table across the room.

"Look! See how them vines have been torn," Strawn directed, pointing to a rambler rose which hugged the outside frame of the window. "And look hard enough at the flower bed down below and you'll see his footprints....

Of course we've measured them and Cain, as you see, is guarding them till my man comes to make plaster casts of them.... Yes, sir, he hoisted himself up to the window ledge, aimed as best he could, then slipped down and beat it across the meadow."

"Then," Dundee began slowly, "I wonder why Mrs. Selim didn't see that figure crouched in the window, since she must have been powdering her face and looking into the middle of the three mirrors—the one which reflects this very window?"

"How do you know she was powdering her face, not looking for something in a drawer?" Strawn demanded truculently.

"For three reasons," Dundee answered almost apologetically. "First: her powder puff, as I'm sure you noticed, is still clutched in her right hand; second: there is no drawer open, and no drawer *was* open, unless someone has closed it since the murder, whereas on the other hand her powder box *is* open; third: the left side of her face is unevenly coated with powder, while the other is heavily but *evenly* powdered. Therefore I can't see why she didn't scream, or turn around when she heard your gunman clambering up to her window, or even when he had crouched in it. I don't see how she could *help* seeing him!"

"Well—what do *you* think?" Strawn asked sourly, after he had tested the visibility of the window from the dressing-table mirror.

"I'm afraid, Captain Strawn, that there are only two explanations possible. The first, of course, is that Nita Selim was quite deaf or very nearsighted. I happen to know from having met her today—"

"*You* met her today?" Strawn interrupted incredulously.

Dundee explained briefly, then went on: "As I was saying I have good reason to know she was not deaf, but I can't say as to her being nearsighted, except that it is my observation that people who are extremely nearsighted do not have very wide eyes and no creases between the brows. I am fairly sure she did not wear glasses at all, because glasses worn even a few hours a day leave a mark across the nose or show pinched red spots on each side of the bridge of the nose."

"You must have had a good hard look at her," Strawn gibed, his grey eyes twinkling, and his harsh, thin-lipped mouth pulling down at one corner in what he thought was a genial smile.

"I did," Dundee retorted. "Well, conceding that she was neither deaf nor half-blind, she would necessarily have heard and seen her assailant before he shot her."

"What's the other explanation?" Strawn was becoming impatient.

"That the person who killed her was so well known to her, and his—or her—presence in this room so natural a thing that she paid no attention to his or her movements and was concentrating on the job of powdering her very pretty face."

"You mean—one of that gang of society folks in there?" and Strawn jerked a thumb toward the left side of the house.

"Very probably," Dundee agreed.

"But where's the gun?" Strawn argued. "I tell you my men—"

"This was a premeditated murder, of course," Dundee interrupted. "The Maxim silencer—unless they are all lying about not hearing a shot—proves that. Silencers are damned hard to get hold of, but people with plenty of money can manage most things. And since the murder was premeditated, it is better to count on the fact that the murderer—or murderess—had planned a pretty safe hiding place for the gun and the silencer.... Oh, not necessarily in the house or even near the house," he hastened to assure Strawn, who was trying to break in.... "By the way, how long after Mrs. Selim was killed was her death discovered? Or do you know?"

"I haven't been able to get much out of that bunch in there—not even out of Penelope Crain, who ought to be willing to help, seeing as how she works for the district attorney. But I guess she's waiting to spill it all to you, if she knows anything, so you and Sanderson will get all the credit."

"Now, look here, chief," Dundee protested, laying a hand on Strawn's shoulder as he reverted to the name by which he had addressed the head of the Homicide Squad for nearly a year, "we're going to be friends, aren't we? Same as always? We know pretty well how to work together, don't we? No use to begin pulling against each other."

"Guess so," Strawn growled, but he was obviously pleased and relieved. "Maybe you'd better have a crack at that crowd yourself. I hear Doc Price's car—always has a bum spark plug. I'll stick around with him until he gets going good on his job; then, if you'll excuse me for butting in, I'll join your party in the living room.... And good luck to you, Bonnie!"

Dundee took the door he knew must lead into the central hall, but found himself in an enclosed section of it—a small foyer between the main hall and Nita Selim's bedroom. There was room for a telephone table and its chair, as well as for a small sofa, large enough for two to sit upon comfortably. He paused to open the door across from the telephone table and found that it opened into a closet, whose hangers and hat forms now held the outdoor clothing belonging to Nita's guests. Nice clothes—the smart but unostentatious hats and coats of moneyed people of good taste, he observed a little enviously, before he opened the door which led into the main hall which bisected the main floor of the house until it reached Nita's room.

Another door in the section behind the staircase leading to the gabled second story next claimed his attention. Opening it, he discovered a beautifully fitted guests' lavatory. There was even a fully appointed dressing-table for women's use, so that none of her guests had had the slightest excuse to invade the privacy of Mrs. Selim's bedroom and bath, unless specifically invited to do so. Rather a well planned house, this, Dundee concluded, as he closed the door upon the green porcelain fixtures, and walked slowly toward the wide archway that led from the hall into a large living room.

He had a curious reluctance to intrude upon that assembled and guarded company of Hamilton's "real society." They were all Penny's friends, and Penny was *his* friend....

But his first swift, all-seeing glance about the room reassured him. No hysterics here. These people brought race and breeding even into the presence of death. Whatever emotions had torn them when Nita Selim's body was discovered were almost unguessable now. A stout, short woman of about thirty was tapping a foot nervously, as she talked to the man who was bending over her chair. John C. Drake, that was. Dundee had met him, knew him to be a vice president of the Hamilton National Bank, in charge of the trust department. Penelope Crain was occupying half of a "love-seat" with Lois Dunlap, the hands of the girl and of the woman clinging together for mutual comfort. That tall, thin, oldish man, with the waxed grey mustache, must be Judge Hugo Marshall, and the pretty girl leaning trustingly against his shoulder must be his wife—Karen Marshall, who had jumped at her first proposal during her first season.

"Yes, well-bred people," he concluded, as his eyes swept on, and then stopped, a little bewildered. Who was *that* man? He didn't belong somehow, and his hands trembled visibly as he tried to light a cigarette. Leaning— not nonchalantly, but actually for support—against the brocaded coral silk drapes of a pair of wide, long windows set in the east wall. Suddenly Dundee had it.... Broadway! This was no Hamiltonian, no comfortably rich and socially secure Middle-westerner. Broadway in every line of his too-well-tailored clothes, in the polished smoothness of his dark hair....

"Why, it's Mr. Dundee at last!" Penny cried, turning in the S-shaped seat before he had time to finish his mental inventory of the room's occupants.

She jumped to her feet and threaded a swift way over Oriental rugs and between the two bridge tables, still occupying the center of the big room, still cluttered with score pads, tally cards, and playing cards.

"I've been wondering if you had stopped to have dinner first," she taunted him. Then, laying a hand on his arm, she faced the living room eagerly. "This is Mr. Dundee, folks—special investigator attached to the district attorney's office, and a grand detective. He solved the Hogarth murder case, you know, and the Hillcrest murder. And he's *my* friend, so I want you all to trust him—and tell him things without being afraid of him."

Then, rather ceremoniously but swiftly, she presented her friends—Judge and Mrs. Hugo Marshall, Mr. and Mrs. Tracey Miles, Mr. and Mrs. John C. Drake, Mrs. Dunlap, Janet Raymond, Polly Beale, Clive Hammond, and—

At that point Penny hesitated, then rather stiffly included the "Broadway" man, as "Mr. Dexter Sprague—of New York."

"Thank you, Miss Crain," Dundee said. "Now will you please tell me, if you know, whether all those invited to both the bridge party and the cocktail party are here?"

Penny's face flamed. "Ralph Hammond, Clive's brother, hasn't come yet.... I—I rather imagine I've been 'stood up,'" she confessed, with a faint attempt at gayety.

And Ralph Hammond was the man who had once belonged rather exclusively to Penny, and who, according to her own confession, had succumbed most completely to Nita Selim's charms!—Dundee noted, filing the reflection for further reference.

"Please, Mr. Dundee, won't you detain us as short a time as possible?" Lois Dunlap asked, as she advanced toward him. "Mr. Dunlap is away on a fishing trip, and I don't like to leave my three youngsters too long. They are really too much of a handful for the governess, over a period of hours."

"I shall detain all of you no longer than is absolutely necessary," Dundee told her gently, "but I am afraid I must warn you that I can't let you go home very soon— unless one or more of you has something of vital importance to tell—something which will clear up or materially help to clear up this bad business."

He paused a long half-minute, then asked curtly: "I am to conclude that no one has anything at all to volunteer?"

There was no answer, other than a barely perceptible drawing together in self-defence of the minds and hearts of those who had been friends for so long.

"Very well," Dundee conceded abruptly. "Then I must put all of you through a routine examination, since every one of you is, of course, a possible suspect."

CHAPTER THREE

"Good-by, dinner!" groaned the plump, blond little man who had been introduced as Tracey Miles, as he sorrowfully patted his rather prominent stomach.

"Don't worry, darling," begged the dark, neurotic-looking woman who was Flora Miles, his wife. "I'm sure Mr. Dundee will ask Lydia—poor Nita's maid, you know—" she explained in an aside to Dundee, "—to prepare a light supper for us if he really needs to detain us long—which I am sure he won't."

"How can you think of food now?" Polly Beale, the tall, sturdy girl with an almost masculine bob and a quite masculine tweed suit, demanded brusquely. Her voice had an unfeminine lack of modulation, but when Dundee saw her glance toward Clive Hammond he realized that she was wholly feminine where he was concerned, at least.

"Of course, we are all *dreadfully* cut up over poor Nita's—death," gasped a rather pretty girl, whose most distinguishing feature was her crop of crinkly, light-red hair.

"I assume that to be true, Miss Raymond," Dundee answered. "But we must lose no more time getting at the facts. Just when was Mrs. Selim murdered?"

At the brutal use of the word a shudder rippled over the small crowd. Dexter Sprague, "of New York," dropped his lighted cigarette where it would have burned a hole in a fine Persian rug, if Sergeant Turner, on guard over the room for Captain Strawn, had not slouched from his corner to plant a big foot upon it.

"We don't know exactly when it happened," Penny volunteered. "We were playing bridge, the last hand of the last rubber, because the men were arriving for cocktails, when Nita became dummy and went to her bedroom to—"

"To make herself 'pretty-pretty' for the men," Mrs. Drake mimicked; then, realizing the possible effect of her cattiness on Dundee, she defended herself volubly: "Of course I *liked* Nita, but she *did* think so terribly much about her effect on men—and all that, and was always fixing her make-up, and besides—you *can't* suspect me, because I was playing against Karen and Nita—"

"Thank you, Mrs. Drake," Dundee cut in. "Does anyone know the exact time Mrs. Selim left the room, when she became dummy?"

"I can tell you, because I had just arrived—the first of the men to get here," Tracey Miles volunteered, obviously glad of the chance to talk—a characteristic of the man, Dundee decided. "I looked at my watch just after I stepped out of my car, because I like to be on time to the dot, and Nita—Mrs. Selim—had said 5:30.... Well, it was exactly 5:25, so I had five minutes to spare."

"Yes?" Dundee speeded him up impatiently.

"Well, I came right into the hall, and hung my hat in the closet out there, and then came in here. It must have been about 5:27 by that time," he explained, with the meticulousness of a man on the witness stand. "I shouted, 'Hello, everybody! How's tricks?...' That's a joke, you know. 'How's tricks?'—meaning tricks in bridge—"

"Yes, yes," Dundee admitted, frowning, but the rest of the company exchanged indulgent smiles, and Flora Miles patted her husband's hand fondly.

"Well, Nita jumped up from the bridge table—that one right there," Miles pointed to the table nearer the arched doorway, "and she said, 'Good heavens! Is it half past five already? I've got to run and make myself 'pretty-pretty' for just such great big men as you, Tracey—"

"'Tracey, darling'!" Judge Marshall corrected, with a chuckle that sounded odd in the tensely silent room.

Tracey Miles flushed a salmon pink, and his wife's fingers clutched at his hand warningly. "Oh, Nita called everybody 'darling,' and didn't mean anything by it, I guess," he explained uneasily. "Just one of her cute little ways—. Well, anyway, she came up to me and straightened my necktie—another one of her funny little ways—and said, 'Tracey, my *own* lamb, won't you shake up the cocktails for poor little Nita?...' You know, a sort of way she had of coaxing people—"

"Yes, I know," Dundee agreed, with a trace of a grin. "Go on as rapidly as you can, please."

"I thought you wanted to know everything!" Miles was a little peevish; he had evidently been enjoying himself. "Of course I said I'd make the cocktails—she said everything was ready on the sideboard. That's the dining room right behind this room," he explained unnecessarily, since the French doors were open. "Well, Nita blew me a kiss from her fingertips, and ran out of the room.... Now, let's see," he ruminated, creasing his sunburned forehead beneath his carefully combed blond hair, "that must have been at exactly 5:30 that she left the room. I went on into the dining room, and Lois—I mean, Mrs. Dunlap came with me, because she said she was simply dying for a caviar sandwich and a nip of—of—"

"Of Scotch, Tracey," Lois Dunlap cut in, grinning. "I'm sure Mr. Dundee won't think I'm a confirmed tippler, so you might as well tell the truth, the whole truth, and nothing but the truth.... Poor Tracey has a deadly fear that we are all going to lose the last shred of our reputations in this deplorable affair, Mr. Dundee," she added in a rather shaky version of the comfortable, rich voice he had heard earlier in the day.

"I'm not going to pry into cellars," Dundee assured her in the same spirit. "What else, Mr. Miles?"

"Nothing much," Tracey Miles confessed, with apparent regret. "I was still mixing—no, I'd begun to shake the cocktails—when I heard a scream—"

"Whose scream?" Dundee demanded, looking about the room, and dismissing Miles thankfully.

"It was—I," Judge Marshall's fair-haired, blue-eyed little bride volunteered in a voice that threatened to rise to hysteria.

"Tell me all about it," Dundee urged gently.

"Yes, sir," she quavered, while her husband's arm encircled her shoulders in courtly fashion. "As Tracey told you, Nita was dummy, and I was declarer—that is, I got the bid, and played the hand. It—it was quite an exciting end for me to the afternoon of bridge, for I'm not usually awfully lucky, so when Penny had figured up the score, because I'm not good at arithmetic, and I knew Nita and I had rolled up an awfully big score, I jumped up and ran into her room to tell her the good news, because she hadn't come back. And—and—there she was—all bowed over her dressing-table, and she—she was—was—"

"She was dead when you reached her?" Dundee assisted her.

"Yes," Karen Marshall answered faintly, and turned to hide her face against her elderly husband's breast.

Dundee's swift eyes took in the varying degrees of whiteness and sick horror that claimed every face in the room as surely as if all present had not already heard Karen tell her story to Captain Strawn. Tracey Miles looked as if he would have no immediate craving for his dinner, and Judge Marshall's fine, thin face no longer looked so "well-preserved" as he prided himself that it did. As for Dexter Sprague, he almost folded up against the coral brocade draperies. It was the women, oddly enough, who kept the better control over their emotions.

"Of course you all rushed in when Mrs. Marshall screamed?" he asked casually.

Twelve heads nodded mutely.

"Did any or all of you touch the body, or things in the room?"

"Mr. Sprague touched her hair, and—and lifted one of her hands," Penny contributed quietly. "But you know how it must have been! We can't any of us tell *exactly* every move we made, but there was some rushing about. The men, mostly, looking for—for whoever did it—"

"Mrs. Marshall, did you see anyone—*anyone at all*—in or near that room when you entered it?"

The white-faced young wife lifted her head, and looked at him dazedly with drowned blue eyes. "There wasn't anyone in—in that room, I know," she faltered. "It felt horrible—being in there with—with *her*—all alone—"

"But near the room? In the main hall or in the little foyer where the telephone is?" Dundee persisted.

"I—don't think so ... I can't—remember—seeing *anyone*.... Oh, Hugo!" and again she crouched against her husband, who soothed her with trembling hands that looked incongruously old against her childish fair hair and face.

"Where were the rest of you—*exactly* where, I mean?" Dundee demanded, conscious that Captain Strawn had entered the room and was standing slightly behind him.

There was such a babel of answers, given and then hastily corrected, that Dundee broke in suddenly:

"I want a connected story of 'the events leading up to the tragedy.' And I want someone to tell it who hasn't lost his—or her—head at all." He looked about the company, as if speculatively, but his mind was already made up. "Miss Crain, will you tell the story, beginning with the moment I left you and Mrs. Dunlap and Mrs. Selim today?"

Penny nodded miserably and was about to begin.

"Just a minute, before you begin, Miss Crain," Dundee requested. "I'd like to make notes on your story," and he drew from a coat pocket a shorthand book, hastily filched from Penny's own tidy desk. "Yes," he answered the girl's frank stare of amazement, "I can write shorthand—of a sort, and pretty fast, at that, though no other human being, I am afraid, could read it but myself.... As for you folks," he addressed the uneasy, silent group of men and women in dead Nita's living room, "I shall ask you not to interrupt Miss Crain unless you are very sure that her memory is at fault."

Penelope Crain was about to begin for the second time, when again Dundee interrupted. "Another half second, please."

On the first sheet of the new shorthand notebook Dundee scribbled: "Suggest you try to locate Ralph Hammond immediately. Very much in love with Mrs. Selim. Invited to cocktail party; did not show up." Tearing the sheet from the notebook, he passed it to Captain Strawn, who read it, frowning, and then nodded.

"Doc Price has done all he can here," Strawn whispered huskily. "Wants to know if you'd like to speak to him before he takes the body to the morgue."

"Certainly," Dundee answered as he grinned apologetically to the girl who was waiting, white-faced but patiently, to tell the story of the afternoon.

Quickly suppressed shudders and low exclamations of horror followed him and the chief of the Homicide Squad from the room.

"Well, Bonnie boy, we meet again, for the usual reason," old Dr. Price greeted the district attorney's new special investigator. "Another shocking affair—that.... A nice clean wound, one of the neatest jobs I ever saw. Shot entered the back, and penetrated the heart.... *Very* nicely calculated. If the bullet had struck a quarter of an inch higher, it would have been deflected by the—"

"But the *path* of the bullet, doctor!" Dundee broke in. "Have you made any calculations as to the place and distance at which the shot was fired?"

"Roughly speaking—yes," the coroner answered. "The gun was fired at a distance, probably, of ten or fifteen feet—perhaps closer, but I don't think so," he amended meticulously. "As for the path of the bullet, I have fixed it, judging from the position of the body, which I am assured had not been moved before my arrival, as coming from a point somewhere along a straight line drawn from the wound, with the body upright, of course, to—here!"

Dundee and Strawn followed the brisk little white-haired old doctor across the bedroom to a window opening upon the drive—the one nearest the door leading out upon the porch.

"I've marked the end of the line here," Dr. Price went on, pointing to a faint pencil mark made upon the window frame—the pale-green strip of woodwork near the chaise longue, which was set between the two windows.

"I told you she was shot from the window!" Strawn reminded Dundee triumphantly. "You see, doc, it's my theory that the murderer climbed up to the sill of this window, which was open as it is now, crouched in it, and shot her while she sat there powdering her face."

"Not necessarily, Captain, not necessarily," Dr. Price deprecated. "I merely say that this pencil mark indicated the *end* of the line showing the path of the bullet. Certainly she was not shot *through* the frame of the window, but she might have been shot by anyone stationed just in front of it, or anywhere along the line, up to, say, within ten feet of the woman.... Now, if that's all, Captain, I'll be getting this corpse into the morgue for an autopsy. And I'll send you both a copy of my findings."

"Just a minute, Dr. Price," Dundee detained him. "How old would you say Mrs. Selim was?"

The little doctor pursed his wrinkled lips and considered for a moment, eyeing the body stretched upon the chaise longue speculatively.

"We-ell, between thirty and thirty-four years old," he answered finally. "Of course, you understand that that estimate is unofficial, and must remain so, until I have completed the autopsy—"

Dundee stared down at the upturned face of the dead woman with startled incredulity. Between thirty and thirty-four years old! That tiny, lovely—But she was not quite so lovely in death, in spite of the serenity it had brought to those once-vivacious features. Peering more closely, he could see—without those luminous, wide eyes to center his attention—numerous fine lines on the waxen face, the slackness of a little pouch of soft flesh beneath her round chin, an occasional white hair among the shoulder-length dark curls.... Dundee sighed. How easy it was for a beautiful woman to deceive men with a pair of wide, velvety black eyes! But he'd bet the women had not been quite so thoroughly taken in by her cuddly childishness, her odd mixture of demureness and youthful impudence!

Back in the living room, whose occupants stopped whispering and grew taut with suspense, Dundee seated himself at a little red-lacquer table, notebook spread, while Strawn settled himself heavily in the nearest overstuffed armchair.

"Now, Miss Crain, I am quite ready, if you will forgive me for having kept you waiting."

In a very quiet voice—slightly husky, as always— Penny began her story:

"I think it lacked two or three minutes of one o'clock when you drove away. Nita, Lois—do you mind if I use the names I am most accustomed to?... Thank you!—and I went immediately into the lounge of Breakaway Inn, where we found Carolyn Drake and Flora Miles waiting for us. Nita soon left us to see about the arrangement of the table, and while she was away the rest of the girls arrived."

"Except—" a woman's voice broke in.

"I was going to say all eight of us were ready for lunch except Polly Beale. She hadn't come," Penny went on, her husky voice a little sharp with annoyance. "When Nita came to ask us into the private dining room, one of the Inn's employees came and told her there was a call for her and showed her to the private booth in the lounge. In a minute Nita returned and told us that Polly wasn't coming to the luncheon, but would join us later for bridge here."

"Why don't you tell him how funny Nita acted?" Janet Raymond prompted.

Penny flushed, but she accepted the prompting. "I think any of us might have been a little—annoyed," she said steadily, as if striving to be utterly truthful. "Nita told us—" she turned to Dundee, whose pencil was flying, "that Polly had made no excuse at all; in fact, she quoted Polly exactly: 'Sorry, Nita. Can't make it for lunch. I'll show up at your place at 2:30 for bridge.'"

"Nita couldn't bear the least hint of being slighted," Janet Raymond explained, with a malicious gleam in her pale blue eyes. "If it hadn't been for Lois and Hugo—Judge Marshall, I mean—Nita Selim would never have been included in any of our affairs—and she *knew* it! The Dunlaps can do anything they please, because they're—"

"Please, Janet!" Lois Dunlap cut in, her usually placid voice becoming quite sharp. "You must know by this time that I make friends wherever I please, and that I liked—yes, I was *extremely* fond of poor little Nita. In fact, I am forced to believe that, of all the women she met in this town, I was her only real friend."

There was a flush of anger on her lovably plain face as her grey eyes challenged first one and then another of the "Forsyte girls." One or two looked a little ashamed, but there was not a single voice to contradict Lois Dunlap's flat assertion.

"Will you please go on, Pen—Miss Crain?" Dundee urged, but he had missed nothing of the little by-play.

"I wish you would call me Penny so I'd feel more like a person than a witness," Penny retorted thornily. "Where was I?... Oh, yes! Nita cooled right off when Lois reminded her that Polly was always abrupt like that—" and here Penny paused to grin apologetically at the girl with the masculine-looking haircut, "and then we all went into the private dining room, where Nita had ordered a perfectly gorgeous lunch, with a heavenly centerpiece of green-striped yellow orchids—Well, I don't suppose you're interested in what we ate and things like that—" she hesitated.

"Was there anything unusual in the conversation—anything like a quarrel?" Dundee prompted.

"Oh, no!" Penny protested. "Nothing happened out of the ordinary at all—No, wait! Nita received a letter by messenger—or rather a note, when we were about half through luncheon—"

There was a low, strangled-in-the-throat cry from someone. Who had uttered it Dundee could not be sure, since his eyes had been on his notebook. But what had really interrupted Penny Crain was a crash.

CHAPTER FOUR

"Pardon! Awfully sorry," Clive Hammond muttered, as he bent to pick up the fragments of a colored pottery ashtray which he and his fiancee, Polly Beale, had been sharing.

"Don't worry—about picking it up," Polly commanded in her brusque voice, but Dundee, listening acutely, was sure of a very slight pause between the two parts of her sentence.

He glanced at the couple—the tall, masculine-looking girl, lounging deep in an armchair, Clive Hammond, rather unusually good-looking with his dark-red hair, brown eyes, and a face and body as compactly and symmetrically designed as one of the buildings which had been pointed out to Dundee as the product of the young architect's genius, now resuming his seat upon the arm of the chair. His chief concern seemed to be for another ashtray, which Sergeant Turner, with a grin, produced from one of the many little tables with which the room was provided.... Rather strange that those two should be engaged, Dundee mused....

"Go on, Miss Crain," the detective urged, as if he were impatient of the delay. "About that note or letter—"

"It was in a blue-grey envelope, with printing or engraving in the upper left-hand corner," Penny went on, half closing her eyes to recapture the scene in its entirety. "Like business firms use," she amended. "I couldn't help seeing, since I sat so near Nita. She seemed startled—or, well maybe I'd better say surprised and a little sore, but she tore it open and read it at a glance almost, which is why I say it must have been only a note. But while she was reading it she frowned, then smiled, as if something had amused or—or—"

"She smiled like any woman reading a love letter," Carolyn Drake interrupted positively. "I myself was sure that one of her *many* admirers had broken an engagement, but had signed himself, 'With all my love, darling—your own So-and-so!'"

Dundee wondered if even Carolyn Drake's husband, the carefully groomed and dignified John C. Drake, bank vice-president, had ever sent *her* such a note, but he did not let his pencil slow down, for Penny was talking again:

"I think you are assuming a little too much, Carolyn.... But let that pass. At any rate, Nita didn't say a word about the contents of the note and naturally no one asked a question. She simply tucked it into the pocket of her silk summer coat, which was draped over the back of her chair, and the luncheon went on. Then we all drove over here, and found Polly waiting in her own coupe, in the road in front of the house. She told Nita she had rung the bell, but the maid, Lydia, didn't answer, so she had just waited.

"Nita didn't seem surprised; said she had a key, if Lydia hadn't come back yet.... You see," she interrupted herself to explain to Dundee, "Nita had already told us at luncheon that 'poor, darling Lydia,' as she called her, had had to go in to town to get an abscessed tooth extracted, and was to wait in the dentist's office until she felt equal to driving herself home again in Nita's coupe.... Yes, Nita had taken her in herself," she answered the beginning of a question from Dundee.

"At what time?" Dundee queried.

"I don't know exactly, but Nita said she'd had to dash away at an ungodly hour, so that Lydia could make her ten o'clock dentist's appointment, and so that she herself could get a manicure and a shampoo and have her hair dressed, so I imagine she must have left not later than fifteen or twenty minutes to ten."

"How did Mrs. Selim get out to Breakaway Inn, if she left her own car with the maid?"

"You saw her arrive with Lois," Penny reminded him.

"Nita had told us all about Lydia's dentist's appointment when she was at my house for dinner Wednesday night," Lois Dunlap contributed. "I offered to call for her anywhere she said, and take her out to Breakaway Inn in my car today. I met her, at her suggestion, in the French hat salon of the shop where she got her shampoo and manicure—Redmond's department store."

"A large dinner party, Mrs. Dunlap?" Dundee asked.

"Not large at all.... Just twelve of us—the crowd here except for Mr. Sprague, Penny and Janet."

"Who was Mrs. Selim's dinner partner?" Dundee asked.

"That's right! He *isn't* here!" Lois Dunlap corrected herself. "Ralph Hammond brought her and was her dinner partner."

"Thank you.... Now, Penny. You were saying the maid had not returned."

"Oh, but she had!" Penny answered impatiently. "If I'm going to be interrupted so much—. Well, Nita rang the bell and Lydia came, tying on her apron. Nita kissed her on the cheek that wasn't swollen, and asked her why she hadn't let Polly in. And Lydia said she hadn't heard the bell, because she had dropped asleep in her room in the basement—dopey from the local anesthetic, you know," she explained to Dundee.

"I—see," Dundee acknowledged, and underlined heavily another note in his scrawled shorthand.

"So Lydia took our hats and summer coats and put them in the hall closet, and then followed Nita, who was calling to her, on into Nita's bedroom. We thought she either wanted to give directions about the makings for the cocktails and the sandwiches, or to console poor Lydia for the awful pain she had had at the dentist's, so we didn't intrude. We made a dive for the bridge tables, found our places, and were ready to play when Nita joined us. Nita and Karen—"

"Just a minute, Penny.... Did any of you, then or later, until Mrs. Marshall discovered the tragedy, go into Mrs. Selim's bedroom?"

"There was no need for us to," Penny told him. "There's a lavatory with a dressing-table right behind the staircase. I, for one, didn't go into Nita's room until after Karen screamed."

There was a chorus of similar denials on the part of every woman present. At Dundee's significant pressing of the same question upon the men, he was met with either laconic negatives or sharply indignant ones.

"All right, Penny. Go ahead, please."

"I was going to tell you how we were seated for bridge, if that interests you," Penny said, rather tartly.

"It interests me intensely," Dundee assured her, smiling.

"Then it was this way," began Penny, thawing instantly. "Karen and Nita, Carolyn and I were at this table," and she pointed to the table nearer the hall. "Flora, Polly, Janet and Lois were at the other. We played at those tables all afternoon. We simply pivoted at our own table after the end of each rubber. When Nita became dummy—"

"Forgive me," Dundee begged, as he interrupted her again. "I'd like to ask a question ... Mrs. Dunlap, since you were at the other table, perhaps you will tell me what your partner and opponents were doing just before Mrs. Selim became dummy."

Lois Dunlap pressed her fingertips into her temples, as if in an effort to remember clearly.

"It's—rather hard to think of bridge now, Mr. Dundee," she said at last. "But—yes, of course I remember! We had finished a rubber and had decided there would be no time for another, since it was so near 5:30—"

"That last rubber, please, Mrs. Dunlap," Dundee suggested. "Who were partners, and just when was it finished?"

"Flora—" Lois turned toward Mrs. Miles, who had sat with her hands tightly locked and her great haggard dark eyes roving tensely from one to another—"you and I were partners, weren't we?... Of course! Remember you were dummy and I played the hand? You went out to telephone, didn't you?... That's right! I remember clearly now! Flora said she had to telephone the house to ask how her two babies—six and four years old, they are, Mr. Dundee, and the rosiest dumplings—. Well, anyway, Flora went to telephone—"

"In the little foyer between the main hall and Mrs. Selim's room?"

"Yes, of course," Lois Dunlap answered, but Dundee's eyes were upon Flora Miles, and he saw her naturally sallow face go yellow under its too-thick rouge. "I played the hand and made my bid, although Flora and I had gone down 400 on the hand before," Lois continued, with a rueful twinkle of her pleasant grey eyes. "When the score was totted up, I found I'd won a bit after all. Our winnings go to the Forsyte Alumnae Scholarship Fund," she explained.

"Yes, I know," Dundee nodded. "And then—?"

"Polly asked the other table how they stood, and Nita said, 'One game to go on this rubber, provided we make it....' Karen was dealing the cards then, and Nita was looking very happy—she'd been winning pretty steadily, I think—"

"Pardon, Mrs. Dunlap.... How did the players at your table dispose of themselves then—that is, immediately after you had finished playing the last hand, and Mrs. Marshall was dealing at the other table?"

Lois screwed up her forehead. "Let me think—I know what *I* did. I went over to watch the game at the other table, and stayed there till Tracey—Mr. Miles—came in for cocktails. I can't tell you exactly what the other three did."

There was a strained silence. Dundee saw Polly Scale's hand tighten convulsively on Clive Hammond's, saw Janet Raymond flush scarlet, watched a muscle jerk in Flora Miles' otherwise rigid face.

Suddenly he sprang to his feet. "I am going to make what will seem an absurd request," he said tensely. "I am going to ask you all—the women, I mean—to take your places at the bridge tables. And then—" he paused for an instant, his blue eyes hard: "I want to see the death hand played exactly as it was played while Nita Selim was being murdered!"

CHAPTER FIVE

"Shame on you, Bonnie Dundee!" cried Penny Crain, her small fists clenched belligerently. "'Death hand', indeed! You talk like a New York tabloid! And if you don't realize that all of us have stood pretty nearly as much as we can without having to play the hand at bridge—the *very* hand we played while Nita Selim was being murdered!—then you haven't the decency and human feelings I've credited you with!"

A murmur of indignant approval accompanied her tirade and buzzed on for a moment after she had finished, but it ceased abruptly as Dundee spoke:

"Who's conducting this investigation, Penny Crain—you or I? You will kindly let me do it in my own fashion, and try to be content when I tell you that, in my humble opinion, what I propose is absolutely necessary to the solution of this case!"

Bickering—Dundee grinned to himself—exactly as if they had known each other always, had quarreled and made up with fierce intensity for years.

"Really, Mr. Dundee," Judge Hugo Marshall began pompously, embracing his young wife protectingly, "I must say that I agree with Miss Crain. This is an outrage, sir—an outrage to all of us, and particularly to this frail little wife of mine, already half-hysterical over the ordeal she has endured."

"Take your places!" Dundee ordered curtly. After all, there was a limit to the careful courtesy one must show to Hamilton's "inmost circle of society."

Penny led the way to the bridge tables, the very waves of her brown bob seeming to bristle with futile anger. But she obeyed, Dundee exulted. The way to tame this blessed little shrew had been solved by old Bill Shakespeare centuries ago....

As the women took their places at the two tables, arguing a bit among themselves, with semi-hysterical edges to their voices, Dundee watched the men, but all of them, with the exception of Dexter Sprague—that typical son of Broadway, so out of place in this company—had managed at least a fine surface control, their lips tight, their eyes hard, narrowed and watchful. Sprague slumped into a vacated chair and closed his eyes, revealing finely-wrinkled, yellowish lids.

"Where shall we begin?" Polly Beale demanded brusquely. "Remember this table had finished playing when Karen began to deal what you call the 'death hand,'" she reminded him scornfully. "And Flora wasn't here at all—she had been dummy for our last hand—"

"And had gone out to telephone," Dundee interrupted. "Mrs. Miles, will you please leave the room, and return exactly when you did return—or as nearly so as you can remember?"

Dundee was sure that Mrs. Miles' sallow face took on a greyish tinge as she staggered to her feet and wound an uncertain way toward the hall. Tracey Miles sprang to his wife's assistance, but Sergeant Turner took it upon himself to lay a detaining hand on the too-anxious husband's arm. With no more than the lifting of an eyebrow, Dundee made Captain Strawn understand that Flora Miles' movements were to be kept under strict observation, and the chief of the Homicide Squad as unobtrusively conveyed the order to a plainclothesman loitering interestedly in the wide doorway.

"Now," he was answering Polly Beale's question, "I should like the remaining three of you to behave exactly as you did when your last hand was finished. Did you keep individual score, as is customary in contract?—or were you playing auction?"

"Contract," Polly Beale answered curtly. "And when we're playing among ourselves like this, one at each table is usually elected to keep score. Janet was score-keeper for us this afternoon, but we all waited, after our last hand was played, for Janet to give us the result for our tally cards."

Dundee drew near the table, picked up the three tally cards—ornamental little affairs, and rather expensive—glanced over the points recorded, then asked abruptly:

"Where is Mrs. Miles' tally? I don't see it here."

There was no answer to be had, so he let the matter drop, temporarily, though his shorthand notebook received another deeply underlined series of pothooks.

"Go on, please, at both tables," Dundee commanded. "Your table—" he nodded toward Penny, who was already over her flare of temper, "will please select the cards each held at the conclusion of Mrs. Marshall's deal."

"Oooh, I'd never remember *all* my cards in the world," Carolyn Drake wailed. "I know I had five Clubs—Ace, King, Queen—"

"You had the Jack, not the Queen, for I held it myself," Penny contradicted her crisply.

"Until this matter of who held which cards after Mrs. Marshall's deal is settled, I shall have to ask you all to remain as you are now," Dundee said to the players seated at the other table.

At last it was threshed out, largely between Penny Crain and Karen Marshall, the latter proving to have a better memory than Dundee had expected. At last even Carolyn Drake's querulous fussiness was satisfied, or trampled down.

Both Judge Marshall and John Drake started forward to inspect the cards, which none of the players was trying to conceal, but Dundee waved them back.

"Please—I want you men—all of you, to take your places outside, and return to this room in the order of your arrival this afternoon. Try to imagine that it is now—if I can trust Mr. Miles' apparently excellent memory—exactly 5:25—"

"Pretty hard to do, considering it's now a quarter past seven and there's still no dinner in sight," Tracey Miles grumbled, then brightened: "I can come right back in then—at 5:27, can't I?"

That point settled, and the men sent away, to be watched by several pairs of apparently indolent police eyes, Dundee turned to the bridge table, Nita's leaving of which had provided her murderer with his opportunity.

"The cards are 'dealt'," Penny reminded him.

"Now I want you other three to scatter exactly as you did before," Dundee commanded, hurry and excitement in his voice.

Lois Dunlap rose, laid down her tally card, and strolled over to the remaining table. After a moment's hesitation, Polly Beale strode mannishly out of the room, straight into the hall. Dundee, watching as the bridge players earlier that afternoon certainly had not, was amazed to see Clive Hammond beckoning to her from the open door of the solarium.

So Clive Hammond had arrived ahead of Tracey Miles! Had somehow entered the solarium unnoticed, and had managed to beckon his fiancee to join him there! Prearranged?... And why had Clive Hammond failed to enter and greet his hostess first? Moreover, *how* had he entered the solarium?

But things were happening in the living room. Janet Raymond, flushing so that her sunburned face outdid her red hair for vividness, was slowly leaving the room also. Through a window opening upon the wide front porch Dundee saw the girl take her position against a pillar, then—a thing she had not done before very probably—press her handkerchief to her trembling lips.

But the bidding was going on, Karen Marshall piping in her childish treble: "Three spades!"

Dundee took his place behind her chair, then silently beckoned to Penny to shift from her own chair opposite Carolyn Drake to the chair Nita Selim had left to go to her death. She nodded understandingly.

"Double!" quavered Carolyn Drake, next on the left to the dealer, and managed to raise her eyebrows meaningly to Penny, her partner, who had not yet changed places.

Penny, throwing herself into the spirit of the thing, scowled warningly. No exchanging of illicit signals for Penny Crain! But the instant she slipped into Nita Selim's chair her whole face and body took on a different manner, underwent almost a physical change. She *was* Nita Selim now! She tucked her head, considered her cards, laughed a little breathless note, then cried triumphantly:

"And I say—*five spades*! What do you think of *that*, partner?"

Then the girl who was giving an amazing imitation of Nita Selim changed as suddenly into her own character as she changed chairs.

"Nita, I don't think it's quite Hoyle to be so jubilant about the strength of your hand," she commented tartly. "I pass."

Karen Marshall pretended to study her hand for a frowning instant, then, under Penny's spell, announced with a pretty air of bravado:

"Six spades!... Your raise to five makes a little slam obligatory, doesn't it, Nita?"

Carolyn Drake flushed and looked uneasily toward Penny, a bit of by-play which Dundee could see had not figured in the original game. But she bridled and shifted her plump body in her chair, as she must have done before.

"I double a little slam!" she declared. Then, still acting the role she had played in earnest that afternoon, she explained importantly: "I always double a little slam on principle!"

Penny, in the role of Nita, redoubled with an exultant laugh, then, as herself, said, "Pass!" with a murderous glance at Mrs. Drake.

"Let's see your hand, partner," Karen quavered, addressing a woman who had been dead nearly two hours; then she shuddered: "Oh, this is too horrible!" as Penny Crain again slipped into Nita Selim's chair and prepared to lay down the dummy hand.

And it *was* horrible—even if vitally necessary—for these three to have to go through the farce of playing a bridge hand while one of the original players was lying on a marble slab at the morgue, her cold flesh insensible to the coroner's expert knife.

But Dundee said nothing, for Tracey Miles was already hovering in the doorway, ready for his cue to enter.

Penny, or rather "Nita," was saying:

"How's *this*, Karen darling?" as she laid down the Ace and deuce of Spades, Karen's trumps.

"I hope you remember *you* are vulnerable, as well as we," Carolyn remarked in a sorry imitation of her original cocksureness, as she opened the play by leading the Ace of Clubs.

"And how's *this*, partner?... A singleton in Clubs!" Nita's imitator demanded triumphantly, as she continued to lay down her dummy hand, slapping the lone nine of Clubs down beside trumps; "and this little collection of Hearts!" as she displayed and arranged the King, Jack, eight and four of Hearts; "*and* this!" as a length of Diamonds—Ace, Jack, ten, eight, seven and six slithered down the glossy linen cover of the bridge table toward Karen Marshall. "Now if you don't make your little slam, infant, don't dare say I shouldn't have jumped you to five!... I figured you for a blank or a singleton in Diamonds, and at least the Ace of Hearts, or you— cautious as you are—wouldn't have made an original three Spade bid without the Ace.... Hop to it, darling!"

"This is where I enter," Tracey Miles whispered to Dundee, and, at a nod from the young detective, the pudgy little blond man strode jauntily into the living room, proud of himself in the role of actor.

"Hello, everybody! How's tricks?" he called genially, but there was a quiver of horror in his voice under its blitheness.

Penny was quite pale when she sprang from her chair, but her voice seemed to be Nita's very own, as she sang out:

"It *can't* be 5:30 already!... Thank heaven I'm dummy, and can run away and make myself pretty-pretty for you and all the other great big men, Tracey darling!"

Dundee's keen memory registered the slight difference in the wording of the greeting as reported by this pseudo-Nita and the man she was running to meet. But Penny, as Nita, was already straightening Tracey Miles' necktie with possessive, coquettish fingers, was coaxing, with head tucked alluringly:

"Tracey, my ownest lamb, won't you shake up the cocktails for Nita? The makings are all on the sideboard, or I don't know my precious old Lydia—even if her poor jaw does ache most horribly."

Then Penny, as Nita, was on her way, pausing in the doorway to blow a kiss from her fingertips to the fatuously grinning but now quite pale Tracey Miles. She was out of sight for only an instant, then reappeared and very quietly retraced her steps to the bridge table.

Unobtrusively, Dundee drew his watch from his pocket, palmed it as he noted the exact minute, then commanded curtly: "On with the game!"

As Tracey Miles passed the first bridge table Lois Dunlap linked her arm in his, saying in a voice she tried to make gay and natural:

"I'm trailing along, Tracey. Simply dying for a nip of Scotch! Nita's is the real stuff—which is more than my fussy old Pete can get half the time!—and you know I loathe cocktails."

The two passed on into the dining room, the players scarcely raising their eyes from their cards, which they held as if the game were real.

Dundee, his watch still in his hand, advanced to the bridge table. Strolling from player to player he made mental photographs of each hand, then took his stand behind Penny's chair to observe the horribly farcical playing of it. Poor little Penny! he reflected. She hadn't had a chance against that dumb-bell across the table from her. Fancy anyone's doubling a little slam bid on a hand like Carolyn Drake's—or even calling an informatory double in the first place! Why hadn't she bid four Clubs after Karen's original three Spade bid, if she simply wanted to give her partner information?... Not that she really had a bid—

Karen's hand trembled as she drew the lone nine of Clubs from the dummy, to place beside Carolyn's Ace, but Penny's fingers were quite steady as she followed with the deuce of Clubs, to which Karen added, with a trace of characteristic uncertainty, the eight.

"There's our book!" Carolyn Drake exulted obediently, but she cast an apologetic glance toward Penny. "If we take one more trick we set them."

"Fat chance!" Penny obligingly responded, and Dundee, relieved, knew that the farcical game would now be played almost exactly, and with the same comments, as it had been played while Nita Selim was being murdered. Thanks to Penny Crain!

With a shamefaced glance upward at Dundee, Carolyn Drake then led the deuce of Diamonds, committing the gross tactical error of leading from the Queen. Karen added the Jack from the dummy, and Penny shruggingly contributed her King, to find the trick, as she had suspected in the original game, trumped by the five of Spades, since Karen had no Diamonds.

"So *that* settles *us*, Carolyn!" Penny commented acidly.

Her partner rose to the role she was playing. "Well, as I said, I always double a little slam on principle. Besides, how could I know they would have a chance for cross-ruffing in *both* Clubs and Diamonds? I thought you would at least hold the Ace of Diamonds and that Karen would certainly have one, as I only had four—"

Penny shrugged. "Oh, well! Let's play bridge!" for Karen was staring at her cards helplessly. "Sorry, Karen! I realize a post mortem is usually held after the playing of a hand—not before."

"I—I guess I'd better get my trumps out," Karen—now almost a genuine actress, too—breathed tremulously. "I *do* wish Nita were playing this hand. I know I'll muff it somehow—"

"Good kid!" Dundee commented silently, and allowed himself the liberty of patting Karen on her slim shoulder.

The girl threw an upward glance of gratitude through misty eyes, then led the six of Spades, Mrs. Drake contributing the four, dummy taking the trick with the Ace, and Penny relinquishing the three.

"Let's see—that makes five of 'em in, since I trumped one trick," Karen said, as she reached across the table to lead from dummy.

As if the words were a cue—which they probably were—Judge Marshall entered the room at that moment, making a great effort to be as jaunty, debonair, and "young for his age" as he must have thought he looked when he made his entrance when the real game was being played.

At his step Karen lifted her head and greeted her elderly husband with a curious mixture of childlike joy and womanly tenderness:

"Hullo, darling!... I'm trying to make a little slam I may have been foolish to bid, but Nita jumped me from three to five Spades—"

"Let's have a look, sweetheart," the retired judge suggested pompously, and Dundee gave way to make room for him behind Karen's chair.

But before Judge Marshall looked at his wife's cards he bent and kissed her on her flushed cheek, and Karen raised a trembling hand to tweak his grey mustache. Dundee, with uplifted eyebrow, queried Penny, who nodded shortly, conveying the information that this was the way the scene had really been played when there was no question of acting.

"I'm getting out my trumps, darling," Karen confided sweetly, as she reached for the deuce of Spades—the only remaining trump in the dummy.

"What's your hurry, child?" her husband asked indulgently. "Lead this!" and he pointed toward the six of Diamonds.

"I wish you'd got a puncture, Hugo, so you couldn't have butted in before this hand was played," Carolyn Drake spluttered. "Remember this is a little slam bid, doubled and redoubled—"

"I should think *you* would like to forget that, Carolyn!" Penny commented bitingly. "But I agree with Carolyn, Hugo, that Karen is quite capable of making her little slam without your assistance."

"Please don't mind," Karen begged. "Hugo just wanted to help me, because I'm such a dub at bridge—"

"The finest little player in town!" Judge Marshall encouraged her gallantly, but with a jaunty wink at the belligerent Penny.

Smiling adoringly at him again, Karen took his suggestion and led the six of Diamonds from the dummy; Penny covered it with the nine; Karen ruffed with the seven of Spades from her own hand, and Mrs. Drake lugubriously contributed the four of Diamonds.

"I can get my trumps out now, can't I, Hugo?" Karen asked deprecatingly, and at her husband's smiling permission, she led the King of Spades, Carolyn had to give up the Jack, which she must have foolishly thought would take a trick; the dummy contributed the deuce, and Penny followed with her own last trump—the eight.

Karen counted on her fingers, her eyes on the remaining trumps in her hand, then smiled triumphantly up at her husband.

"Why not simply tell us, Karen, that the rest of the trumps are in your own hand?" Penny suggested caustically.

"I—I didn't mean to do anything wrong," Karen pleaded, as she led now with the ten of Hearts, which drew in Carolyn's Queen to cover—Carolyn murmuring religiously: "Always cover an honor with an honor—or should I have played second hand low, Penny?"—topped by the King in the dummy, the trick being completed by Penny's three of Hearts.

At that point John C. Drake marched into the room, strode straight to Dundee, and spoke with cold anger:

"Enough of this nonsense! I, for one, refuse to act like a puppet for your amusement! If you are so vitally interested in contract bridge, I should advise you to take lessons from an expert, not from three terrified women who are rather poor players at best. I also advise you to get about the business you are supposed to be here for— the finding of a murderer!"

CHAPTER SIX

Before Drake had reached his side, his purpose plain upon his stern, rather ascetic features, Dundee had taken a hasty glance at the watch cupped in his palm and noted the exact minute and second of the interruption. Time out!

"One moment, Mr. Drake," he said calmly. "I quite agree with you—from your viewpoint. What mine is, you can't be expected to know. But believe me when I say that I consider it of vital importance to the investigation of the murder of Mrs. Selim that this particular bridge hand, with all its attending remarks, the usual bickering, and its interruptions of arriving guests for cocktails, be played out, exactly as it was this afternoon. I thought I had made myself clear before. If you don't wish me to believe that *you have something to conceal* by refusing to take part in a rather grisly game—"

"Certainly I have nothing to conceal!" John C. Drake snorted angrily.

"Then please bow as gracefully as possible to necessity," Dundee urged without rancor. "And may I ask, before we go on, if you made your entrance at this time, and the facts of your arrival?"

Drake considered a moment, gnawing a thin upper lip. Beads of sweat stood on his high, narrow forehead.

"I walked over from the Country Club, after eighteen holes of golf with your *superior*, the district attorney," Drake answered, with nasty emphasis. "I left the clubhouse at 5:10, calculating that it would take me about twenty minutes for the walk of—of about a mile."

Dundee made a mental note to find out exactly how far from this lonely house in Primrose Meadows the

Country Club actually was, but his next question was along another line:

"You *walked*, Mr. Drake?—after eighteen holes of golf on a warm day?"

Drake flushed. "My wife had the car. I had driven out with Mr. Sanderson, but he was called away by a long distance message. I lingered at the club for a while, chatting and—er—having a cool drink or two, then I set out afoot."

"No one offered you a lift?" Dundee inquired suavely.

"No. I presume my fellow-members thought I had my car with me, and I asked no one for a lift, for I rather fancied the idea of a walk across the meadows."

"I see," said Dundee thoughtfully. "Now as to your arrival here—"

"I walked in. The door had been left on the latch, as it usually is, when a party is on," Drake explained coldly. "And I was just entering the room when I heard my wife make the remark about covering an honor with an honor, and then her question of Penny as to whether she should have played second hand low."

"So you entered this time at the correct moment," said Dundee. "Now, Mr. Drake, I am going to ask you to re-enter the room and do exactly as you did upon your arrival at approximately 5:33. I am sure you would not willingly hamper me—or *my superior*—in this investigation."

Drake wheeled, ungraciously, and returned to the doorway, while Dundee again consulted his watch, mentally subtracting the minutes which had been wasted upon this interruption, from the time he had marked upon his memory as the moment at which Drake had interfered. But an undercurrent of skepticism nagged at his mind. Why had Drake chosen to *walk*? And why had it taken him from 5:10 to approximately 5:33 to walk a mile or less? The average walker, and especially one accustomed to playing golf, could easily have covered a mile in fifteen minutes, instead of the twenty-three minutes Drake had admitted to.... If it *was* a mile!... Was it possible that the banker loved wildflowers?

With head up aggressively, Drake was undoubtedly making an effort to throw himself into the role—or perhaps into a role chosen on the spot!

"Where's everybody?" he called from the doorway. "Am I early?"

"Don't interrupt, please, dear," Carolyn Drake answered, her voice trembling now, where before it must have been sharp and querulous.

Silently Drake took his place behind his wife's chair, laying a hand affectionately upon her shoulder. Dundee, watching closely, saw Penny's eyes widen with something like shocked surprise. So Drake *was* trying to deceive him, counting on the oneness of this group, his closest friends!

Karen, obviously flustered, too, reached to the dummy for the Ace of Diamonds, to which Penny played the three, Karen herself discarding the ten of Clubs, and Mrs. Drake the five of Diamonds.

"You asked no questions, Mr. Drake?" Dundee interpolated.

The banker flushed again. "I—yes, I believe I did. Carolyn—Mrs. Drake—explained that Karen was playing for a little slam in Spades, and that she had doubled—'on principle'," he added acidly—a voice which Mrs. Drake must be very well accustomed to, Dundee surmised.

"And when I told you that Nita had redoubled and it looked as if she was going to make it," Carolyn Drake whimpered and shifted her short, stout body in the little bridge chair, "you said—why not tell the truth?—you said it was just like me and I might as well take to tatting at bridge parties."

"That was said jokingly, my dear," Drake retorted, with a coldness that tried to be affectionate warmth.

"Play bridge!" Dundee commanded, sure that the approximate length of the previous dispute had now been taken up, whatever retort Carolyn Drake had made. Then he checked himself, again looking at his watch: "And just what did you answer to your husband's little joke, Mrs. Drake?"

"I—I—" The woman looked helplessly around the table, her slate-colored eyes reddened with tears, then she plunged recklessly, after a fearful glance at Dundee's implacable face. "I said that if it was Nita he was talking to, he wouldn't speak in that tone; that she could make all the foolish mistakes of over-bidding or revoking or doubling that she wanted to, and he wouldn't say a word except to praise her—"

"Then I may as well confess," Drake said acidly, "that I answered substantially as follows: 'Nita is an *intelligent* bridge player as well as a charming woman, my dear!...' Now make the most of that little family tiff, sir—and be damned to you!"

"Did that end the scene, Mrs. Drake?" Dundee asked gently.

"I—I said something about all the men thinking Nita was perfect," Mrs. Drake confessed, "and I cried a little, but we went on with the hand. And Johnny—Mr. Drake went away, walking up and down the room, waiting for Nita to come back, I suppose!"

"Then go on with the game," Dundee ordered.

Silently now, as silently as the real game must have been played, because of the embarrassing scene between husband and wife, the sinister game was carried to its conclusion. Karen led the Jack of Hearts from the dummy, Penny played her seven, Karen contributed her own deuce, and Mrs. Drake followed suit with the five.

Again Karen led from the dummy, with the four of Hearts, followed by Penny's nine, taking it with her own Ace, Mrs. Drake throwing off the five of Clubs. Karen then led the six of Hearts, Carolyn Drake discarded the six of Clubs, dummy took the trick with the eight of Hearts, and Penny sloughed the three of Clubs.

With a faint imitation of the triumph with which she had played the hand the first time, Karen threw down her remaining three trumps.

"I've made it—a little slam!" she tried to sound very triumphant. "Doubled and redoubled!... How much did I—did Nita and I make, Penny?"

"Plenty!" But before putting pencil to score pad, Penny cupped her chin in her hands and stared at Carolyn Drake. "I'd like to know, Carolyn, if it isn't one of your most cherished secrets, *what* possessed you to double in the first place?"

Carolyn Drake flushed scarlet as she protested feebly: "I thought of course I could take two Club tricks with my Ace and King.... That's why I doubled the little slam, of course. And my first double simply meant that I had one good suit.... I thought if you could bid at all that my two doubletons—"

"Oh, what's the use?" Penny groaned. "But may I remind you that it is *not* bridge to lead from a Queen?... You led the deuce of Diamonds, when of course the play, since you had seen the Ace in the dummy, was to lead your Queen, forcing the Ace and leaving my King guarded to take a trick later."

"But Karen didn't have any Diamonds at all," Carolyn defended herself.

"A secret you weren't in on when you led from your Queen," Penny reminded her. "Oh, well! We'll pay up and shut up!" and she made a pretense of totting up the score, while Karen, who had risen, stood over her like a bird poised for flight.

At that instant Dexter Sprague began to advance into the room, Janet Raymond at his side, her face flaming.

"Behave exactly as you did before!" Dundee commanded in a harsh whisper. No time for coddling these people now!

Dexter Sprague's face took on a yellower tinge, but he obeyed.

"Greetings!" he called in the jaunty, over-cordial tones of a man who knows himself not too welcome. "Where's Nita—and everybody? Isn't that the cocktail shaker I hear?"

Having received no answer from anyone present, Sprague strolled through the living room and on into the dining room, Janet following. Judge Marshall had nodded stiffly, and John C. Drake had muttered the semblance of a greeting.... Were they all overdoing it a bit—this reacting of their hostility to the sole remaining outsider of their compact little group?... Dundee stroked his chin thoughtfully.

But Penny was saying in her abrupt, husky voice: "Above the line, 1250; below the line 720, making a total of 1970 on this hand, Karen."

"Won't Nita be glad?" Karen gasped, then began to run totteringly, calling: "Nita! Nita!" But in the hall she collapsed, shuddering, crying in a child's whimper: "No, no! I—can't—go in there—again!"

It was Dundee who reached her first—Dundee and not her outraged and excited old husband.

"Mrs. Marshall—listen, please," he begged in a low voice, as he lifted her so that her head rested against his arm. "You have been splendid—wonderful! Please believe that I am truly sorry to distress you so, and that very soon, I hope, you may go home and rest."

"I—can't bear any—more," Karen whimpered.

Ignoring Judge Marshall's blustering, Dundee continued softly: "You don't want the wrong person to be accused of this terrible crime, do you, Mrs. Marshall?... Of course not! And you *do* want to help us all you can to discover who really killed Mrs. Selim?"

"I—I suppose so," Karen conceded, on a sob.

"Then I'll help you. I'll go to the bedroom with you," Dundee promised her with a sigh of relief. To the others he spoke sharply:

"Go back to the exact positions in living room and dining room and solarium, that you occupied when Mrs. Marshall ran from the room."

"I think you're overdoing it, Bonnie," Captain Strawn protested. "But—sure I'll see that they mind you."

With Karen Marshall clinging to his arm, Dundee walked down the hall, beyond the staircase to an open door on his left—a door guarded by a lounging plainclothesman. Seated at the dressing-table of the guests' lavatory was Flora Miles, her sallow dark face so ravaged that she looked ten years older than when he had first seen her an hour before.

"So you were in here when you heard Mrs. Marshall scream, Mrs. Miles?" Dundee paused to ask.

"Yes—yes!" she gasped, rising. "And that horrible man has made me stay in here—. Of course, the door was closed—before. I telephoned home to ask about my children, and then I came in here to—to do my face over—"

"You didn't hear your husband arrive?"

"No,—I didn't hear him arrive," Flora Miles faltered, her handkerchief dabbing at her trembling, over-rouged lips.

"I—see," Dundee said slowly.

He stepped into the little room, leaving Karen to stand weakly against the door frame. Without a word to Mrs. Miles he looked closely at the top of the dressing-table and into the small wastebasket that stood beside it.

"You—you can see that I cold-creamed my face before I put on fresh powder and—and rouged," Flora Miles pointed out, with an obvious effort at offended dignity. "After I came back, while you were making those poor girls play the hand over again, I went through the same motions—because you told all of us to behave exactly as we had done before—"

"I—see," Dundee agreed.

Pretty clever, in spite of being almost frightened to death, Dundee said to himself. But he had been just a shade cleverer than she, for he had been in this room ahead of her, and there had been no balls of greasy face tissue in the wastebasket then!

He was passing out of the room, offering his arm to Karen, when one of his underlined notes thrust itself upon his memory:

"May I see your bridge tally, please, Mrs. Miles?"

"My—bridge tally!" she echoed blankly. "Why—it must be on the table where I was playing—"

"It is not," Dundee assured her quietly. "Perhaps it is in your handbag?" and he glanced at the rather large raffia bag that lay on the table.

She snatched it up, slightly averting her body as she looked hastily through its contents.

"It—isn't here.... Oh, I don't know *where* it is! What does it matter?"

Without replying, Dundee escorted the trembling little discoverer of Nita Selim's body into the large ornate bedroom, murmuring as he did so:

"Don't be frightened, Mrs. Marshall. The bod—I mean Mrs. Selim isn't here now.... And you shan't have to scream. I'll give the signal myself. I just want you to go through the same motions you did before." On jerky feet the girl advanced to Nita's now deserted vanity dresser.

"I—I was calling to her all the time," she whispered. "I didn't even wait to knock, and I—I began to tell her how much we'd made off that hand, when I—when she didn't answer.... I didn't touch her, but I saw—I saw—" Again she gripped her face with her hands and was about to scream.

"I know," Dundee assured her gently. Then he shouted: "Ready!"

Herded by Strawn, the small crowd of men and women came running into the room, Judge Marshall leading the way, Penny being second in line. Penny *second*! Why not Flora Miles, who had been nearer to that room than any of the others, if her story was true— Dundee asked himself. But all had crowded into the room, including Polly Beale and Clive Hammond, before Mrs. Miles crept in.

"Is this the order of your arrival?" Dundee asked them all.

Penny, who was standing against the wall, just inside the doorway, spoke up, staring at Flora with frowning intentness.

"You're sort of mixed up, aren't you, Flora? I was standing right here until the worst of it was over—I didn't even go near Nita, and I know you didn't pass me. I remember that Tracey stepped away from the—body, and called you, and you weren't here. And then almost the next minute I saw you coming toward him from—from— *over there!*"

And Penny pointed toward that corner of the room which held, on one angle, the door leading to the porch, and on its other angle the window from which, or from near which Nita Selim had been shot.

"You're lying, Penny Crain! I did no such thing!" Flora Miles cried hysterically. "I came running in—with—with the rest of you, and I rushed over there just to see if I could see anybody running away across the meadow—"

"My wife is right, sir," Tracey Miles added his word aggressively. "I saw what she was doing—the most sensible of all of us—and I ran to join her. We looked out of the windows, both the side windows and the rear ones, and out onto the porch. But we didn't see anything."

Surprisingly, Dundee abandoned the point.

"And you were the only one to touch her, Sprague?"

"I—believe so," Dexter Sprague answered in a strained voice. "I—laid my hand on her—her hair, for an instant, then I picked up her hand to see if—if there was any pulse left."

"Yes?"

"She—she was dead."

"And her hand—did it feel cold?"

"Neither cold nor warm—just cool," Sprague answered in a voice that was nearly strangled with emotion. "She—she always had cool hands—"

"What did you do, Judge Marshall?" Dundee asked abruptly.

"I took my poor little wife away from this room, laid her on a couch in the living room, and then telephoned the police. Miss Crain stood at my elbow, urging me to hurry, so that she might ring you—as she did. Your line was busy, and she lost about five minutes before getting you."

"And the rest of you?" Dundee asked.

"Nothing spectacular, I'm afraid, Mr. Dundee," Polly Beale answered in her brusque, deep voice, now edged with scorn.

Further questioning elicited little more, beyond the fact that Clive Hammond had dashed out to circle the house and look over the grounds, and that John Drake had been fully occupied with an hysterical wife.

"Better let this bunch go for the present, hadn't we, boy?" Captain Strawn whispered uneasily. "Not a thing on any of them—"

"Not quite yet, sir, if you don't mind," Dundee answered in a low voice. "Will you take them back into the living room and put them under Sergeant Turner's charge for a while? Then there are one or two things I'd like to talk over with you."

Mollified by the younger man's deference and persuasiveness, Strawn obeyed the suggestion, to return within five minutes, his grey brows drawn into a frown.

"I hope you'll be willing to take full credit for that fool bridge game, Bonnie," he worried. "*I* don't want to look a chump in the newspapers!"

"I'll take the blame," Dundee assured him, with a grin. "But that 'fool bridge game'—and I admit it was a horrible thing to have to do—told me a whole bunch of facts that ought to be very, very useful."

"For instance?" Strawn growled.

"For instance," Dundee answered, "it told me that it took approximately eight minutes to play out a little slam bid, when ordinarily it would have taken not more than two or three minutes. Not only that, but it told me the names of everyone in *this* party who could have killed Nita Selim, and—. Good Lord! Of course!"

And to Captain Strawn's amazement Dundee threw open the door of Nita's big clothes closet, jerked on the light, and stooped to the floor.

CHAPTER SEVEN

Almost immediately Special Investigator Dundee rose from his crouching position on the floor of Nita Selim's closet, and faced the chief of the Homicide Squad of Hamilton's police force.

"I think," he said quietly, for all the excitement that burned in his blue eyes, "that we'd better have Mrs. Miles in for a few questions."

"What have you got there—a dance program?" Strawn asked curiously, but as Dundee continued to stare silently at the thing he held, the older man strode to the door and relayed the order to a plainclothes detective.

"I sent for *Mrs.* Miles," Dundee said coldly, when husband and wife appeared together, Flora's thin, tense shoulders encircled by Tracey's plump arm.

"If you're going to badger my wife further, I intend to be present, sir!" Miles retorted, thrusting out his chest.

"Very well!" Dundee conceded curtly. "Mrs. Miles, why didn't you tell me in the first place that you were *in this room* when Nita Selim was shot?"

"Because I wasn't—in—in the room," Flora protested, clinging with both thin, big-veined hands to her husband's arm.

"Sir, you have no proof of this absurd accusation, and I shall personally take this matter up—"

"I have the best of proof," Dundee said quietly, and took his hand from his pocket. "You recognize this, Mrs. Miles?... You admit that it is the tally card you used while playing bridge this afternoon?"

"No, no! It isn't mine!" Flora cried hysterically, cringing against her husband, who began to protest in a voice falsetto with rage.

Dundee ignored his splutterings. "May I point out that it is identical with the other tally cards used at Mrs. Selim's party today, and that on its face it bears your name, 'Flora'?" and he politely extended the card for her inspection.

"I—yes, it *must* be mine, but I was *not* in this room when Nita was—was shot!"

"But you will admit that you *were* in her clothes closet at some time during the twenty or more minutes that elapsed between your leaving the bridge game, when you became dummy, and the moment when Karen Marshall screamed?"

As Flora Miles said nothing, staring at him with great, terrified black eyes, Dundee went on relentlessly: "Mrs. Miles, when you left the bridge game, you did not intend to telephone your house. You came *here*—into this room!—and you lay in wait, hiding in her closet until Nita Selim appeared, as you knew she would, sooner or later—"

"No, no! That's a lie—a lie, I tell you!" the woman shrilled at him. "I *did* telephone my house, and I talked to Junior, when the maid put him up to the phone.... You can ask her yourself, if you don't believe me!"

"But *after* you telephoned, you stole into this room—"

"No, no! I—I made up my face all fresh, just as I told you—"

Dundee did not bother to tell her how well he knew she was lying, for suddenly something knocked on the door of his mind. He strode to the closet, searched for a moment among the multitude of garments hanging there, then emerged with the brown silk summer coat which Nita Selim had worn to Breakaway Inn that noon. Before the terrified woman's eyes he thrust a hand first into one deep pocket and then another, finding nothing except a handkerchief of fine embroidered linen and a pair of brown suede gauntlet gloves.

"Will you let me have the note, please, Mrs. Miles? The note Nita received during her luncheon party, and which she thrust, before your eyes, into a pocket of this coat?... It is in your handbag, I am sure, since you have had no opportunity, unobserved, to destroy it."

"What ghastly nonsense is this, Dundee?" Tracey Miles demanded furiously.

But Dundee again ignored him. His implacable eyes held Flora Miles' until the woman broke suddenly, piteously. She fumbled in the raffia bag which had been hanging from her arm.

"Good God, Flora! What does it all mean?" Tracey Miles collapsed like a pricked pink balloon. "That's *my* stationery—one of my business envelopes—"

Flora Miles dropped the bag which she need no longer watch and clutch with terror, as she dug her thin fingers into her husband's shoulders and looked down at his puzzled face, for she was a little taller than he.

"Forgive me, darling! Oh, I knew God would punish me for being jealous! I thought *you* were writing love letters to—to that woman—"

Dundee did not miss the slightest significance of that scene as he retrieved the blue-grey envelope she had dropped. It was inscribed, in a curious handwriting: "Mrs. Selim, Private Dining Room, Breakaway Inn."

"Let's see, boy," Strawn said, with respect in his harsh voice.

Dundee withdrew the single sheet of business stationery, and obligingly held it so that the chief of detectives could read it also.

"Nita, my sweet," the note began, without date-line, "Forgive your bad boy for last night's row, but I *must* warn you again to watch your step. You've already gone too far. Of course I love you and understand, *but*—Be good, Baby, and you won't be sorry."

The note was signed "Dexy."

Dundee tapped the note for a long minute, while Tracey Miles continued to console his wife. A new avenue, he thought—perhaps a long, long avenue....

"Mrs. Miles," he began abruptly, and the tear-streaked face turned toward him. "You say you thought this letter to Mrs. Selim had been written by your husband?"

"Yes!" She gasped. "I'm jealous-natured. I admit it, and when I saw one of our own—I mean, one of Tracey's business envelopes—"

"You made up your mind to steal it and read it?"

"Yes, I did! A wife has a right to know what her husband's doing, if it's anything—like that—" Her haggard black eyes again implored her husband for forgiveness, before she went on: "I *did* slip into Nita's room and go into her closet to see if she had left the letter in her coat pocket. I closed the door on myself, thinking I could find the light cord, but it was caught in one of the dresses or something, and it took me a long time to find it in the dark of the closet, but I did find it at last, and was just reading the note—"

"You *read* it, even after you saw that the handwriting on the envelope wasn't your husband's?" Dundee queried in assumed amazement.

Flora's thin body sagged. "I—I thought maybe Tracey had disguised his Handwriting.... So I read it, and saw it was from Dexter—"

"Mr. Miles, do you know how some of your business stationery got into Sprague's hands?"

"He's had plenty of opportunity to filch stationery or almost anything he wants, hanging around my offices, as he does—an idler—"

But Dundee was in a hurry. He wheeled from the garrulity of the husband to the tense terror of the wife.

"Mrs. Miles, I want you to tell me exactly what you know, unless you prefer to consult a lawyer first—"

"Sir, if you are insinuating that *my wife*—"

"Oh, let me tell him, Tracey," Mrs. Miles capitulated suddenly, completely. "I *was* in the closet when Nita was killed, I suppose, but I didn't *know* she was being killed!

Because I was lying in there on the closet floor in a dead faint!"

Dundee stared at the woman incredulously, then suppressed a groan of almost unbearable disappointment. If Flora Miles was telling the truth, here went a-flying his only eye-witness, probably, or rather, his only ear witness.

"Just when did you faint, Mrs. Miles?" he asked, struggling for patience. "Before or after Nita came into this room?"

"I was just finishing the note, with the light on in the closet, and the door shut, when I heard Nita come into the room. I knew it was Nita because she was singing one of those Broadway songs she is—was—so crazy about. I jerked off the light, and crouched way back in a corner of the closet. A velvet evening wrap fell down over my head, and I was nearly smothering, but I was afraid to try to dislodge it for fear a hanger would fall to the floor and make an awful clatter. And then—and then—" She shuddered, and clung to her husband.

"What caused you to faint, Mrs. Miles?"

"Sir, my wife has heart trouble—"

"What did you hear, Mrs. Miles?" Dundee persisted.

"I couldn't hear very well, all tangled up in the coat and 'way back in the closet, but I did hear a kind of bang or bump—no, no, not a pistol shot!—and because it came from so near me I thought it was Nita or Lydia coming to get something out of the closet, and I'd be discovered, so I—I fainted—" She drew a deep breath and went on: "When I came to I heard Karen scream, and then people running in—. But all the time that awful tune was going on and on—"

"Tune?" Dundee gasped. "Do you mean—Nita Selim's—*song?*"

Flora Miles seemed to be dazed by Dundee's vehement question.

"Why, yes—Nita's own tune. That's what she called it—her own tune—"

"But, Mrs. Miles," Dundee protested, ashamed that his scalp was prickling with horror, "do you mean to tell me that Nita was not dead *then*—when Karen Marshall screamed?"

"Dead?" Flora repeated, more bewildered. "Of course she was, or at least, they all said so—. Oh, I know what you mean! And you don't mean what I mean at all—"

"Steady, honey-girl!" Tracey Miles urged, putting his arm about his wife. "I'd better tell you, Dundee.... When we all came running into the room, there was Nita's powder box playing its tune over and over—"

"Oh!" Dundee wiped his forehead. "You mean it's a musical box?"

"Yes, and plays when the lid is off," Tracey answered, obviously delighted to have the limelight again. "Well, of course, since Nita couldn't put the lid back on, it was still playing.... What was the tune, honey?" he asked his wife tenderly. "I haven't much ear for music at best, but at a time like that—"

"It was playing *Juanita*," Flora answered wearily. "Over and over—*'Nita, Jua-a-n-ita, be my own fair bride'*," she quavered obligingly. "Only not the words, of course, just the tune. That's why Nita bought the box, I suppose, because it played her namesake song—"

"Maybe one of her beaus gave it to her," Tracey suggested lightly, patting his wife's trembling shoulder. "Anyway, Dundee, the thing ran on and on, until it ran down, I suppose. I confess I wanted to put the lid back on, to stop the damned thing, but Hugo said we mustn't touch anything—"

"And quite right!" Dundee cut in. "Now, Mrs. Miles, about that noise you heard.... Did you hear anyone enter the room?... No?... Well, then, did you hear Nita speak to anyone? You said you thought it might be Lydia, coming to get something out of the closet."

"I didn't hear Nita speak a word to anybody, though she might have and I wouldn't have heard, all muffled up in that velvet evening wrap and so far back in the closet—"

"Did you hear the door onto the porch—it's *quite* near the closet—"

"The door was open when we came in, Dundee," Tracey interposed. "It must have been open all the time."

"I didn't hear it open," Mrs. Miles confirmed him wearily. "I tell you I didn't hear *anything*, except Nita's coming in singing, then the powder box playing its tune, and that bang or bump I told you about."

"And just where was that?" Dundee persisted.

"*I don't know!*" she shrilled, hysteria rising in her voice again. "I told you it sounded fairly near the closet, as if—as if somebody bumped into something. That's what it was like! That's exactly what it was like. And I was so frightened of being found in the closet that I fainted, and didn't come to until Karen screamed—"

She was babbling on, but Dundee was thinking hard. A very convenient faint—that! For the murderer, at least! But—why not for Mrs. Miles herself? Odd that she should *faint*! Why hadn't she trumped up some excuse immediately and left the closet as Nita was entering the room? Was it, possibly, because she could think of nothing but the great relief of finding that it was Sprague, not her husband, who had been writing love letters to Nita Selim?... A jealous woman—

"Miles," he began abruptly, "I think you'd better tell me how your wife became so jealous of you and Nita Selim that she could get herself into such a false position."

Tracey Miles reddened, but a gesture of one of his sunburned hands restrained his wife's passionate defense of him. "It's the truth that Flora is jealous-natured. And I suppose—" he faltered a moment, and his eyes did not meet his wife's, "—that I liked seeing her a little bit jealous of her old man. Sort of makes a man feel—well, big, you know. And pretty important to somebody!"

"So you were just having a bit of fun with your wife, so far as Mrs. Selim was concerned?" Dundee asked coldly.

The blood flowed through the thinning blond hair. "We-el, not exactly," he admitted frankly. "You see, I *did* take a shine to Nita, and if I do say so myself, she liked me a lot.... Oh, nothing serious! Just a little flirtation, like most of our crowd have with each other—"

"Mrs. Miles," Dundee interrupted with sudden harshness, "are you *sure* you did not know that that letter was from Dexter Sprague before you looked for it?"

"Sir, if you are insinuating that *my wife* carried on a flirtation or—an—an *affair* with that Sprague insect—" Tracey began to bluster.

But Dundee's eyes were on Flora Miles, and he saw that her sallow skin had tightened like greyish silk over her thin cheek bones, and that her eyes looked suddenly dead and glassy.

"You *fainted*, you say, Mrs. Miles," Dundee went on inexorably. "Was it because, by any chance, this note—" and he tapped the sheet which had caused so much trouble—"revealed the fact that Nita Selim and Dexter Sprague were sweethearts or—lovers?"

It was a battle between those two now. Both ignored Tracey's red-faced rage.

Flora licked her dry lips. "No—no," she whispered. "*No!* It was because I was jealous of Tracey and Nita—"

"Yes, and I'd given her cause to be jealous, too!" Tracey forced himself into the conversation. "One night, at the Country Club, Flora saw me and Nita stroll off the porch and down onto the grounds, and she had a right to be sore at me when I got back, because I'd cut a dance with her—my own wife!... And it was only this very morning that I made a point of driving—out of my way too—by this house to see Nita. Not that I meant any harm, but I was being a little silly about her—and she was about me, too! Not that I'd leave my wife and babies for any Broadway beauty under the sun—"

"Oh, Tracey! And you weren't going to tell me—" Was there *real* jealousy now, or just pretense on Flora's part?

"You understand, don't you, Dundee?" Tracey demanded, man to man. "I was just having a little fun on the side—nothing serious, mind you! But of course I didn't tell Flora every little thing—. No man does! There've been other girls—other women—"

"Tracey isn't worse than the other men!" Flora flamed up. "He's such a darling that all the girls pet him, and spoil him—"

Dundee could stand no more of Miles' complacent acceptance of his own rakishness. And certainly a girl like Nita Selim would have been able to bear precious little of it.... Conceited ass! But Flora Miles was another matter—and so was Dexter Sprague!

"You can join me in the living room, if you like," Dundee said shortly, as he wheeled and strode toward the door. Was that quick, passionate kiss between husband and wife being staged for his benefit?

"Pretty near through, boy?" Strawn, who had been silent and bewildered for a long time, asked anxiously, as the two detectives passed into the hall.

"Not quite. I've got to know several things yet," Dundee answered absently.

But in the living room his mind was wholly upon the business in hand.

"I'll keep you all no longer than is absolutely necessary," he began, and again the close-knit group—in which only Dexter Sprague was an alien—grew taut with suspense. "From the playing out of the 'death hand' at bridge," he went on, using the objectionable phrase again very deliberately, "I found that no two of you men arrived together.... Mr. Hammond, you were the first to arrive, I believe?"

"It seems that I was!" Clive Hammond answered curtly.

"And yet you did not enter the living room to greet your hostess?"

"I wanted a private word with Polly—Miss Beale—my fiancee," Hammond explained briefly.

"How and when did you arrive?"

"I don't know the exact time. Never thought of looking at my watch," Hammond offered. "I came out in my own roadster—that tan Stutz you may have noticed in the driveway. As for how I entered the house, I leaped upon the porch and opened a door of the solarium. I walked across the solarium, saw Polly just finishing with bridge for the afternoon, and beckoned to her. She joined me in the solarium, and we stayed there until Karen screamed.... That's all."

"Have you been engaged long, Mr. Hammond—you and Miss Beale?" Dundee asked, as if quite casually.

"Nearly a year,—if it's any of your business, Dundee!"

"And just when had you seen Miss Beale last, before late this afternoon?" Dundee asked.

"I refuse to answer!" Hammond flared. "That at least is none of your damned business!"

"I believe I can answer my own question, Mr. Hammond," Dundee said very softly.

CHAPTER EIGHT

"Then why ask me?" Hammond shrugged, but his eyes flickered toward Polly Beale.

"I thought perhaps you could give me a little additional information," Dundee soothed him. "You see, it happens that I saw you, Miss Beale and another young man come into the Stuart House dining room about half past one today, just when I was thinking of lunch for myself."

"The mysterious 'other young man' was Clive's brother, Ralph Hammond," Polly Beale cut in brusquely.

"Your decision to lunch with your fiance and his brother was quite a sudden one?" Dundee asked courteously. "Just when did you change your mind about Mrs. Selim's luncheon party at Breakaway Inn, Miss Beale?"

The tall girl threw up her mannishly cropped, chestnut head. "There is nothing at all sinister or even queer about it, Mr. Dundee! I was on my way to the luncheon, when I decided to drive past Nita's house, on the chance that she might like me to drive her over."

"Then you didn't know that Mrs. Dunlap had already arranged to meet Mrs. Selim downtown this morning and to take her to the Inn?" Dundee asked.

"No! I didn't hear of the arrangement," Polly answered decidedly.

"You were a close friend of Mrs. Selim's perhaps?" Dundee prodded.

"Not at all! But that would not keep me from doing my hostess a courtesy.... She hated her Ford and liked expensive cars," Polly added unemotionally. "It was about a quarter to one when I got here, I should say. Nita wasn't here, nor was her maid, but I saw Ralph's car parked in front of the house—"

"*Ralph Hammond's car?*" a woman squealed, but Dundee let Polly continue.

"I rang and he answered the door. Said he was alone in the house, going over the premises at Judge Marshall's request," Polly said evenly.

"That's right—that's right!" Judge Marshall agreed hastily. "Nita—Mrs. Selim—wanted the unfinished half of the gabled top story finished up. Wanted a maid's room and bath, and a guest room and bath added to the living quarters already completed. I gave the commission, for an estimate, at least, to the Hammond firm, since they had built the house originally for Crain—Penny's father."

"I see," Dundee agreed. "And you sent your brother, Mr. Hammond?"

"He was the natural one to send," Clive Hammond retorted. "Small job. All he had to do was to get together an estimate on additional furnace lines and radiators, electric wiring, plumbing, plastering, etc."

"Go on, Miss Beale," Dundee directed.

"Thanks!" There was sarcasm in her brusque voice. "But that's really about all I have to tell. Ralph complained that he was hungry and charged me with giving him too little of my time—the usual thing. I picked up Nita's phone, called Clive and made the date for the three of us. Then I called Breakaway Inn, cancelled the luncheon part of the bridge party with Nita, and Ralph and I drove back to Hamilton."

Dundee studied her strong, clever, almost plain face for a long minute. Certainly Polly Beale did not look like a liar—but he would have taken his oath that she was lying now. Or rather not revealing the whole truth behind the actual facts of her movements that day. For instance, could a simple plea of her future brother-in-law make her do so discourteous a thing as to break a luncheon appointment, especially when such a course would not only disappoint her hostess and her friends but disarrange the seating plan of a rather formal party?

Of course the explanation was obvious. She had wanted, first, to see Nita and remonstrate privately with her for having so enslaved Ralph Hammond, when he was tacitly known to "belong" to Penny Crain—one of the sacred crowd. Failing that, she had found Ralph himself, and had not expected to find him; had talked with him about Nita, and had quarreled a bit with him, perhaps, over his love-sodden behavior. And the crisis had become so acute that Polly had arbitrarily called upon Clive Hammond and then had forced Ralph to accompany her.

"Do you know, Miss Beale, why Ralph Hammond did not keep *his* engagement with Mrs. Selim this afternoon? Or rather, his promise to appear for cocktails and to be Miss Crain's partner for the rest of the evening—dinner and dancing at the Country Club?"

"I do not!" Polly said crisply.

"Hammond?"

"Neither do I," Hammond retorted angrily.

"Then it was not to discuss Ralph Hammond and his—affairs, that you beckoned Miss Beale to meet you in the solarium upon your arrival?"

"It—*was not!*"

A shade too much anger and emphasis, Dundee decided. And he wished heartily that Strawn's detectives would not delay much longer in bringing the missing young man into this already involved examination.

"You say that you both were in the solarium from the time of your arrival, Hammond, until Mrs. Marshall screamed," Dundee continued. "Just what did you see and hear?"

Dundee watched their faces keenly, but again they were well-bred, expressionless. It was Polly Beale who answered: "Naturally there was not absolute silence, but I am afraid we were not listening. We were rather engrossed in our conversation. We were seated—near no windows—and I for one *saw* nothing, as well as heard nothing that I can recall."

"Hammond?"

"That goes for me, too—absolutely!"

Abruptly abandoning the engaged couple, Dundee returned to Miles. "You were the second arrival, then?"

"Yes. I parked my car along the curb in front of the house," Tracey answered readily. "And I came right on in, and Nita jumped up—"

"Yes. We've had all that twice before," Dundee interrupted cruelly. "Now, Judge Marshall—"

"One of my friends gave me a lift from town," Judge Marshall volunteered pompously. "Chap named Sampson. You may have heard of him—fine fellow, splendid lawyer. We played billiards together at the Athletic Club, and when I was about to call a taxi—my wife having the car here—he offered to drop me here on his way to the Country Club.... N-no, I don't remember the exact time, did not consult my watch."

"You came directly from the road into the house, Judge Marshall?"

"Certainly, sir!"

"Did you—er, see anyone?"

"You mean, sir, did anyone see *me*?" Judge Marshall demanded with pompous indignation. "No, no one, sir! If my word is not good enough for you, you can think what you damned please!"

"I think we are all getting a little too tired, Mr. Dundee," Penny Crain suggested, almost humble in her weariness.

"I'm truly sorry," the young detective apologized. "But I can't leave things like this ... Mr. Drake, you have said you walked over from the Country Club. You must have approached the house from the driveway side, the side of the house which contains Mrs. Selim's bedroom.... Is that right?"

"More or less, except that I skirted the house rather widely and arrived from the road, stepping upon the front porch, and walking directly into the hall. I saw no one outside or near the house when I arrived," Drake answered, with less than his usual nastiness.

"And saw no one running away across the meadows?" Dundee pressed.

"No one at all," Drake retorted. "I wish to God I could truthfully say that I saw a gunman, with a mask and a smoking revolver, skulking through the wildflowers, but the absolute truth is that I saw no one."

"Thank you, Mr. Drake.... Now—Mr. Sprague, 'of New York'!"

Sprague's nervously twitching face reddened darkly. "I—I took a bus. I have no car of my own. I got off the bus on Sheridan Road, at the entrance to Primrose Meadows."

"I see. And you walked the quarter of a mile to this house?"

Sprague's hand fumbled with his cravat. "I—of course I did!"

"I see.... Now, Miss Raymond," Dundee pounced unexpectedly, so that the red-haired girl went very white beneath her freckles, "you observed Mr. Sprague toiling down the rutty road, hot and weary, but romantic in the sunset?"

Mrs. Drake let out a nervous giggle, then clapped her hand over her mouth.

"I—I wasn't looking that way," Janet Raymond stammered. "I—I just went out on the porch for a breath of fresh air—"

"And you were *completely* surprised when Mr. Sprague came walking up the flagstone path?" Dundee persisted, for he knew she was lying, knew that she had stationed herself there to watch for Sprague.

"I—yes, I was! He stopped and talked for a while, before we came in and joined Tracey and Lois in the dining room, where Tracey was mixing cocktails.... But," she flared suddenly, "I don't see why you have to badger all of us, when it *must* have been Lydia, the maid, who killed Nita, because—"

"Oh, Janet! Shame on you!" Penny cried furiously.

"Where is the maid now, Captain Strawn?" Dundee asked. "I haven't seen her yet—"

"Because she's in her room in the basement, Bonnie," Strawn answered. "Sort of forgot about her, didn't you?" and he chuckled at the younger man's discomfiture. "But *I* got her story out of her, you bet! Nothing to it, though. One of my boys—Collins, it was—found her in that short, dark hall that runs between the Selim woman's bedroom and the kitchen. Sicker'n a pup she was; it was a mess. Said she'd—"

"I'd better have her up and question her, if she's well enough," Dundee interrupted, as tactfully as possible. "It seems that she had an abscessed tooth out today, with gas and a local anesthetic.... Now, Miss Raymond, will you tell me exactly what you meant by saying it must have been Lydia who killed her mistress?"

"I certainly will!" the red-haired girl cried defiantly. "What I can't see is why Tracey and Lois and Dex—Mr. Sprague—didn't think of it, too. It's as plain as—"

"Yes, as the nose on my face," Dundee cut in grimly, but with a glance at Strawn. "Just stick to the facts, however, Miss Raymond, and maybe we can all agree with you."

"Well, when Mr. Sprague and I went into the dining room, there were Lois and Tracey cutting up like a couple of children," Janet began, determined to take her time. "When they saw us, Lois said: 'Good Lord, Tracey! Get busy! Or your job as bartender will be taken away from you,' and Tracey began to shake cocktails at the sideboard—"

"Guess I'd better tell it, Janet, for what it's worth," Lois cut in impatiently. "It's nothing more nor less than that I had to ring twice for poor Lydia before she came," she explained to Dundee. "Tracey is full of original ideas about cocktails, and wanted some sort of bitters. He was going to shout for Lydia, but I stepped on the button under the dining table, and the poor thing—in the basement nursing her jaw, probably—didn't hear. Tracey and I got to kidding, as Janet says, and had scarcely noticed how long Lydia was in coming. I rang again, and she came.... That's all!"

"That isn't all!" Janet denied angrily. "I was there when Lydia came in, and she was looking white as a ghost—except for her swollen jaw. What's more, she acted so dumb Tracey had to tell her twice what he wanted.... And then she said Nita didn't have any of those bitters anyway."

"An open-and-shut case against poor Lydia!" Penny Crain broke in derisively. "Go pluck daisies, Janet! You'd be of a lot more help!"

"Here's your maid, Bonnie," Captain Strawn announced lazily, as one of his plainclothesmen appeared in the arch between dining and living room, dragging by the hand a woman who was resisting strangely, her apron pressed to her face.

"You are Lydia?" Dundee asked, his voice kinder than it had been for many minutes. "Oh, it's Lydia Carr, Captain Strawn? Thank you.... Don't be afraid. And I'm sorry about the tooth.... Come along in. I'll not keep you long."

The woman's knees seemed about to fail her, but with a sudden effort she released the detective's grip on her wrist. Very tall she was, very bony in her black cotton dress. Pathetic, too, with her thin, iron-grey hair, and that apron concealing the left half of her face. It was odd, Dundee thought, that it was not the swollen jaw she chose to cover.

Mrs. Dunlap sprang to her feet and hurried across the room.

"Don't mind, Lydia, please. You must not be so sensitive," she said gently, and even more gently pulled down the concealing apron....

"Good God!" Dundee breathed, and Strawn nodded his understanding of the younger man's horror.

For the left half of Lydia Carr's face was drawn and puckered and ridged almost out of human semblance. Even the eye was ruined—a milky ball which the puckered, hairless eyelid could never cover again.

"Poor Lydia is ashamed of her scarred face," Lois Dunlap explained, her arm still about the maid's shoulder. "She isn't quite used to it yet, but none of *us* mind—"

"You were burned recently, Lydia?" Dundee asked pityingly.

"That's my business!" the woman astounded him by retorting harshly.

"How did it happen, Lydia?" Dundee persisted, puzzled.

"I had an accident. It was my own fault."

Lois Dunlap's kind grey eyes caught and held Dundee's firmly. "I think, if Nita could speak to you now, Mr. Dundee, that she would beg you not to try to force Lydia's confidence on this subject. Nita was devoted to Lydia—we can all testify to that!—and one of the sweetest things about her was her constant effort to protect Lydia from questions and curious glances. I, for one, know that Nita often begged Lydia to submit to a skin-grafting operation, regardless of expense—"

When that kind voice choked on tears, Dundee abruptly abandoned his intention to press the matter further.

"Lydia, your mistress had been married, or was still married, wasn't she?"

The woman's single, slate-grey eye stared into his expressionlessly. "She had 'Mrs.' in front of her name, to use when she felt like it. That's all I know. I never saw her husband—if she had one. I only worked for her about five years."

"You say she used her married name 'when she felt like it....' What do you mean by that, Lydia?"

"I mean she was an actress, and used her stage name—Juanita Leigh—pronounced like it was spelled plain 'Lee'; but she was mostly called 'Nita Leigh'."

"An actress, you say?" Dundee repeated thoughtfully. "I had heard of her only as director of the Forsyte School plays.... What shows was she in?"

"She was what they call a specialty dancer in musical comedy," Lydia answered. "Sometimes she had a real part and sometimes she only danced. She was a good hoofer and a good trouper," she added, the Broadway terms falling strangely from those austere lips. "And when she wasn't in a show she sometimes got a job in the pictures. She never had a real chance in the movies, though, because they mostly wanted her to double for the star in long shots, where dancing comes into the picture, or in close-ups where they just show the legs, you know."

"I see," Dundee agreed gravely. "Where were you during the fifteen minutes or so before your mistress was shot, Lydia?"

"I was down in my room in the basement," the woman answered. "Nita—I mean Miss Nita was going to get Judge Marshall to build me a room on the top floor. She hated for me to have to sleep in the basement, but I didn't mind."

"You were not required to be on duty for the party?"

"No," she answered in her harsh, flat voice. "I'd fixed the sandwiches and put out the liquors for the cocktails—set them all out on the dining table and sideboard, and Miss Nita had told me to go and lie down as soon as I was through. So I did. I had an abscessed tooth pulled this morning, and I was feeling sick."

"Did you hear the kitchen bell at all?" Dundee went on.

"I dropped off to sleep—that fool dentist had shot me full of dope—but I did hear the bell and I come up to answer it. Mrs. Dunlap said she'd rung twice, and I said I was sorry—"

"Lydia, did you go into your mistress' bedroom before or after you answered that bell?" Dundee asked with sudden sharpness.

"I did not! I didn't even know she was in her bedroom, until I saw her sitting at her dressing-table—dead." The harsh voice hesitated over the last word, but it did not break.

"And just when did you first see her—after she was dead?"

"I went into the kitchen, thinking something else might be needed. Then I heard a scream. It sounded like it come from Nita's—Miss Nita's bedroom, and I run along the back hall that leads from the kitchen to her bedroom. I heard a lot of people running and yelling. Nobody paid any attention to me."

"You came into the room?"

"No, sir, I did not. I stopped in the doorway. I heard Mr. Sprague say she was dead. I was sick and dizzy anyway, and I couldn't move for a minute. I sort of slipped down to the floor, and I guess I must have passed out. And then I was sick to my stomach, and—I didn't seem to care if I never moved again."

"Why, Lydia?" Dundee asked gently.

"Because she was the only friend I had in the world, and I couldn't have loved her better if she'd been my own child," Lydia answered. And the stern voice had broken at last. "I was still there in the back hall when a cop come and asked me a lot of questions, and then that man—" she pointed to Captain Strawn, "—said I could go and lay down. He helped me down the basement stairs."

Dundee tapped his teeth with the long pencil he had kept so busy that evening—tapped them long and thoughtfully. Then:

"Lydia, did you see anyone—*anyone at all!*—from your basement room window before you answered Mrs. Dunlap's ring?"

CHAPTER NINE

For the first time during the difficult interview Dundee was sure that Lydia Carr was lying. For a fraction of a second her single eye wavered, the lid flickered, then came her harsh, flat denial:

"I didn't see nobody."

"I presume your basement room has a window looking out upon the back garden?" Dundee persisted.

"Yes, it has, but I didn't waste no time looking out of it," Lydia answered grimly. "I was laying down, with an ice cap against my jaw."

She *had* seen someone, Dundee told himself. But the truth would be harder to extract from that stern, scar-twisted mouth, than the abscessed tooth had been.

Finally, when her lone eye did not again waver under his steady gaze, he dismissed her, or rather, returned her to Captain Strawn's custody.

"Well, Janet, I hope you're satisfied!" Penny Crain said bitingly, as she dashed unashamed tears from her brown eyes. "If ever a maid was absolutely crazy about her mistress—"

"I'm *not* satisfied!" Janet Raymond retorted furiously. "She's just the sort that would harbor a grudge for *years*, and then, all hopped up with dope—"

"Stop it, Janet!" Lois Dunlap commanded with a curtness that set oddly upon her kind, pleasant face.

"Listen here, Dundee," Tracey Miles broke in, almost humbly. "My wife is getting pretty anxious about the kiddies. The nurse quit on us yesterday, and—"

"And *my* little wife is worrying herself sick over our boy—just three months old," Judge Marshall joined the protest. "I'm all for assisting justice, sir, having served on the bench myself, as you doubtless know, but—"

"I'm all right, really, Hugo," Karen Marshall faltered.

"Please be patient a little longer," Dundee urged apologetically. After all, only one of these people could be guilty of Nita Selim's murder, and it *was* beastly to have to hold them like this.... *But one was guilty!*

"You knew Mrs. Selim in New York, Sprague?" he asked, whirling suddenly upon the man with the Broadway stamp.

"I met Nita Leigh, as I always heard her called, when I was assistant director in the Altamont Studios, out on Long Island," Sprague answered, his black eyes trying to meet Dundee's with an air of complete frankness. "Wonderful little girl, and a great dancer ... Screened damned well, too. I had hoped to give her a break some day, at something better than doubling for stars who can't dance. But it happened that Nita, who never forgot even a casual friend, had a chance to give me a leg up herself—a chance to show what I can really do with a camera."

"I knew I'd seen your name somewhere!" Dundee exclaimed. "So you're the man the Chamber of Commerce is dickering with.... Going to make a movie of the founding, growth and beauties of the city of Hamilton, aren't you?"

"If I get the contract—yes," Sprague answered with palpably assumed modesty. "My plans, naturally, call for a great deal of research work, a large expenditure of money, a very careful selection of 'stars'—"

"I see," Dundee interrupted. Then his tone changed, became slow and menacing in its terrible emphasis: "*And you really couldn't let even a good friend like Nita Selim upset those fine plans of yours, could you, Sprague?*"

Even as he put the sinister question, the detective was exulting to himself: "Light at last! Now I know why this Broadway bounder was received into an exclusive crowd like this! Every last female in the bunch hoped to be the star of Sprague's motion picture!"

"I don't know what you're driving at, Dundee!" Sprague was on his feet, his black eyes blazing out of a chalky face. "If you're accusing me of—of—"

"Of killing Nita Selim?" Dundee asked lazily. "Oh, no! Not—yet, Sprague! I was just remembering a rather puzzling note of yours I happened to read this afternoon.... That note you sent by special messenger to Breakaway Inn this noon, you know."

He had little interest for the sudden crumpling of Dexter Sprague into the chair from which he had risen. Instead, as Dundee drew the note from his coat pocket, his eyes swept around the room, noted the undisguised relief on every face, the almost ghoulish satisfaction with which that close-knit group of friends seized upon an outsider as the probable murderer of that other outsider whom they had rashly taken into their sacred circle. Even Penny Crain, thorny little stickler for fair play that she was, relaxed with a tremulous sigh.

"You admit that this note, signed by what I take to be your 'pet name,' was written by your hand, Sprague?" Dundee asked matter-of-factly, as he extended the sheet of bluish notepaper.

"I—no—yes, I wrote it," Sprague faltered. "But it doesn't mean a thing—not a damned thing! Just a little private matter between Nita and myself—"

"Rather queer wording for an unimportant message, Sprague," Dundee interrupted. "Let me refresh your memory: 'Nita, my sweet,'" he began to read slowly, "'Forgive your bad boy for last night's row, but I *must* warn you again to watch your step. You've already gone too far. Of course I love you and understand, *but*—Be good, Baby, *and you won't be sorry!*—Dexy....' Well, Sprague?"

Sprague wiped his perspiring hands on his handkerchief. "I know it sounds—odd, under the circumstances," he admitted desperately, "but listen, Dundee, and I'll try to make that damned note as clear as possible to a man who doesn't know his Broadway....

Why, man, it isn't even a love letter! Everybody on
Broadway talks and writes to each other like that,
without meaning a thing!... As I told you, Nita Leigh, or
Mrs. Selim, remembered some little kindnesses I had
done her on the Altamont lot, when they got her to take
up that Little Theater work Mrs. Dunlap is interested in,
and found that the Chamber of Commerce was interested
in putting Hamilton into the movies, in a big booster
campaign. She wired me and I thought it looked good
enough to drop everything and come.... Of course Nita
and I got to be closer friends, but I swear to God we were
just friends—"

"And what was the 'friendly' row about last night,
Sprague?"

"There wasn't a row, really," Sprague protested with
desperate earnestness. "It was merely that Nita insisted
on my casting her for the heroine of the movie—a thing I
knew would alienate the whole crowd that's been so kind
to us—"

"Why—since she was a professional actress?" Dundee
demanded.

"Because she isn't a Hamilton girl, of course, and the
Chamber of Commerce wants the cast to be all local
talent," Sprague answered, lapsing unconsciously into the
present tense.

"And just what were you warning her against?"

"I'd told her before to watch her step," Sprague went
on more easily. "You see, Dundee, Nita Leigh is—was—a
first-class little vamp, and I could see she was playing her
cards with the men here—" he indicated four of
Hamilton's most prominent Chamber of Commerce
members with a wave of his hand—"to get them all so
crazy about her that they'd vote for her as the star of the
picture. I could see her point, all right. It would have
been a big chance for her to show how she could act....
Well, I could see it was dangerous business, and that the
girls—" and he smiled jerkily at the tense women in the
living room, "—were getting pretty wrought up over the

way Nita was behaving.... All except Mrs. Dunlap," he added. "*She* didn't want to act in the picture, and Nita didn't make any headway at all with Peter Dunlap."

"Thanks, Mr. Sprague," Lois Dunlap drawled, with an amused quirk of her broad mouth.

"Get along with the row, Sprague!" Dundee commanded impatiently.

"As I said, it wasn't really a row. I just pleaded with Nita last night to smooth down the girls' rumpled feathers, and to make it clear to them that she didn't want the star part in the picture any more than she wanted any other woman's husband or sweetheart.... Just a friendly warning—" Sprague drew a deep breath. "And that's all the note meant—absolutely!"

"I see," Dundee said quietly, then quoted: "*'Be good, Baby, and you won't be sorry!'*"

"That meant, of course," Sprague took him up eagerly, "that I'd see she got a real part in a regular movie, after I'd made my hit with the Hamilton picture."

Very plausible, very plausible indeed, Dundee reflected. And yet—

Finally he lifted his head and let his eyes dart from face to face.

"All of you have stated, separately and collectively, that you heard no shot fired in Nita Selim's bedroom this afternoon," he said sharply. "Is that true?"

He was answered by weary nods or sullen affirmations.

"Then," he continued, "I must conclude that you are all lying or that Nita Selim was killed with a gun equipped with a Maxim silencer."

Never was a detective more unprepared for the effect of his words upon a group of possible suspects than was Special Investigator Dundee....

CHAPTER TEN

As Dexter Sprague had glibly and plausibly explained away every sinister aspect of the note he had written to Nita Selim that day, Special Investigator Dundee was recalling with verbatim vividness his argument with Captain Strawn of the Homicide Squad immediately after his arrival into the house of violent death.

He had said then: "The person who killed Nita Selim, was so well known to her, and his—or her—presence in this room so natural a thing that she paid no attention to his or her movements and was concentrating on the job of powdering her very pretty face."

And he had said further, in face of the disappearance of the gun and in explanation of the fact that all twelve of these people had immediately protested to Strawn that they had heard no shot:

"This was a premeditated murder, of course. The Maxim silencer—unless they are all lying about not hearing a shot—proves that. Silencers are damned hard to get hold of, but people with plenty of money can manage most things."

And as Dexter Sprague had talked on, more and more glibly, Dundee had suddenly found an explanation which fitted his own argument with such perfection that he wondered, naively, if he were perhaps gifted with clairvoyance.

Of all these twelve people, whom he had questioned so relentlessly, only Dexter Sprague could easily have come into possession of a Maxim silencer. He had dilated proudly upon the fact that he had been an assistant director at the Altamont Studios on Long Island. And the Altamont company had recently finished making a series of "underworld" motion pictures—crook dramas featuring gunmen with "rods" made eerily noiseless by Maxim silencers.

A bit of information he had picked up in a motion picture magazine had hurtled into the logical chain of Dundee's reasoning: assistant directors were in charge of "props"; it was their business to see that no article needed for the production of a picture was lost or missing when the director needed it. Dexter Sprague had said that he had "dropped everything" to come when Nita Selim wired him of the Chamber of Commerce project to make a "booster" movie of Hamilton.

Perhaps he *had* dropped everything. But—*had he hesitated long enough to pick up a Maxim silencer and a blunt-nosed automatic?* And was the "row" which Sprague had been so glibly explaining away an ancient one—a row so deadly that, when Nita Selim had refused to heed his written warning, her murder had become necessary?

It was with all this in mind that Bonnie Dundee flung his challenge: "I must conclude that you are all lying or that Nita Selim was killed with a gun equipped with a Maxim silencer."

And his eyes, terrible with their command that the weakling should break and confess, were upon Dexter Sprague. But Sprague did not break. He stared back blankly....

If his eyes and his attention had included the whole group it is possible that what happened would not have taken Dundee so completely by surprise. He had paid little attention to a sort of concerted gasp, a slight movement among the group farthest from him.

But not even his intense concentration upon Sprague could prevent his hearing Karen Marshall's childish voice, tremulous with fear:

"No, no, Hugo! Don't—don't!"

He whirled from Sprague in time to see Judge Marshall disengaging his arm from his young wife's clinging fingers, to note, with profound astonishment, that Drake was stepping hastily aside, so that not even his coat sleeve might be brushed by the advancing figure of the elderly, retired judge. And before Judge Marshall had time to speak, Dundee saw that a blight had touched, at last, the solid friendship of the women; that they did not look at each other with that air of standing together whatever happened, but that their eyes, not meeting at all, became secret, calculating, afraid....

"Sir!" Judge Marshall began pompously, when he had planted himself squarely before the young detective, "It shall never be said of me that I have tried, even in the slightest way, to hamper the course of justice."

"I am sure of that, Judge Marshall," Dundee replied courteously, but his pulses were hammering. What, in God's name, did this long-winded old fool have to tell him?... "You have some information you believe may be valuable, Judge?"

"I do not believe it will be at all valuable, sir. On the contrary!" the old man retorted indignantly. "But to suppress the fact at this juncture might lead to grave misunderstandings later, when it inevitably comes to light. So, sir, it is my duty to inform you that I myself own a Colt's .32, as well as a Maxim silencer."

"What!" Dundee exclaimed incredulously. He was conscious that, behind him, Captain Strawn was getting to his feet.

"There is no need to get out your handcuffs, Captain Strawn!" Judge Marshall warned him majestically. "I assure you that I have not violated the law. Every judge, active and retired, is entitled to a permit to carry a weapon, and I long ago availed myself of the privilege. Nor am I about to make a confession of murder!"

"There ain't no permit, so far as I know, Judge," Strawn growled, "for any man, whoever he may be—God A'mighty himself not excepted—to tote a gun with a silencer on it."

Karen Marshall was crying now, with the abandoned grief of a petted child.

"Granted, Captain!" Judge Marshall snapped. "But it happens that I do not 'tote' my gun with the silencer on it. If it interests you, I may as well explain that I came by the silencer several years ago, when I was on the bench. A notorious Chicago gunman, on trial for murder here, and acquitted by a feeble-minded jury, made me a present of the very silencer he had used in killing his victim—an ironic gesture, a gesture of supreme insolence, but an entirely safe gesture, since he well knew that a man once acquitted of a crime cannot again be placed in jeopardy for the same offence."

"So you kept the silencer as a curiosity, Judge Marshall?" Dundee interrupted the pompous flow of rhetoric.

"For years—yes," the ex-judge answered, then his face went yellow and very old. "As I told you just now, I will withhold no fact that may be of any relevance whatever.... About two months ago—in March, I believe—our little group here took up target-shooting as a fad. Several of us became quite expert with revolver and rifle. Mr. Drake—" and he nodded toward the banker, who instantly averted his eyes, "—conceived the idea of practising the draw-from-the-hip sort of revolver-shooting—the kind one sees in Wild West movies, you know—"

"I think you might add, Hugo," Drake cut in angrily, "that I had in mind the hope of being able to protect the bank in case of a holdup!"

"And the silencer, Judge Marshall?" Captain Strawn prodded.

Judge Marshall flushed, and fingered the end of a waxed mustache. "The silencer, sir, was my wife's idea. You see, sir, we are fortunate enough to be the parents of an infant son. He was just a month old when I painted a bull's eye upon the brick wall of our back garden and invited our friends to indulge their fad as our guests. The shooting awakened the baby so frequently that Karen—Mrs. Marshall—dug up the silencer, which I had shown her as a memento of my career on the bench. Thereafter we confined our practice almost exclusively to drawing from the hip and shooting without sighting. It is impossible to sight with a gun equipped with a silencer, you know, since the silencer covers the sighter on the barrel."

"It sure does," Strawn drawled. "So every last one of you folks had a good deal of this sort of practice, I take it?"

Judge Marshall glanced about the room, as if he could not recall the face of everyone present.

"Yes, all of us—except Mr. Sprague and—Penny, my dear, did you join us at all?"

The girl who had once been in on every sport that this crowd of Hamilton's socially elect indulged in, flushed a painful red.

"No, Hugo. I—I have to stay with Mother on Sunday mornings, you know."

"Your target practice was a Sunday morning diversion, then, Judge Marshall?" Dundee asked.

"Yes. We usually have an hour of the sport—between eleven and noon, on Sundays. We've been having a sort of tournament—quite sharply competitive—"

"When did you and your friends practise last?" Dundee asked.

"Last Sunday. Tomorrow was to mark the end of the 'tournament'," the Judge answered.

"And when did you last see your gun and silencer?" Dundee persisted.

"Last Sunday, of course.... Why, Good Lord!" Marshall ejaculated. *"It was Nita herself who put the gun away!"*

There was a collective gasp of relief. Eyes could meet eyes—now. But it was Flora Miles who voiced the thought or hope that seemed apparent on every face.

"That's why I didn't hear anyone talking when I was in the closet!" she cried, her voice almost hysterical in its vehemence. *"There wasn't anybody but Nita in the room!* She committed suicide! She stole poor Hugo's gun and the silencer and committed suicide!"

"At a distance of from ten to fifteen feet?" Dundee asked with ill-concealed sarcasm. "And when she was powdering her face? And just after entering the room, blithely singing a Broadway hit?"

"Maybe the lady is right, boy," Captain Strawn interposed mildly. "I've heard of people rigging up contrivances—"

"Which make the gun and the silencer disappear by magic?" Dundee demanded. "No, folks, I'm afraid the suicide theory is no good.... Now, Judge Marshall," and he turned again to the creator of the biggest sensation since the investigation into Nita Selim's death had got under way, "you say that Mrs. Selim herself put the gun away.... Will you explain the circumstances?"

The elderly man's face had gone yellowish again. "Certainly! Nita Selim and I were the last to leave the back garden. She was particularly poor at the sport— never made a bull's eye during the four or five Sunday mornings after Lois—Mrs. Dunlap—drew her into our set. She begged for a few more shots, and I stayed with her, after the others had gone into the house for—er— refreshment. She fired the last bullet in the chamber of the Colt's, and together we walked to the house, entering the little room at the rear where all sorts of sports equipment are kept—fishing rods and tackle, golf clubs, bows and arrows, skis, etc. She was carrying the gun, unscrewing the silencer as we walked. It is my habit to keep the pistol and the silencer in a drawer in a little corner cupboard—"

"Locked, up?" Dundee asked sharply.

"Usually locked, but not always, I am afraid," Judge Marshall answered reluctantly.

"And you saw Mrs. Selim place the gun and the silencer in the drawer?"

"I—thought I did, but I was really not watching closely. As a matter of fact, I stopped to look over a fishing rod, with a view to trying it out the first good fishing weather—"

"Was Mrs. Selim wearing a coat or cloak?" Dundee cut in impatiently.

"Why, I don't know—"

"Yes, she was, Hugo!" Karen cried out eagerly. "It was quite chilly last Sunday morning. Remember? We all had on coats or sweaters. Nita wore a dark-green leather jacket with big pockets—"

"And she left in a great hurry, without even waiting for a drink," Flora Miles contributed triumphantly. "I tell you, she took them away in her pockets."

"Your guess may be correct, Mrs. Miles," Dundee agreed, "but I think we had better not come to any definite conclusion until we know that Judge Marshall's automatic and silencer are really missing.... Is there anyone at your house now, Judge, whom you can ask to look for it?"

"Certainly. The butler.... Shall I telephone him?"

Accompanied by Captain Strawn, the ex-judge went to the telephone in the little foyer between Nita Selim's bedroom and the main hall. And within five minutes he was back, nodding his head gravely.

"Hinson tells me that the Colt's and the silencer are both missing, sir.... May I express my profound regret that my possession of—"

"Some other time, Judge Marshall!" Dundee interrupted curtly, and hurried from the room, followed by Strawn, who nodded to Sergeant Turner, still lounging wearily in a far corner of the living room, to stand guard vigilantly.

"Well, Bonnie, here's the devil to pay," Strawn gloomed, but Dundee made for the telephone without answering.

He called a number, then curtly demanded: "Dr. Price, please!... Yes, I know he's busy on an autopsy. Just tell him that Dundee, of the district attorney's office, wants to speak to him."

There was a long pause, then: "Hello, Dr. Price!... Dundee.... What are the caliber and type of bullet that

killed Nita Selim?... Thanks much, doctor.... Anything
new?... Fine! Thanks again!"

He hung up the receiver and faced Strawn. "Bullet
from a Colt's .32," he said grimly. "I suggest you send one
of your men around to the Marshall home to pick up a
bullet that was shot in their damned target practice. If
you send the two bullets tonight, registered mail, to
Wright, the ballistics expert in Chicago, he can probably
wire you tomorrow morning as to whether the same gun
was used to fire both."

"Sure, Bonnie," Strawn agreed lugubriously. "I was
going to do just that.... Say, this town is getting to be
worse than Chicago!"

When he re-entered the living room Dundee began
upon the judge again, regardless of the fact that the
elderly   husband   was   murmuring   consolatory
endearments to his young wife.

"Judge Marshall, how many keys are there to the
cupboard drawer in which your gun and silencer were
kept?"

"Just one. I have it with me," the old man answered
wearily.

"Then when Hinson, your butler, looked for them, he
found the drawer unlocked?"

"He did. I confess to almost criminal negligence—"

"Then so far as you know, the gun and silencer could
have been removed at any time by any guest of yours
between noon last Sunday and—today?" Dundee went on
relentlessly.

"I—suppose so. But these people have been my close
friends for years," the judge answered. "Not one of them,
sir—"

"After Mrs. Selim's departure last Sunday, did your
other guests remain for any length of time?"

"For an hour or more, I think. Lois and Peter Dunlap
remained for our two o'clock Sunday dinner, but the
others drifted away to various engagements."

"Did any of you return to the room where the gun was kept?"

"I can speak only for myself and Peter—Mr. Dunlap," Judge Marshall answered, flushing with indignation. "The two of us went down just before dinner was served. I wanted to show him some new flies for trout casting."

"Your home is a popular rendezvous for your intimates, is it not?"

"I pride myself that it is, sir!"

"And guests run in and out, having the freedom of the place?"

"Certainly, sir!... And since I am not so stupid as you imagine, I can tell you now that I understand the drift of your questions, and can forestall them: Yes, all of these people—*my friends!*—have had opportunity to take the gun and the silencer from the cupboard since it was placed there last Sunday, if it *was* placed there by Mrs. Selim. But may I remind you, sir, that opportunity alone is not sufficient; that *motive*—"

"Since Mrs. Selim is dead, murdered by the weapon which was stolen, we can assume, Judge Marshall, that someone had motive," Dundee reminded him implacably, for in his mind there was no doubt that the ballistics expert would bear him out.

There was a heavy, throbbing silence. The group that, with the exception of Dexter Sprague, had been so united, so cemented with long-sustained friendship, again dissolved visibly before Dundee's eyes into eleven individuals, each shrinking into himself, mentally drawing away from any possible contamination with a murderer....

"You have said, Judge Marshall," Dundee went on at last, "that Miss Crain and Mr. Sprague were not at your home for target practice Sunday. Has either of them been in your home during this past week?"

"Penny—Miss Crain—spent an evening with my wife when I was—er—away from home on business. That was last Tuesday, I believe—"

"Yes, it was Tuesday, Hugo," Penny Crain interrupted firmly. "And Karen can vouch for the fact that I did not go into the gun room."

"Don't be silly, Penny!" Carolyn Drake scolded, as if she had long been bursting to speak. "Giving an alibi! As if *any* of us who were playing bridge while that woman was being shot *needs* any alibi!... But I'll tell you what *I* think, Mr. Detective! I think Nita herself stole the gun and the silencer, to kill Dexter Sprague with, and that *he* stole it from her and murdered *her*! Nobody else has the slightest scrap of a motive, and that note he wrote her ought to be enough to hang him on!"

Dexter Sprague had struggled to his feet during the woman's hysterical attack, his face like chalk, his eyes blazing. But Dundee waved him aside peremptorily.

"One more question, Judge Marshall," he said suavely, as if he had not heard a word that Carolyn Drake had said. "You knew Mrs. Selim before her arrival in Hamilton with Mrs. Dunlap, I believe.... Just when and where did you meet her?"

CHAPTER ELEVEN

"You are damned impertinent, sir!" Judge Marshall shouted, the ends of his waxed grey mustache trembling with anger.

"Then I take it that you do not wish to divulge the circumstances of your friendship with Mrs. Selim?" Dundee asked.

"Friendship!" the old man snorted. "Your implications, sir, are dastardly! I met Mrs. Selim, or rather, Nita Leigh, as she was introduced to me, only once, several years ago when I was in New York. Naturally—"

"Just a moment, Judge. You say she was introduced to you as Nita Leigh. Then you knew her as an actress, I presume?"

"I refuse to submit to such a cowardly attack, sir!"

"*Attack*, Judge?" Dundee repeated with assumed astonishment. "I merely thought you might be able to shed a little light on the past of the woman who has been murdered here today, with a weapon you admit to having owned.... However—"

The elderly ex-judge stared at his tormentor for a moment as if murder was in his heart. He gasped twice, then suddenly his whole manner changed.

"I apologize, Dundee. You must realize how—But that is beside the point. I met Nita Leigh at—er—at a social gathering, arranged by some New York friends of mine. She was young, attractive, more refined than—er—than the average young woman in musical comedy. Naturally I told her if she was ever in Hamilton to look me up. And she did."

"And because she was 'more refined than the average young woman in musical comedy'—than the average chorus girl, to put it simply," Dundee took him up, "you co-operated with Mrs. Dunlap to introduce her to your most intimate friends—including your wife?"

"Oh, Hugo! Why didn't you tell me?" Karen Marshall wailed.

"You see, sir, what you are doing!" Judge Marshall stormed.

"I am truly sorry if I have distressed you, Mrs. Marshall," Dundee protested sincerely. "But—" He shrugged and turned again to the husband. "I understand you were Mrs. Selim's landlord.... May I ask how much rent she paid?"

"The house rents for one hundred dollars a month—furnished."

"And did Mrs. Selim pay her rent promptly?" Dundee persisted.

"Since this is the 24th of May, sir, Mrs. Selim's rent for June was not yet due."

Not before poor little Karen could Dundee force himself to ask what, inevitably, would have been his next question—one which could not have been evaded, as the ex-judge had evaded the other two questions: "*Is it not true, Judge Marshal, that Nita Leigh Selim paid you no rent at all?*" But there were other ways to find out....

"Look here, Dundee!" a brusque voice challenged, and the detective whirled to face Polly Beale. It was like her, he thought with a slight grin, to address him as one man to another....

"Yes, Miss Beale?"

"I'm no fool, and I don't think any of my friends here are either—though two or three of them have acted like it today," the masculine-looking girl stated flatly. "You've made it very plain that any one of us here, except the Sprague man, could have stolen Hugo's gun and silencer.... Has the gun been found?"

"It has not, Miss Beale."

"O. K.!" The queer girl snapped her fingers. "I move that you or Captain Strawn search the men for the weapon, and that I search the Women.... Wait!" she harshly stopped a flurry of feminine protests. "I'll ask you, Dundee, to search me first yourself. I believe the technical term is 'frisking,' isn't it?... Then 'frisk' me.... Here is my handbag. I wore no coat, except this—" and she pointed to the jacket of her tweed suit.

As she strode toward the detective Clive Hammond sprang after her with an oath and a sharp command.

"Shut up, Clive! I'm not married to you yet!" she retorted, but her eyes were gentler than her voice.

His face burning with embarrassment, Dundee went through the traditional gestures of police "frisking"— running his hands rapidly down the girl's tall, sturdy body, slapping her pockets. And his fingers fumbled sadly as he opened her tooled leather handbag.

"Satisfied?" Polly Beale demanded, and at Dundee's miserable nod, the girl faced her friends: "Well, come along, girls!"

"Lord! What a girl!" Dundee muttered to Strawn, as the young Amazon herded Flora Miles, Penny Crain, Karen Marshall, Carolyn Drake, Lois Dunlap and Janet Raymond into the dining room.

Silently, and almost meekly, as if shamed into submission by Polly Beale's example, John Drake, Tracey Miles, Clive Hammond, Judge Marshall, and Dexter Sprague permitted Captain Strawn and Sergeant Turner to search them.

"How about the guest closet and the cars?" Dundee asked of Strawn in a low voice, when the fruitless, unpleasant task was finished.

"Gone over with a fine tooth comb long ago," Strawn assured him gloomily. "And not a hiding place in or outside the house that the boys haven't poked into— including the meadow as far as anyone could throw from the bedroom window."

The women were filing back into the room, some pale, some flushed, but all able to look each other in the eye again.

With surprising jauntiness Polly Beale saluted Dundee. "Nothing more deadly on any of us than Flora's triple-deck compact."

"I thank you with all my heart, Miss Beale," Dundee said sincerely. "And now I think you may all go to your homes.... Of course you understand," he interrupted a chorus of relieved ejaculations, "that all of you will be wanted for the inquest, which will probably be held Monday."

"And what's more," Captain Strawn cut in, to show his authority, "I want all of you to hold yourselves ready for further questioning at any time."

There was a stampede for coats and hats, a rush for cars as if the house were on fire, or—Dundee reflected wryly—as if those he had tortured were afraid he would change his mind. Rushing away with hatred of him in their hearts....

Only Penny Crain held back, maneuvering for a chance to speak with him.

"I don't have to go with the rest, do I?" she begged in a husky whisper.

"And why not?" Dundee grinned at her, but he was glad there was no hatred in *her* eyes.

"I'm 'attached' to the district attorney's office, too, aren't I?"

"Right! And you've been a brick this evening. I don't know what I should have done without you—"

"Well, I can't see that you've done much *with* me," she gibed. "But I'd like to stick around, if you're going to do some real Sherlocking—"

"Can't be done, Penny. I want to stay here alone for a while and mull things over. But I'd like to have a long talk with you tomorrow."

"Come to Sunday dinner. Mother loves murder mysteries," she suggested. Then realization swept over her. Her brown eyes widened, filled with terror. "Stop thinking one of us did it! *Stop*, I tell you!"

"Can *you* stop, Penny?" he asked gently.

But she fled from him, sobbing wildly for the first time that long, horrible evening. Dundee, watching from the doorway of the lighted hall, saw the chauffeur open the rear door of the Dunlap limousine, saw Penny catapult herself into Lois Dunlap's outstretched arms....

"When did the Dunlap chauffeur call for his mistress?" he asked Strawn, who stood beside him.

"About ten minutes after you arrived," Strawn answered wearily. "Said he'd dropped Mrs. Dunlap and the Selim woman at about 2:30 and had been ordered to return around 6:30.... Knows nothing, of course." The chief of the Homicide Squad drew a deep breath. "Well, Bonnie, he has nothing on me. In spite of all the palaver I don't know nothing either."

"You need some dinner, chief," Dundee suggested. "And the boys must be getting hungry, too."

"Somebody's got to guard the house, I suppose," Strawn gloomed. "Not that it will do any good.... And what about that maid—that Carr woman? Shall I lock her up on general principles?"

"No. I want to have another talk with her, and if she bucks at spending the night here, I'll take her to the Rhodes House, and turn her over to my old friend, Mother Rhodes. We haven't anything on her, you know."

"No, nor on anybody else, except that old fool, Marshall, and we can't clap him into jail—yet," Strawn agreed, his grey eyes twinkling.

"Take your crew on in, chief," Dundee urged. "I'll stick till midnight or longer, if you don't mind. You can arrange to have a couple of the boys to relieve me about twelve.... And by the way, will you telephone me the minute you get hold of Ralph Hammond?"

"Well, maybe not so quick as all that," Strawn drawled. "I'll take the first crack at *that* baby, my lad!... Not so dumb, am I, Bonnie-boy? Not so dumb! I can put two and two together as well as the next one—pretty near as well as the district attorney's new 'special investigator!'"

*   *   *   *   *

Although Bonnie Dundee had taken Captain Strawn's
none-too-gentle parting gibe with good grace, it was a
very thoughtful young detective who set about locking
himself into the house in which Nita Selim had been
murdered.

Captain Strawn had beaten him to the job that
evening by at least twenty minutes. Had the old detective
stumbled upon something which Dundee, for all his
spectacular thoroughness, had overlooked or had been
unable to turn up because Strawn had suppressed it?

What if Strawn's parting boast was not an idle one,
and he really had "the goods" on Ralph Hammond? Had
the old chief been laughing up his sleeve during the farce
of playing out the "death hand at bridge," and during the
merciless quizzing of old Judge Marshall?

But Dundee's native common sense quickly routed his
gloom. Captain Strawn was too direct in his methods, too
afraid of antagonizing the rich and influential, to have
permitted even a "special investigator" from the district
attorney's   office   to   torment   those   twelve   people
needlessly. Probably Strawn, feeling a little hurt at
having played second fiddle all evening, had simply
wanted to get him fussed, was even now chuckling over
the effect of his parting boast....

Much cheered, Dundee lingered in the dining room
whose windows he had made fast against any intrusion,
so that his task of guarding the house alone might be
minimized. As he glanced at the table, with its silver
plates heaped with tiny sandwiches of caviar and anchovy
paste, its little silver boats of olives and sweet pickles, he
discovered that he was very hungry indeed....

As he munched the drying sandwiches and sipped
charged water—the various liquors for cocktails on the
sideboard   offered   a   temptation   which   he   sternly
resisted—Dundee's thought boiled and churned, throwing
up picture after picture of Nita Selim, alive and then

dead; of Penny Crain—bless her!—helping him at the expense of her loyalty to life-long friends; of Flora Miles, lying desperately and then confessing to a shameful theft; of Karen Marshall gallantly playing out the "death hand"; of Karen's stricken, childish face when she learned that her elderly husband had met and at least flirted with Nita Selim at a chorus girls' party....

At that last picture Dundee flushed so that his skin prickled. Had he made a fool of himself, or was he right in his suspicion that Hugo Marshall had given Nita Selim this cottage rent free? That point should be easily settled, at any rate....

Ruefully reflecting that appetizers do not make a satisfactory meal he betook himself to the dead woman's bedroom.... Yes, his memory had served him well. Here was her desk—a small feminine affair of rosewood, set in the corner of the room nearest the porch door.

The desk was not locked. As Dundee let down the slanting lid, whose polish was marred with many fingerprints, he saw that its contents were in a hopeless jumble. So Strawn had beaten him to this, too! Had he found an all-important clue in one of the many little pigeon-holes and drawers, stuffing it into his pocket just before a bumptious young "special investigator" had arrived?

But Dundee's returning gloom was instantly dispelled. Here was Nita's checkbook, a flutter of filled-in stubs attached to only one remaining blank check. So Nita had banked with the Hamilton National Bank, of which John C. Drake—who apparently hated his fattish, fussy wife—was a vice president! Another tiny fact to be tucked away.... She had opened her account, apparently, on April 21, the day of her arrival in Hamilton—the guest and employe of Mrs. Peter Dunlap. Probably Lois Dunlap had advanced her the two hundred dollars as first payment for her prospective work in organizing a Little Theater movement in Hamilton.

Turning rapidly through stubs, Dundee stopped twice, whistling softly with amazement each time. For on April 28th, and again on May 5th, Nita Selim had deposited $5,000! Where had she got the money? Were the sums transfers from accounts in New York banks? But it was hardly likely that a little Broadway hanger-on had had so much hard cash on deposit. Then where had she got it— $5,000 at a time, here in Hamilton?

Blackmail!

Hastily but thoroughly Dundee ran through the remaining check stubs.... *No record at all of a check for rent made out to Judge Hugo Marshall!*

But there was a stub that interested him. Check No. 17—Nita had spent her money lavishly—was filled in as follows, in Nita's pretty backhand:

No. 17 $9,000
May 9, 1930
To *Trust Dept.*
For *Investment*

Had John C. Drake, who as vice president in charge of trusts and investments had doubtless handled the check, wondered at all where the $9,000 had come from?

One other revelation came out of the twenty-three filled-in stubs. On every Monday Nita Selim had drawn a check for $40 to her maid, Lydia Carr.

Again Dundee whistled. Forty dollars a week was, he wagered to himself, more money than any other maid in Hamilton was lucky enough to receive! Nita in a new light—an over-generous Nita! Or—*was Nita herself paying blackmail on a small scale?*

He reached into a pigeon-hole whose contents—a thick packet of unused envelopes—had not been disturbed by Strawn, and was about to remove an envelope in which to place the all-important checkbook, when he noticed something slightly peculiar. An envelope in the middle of the packet looked rather thicker than an empty case should....

But it was not empty. And across the face of the expensive, cream-colored linen paper was written, in that same pretty, very legible backhand:

TO BE OPENED IN CASE OF MY DEATH — JAUNITA LEIGH SELIM

His heart hammering painfully, and his fingers trembling, Dundee drew out the two close-written sheets of creamy notepaper. After all, who had better right than he to open it? Was he not the representative of the district attorney?... And he hadn't damaged the envelope. It had opened very easily indeed—its flap had yielded instantly to his thumb-nail....

Wait! It had been *too easy*! Before unfolding the letter or whatever it was, Dundee examined the flap of the envelope.... Yes! He was not the first to open it since its original sealing. God grant he hadn't destroyed any tell-tale fingerprints in his criminal haste to learn any secret that Nita Selim had recorded here!... Perhaps Nita herself had unsealed the letter to make an addition or a correction?

Well, whatever damage had been done was done now, and he might as well read....

Five minutes later Bonnie Dundee was racing through the dining room, pushing open the swinging door that led into the butler's pantry. Where the devil were the steps that led down into the basement? A precious minute was lost before he discovered that a door in the dark back hall opened upon the steep stairs....

An unshaded light, dangling from the ceiling, revealed the furnace in one corner of the big basement, laundry equipment in another. He plunged on.... That must be the maid's room, behind that closed door.... God! What if she had escaped, while he had been munching caviar and anchovy sandwiches? A fine guard he'd been!... And it wasn't as if he hadn't had a dim suspicion of the truth....

The knob turned easily. He flung open the door. And then his knees nearly gave way, so tremendous was his relief. For there, on the thin mattress of a white-enameled iron bed, lay the woman he so ardently desired to see.

She had apparently been asleep, and the noise he had made had startled her into panicky wakefulness. Instinctively her hand flew to the ruined left side of her face—that hideous expanse of livid flesh, scarred and ridged so that it did not look human....

"What—? Who—?" Lydia Carr gasped, struggling to a sitting position, only to fall back as nausea swept over her.

"You remember me?" Dundee panted. "Dundee of the district attorney's office. I questioned you this afternoon—"

The woman closed the single eye that had escaped the accident which had marred her face so hideously. "I—remember.... I'm sick.... I told you all I know—"

"Lydia, why didn't you tell me that it was your mistress, Mrs. Selim who did—that?" Dundee demanded sternly, pointing to the woman's sightless left eye and ruined cheek.

CHAPTER TWELVE

Lydia Carr, still clothed in the black cotton dress and white apron of her maid's uniform, struggled to a sitting position on the edge of her basement room bed.

"No, no! That's a lie! It was an accident, I tell you—my own fault!... Who dared to say Nita—Miss Nita—did it?"

"Better lie down, Lydia," Dundee suggested gently. "I won't want you fainting. You've had a hard day with the abscessed tooth, the dope the dentist gave you, and—other things. I don't wonder that you lost your head, went a little crazy, perhaps—"

The detective's sinister implication seemed to make no impression at all upon the woman with the scarred face.

"I asked you—" she gasped, her single eye glaring at him, "who dared say Nita burned me?"

"It was Nita herself who told me," Dundee answered softly. "Just a few minutes ago."

"Holy Mother!" the maid gasped, and crossed herself dazedly.

Let her think the dead woman had appeared to him in a vision, Dundee told himself. Perhaps her confession would come the quicker—

The maid began to rock her gaunt body, her arms crossed over her flat chest. "My poor little girl! Even in death she thinks of me, she's sorry—. She sent me a message, didn't she? Tell me! She was always trying to comfort me, sir! The poor little thing couldn't believe I'd forgiven her as soon as she done it—. Tell me!"

"Yes," Dundee agreed, his eyes watching her keenly. "She sent you a message—of a sort.... But I can't give it to you until you have told me all about the—accident in which you were burned."

"I'll tell," Lydia promised eagerly. Gone were the harshness and secretiveness with which she had met his earlier questioning.... "You see, sir, I loved Miss Nita—I called her Nita, if you don't mind, sir. I loved her like she was my own child. And she was fond of me, too, fonder of me than of anybody in the world, she used to tell me, when some man had hurt her bad.... And there was always some man or other, she was so sweet and so pretty.... Well, I found her in the bathroom one day, just ready to drink carbolic acid, to kill her poor little self—"

"When was that, Lydia?" Dundee interrupted.

"It was in February—Sunday, the ninth of February," Lydia went on, still rocking in an agony of grief. "I tried to take the glass out of her hands. She'd poured a lot of the stuff out of the bottle.... You see, she was already in a fit of hysterics, or she'd never have tried to kill herself.... It was my own fault, trying to take the glass away from her, like I did—"

"She flung the acid into your face?" Dundee asked, shuddering.

"She didn't know what she was doing!" the woman cried, glaring at him. "Nearly went out of her mind, they told me at the hospital, because she'd hurt me.... A private room in the best hospital in New York she got for me, trained nurses night and day, and so many doctors fussing around me I wanted to fire the whole outfit and save some of my poor girl's money—which I don't know till this day how she got hold of—"

Dundee let her sob and rock her arms for a while unmolested. In February Nita Selim had had to borrow money to pay doctor and hospital bills. Had borrowed it or "gold-dug" it.... And in May she had been rich enough to have $9,000 to invest!

"Lydia, you never forgave Nita Selim for ruining your life as well as your face!" Dundee charged her suddenly.

"You're a liar!" she cried passionately. "I know what I felt. It's *my* face and *my* life, ain't it? I tell you I didn't even bear a grudge against her—the poor little thing!

Eating her heart out with sorrow for what she'd done—
till the very day of her death! Always trying to make it up
to me—paying me too much money for the handful of
work I had to do, what with her eating out nearly all the
time and throwing away stockings the minute they got a
run in 'em—. Forgive her? I'd have crawled from here to
New York on my hands and knees for Nita Leigh!"

Dundee studied her horribly scarred face, made more
horrible now by what looked like genuine grief.

"Lydia, who was the man over whom your mistress
wanted to commit suicide?"

The single, tear-reddened eye glared at him
suspiciously, then became wary. "I don't know."

"Was it Dexter Sprague, Lydia?"

"Sprague?" She spat the name out contemptuously.
"No! She didn't know him then, except to speak to at the
moving picture studio."

"When did he become her—lover, Lydia?" Dundee
asked casually.

The woman stiffened, became menacingly hostile.
"Who says he was her lover? You can't trick me, Mr.
Detective! I'd cut my tongue out before I'd let you make
me say one word against my poor girl!"

Dundee shrugged. He knew a stone wall when he ran
up against one.

"Lydia," he began again, after a thoughtful pause, "I
have proof that Nita Selim was sure you had never
forgiven her for the injury she did you." His fingers
touched the letter in his pocket—that incredible "Last
Will and Testament" which Nita had written the day
before she was murdered....

"And that's another lie!" the woman cried, shaking
with anger. She struggled to her feet, stood swaying
dizzily a moment. "Come upstairs with me to her room,
and I'll show *you* some proof that I had forgiven her!...
Come along, I tell you!... Trying to make me say *I* killed
my poor girl, when I'd have died for her—Come on, I tell
you!"

And Dundee, wondering, beginning to doubt his own conviction a little—that conviction which had sprung full-grown out of Nita's strange, informal will, and which had seemed to explain everything—followed Lydia Carr from her basement room to the bedroom in which Nita had been murdered....

"See this!" and Lydia Carr snatched up the powder box from the dressing-table. Her long, bony fingers busied themselves with frantic haste, and suddenly, into the silence of the room came the tinkle of music. "*I* bought her this—for a present, out of my own money, soon as I got out of the hospital!" the maid's voice shrilled, over the slow, sweet, tinkly notes. "It's playing her name song—*Juanita*. It was playing that song when she died. I stood there in the doorway and heard it—" and she pointed toward the door leading from Nita's room into the back hall. "She loved it and used it all the time, because I gave it to her.... And *this*!"

She set the musical powder box upon the dressing-table and rushed across the room to one of the several lamps that Dundee had noticed on his first survey of the room. It was the largest and gaudiest of the collection—a huge bowl of filigreed bronze, set with innumerable stones, as large as marbles, or larger. Red, yellow and green stones that must have cast a strange radiance over the pretty head that had been wont to lie just beneath it, on the heaped lace pillows of the chaise lounge, Dundee reflected.

As if Lydia had read his thoughts, she jerked at the little chain which hung from the bottom of the big bronze bowl against the heavy metal standard.

"I gave her this—saved up for it out of my own money!" she was assuring him with savage triumph in proving her point. "And she loved it so she brought it with us when we came from New York—It won't light! It was working all right last night, because my poor little girl was lying there, looking so pretty under the colored lights—"

With strong twists of her big hands Lydia began to unscrew the filigreed bronze bowl. As she lifted it off she exclaimed blankly:

"Why, look! The light bulb's—*broke!*"

But Dundee had already seen—not only the broken light bulb but the explanation of the queer noise that Flora Miles had described hysterically over and over, as "a bang or a bump." The chaise lounge stood between the two windows that opened upon the drive. And at the head of it stood the big lamp, just a few inches from the wall and only a foot from the window frame upon which Dr. Price had penciled the point to indicate the end of the imaginary line along which the shot which killed Nita Leigh Selim had traveled.

The "bang or bump" which Flora Miles had heard had been made by the knocking of the big lamp against the wall. Undoubtedly the one who had bumped into the lamp was Nita's murderer—or murderess—in frantic haste to make an escape.

And that meant that the murderer had fled toward the back hall, not through the window in front of which he had stood, not through the door leading onto the front porch.... A little progress, at least!

But Lydia was not through proving that she had forgiven her mistress. She was snatching things from Nita's clothes closet—

"See these mules with ostrich feathers?—I give 'em to my girl!... And this bed jacket? I embroidered the flowers on it with my own hands—"

Through her flood of proof Dundee heard the whir of a car's engine, then the loud banging of a car's door.... Running footsteps on the flagstone path.... Dundee reached the front door just as the bell pealed shrilly.

"Hello, Dundee! Awfully glad I caught you before you left.... Is poor Lydia still here?"

"Come in, Mr. Miles," Dundee invited, searching with a puzzled frown the round, blond face of Tracey Miles. "Yes, Lydia is still here.... Why?"

"Then I'm in luck, and I think Lydia is, too—poor old girl!... You see, Dundee," Miles began to explain, as he took off his new straw hat to mop his perspiring forehead, "the crowd all ganged up when our various cars reached Sheridan Road, and by unanimous vote we elected to drive over to the Country Club for a meal in one of the small private dining rooms—to escape the questions of the morbidly curious, you know—"

"Yes.... What about it?" Dundee interrupted impatiently.

"Well, I admit we were all pretty hungry, in spite of—well, of course we were all fond of Nita, but—"

"What about Lydia?" Dundee cut him short.

"I'm getting to it, old boy," Miles protested, with the injured air of an unappreciated small boy. "While we were waiting for our food, somebody said, 'Poor Lydia! What's going to become of *her*?' And somebody else said that it was harder on her—Nita's death, I mean—than on anybody else, because Nita was all she had in the world, and then Lois—Lois is always practical, you know—ran to telephone Police Headquarters, to see what had been done with Lydia, and to see if it would be all right for Flora and me to take her home with us—"

"Just a minute, Miles! Whom did Mrs. Dunlap talk to at Headquarters?"

"Why, Captain Strawn, of course," Miles answered. "He told Lois that you were still out here, questioning Lydia again, and that it was all right with him, whatever you decided. So as soon as I had finished eating, I drove over—"

"Is Mrs. Miles with you?" Dundee interrupted again.

"Well, no," Miles admitted uncomfortably. "You see, the girls felt a little squeamish about coming back, even on an errand of mercy—"

Dundee grinned. He had no doubt that Flora Miles had emphatically refused the possibility of another gruelling interview.

"Why do you and Mrs. Miles want to take Lydia home with you?" he asked.

"To give her a home and a job," Miles answered promptly. "She knows us, we're used to her poor old scarred face, and the youngsters, Tam and Betty, are not a bit afraid of her. In fact, Betty pats that scarred cheek and says, over and over, 'Poo Lyddy! Poo Lyddy! Betty 'oves Lyddy!' and Tam—he's T. A. Miles, junior, you know, and we call him Tam, from the initials, because he hates being called Junior and two Tracey's are a nuisance—"

"I gather that you want to hire Lydia as a nurse for the children," Dundee interrupted the fond father's verbose explanations.

"Right, old man! You see, our nurse left us yesterday—"

"Wait here, Miles. I'll speak to Lydia. She's in Mrs. Selim's bedroom.... By the way, Miles, since you and your wife are kind enough to want to take Lydia in and give her a home and a job, I think it only fair to tell you that it is highly improbable that Lydia Carr will take any job at all."

"You mean—?" Miles gasped, his ruddy face turning pale. "I say, Dundee, it's absurd to think for a minute that good old faithful Lydia had a thing to do with Nita's murder—"

"I rather think you're right about that, Miles," Dundee interrupted. "Now will you excuse me?"

He found Lydia where he had left her—in her dead mistress' bedroom. The tall, gaunt woman was crouching beside the chaise longue, her arms outstretched to encircle a little pile of the gifts she claimed to have given Nita Selim to prove that she bore no grudge for the terrible injury her mistress had done her. At Dundee's entrance she flung up her head, and the detective saw that tears were streaming from both the sightless eye and the unharmed one.

Taking his seat on the chaise longue, Dundee explained gently but briefly the offer which Tracey Miles had just made.

"They want—*me*?" she gasped brokenly, incredulously, and her fingers faltered to her horrible cheek. "I didn't think anybody but my poor girl would have me around—"

"It is true they want you," Dundee assured her. "But you don't have to take a job now unless you wish, Lydia."

"What do you mean?" the maid demanded harshly, her good eye hardening with suspicion.

"Lydia," the young detective began slowly, and almost praying that he was doing the right thing, "when I woke you up tonight to question you, I said that Nita herself had just told me that it was she who had burned your face.... And you asked me if she had also given you a message—"

"Yes, sir!" the maid interrupted with pitiful eagerness. "And you'll tell me now? You don't still think *I* killed her, do you?"

"No, I don't think you killed your mistress, Lydia, but I think, if you would, you could help me find out who did," Dundee assured her gravely. "No, wait!" and he drew from his pocket the envelope inscribed: "To Be Opened In Case of My Death—Juanita Leigh Selim."

"Do you recognize this handwriting, Lydia?"

"It was wrote by her own hand," the maid answered, her voice husky with tears. "Is that the message, sir?"

"You never saw it before?" Dundee asked sharply.

"No, no! I didn't know my poor girl was thinking about death," Lydia moaned. "I thought she was happy here. She was tickled to pieces over being taken up by all them society people, and on the go day and night——"

"Lydia, this is Mrs. Selim's last will and testament," Dundee interrupted, withdrawing the sheets slowly and unfolding them. "It was written yesterday, and it begins:

"'Knowing that any of us may die any time, and that I, Juanita Leigh Selim, have good cause to fear that my own life hangs by a thread that may break any minute—'"

"What did my poor girl mean?" Lydia Carr cried out vehemently. "She wasn't sick, ever—"

"I think, Lydia, that she feared exactly what happened today—murder! And I want you to tell me who it was she feared. *For I believe you know!*"

The woman shrank from him, until she was sitting on her lean haunches, her hands flattening against her cheeks. For a long minute she did not attempt to answer. Her right eye widened enormously, then slowly grew as expressionless as the milky left ball.

"I—don't—know," she said dully. Then, with vehement emphasis: "*I don't know!* If I did, I'd kill him with my own hands!"

Dundee had no choice but to take her word.

"You said there was a message for me," Lydia reminded him.

"I'll read you her will first," Dundee said quietly, lifting the sheets again: "I am herewith setting down my last will and testament, in my own handwriting. I do here and now solemnly will and bequeath to my faithful and beloved maid, Lydia Carr, all property, including all moneys, stocks and personal belongings of which I die possessed—"

"To—*me*?" Lydia whispered. "To me?"

"To you, Lydia," Dundee assured her gravely.

"Then I can have all her pretty clothes to keep always?"

"And her money, to do as you like with, if the court accepts this will for probate—as I think it will, regardless of the fact that it is very informal and was not witnessed."

"But—she didn't have any money," Lydia protested. "Nothing but what Mrs. Dunlap paid her in advance for the work she was going to do—"

"Lydia, your mistress died possessed of nearly ten thousand dollars!" Dundee fixed her bewildered grey eye with his blue ones. "*Ten thousand dollars!* All of which she got right here in Hamilton! And I want you to tell me how she got it!"

"But—I don't know! I don't believe she had it!"

Dundee shrugged. Either this woman would perjure her soul to protect her mistress' name from scandal, or she really knew nothing.

"That is all of the will itself, Lydia," he went on finally, "except her command that her body be cremated without funeral services of any kind, and that nobody be allowed to accompany the remains to the crematory except yourself and Mrs. Peter Dunlap, in case her death takes place in Hamilton—"

"She *did* love Mrs. Dunlap," Lydia sobbed. "Oh, my poor little girl—"

"And there is also a note for you, which I took the liberty of reading, in which Mrs. Selim minutely describes the clothes in which she wishes to be cremated, as well as the fashion in which her hair is to be dressed—"

"Let me see it!" Lydia plunged forward on her knees and snatched at the papers he held. "For God's sake, let me see!"

CHAPTER THIRTEEN

"I'll read you the note, Lydia, but I can't let you touch it," Dundee said sternly, taking good care that she should not touch either the paper on which the note to herself had been written or the sheet which contained that strange, informal will. Informal, in spite of the dead woman's obvious effort to couch it in legal phraseology....

Was Lydia's frenzy assumed? Did she hope to leave fingerprints now which would account for fingerprints she had already left upon it? Was it not possible that Lydia's had been the prying fingers which had opened the envelope after Nita Selim had sealed it with God only knew what fears in her heart? If so, Lydia Carr had found that she was her mistress' sole legatee.... *Revenge, coupled with greed....* What better motive for murder could a detective ask? And who had had so good an opportunity as Lydia Carr to dispose of the weapon?

The woman crouched back on her haunches, an agony of pleading in her single eye.

"Lydia, I think you know already what this note tells you," Dundee said slowly.

To his astonishment the maid nodded, the tears starting again. "I asked her once what she wanted to keep that old dress for, and she—she said I'd find out some day, but I never dreamed she'd want it for a—oh, my God!—for a *shroud!*"

For the second time that evening Lydia Carr completely routed Dundee's carefully worked-up case against her. It was inconceivable, he told himself, that a mind cunning enough to have executed this murder would give itself away in such a fashion. If she had indeed pried among her mistress' papers and found the will and note, would she not, from the most primitive instinct of self-preservation, have pretended total ignorance of the note's contents?

"I'll read the note, Lydia," he said gently. "It is addressed: 'My precious old Lydia'—"

"She was always calling me that!" the maid sobbed.

"And she writes: 'If you ever read this it will be because I'm dead, and you'll know that I've tried to make it up to you the only way I knew. I never could believe you really forgave me, but maybe you will now. And there is one last thing I want you to do for me, Lydia darling. You remember that old royal blue velvet dress of mine that you were always sniffing at and either trying to make me give away or have made over? And remember that I told you that you'd know some time why I kept it? Well, I want you to lay me out in it, Lydia. Such a funny old-fashioned shroud, isn't it?... But with dresses long again, maybe it won't look so funny, and there'll be nobody but you and Lois to see me in it, because I've said so in my will. And I want my hair dressed as it was the only time I ever wore the royal blue velvet. A French roll, Lydia, with little curls coming out the left side of it and hanging down to the left ear. You brush the hair straight up the back of the head, gather it together and tie a little bit of black shoestring around it, then you twist the hair into a roll and spread it high, pinning it down on each side of the head. *And don't forget the little curls on the left side!* I hope I have enough hair, but if it hasn't grown long enough, you know where those switches are that I had made when I first bobbed my hair.... You won't mind touching me when I'm dead, will you, Lydia? I do love you.... Nita.'"

Dundee was silent for a minute after he had finished reading the strange note and had returned it to the envelope, along with the will. At last, speaking against a lump in his throat, he broke in on the desolate sobbing of Nita's maid:

"Lydia, how old was your mistress?"

"You won't put it in the papers, will you?" Lydia pleaded. "She—she was—thirty-three. But not a soul knew it except me—"

"And will you tell me how old the royal blue velvet dress is?" he continued. "Also, how long since girls dressed their hair in a French roll?"

"The dress is twelve or thirteen years old," Lydia said, her voice dull now with grief. "I know, because I used to do dressmaking during the war. And it was during the war that girls wore their hair that way—I did mine in a Psyche knot, but the French roll was more stylish."

"Did your mistress ever tell you about the one time she wore the dress?"

Lydia shook her head. "No. She wouldn't talk about it—just said I'd know sometime why she kept it.... Royal blue velvet, it is, the skirt halfway to the ankles, and sleeves with long pointed ends, lined with gold taffeta, and finished off with gold tassels. It's in a dress bag, hanging in her closet."

"Do you think it was her wedding dress, Lydia?" Dundee suggested, the idea suddenly flashing into his mind.

"I don't know. I didn't ask her that," Lydia denied dully. "Can I take it with me—and the switches she had made out of her curls?"

"I'll have to get authority to remove anything from the house, Lydia," Dundee told her. "But I am sure you will be permitted to follow Mrs. Selim's instructions.... So you're going to accept the Miles' offer of a job as nurse?"

"Yes. I'd rather work. Mr. and Mrs. Miles have always been specially nice to me, and I—I could love their children. They're not—afraid of me—"

"Perhaps you're wise," Dundee agreed. "By the way, Lydia, did Mrs. Selim have a pistol in her possession at any time during the past week?"

The maid shook her head. "Not that I seen. And if she'd got one because she was afraid, she'd a-kept it handy and I'd a-been bound to see it."

Convinced of her sincerity, he was about to let her go to pack her bag when another belated question occurred to him. "Lydia, will you tell me what engagements Mrs. Selim had this last week?"

The woman scowled, fanatically jealous, Dundee guessed, of her mistress' reputation, but at last she answered defiantly: "Let me see.... Mr. Sprague had Sunday dinner here, and spent the afternoon, but Sunday night it was young Mr. Ralph Hammond. He come whenever she'd let him.... Monday night?... Oh, yes! She had dinner at the Country Club with the Mileses and the Drakes and the Dunlaps. Mr. Miles brought her home, because Mr. Sprague wasn't invited.... Tuesday night—let me think!... Yes, that's the night Judge Marshall was here. Nita had sent for him to talk about finishing up the attic—"

So that was the "business engagement" which Judge Marshall had hemmed and hawed over, Dundee reflected triumphantly.

"—and Wednesday night," Lydia was continuing, with a certain pride in her mistress' popularity, "she was at a dinner party at the Dunlaps'."

"Did Mr. Peter Dunlap ever call on Mrs. Selim—alone?"

"*Him?*" Lydia was curiously resentful. "He wasn't ever here. Nita said to me she wished Mr. Peter liked her as well as Mis' Lois did."

"Thursday night?"

"Mr. Ralph Hammond took her somewhere to dinner, to some other town, I think, but I wasn't awake when they got home. Nita never would let me set up for her— said I needed my rest. So I always went to bed early."

"And yesterday—Friday?" Dundee demanded tensely. For Friday she had been driven to making her last will and testament....

"She was home all day, but about half past four Mr. Drake came," Lydia said slowly, as if she too were wondering. "She was awfully restless, couldn't set still or eat. I ought to have suspicioned something, but she was often like that—lately. Mr. Drake stayed about an hour. I didn't see him leave, because I was cooking Nita's dinner.... But little good it did, because she didn't eat it, so there was plenty for Mr. Sprague when he dropped in about seven."

"Did Sprague spend the evening?"

"I guess so, but I don't know. Nita made me take the Ford and drive into town for a picture show. She was in bed when I got back, and—" but she checked herself hastily.

"Did Nita seem strange—troubled, excited? Did she look as if she'd been crying?" Dundee prodded.

"I didn't see her," the maid acknowledged. "I knocked on her door, but she told me to go on to bed, that she wouldn't need me. But now I think back, her voice sounded queer.... Maybe she *was* crying, but I don't know—"

"And this morning?"

"She seemed all right—just excited about the party and worried about my tooth. Mr. Ralph Hammond come to make the estimates on finishing up the top floor, and we left him here—"

"What was her attitude toward Mr. Miles when he dropped in on her this morning?" Dundee interrupted.

"Mr. Miles?" Lydia echoed, frowning. "He wasn't here this morning, or if he was, it was after Nita and I left for town."

While the maid was packing a bag, which Dundee would examine before she was allowed to take it away with her, the detective rejoined Tracey Miles, who had made himself as comfortable as possible in the living room.

"Lydia's going with you, and is grateful for your wife's kindness," Dundee informed him, and felt his heart warm to the boresome, egotistical little cherub of a man when he saw how Miles' face lit up with real pleasure. "By the way, Miles, you saw Ralph Hammond when you called here this morning, didn't you?"

"Yes," Miles answered with some reluctance. "He answered the door when I rang and told me Lydia and Nita had gone into town."

"Mr. Miles," Dundee began slowly, throwing friendliness and persuasion into his voice, "I know how all you folks stick together, but I'd appreciate it a lot if you'd tell me frankly whether you noticed anything unusual in Hammond's manner this morning."

"Unusual?" Miles repeated, frowning. "He was a little short with me because he was busy, and, I suspect, a little jealous because I'd come calling on Nita—" He broke off abruptly, in obvious distress. "Look here, Dundee! I didn't mean to say that, but I suppose you'll find out sooner or later.... Well, the fact is, the whole crowd knows Ralph Hammond was absolutely mad about Nita Selim. Wanted to marry her, and made no secret of it, though we all thought or hoped it would be little Penny Crain. He's been devoted to Penny for years, and since Roger Crain made a mess of things and skipped out, leaving Penny and her poor mother high and dry, we've all done our best to throw Penny and Ralph together. But since Nita came to town—"

"Was Nita in love with Ralph?" Dundee cut in, rather curtly, for he had a curious distaste for hearing Penny Crain discussed in this manner.

"Sometimes we were sure she was," Miles answered. "She flirted with all of us men—had a way with her of making every man she talked to think he was the only pebble on the beach. But there was something special in the way she looked at Ralph.... Yes, I think she *was* in love with him! But then again," he frowned, "she would treat him like a dog. Seemed to want to drive him away from her—but she always called him back—Oh, Lord!" he interrupted himself with a groan. "Now I suppose I *have* put my foot in it! You've got the damnedest way of making a chap tell everything he would cut his tongue out rather than spill, Dundee! But just because a young man's in love, and happens not to show up at a party, is no reason to think he sneaked up to the house and killed the woman he loved and wanted to marry. For I'm not so dumb that I haven't seen the drift of your damnable questions, Dundee!... Do you know Ralph Hammond, by any chance?" he concluded, his round face red with anger.

"No—but I should like to meet him," Dundee retorted. "He seems quite hard to locate this evening."

"Well, when you do meet him," Tracey Miles began violently, his blue eyes blazing with anger, "you'll soon find you've been barking up the wrong tree! There's not a cleaner, finer, straighter—"

"In fact, he is a friend of yours, Miles," Dundee answered soothingly, "and I respect you for every word you've said.... By the way, did all of you go to the Country Club for dinner after you left here?"

Somewhat mollified, Miles answered: "All of us but Clive Hammond. He said he was going to have a look around for Ralph himself. Seemed to have an idea where he might find him.... And, oh, yes, Sprague disappeared in the scramble. He hasn't a car and nobody thought of offering him a lift. Guess he took a bus into Hamilton.... Ah! Here's Lydia!... Hello, Lydia!" he called heartily to the woman who was standing, tall and gaunt, in the doorway. "Mighty glad you're coming to look after the kids!"

From behind the black veil which draped her ugly black hat and hid her scarred face, Lydia answered in the dull, harsh voice that was characteristic of her:

"Thank you, sir. I'll do my best."

She made no protest when Dundee, with a word of embarrassed apology, went rapidly through the heavy suitcase she had brought up from the basement with her. And when he had finished his fruitless search, she knelt and silently smoothed the coarse, utilitarian garments he had disarranged.

Five minutes later Dundee was alone in the house where murder had been committed under such strange and baffling circumstances that afternoon. He was not nervous, but again he made a tour of inspection of the first floor and basement, looking into closets, and testing windows to make sure they were all locked. Everywhere there were evidences of the thoroughness of the police detectives who had searched for the weapon with which Nita Selim had been murdered. In the basement, as he had subconsciously noted on his headlong dash to question Lydia Carr, the furnace doors swung open, and the lids of the laundry tubs had been left propped up, after the unavailing search....

He plodded wearily up the basement stairs and on into the kitchen. Perhaps the ice-box had something fit to eat in it—the fruit intended for Nita's and Lydia's Sunday breakfast. Those caviar and anchovy sandwiches had certainly not stuck with him long....

He was making his way toward the electric refrigerator when he stopped as suddenly as if he had been shot.

The kitchen door, which he had taken especial pains to assure himself was locked, when he had made the rounds immediately after the departure of Captain Strawn and his men, was standing slightly ajar!

Someone had entered this house!

Dundee stared blankly at the door, which was equipped with a Yale lock. Someone with a key.... But why had the door been left ajar? *To make escape more noiseless?*

With the toe of his shoe Dundee pushed the door to and heard the click of the lock, then, all thought of food routed from his mind, made a quick but almost silent dash into the dining room to secure one of the pair of tall wax tapers, which, in their silver candlesticks, served as ornaments for the sideboard.

If the intruder was still in the house he could be nowhere but in that unfinished half of the gabled top story. The nearer stairs were those in the back hall, and Dundee took them two at a time, regardless of the noise.

Who had preceded him stealthily?... By the aid of his lighted candle he discovered an electric switch at the head of the stairs, flicked it on, and found himself in a wide hall, one wall of which was finished with buff-tinted plaster and with three doors, the other of rough boards with but a single door.

With his candle held high, so that its light should not blind him, and well aware that it made him a perfect target, Dundee opened the unpainted door and found himself in the dark, musty-smelling room that had served Nita Selim and the Crains before her as a storeroom. From the ceiling dangled a green cord ending in a cheap, clear-glass bulb, but its light was sufficient to penetrate even the farthest low nooks made by the three gables. He blew out his candle and dropped it, as useless now.

A quick tour convinced him that nothing human was concealed behind one of Nita Selim's empty wardrobe trunks, or behind one of the several pieces of heavy old furniture, undoubtedly left behind by the dispossessed Crain family.

Big footprints on the thick dust which coated the floor showed him that he was being no more thorough than Captain Strawn's brace of plainclothes detectives had been much earlier that evening. Two pairs of giant footprints....

With an exclamation he discovered a smaller, narrow pair of prints, and followed their winding trail all around and across the attic. And then he remembered.... Ralph Hammond's footprints, of course, made that morning as he went about his legitimate business of measuring and estimating for the job of turning the storeroom into bedrooms and bathrooms.

Dundee had not realized that he was frightened until he was in the hall again, facing one of the three doors in the plastered wall. With surprise, and some amusement, he became aware that his hands were trembling, and that his knees had a curious tendency to buckle.

The fact that the door directly in front of him was open about two inches served, for some odd reason, to steady his nerves. Pushing the door wide open with his foot—for he never forgot the possibility of incriminating fingerprints which might easily be obliterated, he discovered a light switch near the door frame.

The instant illumination from a ceiling cluster revealed a large bedroom, and less clearly, another and smaller room beyond it, facing as the house faced— toward the south. Knees and hands steady again, he investigated the finished portion of the gabled story swiftly. A charming layout, he told himself. Had Penny Crain once enjoyed this delightful little sitting-room, with its tiny balcony built out upon the sloping roof?... And it gave him pleasure to think that this big, well-furnished but not fussily feminine bedroom had once been hers, as well as the small but perfect bathroom whose high narrow window overlooked the back garden. The closets, dresser drawers and highboy drawers were completely empty, however, of any traces of her occupancy or that of any other....

With these rooms going to waste, why—he suddenly asked himself—had Nita Selim coaxed Judge Marshall to have the unfinished half of the gabled attic turned into bedrooms and baths? Why couldn't Lydia have slept up here, if Nita thought so much of her "faithful and beloved maid"?

But even as he asked himself the question Dundee realized that the answer to it had been struggling to attract his attention.

These rooms had not been wasted! Someone had been occupying them as late as last night! Weaving swiftly through the three rooms, like a bloodhound on the scent, Dundee collected the few but sufficient proofs to back up his intuitive conviction. A copy of *The Hamilton Evening Sun*, dated Friday, May 23, left in an armchair in the sitting-room. All windows raised about six inches from the bottom, so that the night breeze stirred the hand-blocked linen drapes. And, clinging to these drapes, the faint but unmistakable odor of cigarette smoke. Finally, with a low cry of triumph, Bonnie Dundee flung back the colored linen spread which covered the three-quarter bed and discovered that the sheets and pillow cases, though clean, had, beyond the shadow of a doubt, been slept upon.

Bending so that his nose almost touched a pillow case he sniffed. *Pomade!*... Who was the man who had slept in this bed last night?

CHAPTER FOURTEEN

With the thrill of his discovery singing blithely along his nerves, Bonnie Dundee, Special Investigator for the District Attorney, had at first hugged the intention of following the new trail alone. Hadn't Captain Strawn taunted him not too good-naturedly about his ability to get along without the younger man's help?

But he was glad, both selfishly and unselfishly, when, half an hour later, he threw open the front door of dead Nita's house to the chief of the Homicide Squad, Carraway, the fingerprint expert, and the two plainclothesmen who had searched the top floor for the missing weapon or the murderer himself soon after the murder had been committed. For if Strawn needed his help, Dundee needed the expert machinery which Strawn captained. And it was good to feel the grip of gratitude in the old chief's handclasp and to see the almost shy twinkle of apology in his hard old grey eyes....

Dundee led the way up the front stairs to the upper floor, glad to hear the heavy tread of official feet behind him.

"I guess you've got it all doped out who the Selim woman's gentleman friend was," Strawn commented genially, as he followed Dundee into the pleasant, big bedroom.

"I believe I have, but I need Carraway to prove my hunch," Dundee acknowledged.

Eagerly, swiftly, he displayed his first tangible finds— the open windows, the drapes smelling of cigarette smoke, the evening paper of the day before, the faint odor and greasiness of barber's pomade upon the pillow case of the bed which had clearly been slept in since the linen was changed.

"Now, Collins—Harmon—" Dundee whirled upon the two silent plainclothesmen, "I want to know what you saw in these rooms when you searched them early this evening that you don't see now. You looked into the closets and drawers, of course?"

"Yes, sir," Collins answered. "And they was all empty, Dundee. Me and Harmon didn't waste time smelling pillow cases, and I admit we didn't pay no attention to that there newspaper—"

"*Empty!*" Dundee echoed. "Are you sure?... You, too, Harmon?"

"What are you driving at, boy?" Captain Strawn asked indulgently.

Briefly, with disappointment flattening his voice, Dundee told of his finding the kitchen door ajar, after he had made sure it was locked on his first rounds of the house.

"I worked it out this way," he continued, despite Strawn's grin. "Dexter Sprague was Nita's lover, as I had thought all along. He was in the habit of spending the night here whenever Nita would give him an evening of her company. He was here last night, according to the maid, Lydia Carr. Nita sent her into Hamilton to a picture show. Nita and Sprague quarreled last night, but I am positive he spent the night here anyway. Certainly there was no actual rupture, since Sprague worded his note to her as he did. I have another strong reason for thinking his belongings were here at least until noon today, but that can wait for the moment. Furthermore, I am positive that Sprague descended by the backstairs and went around the house to join the cocktail party which was to follow the hen bridge party."

"How do you make that out, Bonnie?" Strawn asked, his grin wiped away.

"Try to remember how Sprague looked when you first got here," Dundee suggested. "I saw him twenty minutes after you did, but—*he was wearing an immaculate stiff collar, and there were still traces of talcum powder over a close shave*! And you will remember that he said he had made a half hour's trip by bus, and had walked the quarter of a mile from the bus stop on Sheridan Road to this house. It was a mighty hot afternoon, chief!"

"Not conclusive," Strawn growled.

"Then here's another straw to add to the weight of my conclusion," Dundee went on unshaken. "You remember that Janet Raymond was on the front porch *watching for Sprague*, while the 'death hand of bridge' was being played?... Oh, she tried to protect him.... Wait, I'll read you the notes I made when I was questioning her. I looked them up while I was waiting for you.... Here! I had said to Miss Raymond: 'You observed Mr. Sprague toiling down the rutty road, hot and weary, but romantic in the sunset?' And she answered, stammering: 'I—I wasn't looking that way....' And I knew she was lying, knew that she had been taken completely by surprise when Sprague suddenly appeared *from the rear of the house*! What's more, she betrayed herself and him by admitting that she was surprised. Then—because the girl is undoubtedly in love with Sprague and was mortally afraid he had killed Nita Selim, she tried frantically to throw suspicion on Lydia Carr, by telling how Lydia had failed to answer Mrs. Dunlap's first ring—Good Lord! Wait a minute! I want to think!" he interrupted himself to exclaim.

After a full minute, while he had stood very still, with his fingers pressed against his closed eyes, Dundee began slowly:

"I believe that's it.... Listen, boys!" He turned to the two plainclothesmen, urgent pleading in his voice. "Would you both take your oath that there was no bag—say a small Gladstone overnight bag—anywhere in these rooms when you searched them this evening?"

The two detectives glanced at each other, their faces reddening. It was Harmon, the older of the pair, who swallowed hard before answering:

"We'd been told to look for a man hiding, and for a gun—" Then he squared his shoulders as if to receive the blame like a man. "Yes, sir! There was a little black grip on the closet shelf. I went through it myself, but there wasn't no gun in it. Just a pair of pajamas and a couple of shirts, one of 'em dirty, some socks and collars and a shaving-kit—"

Dundee drew a deep breath, and clapped the red-faced detective on the back in high good humor.

"There simply *had* to be a bag somewhere!" he laughed.

"This is the way of it, Strawn.... Nita and Sprague rowed last night. Sprague tried to make it up, but Nita must have been through with him. Probably told him last night to clear his things out and not come back. She thought he had done so; probably he did leave before she got up. At any rate she was so sure he was gone and his things with him that she and Lydia went to town this morning and left Ralph Hammond here to go through the place as freely as he liked, making his estimates on the job of finishing up the other half of this floor. And Ralph—but let that wait for the moment."

"Got any real proof that it was Sprague who stayed here and not the Hammond boy?" Strawn interrupted shrewdly.

"I'm coming to the proof," Dundee assured him, "or rather, the rest of the proof that I haven't already given you. You're damned hard to convince, chief! But let me go on with my theory, which I think covers the facts.... At luncheon, when Nita received that note from Sprague, I imagine she got a hunch that he hadn't taken her seriously, that he had not removed his belongings. You remember Penny Crain said Nita had Lydia follow her into her bedroom, as soon as Nita got home from the luncheon?... Well, it's my hunch that Nita asked Lydia if Sprague's things were gone when she cleaned these rooms this morning, and that Lydia said no. Nita then probably told Lydia to pack them herself, and I feel positive that Lydia did so, for she must have felt safe when she protested to me that Sprague was not Nita's lover. I also feel sure that Sprague arrived at least half an hour before he said he did, by some back path across the meadow; that he came up to these rooms that he considered his, found his things packed, but went about shaving and changing his shirt and collar, regardless. I also feel sure that Lydia followed him upstairs to explain and impress upon him that Nita had meant what she said. And it is quite likely that she was not through picking up after him when he descended by the back stairs and surprised Janet Raymond on the front porch. That accounts, of course, for Lydia's not hearing the kitchen bell the first time Mrs. Dunlap rang."

"Umm," Strawn grunted. "What about the proofs you're holding back?"

"Come along, chief—you, too, Carraway!" Dundee answered, and led the way into the bathroom. "I felt sure these rooms would yield a very definite clue, even though Sprague, when he sneaked back tonight to get his telltale bag, apparently made every effort to wipe his fingerprints off the furniture and bathroom fixtures.... Now, Carraway, if you'll step upon this little stool and look along the top of this medicine cabinet, you'll find what I found—and didn't touch."

The fingerprint expert did as he was told. When he stepped down he was holding, between the very tips of his fingers, a safety razor blade.

"No dust on it, you see," Dundee pointed out. "Now if you don't find Dexter Sprague's fingerprints on it, my whole theory topples."

"How am I going to know whose fingerprints they are till we get hold of Sprague?" Carraway asked reasonably.

"We don't need him—for that purpose, at least," Dundee assured him. "Downstairs in the living room, on a little table in the southeast corner of the room, you'll find a red glass ashtray which no one but Dexter Sprague used all evening. It was clean and empty when I saw him use it first. I think you'll find on it all the prints you need."

"So you think Sprague killed her because she was through with him?" Strawn asked.

Dundee shook his head. "Since I don't like Dexter Sprague a little bit, chief, I'd like to think so, but—"

CHAPTER FIFTEEN

Bonnie Dundee's first thought upon awakening that Sunday morning was that it might prove to be rather a pity that his new bachelor apartment, as he loved to call his three rooms at the top of a lodging house which had once been a fashionable private home, faced south and west, rather than east. At the Rhodes House, whose boarding-house clamor and lack of privacy he had abandoned upon taking the flattering job and decent salary of "Special Investigator attached to the District Attorney's office," he had grown accustomed to using the hot morning sun upon his reluctant eyelids as an alarm clock.

But—he continued the train of thought, after discovering by his watch that it was not late; only 8:40— it was pretty darned nice having "diggings" like these. Quiet and private. For he was the only tenant now on the top floor. His pleased, lazy eyes roved over the plain severity but solid comfort of his bedroom, and on past the open door to take in appreciatively the equally comfortable and masculine living room.... Pretty nice! That leather-upholstered couch and armchair had been a real bargain, and he liked them all the better for being rather scuffed and shabby. Then his eyes halted upon a covered cage, swung from a pedestal....

"Poor old Cap'n!... Must be wondering when the devil I'm going to get up!" and he swung out of bed, lounged sleepily into the small living room and whisked the square of black silk from the cage.

The parrot, formerly the property of murdered old Mrs. Hogarth of the Rhodes House, but for the past year the young detective's official "Watson," ruffled his feathers, poked his green-and-yellow head between the bars of his cage and croaked hoarsely: "Hullo! Hullo!"

"Hullo, yourself, my dear Watson!" Dundee retorted. "Your vacation is over, old top! It's back on the job for you and me both!... Which reminds me that I ought to be taking a squint at the Sunday papers, to see how much Captain Strawn thought fit to tell the press."

He found *The Hamilton Morning News* in the hall just outside his living room door.

"Listen, Cap'n.... 'NITA SELIM MURDERED AT BRIDGE'.... Probably the snappiest streamer headline the News has had for many a day.... Now let's see—" He was silent for two minutes, while his eyes leaped down the lesser headlines and the column one, page one story of the murder. Then: "Good old Strawn! Not a word, my dear Watson, about your absurd master's absurd performance in having 'the death hand at bridge' replayed. Not a word about Ralph Hammond, the missing guest! Not a word about Mrs. Tracey Miles' being hidden away in the clothes closet while her hostess was being murdered!... In fact, my dear Watson, not a word about anything except Strawn's own theory that a hired gunman from New York or Chicago—preferably Nita's home town, New York, of course—sneaked up, crouched in her window, and bumped her off. *And* life-size photographs of the big footprints under the window to prove his theory!... By golly, Cap'n! I clean forgot to tell my former chief that I'd found Nita's will and note to Lydia! He'll think I deliberately held out on him.... Well— I can't sit here all day gossiping with you, 'my dear Watson....' Work—much work—to be done; then—Sunday dinner with poor little Penny."

Four hours later a tired and dispirited young detective was climbing the stairs of an ugly, five-story "walk-up" apartment house in which Penny Crain and her mother had been living since the financial failure and flight of the husband and father, Roger Crain.

"Hello, there!" It was Penny's friendly voice, hailing him from the topmost landing of the steep stairs. "All winded, poor thing?"

His tired, unhappy eyes drank her in—the freshness and sweetness of a domestic Penny, so different from the thorny little office Penny who prided herself on her efficiency as secretary to the district attorney.... Penny in flowered voile, with a saucy, ruffled white apron.... But there were purplish shadows under her brown eyes, and her gayety lasted only until he had reached her side.

"Sh-h-h!—Have they found Ralph?" she whispered anxiously.

He could only answer "No," and he almost choked on the word.

"Mother's all of a twitter at my having a detective to dinner," she whispered, trying to be gay again. "She fancies you'll be wearing size 11 shoes and a 'six-shooter' at your belt—Yes, Mother! It's Mr. Dundee!"

She did not look "all of a twitter," this pretty but rather faded middle-aged little mother of Penny's. A gentle dignity and patient sadness, which Dundee was sure were habitual to her, lay in the faded blue eyes and upon the soft, sweet mouth....

But Mrs. Crain was ushering him into the living room, and its charm made him forget for the moment that the Crains were to be pitied, because of their "come-down" in life. For every piece of furniture seemed to be authentic early American, and the hooked rugs and fine, brocaded damasks allied themselves with the fine old furniture to defeat the ugliness with which the Maple Court Apartments' architect had been fiercely determined to punish its tenants.

"'Scuse me! Gotta dish up!" Penny flung over her shoulder as she ran away and left him alone with her mother.

Dundee liked Mrs. Crain for making no excuses about a maid they could not afford, liked the way she settled into a lovely, ancient rocking-chair and set herself to entertain him while her daughter made ready the dinner.

Not a word was said about the horrible tragedy which had occurred the day before in the house which had once been her home. They talked of Penny's work, and the little gentlewoman listened eagerly, with only the faintest of sighs, as Dundee humorously described Penny's fierce efficiency and District Attorney Sanderson's keen delight in her work.

"Bill Sanderson is a nice boy," the woman of perhaps 48 said of Hamilton's 35-year-old district attorney. "It is nice for Penny to work with an old friend of the family, or was—until—"

And that was the nearest she came to mentioning the murder before Penny summoned them to the little dining room.

Because Penny was watching him and was obviously proud of her skill as a cook—skill recently acquired, he was sure—Dundee ate as heartily as his carefully concealed depression would permit. There was a beautifully browned two-rib roast of beef, pan-browned potatoes, new peas, escalloped tomatoes, and, for dessert, a gelatine pudding which Penny proudly announced was "Spanish cream," the secret of which she had mastered only that morning.

"I was up almost at dawn to make it, so that it would 'set' in time," she told him, and by the quiver of her lip Dundee knew that it was not Spanish cream which had got her up....

"I'm going to help wash dishes," he announced firmly, and Penny, with a quick intake of breath, agreed.

"Hadn't you better take a nap, Mother?" she added a minute later, as Mrs. Crain, with a slight flush on her faded cheeks, began to stack the dessert dishes. "You mustn't lay a hand on these dishes, or Bonnie and I will have our dishwashing picnic spoiled.... Run along now. You need sleep, dear."

"Not any more than you do, poor baby!" Mrs. Crain quavered, and then hurried out of the room, since gentlewomen do not weep before strangers.

"I called you 'Bonnie' so Mother would know we are really friends," Penny explained, her cheeks red, as she preceded him through the swinging door into the miniature kitchen.

"You'll stick to that—being friends, I mean, no matter what happens, won't you, Penny?" Dundee said in a low voice, setting the fragile crystal dishes he carried upon the porcelain drainboard of the sink.

"I knew you had something bad to tell me.... It's about—Ralph, I suppose?" Her husky voice was scarcely audible above the rush of hot water into the dishpan. "You'd better tell me straight off, Bonnie. I'm not a very patient person.... Are they going to arrest Ralph when they find him? There wasn't a word in the paper about him this morning—"

"I'm afraid they are, Penny," Dundee told her miserably. "Captain Strawn has a warrant ready, but of course—"

"Oh, you don't have to tell me you hope Ralph isn't guilty!" she cut in with sudden passionate vehemence. "Don't *I* know he couldn't have done it? They always arrest the wrong person first, the blundering idiots—"

It was the thorny Penny again, the Penny with glittering eyes which matched her nickname. But Dundee felt better able to cope with this Penny....

"I'm afraid I'm the chief idiot, but you must believe that I'm sorry it should be a friend of yours," he told her, and reached for the plate she had rinsed of its suds under the hot water tap.

"Shoot the works!" she commanded, with hard flippancy. "Of course I might have known that Captain Strawn's theory about a gunman was just dust in our eyes, and that only a miracle could keep you from fastening on poor Ralph, since he and the gun are both missing.... Naturally it wouldn't occur to you that it might be an outsider, someone who had followed Nita and her lover, Sprague, from New York, to kill her for having left him for Sprague.... Oh, no! Certainly not!" she gibed, to keep from bursting into tears.

"An outsider would hardly have had access to Judge Marshall's pistol and Maxim silencer," he reminded her. "And Captain Strawn received a wire from a ballistics expert in Chicago this morning, confirming our conviction that the same gun which fired the bullets against Judge Marshall's target fired the bullet which killed Nita Selim.... You've washed that plate long enough. Let me dry it now.... And there are other things, Penny—"

"Such as—" she challenged in her angry, husky contralto.

"Sprague admitted to me this morning, after I had confronted him with proofs, that he sometimes slept in the upstairs bedroom—"

"I told you they were lovers!" Penny interrupted.

"—and that he slept there Friday night, after he and Nita had quarreled. He still contends that the row was over that movie-of-Hamilton business," Dundee went on, as if she had not spoken. "He admitted also that Nita had told him to take his things away when he left Saturday morning, but he says it was only because she didn't want Ralph Hammond to find a man's belongings there if he had occasion to go into the upstairs rooms in making his estimates for the finishing-up of the other side. But he contends, and Lydia Carr, whom I also saw again this morning, supports him in it, that he stayed in the house occasionally when Nita was particularly nervous about being alone, and that they were *not* lovers."

"Pooh!... Don't wipe the flowers off that plate. Here's another."

"I'm inclined to say 'Pooh!', too, Penny," Dundee assured her, "but Tracey Miles told me last night when he came to get Lydia that Nita really seemed to be in love with Ralph—part of the time, at least."

"Nita thought enough of Dexter Sprague to send for him to come down here, and to root her head off for him to get the job of making the movie," Penny reminded him fiercely, making a great splashing in the dishpan.

"Then—*you* don't think she was in love with Ralph?" Dundee asked.

"Oh, *I don't know!*" the girl cried. "I thought sometimes—had the grace to hope so, anyway, since Ralph was so crazy about her."

"That's the point, Penny," Dundee told her gently. "Everyone I've talked to this morning, including Sprague, seems sure that Ralph Hammond was mad about Nita Selim."

"So of course he would kill her!" Penny scoffed bitterly.

"Yes, Penny—when he discovered Sprague's easily-recognized cravats draped over the mirror frame in a bedroom in Nita's house.... For they were there to be seen when Ralph went into that bedroom yesterday morning."

"How do you know he saw them?"

"Because he left this behind him," Dundee admitted reluctantly, and wiped his hands before drawing an initialed silver pencil from his breast pocket. "I found it under the edge of the bed. The initials are R. H."

"Yes, I recognize it," Penny admitted, turning sharply away. "I gave it to him myself, for a Christmas present. I thought I could afford to give silver pencils away then. Dad hadn't bolted yet " She crooked an elbow and leaned her face against it for a moment. Then she flung up her brown bobbed head defiantly. "Well?"

"Ralph must have been—well, in a pretty bad way, since he loved Nita and wanted to—marry her," Dundee persisted painfully. "Remember that Polly Beale found him still there when she stopped to offer Nita a lift to Breakaway Inn. It is not hard to imagine what took place. We *know* that Polly curtly cancelled her luncheon engagement with Nita and the rest of you, and went into town with Ralph, after making sure that Clive would join them. I saw young Hammond myself for an instant, without knowing who he was, and I remember now thinking that he looked far too ill to eat. I was lunching at the Stuart House myself when they came into the dining room, you know."

"Plenty to hang him on, I see!" Penny cried furiously.

"There's a little more, Penny," Dundee went on. "Polly Beale and Clive Hammond were mortally afraid that Ralph *would* come to the cocktail party! I'm sure Clive made Ralph promise to stay away, and that both Clive and Polly did not trust him to keep his promise. That is why, I am sure, Clive beckoned Polly to join him in the solarium, without entering the living room to speak to Nita. You remember they said they stayed there all during the playing of—"

"If you call it the 'death hand' again, I'll scream!"

"All right.... They stayed there until Karen discovered the murder. I am sure they chose that place because of its many windows—they could watch for Ralph's car, dash out and head him off. Take him away by force, if necessary, to keep him from making a scene. I believe they knew he had murder in his heart, and that he would find a way to get a gun—"

"Have you also found out that he stole Hugo's gun yesterday?"

"I have found that it was possible for him to do so," Dundee said slowly. "The butler was off for the afternoon until six o'clock. There was no one in the house but the nursemaid and the-three-months-old baby."

"Well? And I suppose you think Clive and Polly didn't have a chance to head Ralph off, as you say, but that they did see him running away after he killed her?" Her voice was still brittle with anger, but there were indecision and fear in it, too.

"No," Dundee replied. "I don't think they saw him. I feel pretty sure he came into the house by the back way, and through the back hall into Nita's room. He must have known Clive and Polly would be on the lookout for him....

At any rate, I have proof that whoever shot Nita from in front of that window near the porch door fled toward the back hall."

And he told her of the big bronze lamp, whose bulb had been broken, reminding her of its place at the head of the chaise longue which was set between the two west windows.

"That was the 'bang or bump' Flora Miles heard while she was hiding in the closet," he explained. "I suppose Flora has told all of you about it?... I thought so. Muffled as she was in the closet, it is unlikely that she could have heard Nita's frantic whisperings to Ralph.... I doubt if he spoke at all. Nita must have been sure he was about to leave by the porch door—"

Dimly there came the ring of the telephone. With a curt word, Penny excused herself to answer it. Dundee went on polishing glasses with a fresh towel....

"Bonnie!" Penny was coming back, walking like a somnambulist, her brown eyes wide and fixed. "That was—Ralph!... *And he doesn't even know Nita is dead!*"

CHAPTER SIXTEEN

"Of course I recognized his voice instantly when he said, 'That you, Penny?' and it's a wonder I didn't scream," said Penny Crain, fighting her way up through dazed bewilderment to explain in detail, in answer to Dundee's pelting questions. "I said, 'Of course, Ralph.... Where *have* you been?...' And *he* said, in that coaxing, teasing voice of his that I know so well: 'Peeved, Penny?... I don't blame you, honey. You really ought not to let me come over and explain why I stood you up last night, but you will, won't you?... Ni-i-ze Penny!...' That's exactly how he talked, Bonnie Dundee! Exactly! *Oh, don't you see he couldn't know that Nita is dead?*"

"Did you ask him where he was?" Dundee asked finally.

"No. I just told him to come on over, and he said I could depend on it that he wouldn't waste any time.... Oh, Bonnie! What shall we *do*?"

"Listen, Penny!" Dundee urged rapidly. "You must realize that I've got to see and hear, but I don't want Ralph Hammond to see *me* until after he's had a talk with you. Will you let me eavesdrop behind these portieres?... I know it's a beastly thing to do, but—"

Penny agreed at last, and within ten minutes after that amazing telephone call Dundee, from behind the portieres that separated the dining and living room, heard Penny greeting her visitor in the little foyer. She had played fair; had not gone out into the hall to whisper a warning—if any warning was needed.

He had seen Ralph Hammond enter the dining room of the Stuart House the day before, in company with Clive Hammond and Polly Beale, when the three had been strangers to him; but Dundee told himself now that he would hardly have recognized the young man whom Penny was preceding into her living room. The Ralph Hammond of Saturday had had a white, drawn face and sick eyes. But this boy....

Like his older brother, Clive, Ralph Hammond had dark-red, curling hair. But unlike his brother's, his eyes were a wide, candid hazel—the green iris thickly flecked with brown. A little shorter than Clive, a trifle more slender. But that which held the detective's eyes was something less tangible but at once more evident than superlative masculine good looks. It was a sort of shy joyousness and buoyance, which flushed the tan of his cheeks, sang in his voice, made his eyes almost unbearably bright....

Before Penny Crain, very pale and quiet, could sink into the chair she was groping toward, Ralph Hammond was at her side, one arm going out to encircle her shoulders.

"Don't look like that, Penny!" Dundee heard him plead, his voice suddenly humble. "You've every right to be sore at me, honey, but please don't be. I know I've been an awful cad these last few weeks, but I'm myself again. I'm cured now, Penny—"

"Wait, Ralph!" Penny protested faintly, holding back as he would have hugged her hard against his breast. "What about—Nita?"

Dundee saw the young man's face go darkly red, but heard him answer almost steadily: "I hoped you'd understand without making me put it into words, honey.... I'm cured of—Nita. I can't express it any other way except to say I was sick, and now I'm cured—"

"You mean—" Penny faltered, but with a swift, imploring glance toward Dundee, "—you don't love Nita any more? You can't deny you were terribly in love with her, Ralph. Lois told us—told *me* last night that Nita had told her in strictest confidence that she had promised to marry you, just Thursday night—"

The boy's face was very pale as he dropped his hands from Penny's shoulders, but Dundee, from behind the portieres, was not troubling to spy for the moment. He was too indignant with Penny for having withheld from him the vital fact of Nita's engagement to Ralph Hammond....

"That's true, Penny," Ralph was saying dully. "You have a right to know, because I'm asking *you* to marry me now.... I did propose to Nita again Thursday night, and she did accept me. I confess now I was wild with happiness—"

"Why did she refuse you before?" Penny cut in, and Dundee silently thanked her for asking the question he would have liked to ask himself. "Was it because she wasn't sure she was in love with you?"

"You're making it awfully hard for me, honey," the boy protested, then admitted humbly, "Of course you want to know, and you should know.... No, she said all along, almost from the first that she loved me more than I could love her, but that there were—reasons.... *Two reasons*, she always said, and once I asked her jealously if they were both men, but she looked so startled and then laughed so queerly that I didn't ask again.... Then I thought it might be because I was younger than she was, though I can't believe she is more than twenty-three or so, and I'm twenty-five, you know. And once I got cold-sick because I thought she might still be married, but she said her husband was married again, and I wasn't to ask questions or worry about him—"

"But she *did* accept you Thursday night?" Penny persisted.

"Yes," the boy admitted, his face darkly flushed again. "This is awfully hard, honey, but I'll tell you once for all and get it over with.... I took her to dinner. We drove to Burnsville because she said she was sick of Hamilton. When we were driving back she suddenly became very queer—reckless, defiant.... And she asked me if I still wanted to marry her, and I said I did. I asked her right then to say when, and she said she'd marry me June first, but she added—" and the boy, to Dundee's watching eyes, seemed to be genuinely puzzled again by what must have sounded so odd at the time—"that she'd marry me June first *if she lived to see the day*."

"Oh!" Penny gasped, then, controlling her horror, she asked with what sounded like real curiosity, "Then what—happened, Ralph? Why do you propose to *her* on Thursday and to *me* on—on Sunday?"

"A gorgeous actress sacrificed to the typewriter," Dundee told himself, as he waited for Ralph Hammond's reluctant reply.

"Can't we forget it, honey?... You do love me a little, don't you? Can't you take my word for it that—I'm cured now—forever?"

Penny's hands went up to cover her face, and Dundee had the grace to feel very sorry indeed for her—sorry even if she intended to give her promise to Ralph Hammond, as a sick feeling in his stomach prophesied that she was about to do....

"How can I know you're really—cured, if I don't know what cured you?"

"I suppose you're right," the boy admitted miserably. "There's no need to ask you not to tell anyone else. Although I don't want to see her again ever—. Why, Penny, I wouldn't even tell Polly and Clive yesterday, after it happened, though Polly guessed and went upstairs—. I tried to keep her back—."

"I don't—quite understand, Ralph," Penny interrupted. "You mean something happened when you were at Nita's house yesterday morning?"

"Yes. Judge Marshall had promised Nita to have the unfinished half of the top story turned into a maid's bedroom and bath and a guest bedroom and bath. Clive let me go to make the estimates. Of course I was glad of the chance to see Nita again—I hadn't been with her since Thursday night. But she had to take Lydia in for a dentist's appointment, and they left me alone in the house. I had to go into the finished half to make some measurements, and in the bedroom I found—oh, God!" he groaned, and pressed a fist against his trembling mouth.

"You found that Dexter Sprague was staying there, was using the bedroom that used to be mine—didn't you?" Penny helped him at last, in desperation.

"How did you know?" The boy stared at the girl blankly for a moment, then seemed to crumple as if from a new blow. "I suppose it was common gossip that Nita and Sprague were lovers, and I was the only one she fooled!... My God! To think all of you would stand by and let me *marry* her—a cheap little gold-digger from Broadway, living with a cheap four-flusher she couldn't get along without and had to send for—"

"Did you—want to kill her, Ralph?" Penny whispered, touching one of his knotted fists with a trembling hand.

"Kill her?... Good Lord, *no!*" the boy flung at her violently. "I'm not such an ass as that! You girls are all alike! Polly had so little sense as to think I'd want to kill Nita and Sprague both! She couldn't see, and neither could Clive, that all I wanted was to get away from everybody and get so drunk I could forget what a fool I'd been—"

"What *did* you do, Ralph?" Penny asked urgently.

"Why, I got drunk, of course," the boy answered, as if surprised at her persistence. "Darling, you wouldn't believe me if I told you how much rot-gut Scotch it took to put me under, but that filthy bootlegging hotel clerk would have charged me twice what he did for the stuff if he had known how much good it would do me."

"Hotel?" Penny snatched at the vital word. "Where did you go to get drunk, Ralph?"

"I never realized before you had so much curiosity, honey," the boy grinned at her. "After I shook Clive—Polly went on to Nita's bridge party, because she couldn't throw her down at the last minute—I wandered around till I came to the Railroad Men's Hotel, down on State Street, you know, the other side of the tracks. It's a miserable dump, but I sort of hankered for a place to hide in that was as miserable and cheap as I felt—"

"Did you register under your own name?"

"Ashamed of me, Penny?... No, I registered under my first two names—Ralph Edwards. And the rat-faced, filthy little hotel clerk turned out to be a bootlegger.... Well, when I woke up about eleven this morning I give you my word I wasn't sick and headachy, though God knows I'd drunk enough to put me out for a week.... Penny, I woke up feeling—well, I can't explain it but to say I felt light and new and—and clean.... All washed-up! At first I thought my heart was empty—it felt so free of pain. But as I lay there thanking God that *that was that*, I found my heart wasn't empty at all. It was brimming full of love—Gosh, honey! I sound like a Laura Jean Libbey hero, don't I?... But before I rang you from the lunch room where I ate breakfast I wrote Nita a special delivery note, telling her it was all off. I had to be free actually, before I could ask you.... You *will* marry me, won't you, Penny honey?... I knew this morning I had never really loved anyone else—"

Penelope Crain remained rigid for a moment, then very slowly she laid both her hands on his head, for he had knelt and buried his face against her skirt. But as she spoke, her brown eyes, enormous in her white face, were upon Dundee, who had stepped silently from behind the portieres.

"Yes. I'll marry you, Ralph!... You may come in now, Mr. Dundee!"

CHAPTER SEVENTEEN

It was nearly nine o'clock Monday morning, and Special Investigator Dundee sat alone in the district attorney's office, impatiently awaiting Sanderson's arrival. Coroner Price, with the approval of Captain Strawn of the Homicide Squad, had set the inquest into the murder of Juanita Leigh Selim for ten o'clock, and there was much that Dundee wished to say to the district attorney before that hour arrived.

When the thoroughly tired and dispirited young detective had returned to his apartment late Sunday afternoon, after having seen Ralph Hammond completely exonerated of any possible complicity in the murder of Nita Selim, he had found a telegram from the district attorney, filed in Chicago:

"CALLED CHICAGO SERIOUS ILLNESS OF MOTHER STOP RETURNING HAMILTON EIGHT TEN MONDAY MORNING STOP SEE BY PAPERS YOU ARE ON SELIM JOB STOP GOOD BUT WATCH YOUR STEP—SANDERSON"

Well—and Dundee grinned ruefully—he had been on the job all right, but would Sanderson consider that he had "watched his step"? At any rate, he had been thorough, he congratulated himself, as he weighed the big manilla envelope containing his own transcription of the copious shorthand notes he had taken during the first hours of the investigation. A smaller envelope held Nita's tell-tale checkbook, her amazing last will and testament, and the still more startling note she had written to Lydia Carr. The last two Dundee had retrieved from Carraway only this morning, after having submitted them to the fingerprint expert on Sunday.

Carraway's report had rather dashed him at first, for it proved that no other hands than Nita's—and his own, of course—had touched either envelope or contents. But he was content now to believe that Nita herself had unsealed the envelope she had inscribed, "To Be Opened in Case of My Death".... Why?... Had she been moved by an impulse to give a clue to the identity of the person of whom she stood in fear, but had stifled the impulse?

Strawn had said, too, that the little rosewood desk had been in a fairly orderly condition, before his big, official hands had clawed through it in search of a clue or the gun itself.... Well, Strawn had been properly chagrined when Dundee had produced the will and note....

"Why did she stick it away in a pack of new envelopes, if she wanted it to be found?" Strawn had demanded irritably, and had not been appeased by Dundee's suggestion: "Because she did not want Lydia, in dusting the desk, to see it and be alarmed."

Yes, he had been busy enough, but what, actually, had he to show for his industry? He had worked up three good cases—the first against Lydia Carr, the second against Dexter Sprague, and the third against Ralph Hammond—only to have them knocked to pieces almost as fast as he had conceived them.... Of course Lydia Carr might be lying to give Sprague an alibi, but Dundee was convinced that she was telling the truth and that she hated Sprague too much to fake an alibi for him.... Of course there was always Judge Marshall, but—

Through the closed door came sounds which Dundee presently identified as connected with Penny Crain's arrival—the emphatic click of her heels; the quick opening and shutting of desk drawers....

The down-hearted young detective debated the question of taking his perplexities out to her, but decided against it. She probably wanted to hear no more of his theories, was undoubtedly burning with righteous indignation against him because of Ralph Hammond.... Did she still consider herself engaged to Ralph, in spite of the fact that young Hammond had gallantly insisted upon releasing her from her promise as soon as he suspected that it had been given merely to prove her faith in his innocence?

It was a decidedly unhappy young detective whom Sanderson greeted upon his arrival at nine o'clock.

The new district attorney, who had held office since November, was a big, good-natured, tolerant man, who looked younger than his 35 years because of his freckles and his always rumpled mop of sandy hair. But those who sought to take advantage of his good nature in the courtroom found themselves up against as keen a lawyer and prosecutor as could be found in the whole state, or even in the Middle West.

"Well, boy!" he greeted Dundee genially but with an undertone of solemnity in his rich, jury-swaying baritone. "Looks like we've got a sensational murder on our hands. It's not every day Hamilton can rate a headline like 'BROADWAY BELLE MURDERED AT BRIDGE'—to quote a Chicago paper.... But I'm afraid there's not enough mystery in it to suit your tastes."

Dundee grinned wryly. "I've been pretty down in the mouth all morning because there's a little too much mystery, chief."

"Fairly open-and shut, isn't it?" Sanderson asked, obviously surprised. "New York gets too hot for this Selim baby—probably mixed up with some racketeer, racketeers being the favorite boy-friends of 'Broadway belles', if one can believe the tabloids. Lois Dunlap offers her a job to organize a Little Theater in Hamilton—which the fair Nita would certainly have described as a hick town and which she wouldn't have been found dead in if she could have helped it—" and the district attorney grinned at his own witticism, "—but Broadway Nita jumps at it. Her racketeer sweetie has a long arm, however, and Nita gets hers. Justly enough, probably, but I wish to the Lord she had chosen some other town to hide in. Lois Dunlap is the finest woman in Hamilton, but she's too damned promiscuous in her friendships. As it is now, some of the best friends I have in the world are mixed up in this mess, even if it is only as innocent victims of circumstance—"

Until then Dundee had let his chief express his pent-up convictions without interruption, and indeed Sanderson's courtroom training had fitted him admirably for long speeches. But he could keep silent no longer.

"That is what has been worrying me, chief," he interrupted. "Captain Strawn has given the papers very little real information, but the truth is I am afraid *one* of your friends was not an innocent victim of circumstance."

District Attorney Sanderson sat down abruptly in the swivel chair at his desk. "Just what do you mean, Dundee?"

"I mean I am convinced that one of Mrs. Selim's *guests* was her murderer, but I'd like to tell you the whole story, and let you judge for yourself."

"My God!" Sanderson ejaculated. Slowly he drew out a handkerchief and mopped his freckled brow. "If I hadn't had a good many years of experience with criminals, Dundee, I'd say it is obvious on the face of it that none of those four men—Judge Marshall, Tracey Miles, Johnny Drake, Clive Hammond—could have committed such a cheap, sensational crime as murdering a hostess during a bridge game.... Not that I haven't wanted to commit murder myself over many a game of bridge," he added, with the irrepressible humor for which he was famous. Then he groaned, the rueful twinkle still in his eye: "I'm afraid we're in for a lot of gruesome kidding. Why, last night, in the club car of my train, three tables of bridge players could scarcely play a hand for wisecracking about the dangers of being dummy!... Well, boy, now that I've talked myself past the worst shock, suppose you give me the low-down. But I warn you I'm going to take a powerful lot of convincing."

Painstakingly, and in the greatest detail, Dundee told the whole story, beginning with his arrival Saturday evening at the Selim house, including the ghastly replaying of the "death hand at bridge"—a phrase, by the way, which the prosecutor instantly adopted—and ending with Ralph Hammond's establishing of an alibi, to the entire satisfaction of Captain Strawn, as well as of Dundee himself. He was interrupted frequently of course, scoffingly at first, then with deepening solemnity and respect on the part of the district attorney.

"Let me see the plan of the house again," he said, when Dundee had finished. "Also that table you've worked up showing the approximate time and order of arrival of the four men.... Thanks!... Hmm!... Hmm!"

"You see, sir," Dundee repeated at last, "the list of possible suspects includes Lydia Carr, Dexter Sprague, John C. Drake, Judge Marshall, Polly Beale, Flora Miles, Janet Raymond, Clive Hammond—"

"But Polly and Clive were in the solarium *together* all the time!" Sanderson objected.

"So they said," Dundee agreed. "But it is a very short trip from the solarium by way of the side porch into Nita's bedroom. And either Polly Beale or Clive Hammond could have made that trip, on the pretext of speaking to Nita about Ralph!... Motive: murder to end blackmail. Naturally such a theory would not include *both* of them, but if *one of them* was being blackmailed and made use of the pretext of warning Nita of Ralph's overwrought condition—"

"Sprague's your man!" Sanderson interrupted with relief. "Motive: jealousy because Nita was ditching him to marry Ralph.... As for the gun and silencer, it seems pretty clear to me that Nita herself stole it from Judge Marshall, and that Sprague got it away from her. You say the maid, Lydia, went upstairs to tell Sprague he had to pack his things and take them away—for good!... Very well! Sprague goes down the backstairs with the gun in his pocket, through the back hall into Nita's bedroom, shoots her, bumps into the lamp, goes out by the back door, and comes around front to join the party.... You say yourself he has admitted to everything but the trip to Nita's room and the shooting—even to sneaking back to get his bag, which I believe also contained the gun until he had a chance to dispose of it on his way to his hotel in Hamilton."

Dundee shook his head. "I'd like to agree, chief, but I believe Lydia is telling the truth. She says she was in the upstairs bedroom with Sprague and remained behind only two or three minutes at most, to put his shaving kit into the packed bag, and to clean up the bathroom basin. On her way down the backstairs she says she heard Lois Dunlap's second ring and went to answer it. Sprague and Janet Raymond, with whom Janet says he stopped to talk a minute on the front porch, were in the dining room *before* Lydia entered it.... I'm convinced Lydia hates Sprague and would be glad to believe him guilty.... No, Mr. Sanderson, I don't believe Sprague did it, but I do believe it was Sprague's revenge that Nita was afraid of when she made her will Friday night. Naturally she figured she'd have time to tell the person she was blackmailing that she was through with him—or her, but I believe Sprague and Nita were lovers, even partners in blackmail, and that she feared he would kill her when he knew she was going to marry Ralph Hammond and give up their source of income."

Sanderson considered for a long minute, pulling at his full lower lip. "Well, thank God for those precious footprints Strawn is building on! Don't think I fail to follow your reasoning that the crime *must* have been committed in the bedroom, and not from the window sill, but those footprints may save us yet, and will certainly get us through the inquest. You agree, of course, that none of all this you've told me must even be hinted at during the inquest?... Good! Let's be going. It's nearly ten."

Dundee's whole soul revolted at the very thought of the barbaric farce of an inquest—the small morgue chapel crowded to the doors with goggle-eyed, blood-loving humanity; the stretcher with its sheeted corpse; reporters avid of sensation and primed with questions which, if answered by indiscreet witnesses, would defeat the efforts of police and district attorney; news photographers with their insatiable cameras aimed at every person connected with the case in any way.

Mercifully, this particular inquest upon the body of Juanita Leigh Selim promised to be quickly over. For Coroner Price, in conference with Sanderson, Dundee and Captain Strawn, had gladly agreed to call only those witnesses and extract from them only such information as the authorities deemed advisable.

Lydia Carr, whose black veil had defeated the news camera levelled at her poor scarred face, was the first witness called by Coroner Price, and she was required for the single purpose of identifying the body as that of her mistress. To two perfunctory questions—"Have you any information to give this jury regarding the cause and manner of the deceased's death?" and "Have you any personal knowledge of the identity of any person, man or woman, of whom the deceased stood in fear of her life?"— Lydia answered a flat "No!" and was then dismissed.

Karen Marshall, looking far too young to be the wife of the elderly ex-judge, Hugo Marshall, was the second witness called. Dr. Price guided her gently to a brief recital of her discovery of the dead body of her hostess, emphasizing only the fact that, so far as she could see, the bedroom was unoccupied except by the corpse at the time of the discovery.

He then handed her the photostatic copy of a blueprint of the ground floor of the Selim house, with a pencilled ring drawn around the bedroom. Karen falteringly identified it, as well as the pencil-drawn furniture, and was immediately dismissed—to the packed rows of spectators and reporters.

Dr. Price himself took the stand next and described, in technical terms, the wound which had caused death and the caliber of the bullet he had extracted from the dead woman's heart.

"I find, also, from the autopsy," he concluded, "that the bullet traveled a downward-slanting path. I should add, moreover, that I have made exact mathematical calculations, using the position of the body and of the wound as a basis, and found that a line drawn from the wound, and extended, at the correct slant, ends at a point 51.8 inches high, upon the right-hand side of the frame of the window nearest the porch door." And he obligingly passed the marked blueprint among the jury. When it was in his own hands again, he added: "It is impossible to state the exact distance the bullet traveled, more nearly than to say the shot was fired along the line I have indicated, at a distance of not more than fifteen feet and not less than ten."

Captain Strawn rose and was permitted to question the witness:

"Dr. Price, that blueprint shows that the bedroom is fifteen feet in width, don't it?"

"That is correct."

"Have you also measured the height of that window sill from the floor?"

"I have," the coroner answered. "The height from floor to sill is 26 inches."

"Now, doctor, from your calculations, would it be possible for a man crouching in the open window to fire a shot along the path you have calculated?"

"It would," Dr. Price answered. "But as I have pointed out, it is impossible for me to say at exactly what distance from the body the shot was fired."

But Strawn, of course, was amply satisfied. And so were Dundee and the district attorney, for it suited their purposes admirably for the public to be convinced at this time that an intruding gunman had murdered Nita Selim.

Captain Strawn, sworn in, told briefly of his being called to the scene of the crime, of the activities of Carraway, the fingerprint expert, and of the exhaustive search of his squad of detectives.

"Did you find any person concealed upon the premises, that is, within the house itself, or in the garage or on the grounds?" Dr. Price asked.

"No, sir."

"Did you or your men discover the weapon with which the deceased was killed?"

"No, sir."

"Did you question all persons in the house at the time of the crime, as to whether or not a shot had been heard?"

"I did. The answer in every case was that they heard no shot."

"And you also questioned every person present in an effort to place responsibility for the death of Mrs. Selim?"

"I did. I couldn't find that anyone present had anything to do with it."

"Who were these persons?" Dr. Price then asked.

"Judge and Mrs. Hugo Marshall, Mr. and Mrs. Tracey A. Miles, Mr. and Mrs. John C. Drake, Mrs. Peter Dunlap, Miss Janet Raymond, Miss Polly Beale, Miss Penelope Crain, Mr. Clive Hammond, Mr. Dexter Sprague—of New York, and Mrs. Selim's maid, Lydia Carr," Captain Strawn answered promptly, rolling out the names of Hamilton's elect with sonorous satisfaction, which obviously had the desired effect in convincing the jury that not among those proud names, at least, could be found the name of the murderer.

"Did you find on the premises any clue which you consider of importance to this jury?"

"I did! A bunch of footprints under the window you've been talking about. Here are life-size photographs of 'em, doctor.... And the rambler rose vines that climb up the outside of the window had been torn."

After the photographs had been duly inspected by the jury of six Dr. Price said: "That is all, and thank you, Captain Strawn.... Mr. Dundee!"

As had been agreed between the coroner and the district attorney, Dundee's testimony, after the preliminary questions, was confined to the offering of Nita Selim's "last will and testament" and the note to Lydia.

The reporters, who had obviously feared that nothing new would eventuate, sat up with startled interest, then their pencils flew, as Dundee read the two documents, after he had told when and where he had discovered them. As District Attorney Sanderson had said; "Better give the press something new to chew on, but for God's sake don't mention that checkbook of Nita's. It's dynamite, boy—dynamite!"

While the morgue chapel was still in a buzz of excitement, Dundee was dismissed, and District Attorney Sanderson requested an adjournment of the inquest for one week.

The police were urging the crowd upon its way before it became fully aware that it had been cheated of the pleasure of hearing, at first hand, the stories of that fatal bridge and cocktail party from the guests themselves.

"Tell the Carr woman I want to speak to her," Sanderson directed Dundee. "She'll thank you for rescuing her from the reporters."

As Dundee pushed his way through the jam he heard a reporter earnestly pleading with Lois Dunlap: "But I'm sure you can remember the cards each player held in that 'death hand,' Mrs. Dunlap—"

Cheerfully sure that he could trust Lois Dunlap's discretion and distaste for publicity, Dundee went on, grinning at the reporter's use of his own lurid phrase.

Two minutes later Sanderson, Strawn and Dundee were closeted in Dr. Price's own office with Lydia Carr.

"First, Lydia," began Sanderson, "I want to warn you to give the reporters no information at all regarding the nature or extent of your mistress' bequest."

"It was little enough she had, poor girl, beyond her clothes and a few pieces of jewelry," Lydia answered stubbornly. "Are you going to let me do what she told me to, in that note?... Not that I hold with burning—"

"I see no reason why you should not take charge of the body, Lydia, and arrange it immediately for cremation.... Do you, Captain Strawn?" Sanderson answered.

"No, sir. The quicker the better."

"Then, Lydia, if Captain Strawn will send you out to the Selim house with one of his boys, you may get the dress described in Mrs. Selim's note—"

"And the curls she cut off and had made into switches," Lydia interrupted. "I can't dress my poor girl's hair in a French roll without them!"

"The curls, too," Sanderson agreed. "Now as to the cremation—"

"Mrs. Miles let me come in early to see about that," Lydia interrupted again. "They can do it this afternoon, and you don't need to worry about the expense. I've got money enough of my own to pay my girl's funeral expenses."

"Good!" Sanderson applauded. "The will shall be probated as soon as possible, of course, but it makes it simpler if you will pay the necessary expenses now."

"Just a minute, chief," Dundee halted the district attorney as he was about to leave. "Under the circumstances, I think it highly advisable that we get pictures of the burial dress. I suggest you have Lydia bring the things to your office before she lays out the body, and that Carraway photograph the dress there, from all angles. I should also like to have a picture of the body after Lydia has finished her services."

The maid's scarred face flushed a deep, angry red, but she offered no protest when the district attorney accepted both of Dundee's suggestions.

"Then you'll have Carraway with his camera at my office in about an hour?" Sanderson turned to Captain Strawn. "Let's say twelve o'clock. By the way, Lydia, you may bring in with you the few pieces of jewelry you mentioned. I'll keep them safely in my offices until the will is probated and they are turned over to you."

"I don't know where she kept them," Lydia answered.

"*What?*" exclaimed Bonnie Dundee.

"I said I don't know where she kept her jewelry," Lydia Carr retorted. "It wasn't worth much—not a hundred dollars altogether, I'll be bound, because Nita sold her last diamond not a week before we left New York. She owed so many bills then that the money she got for directing that play at the Forsyte School hardly made a dent on them."

"Do you know whether the jewelry was kept in the house or in a safe deposit box?" Dundee asked, excitement sharpening his voice.

"It must have been in the house, because she wore the different pieces any time she pleased," the maid answered. "I didn't ask no questions, and I didn't happen to see her get it out or put it away. I didn't ever do much lady's-maid work for her, like dressing her or fixing her hair—just kept her clothes and the house in order, and did what little cooking there was to do—"

"Her dressing-table?" Dundee prodded. "Her desk?"

The maid shook her head. "I was always straightening up the drawers in both her dressing-table and her desk, and she didn't keep the jewelry in either one of them places."

"Captain Strawn, when you searched the dressing-table and desk for the gun or anything of importance, did you have any reason to suspect a secret drawer in either of them?"

"No, Bonnie. They're just ordinary factory furniture. I tapped around for a secret drawer, of course, but there wasn't even any place for one," Strawn assured him with an indulgent grin.

"I want to see Penny Crain!" Dundee cried, making for the door.

"Then you'd better come along to the courthouse with me," Sanderson called after him. "I sent her back to the office as soon as the inquest was adjourned."

The two men passed through the now deserted morgue chapel and almost bumped into a middle-aged man, obviously of the laboring class in spite of his slicked-up, Sunday appearance.

"You're the district attorney, ain't you, sir?" he addressed Sanderson in a nervous, halting undertone.

"Yes. What is it?"

"I come to the inquest to give some information, sir, but it was adjourned so quick I didn't have time—"

"Who are you?" Sanderson interrupted impatiently.

"I'm Rawlins, sir. I worked for the poor lady, Mrs. Selim—gardening one day a week—"

"Come to my office!" Sanderson commanded quickly, as a lingering reporter approached on a run.... "No, no! I'm sorry, Harper," he said hastily, cutting into the reporter's questions. "Nothing new! You may say that the police have thrown out a dragnet—" and he grinned at the trite phrase "—for the gunman who killed Mrs. Selim, and will offer a reward for the recovery of the weapon—a Colt's .32 equipped with a Maxim silencer.... Come along, George, and I'll explain just what Mrs. Sanderson and I have in mind."

The district attorney and Dundee strode quickly away, and the man, Rawlins, after a moment of indecision, trotted after them.

"I don't understand, sir, and my name ain't George. It's Elmer."

"You don't have to understand anything, except that you're not to answer any question that any reporter asks you," Sanderson retorted.

When the trio entered the reception room of the district attorney's suite in the courthouse Sanderson paused at Penny Crain's desk:

"Bring in your notebook, Penny. This man has some information he considers important."

A minute later Sanderson had begun to question his voluntary but highly nervous witness.

"Your name?"

"It's Elmer Rawlins, like I told you, sir," the man protested, and flinched as Penny recorded his words in swift shorthand. "It was my wife as made me come. She said as long as me and her knowed I didn't do nothing wrong, I'd oughta come forward and tell what I knowed."

"Yes, yes!" Sanderson encouraged him impatiently. "You say you worked for Mrs. Selim as gardener one day a week—"

"Yes, sir, but I 'tended to her hot water and her garbage, too—twice a day it was I had to go and stoke the little laundry heater that heats the hot water tank in summertime when the steam furnace ain't being used. I live about a mile beyant the Crain place, that is, the house the poor lady was killed in—"

"Did you come to stoke the laundry heater Saturday evening?" Dundee interrupted. "Excuse me, sir," he turned to the district attorney, "but this is the first time I've seen this man."

"No, sir, I didn't stoke it Sat'dy night," Rawlins answered uneasily. "You see, I was comin' up the road to do my chores at half past six, like I always do, but before I got to the house I seen a lot of policemen's cars and motorcycles, and I didn't want to get mixed up in nothing, so I turned around and went home again. I didn't know what was up, but when me and the wife went into Hamilton Sat'dy night in our flivver we seen one of the extries and read about how the poor lady was murdered. But that ain't what I was gittin' at, sir—"

"Well, what *are* you getting at?" Sanderson urged.

"Well, the extry said the police had found some footprints under the frontmost of them two side windows to Mis' Selim's bedroom, and went on to talk about the rose vines being tore, and straight off I said to the missus,

'Them's *my* footprints, Minnie'—Minnie's my wife's name—"

"*Your* footprints!" Sanderson ejaculated, then shook with silent laughter. "There goes Strawn's case, Bonnie!" But immediately he was serious again, as the import of this new evidence came to him. "Tell us all about it, Rawlins.... When did you make those footprints?"

"Friday, sir. That's the day I gardened for Mis' Selim.... You see, sir, the poor little lady told me she was kept awake nights when they was a high wind, by the rose vines tapping against the windows. Says she, 'I think they's somebody tryin' to git into my room, Elmer,' and I could see the poor little thing was mighty nervous anyway, so I didn't waste no time. I cut away a lot of the rose vine and burned it when I was burnin' the garbage and papers in the 'cinerator out back."

"Is that all, Rawlins?" Sanderson asked.

"'Bout all that 'mounts to anything," the laborer deprecated. "But they was somethin' else that struck me as a little funny, when I come to think of it—"

"Well?" Sanderson prodded, as the man halted uncertainly.

"Well, it's like I told you, it was my job to burn the papers. That scar-face maid of Mis' Selim's put everything—garbage and trash—in a big garbage can outside the back door, and I burnt 'em up. So I was kinder surprised Sat'dy mornin', when I went to stoke up the laundry heater, to find somebody'd been meddlin' with my drafts and had let the fire go clean out. I had to clean out the ashes and build a new fire—"

"You're trying to say, I suppose, that you could tell by the ashes that someone had been burning papers in the laundry heater?" Sanderson asked, with a quick glance at Dundee's tense face.

"That's right, sir," Rawlins agreed eagerly. "You know what kind of ashes a mess o' paper makes—layers of white ashes, sir, that kinder looks like papers yit."

"Yes, I know.... And you found layers of white ashes, which you took particular pains to clean out?" Sanderson asked bitterly.

"Yes, sir. So's I could build a new fire—"

"Did you speak to the maid—ask her if she'd been 'meddlin' with your drafts'?"

"Yes, sir, I did!" the man answered with a trace of the belligerence he had undoubtedly shown to Lydia. "She said *she* didn't open no dampers, claimed the heater was the same as usual when she left Friday night to go to a movie. So I reckin it was the poor lady herself, burnin' up love letters, maybe, or some such truck—"

"You're to keep your 'reckins' to yourself, Rawlins," Sanderson cut in emphatically. "Remember, now, you're not to tell anybody else what you've just told me.... If that's all, you can go now, and I'm much obliged to you. Leave your address with the young lady here. You'll be needed later, of course."

The relieved man hurried out of the room on Penny's heels. Sanderson shrugged, then, when the door had closed, began heavily:

"It looks like you're right, Bonnie, about that blackmail business. As the astute Rawlins says, 'love letters, maybe, or some such truck....' Of course it all fits in with your theory that Nita had made up her mind to reform, marry Ralph Hammond, and be a very good girl indeed.... All right! You can have Penny in now. I think I know pretty well what you're going to ask her. And I may as well tell you that when Roger Crain skipped town with some securities he was known to possess, he hadn't got them from a safe deposit box, because he didn't have one," and Sanderson pressed a button on the edge of his desk....

"Penny, do you know whether there is a concealed safe in the Selim house?"

The girl, startled, began to shake her head, then checked herself. "Not that I ever saw, or knew of when Dad and Mother and I lived there, but—" She hesitated, her cheeks turning scarlet.

"Out with it, Penny!" Sanderson urged, his voice very kind.

"It's just that, if you really think there's a secret hiding place in the house, I believe I understand something that puzzled me when it happened," Penny confessed, her head high. "I was at the Country Club one night—a Saturday night when the whole crowd is usually there for the dinner and dance. I'd been dancing with— with Ralph, and when the music stopped we went out on the porch, where several of our crowd were sitting. It was—just two or three weeks after—after Dad left town. Lois wouldn't let me drop out of things.... Anyway, it was dark and I heard Judge Marshall saying something about 'the simplest and most ingenious arrangement you ever saw. Of course that's where the rascal kept his securities—...' I knew they were talking about Dad, from the way Judge Marshall shut up and changed the subject as soon as he saw me."

"Who was on the porch, Penny?" Dundee asked tensely.

"Why, let's see—Flora, and Johnny Drake, and Clive," she answered slowly. "I think that was all, besides Judge Marshall. The others hadn't come out from dancing.... Of course I don't know whether or not it was some 'arrangement' in the house—"

"Where are you going, boy?" Sanderson checked Dundee, who was already on his way to the door.

"To find that gun, of course!"

"Well, if it's tucked away in the 'simplest and most ingenious arrangement you ever saw' it will stay put for a while," Sanderson said. "Lydia's due here within half an hour, and you don't want to miss her, do you?"

CHAPTER EIGHTEEN

It was exactly twelve o'clock when Lydia Carr, accompanied by Detective Collins of the Homicide Squad carrying a small suitcase, arrived at the district attorney's office.

"I kept my eye on her every minute of the time, to see that there wasn't no shenanigans," Collins informed Dundee and Sanderson importantly, callous to the fact that the maid could hear him. "But I let her bring along everything she said she needed to lay the body out in.... Was that right?"

"Right!" agreed the district attorney, as Dundee opened the suitcase upon Sanderson's desk.

The royal blue velvet dress lay on top, neatly folded. Dundee shook out its folds. It looked remarkably fresh and new, in spite of the years it had hung in Nita Selim's various clothes closets, preserved because of God alone knew what tender memories. Perhaps the beautiful little dancer had intended all those years that it should be her shroud....

"Oh, it's lovely!" Penny Crain, who was looking on, cried out involuntarily. "It looks like a French model."

"It's a copy of a French model. You can see by the label on the back of the neck," Lydia answered, her one good eye softening for Penny.

"So it is!" Dundee agreed, and took out his penknife to snip the threads which fastened the white satin, gold-lettered label to the frock. "'Pierre Model. Copied by Simonson's—New York City'," he read aloud, and slipped the little square of satin into the envelope containing the murdered woman's will. "Well, Penny, I'm glad you like the dress, for I'm going to ask you to do the mannikin stunt in it as soon as Carraway arrives with his camera."

Penny turned very pale, but she said nothing in protest, and Dundee continued to unpack the suitcase. His masculine hands looked clumsy as they lifted out the costume slip and miniature "dancing set"—brassiere and step-ins—all matching, of filmiest white chiffon and lace. His fingers flinched from contact with the switch of long, silky black curls....

"She bought them after we came to Hamilton," Lydia informed him, pointing to the undergarments. "Them black moire pumps and them French stockings are brand new, too—hundred-gauge silk them stockings are, and never on her feet—"

"Ready for me?" Carraway had appeared in the doorway, with camera and tripod.

"Yes, Carraway.... Just the dress, Penny.... I want full-length front, back and side views of Miss Crain wearing this dress, Carraway.... Flashlights, of course. Better take the pictures in Miss Crain's office," Dundee directed. "You stay here, Lydia. I want to talk with you while that job is being done."

"Yes, sir," Lydia answered, and accepted without thanks the chair he offered.

"I suppose you have read *The Hamilton Morning News* today, Lydia?"

"I have!"

"May I have that paper, chief?... Thanks!... Now, Lydia, I want you to read again the paragraphs that are headed 'New York, May 25—' and tell us if the statements are correct."

Lydia accepted the paper and her single eye scanned the following lines obediently:

New York, May 25 (UP)
Mrs. Juanita Leigh Selim, who was murdered Saturday afternoon in Hamilton, ——, was known along Broadway as Nita Leigh, chorus girl and

specialty dancer. Her last known address in New York was No. — West 54th St., where she had a three-room apartment. According to the superintendent, E. J. Black, Miss Leigh, as he knew her, lived there alone except for her maid, Lydia Carr, and entertained few visitors.

Irving Wein, publicity director for Altamont Pictures, when interviewed by a reporter in his rooms at the Cadillac Hotel late today, said that Nita Leigh had been used for "bits" and as a dancing "double" for stars in a number of recent pictures, including "Night Life" and "Boy, Howdy!", both of which have dancing sequences. Musical comedy programs for the last year carry her name only once, in the list of "Ladies of the Ensemble" of the revue, "What of it?"

Miss Eloise Pendleton, head-mistress of Forsyte-on-the-Hudson, mentioned in the dispatches from Hamilton, confirms the report that Mrs. Selim, as she was known there, twice directed the annual Easter musical comedy presented by that fashionable school for young ladies, but could add nothing of interest to the facts given above, beyond asserting that Mrs. Selim had proved to be an unusually competent and popular director of their amateur theatricals.

"Yes, that's correct, as far as it goes," Lydia commented, resentment strong in her harsh voice as she returned the paper to Dundee.

"Have you anything to add?" Dundee caught her up quickly.

"No, sir!" Lydia shook her head, her lips in a grim line. Then resentment burst through: "They don't have to talk like she was a back number on Broadway, just because she was tired of the stage and going in for movies!"

District Attorney Sanderson took her in hand then, pelting her with questions about Nita's New York "gentlemen friends," but he made no more headway than Dundee.

"We *know* that Nita Selim was afraid of *someone!*" Sanderson began again, angrily. "Who was it—someone she'd known in New York, or somebody in Hamilton?"

"I don't know!" Lydia told him flatly.

"But you do know she was living in fear of her life, don't you?" Dundee interposed.

"I—well, yes, I suppose she was," Lydia admitted reluctantly. "But I thought she was just afraid to live out there in that lonesome house away off at the end of nowhere."

"Was she afraid of Dexter Sprague?" Sanderson shot at her.

"Would she have asked him to stay all night if she'd been afraid of *him?*" Lydia demanded scornfully. "And would she have asked *him* to rig up a bell from her bedroom to mine, if it was *him* she was afraid of?"

"A bell?" Dundee echoed.

"Yes, sir. It has a contraption under the rug, right beside her bed, so's she could step on it and it would ring in my room, which was underneath hers.... Mr. Sprague bought the wire and stuff, bored a hole through her bedroom floor, and fixed it all hisself."

"Did anyone know Nita had taken this precaution to protect herself?" Dundee asked.

"Mis' Lois did, because one day not long ago she stepped on it accidentally, when she was in Nita's room. The bell buzzed in my room and I come up to answer it, and Nita explained it to Mis' Lois."

So that was why no attempt had been made to murder Nita while she slept!—Dundee told himself triumphantly. For of course it was more than probable that Lois Dunlap had innocently spread the news of Nita's nervousness and her ingenious method of summoning help instantly....

There was a knock at the door.

"Come in!... All finished, Carraway?... Fine! I'd like to see the prints as soon as possible, and now I'd like you to go over to the morgue with Lydia, and wait there until she has the body dressed in these clothes, and the hair done according to the instructions Mrs. Selim left.... I'll leave the posing to you, but I want a full-length picture as well as a head portrait."

As Lydia's work-roughened, knuckly hands were returning the funeral clothes to the suitcase, another question occurred to Dundee:

"Lydia, did you know, before I questioned you at the Miles home yesterday, that Sprague had returned for that bag he had left in the bedroom upstairs?"

Her scarred cheek flushed livid, but the maid answered with defiant honesty: "Yes, I did! He spoke to me through my basement window just before you come running down to talk to me. He'd sneaked back, but he could tell from seeing your car outside that you was there, and he asked me to go up and get the bag and set it outside the kitchen door for him. I said I wouldn't do it; it was too risky."

"Then you were pretending to be asleep when I entered your room?"

"Yes, I was! But I *had* been asleep before Mr. Sprague called me. While you was ding-donging at me about Nita burning my face I heard Mr. Sprague open the kitchen door. He had a key Nita had give him, so's he could slip in unnoticed if he happened to come when Nita had other company. He didn't hardly make any noise at all, but I heard it, because I was listening for it.... You'd left the door to the basement stairs open, and my door, too, so I heard him."

"Did you hear him come down?"

"Yes, I did! There's a board on the backstairs that squeaks, and I heard it plain, while you was still at me, hammer and tongs," Lydia answered. "He was in the house not more'n two minutes, all told, and when I figured he was safely out, I went upstairs with you to

show you the presents I'd give Nita after she burnt me, to
prove I'd forgive her."

"Why didn't you tell me, Lydia? Why did you protect
Sprague? I know you don't like him," Dundee puzzled.

"I wasn't thinking about him," Lydia told him flatly. "I
was thinking about Nita. I didn't want any scandal on
her, and I knew what the police and the newspapers
would say if they found out Mr. Sprague had been staying
all night sometimes."

"Are you prepared to swear Sprague had time to do
nothing but go up to the bedroom and get his bag?"

"I am!"

When Lydia and Carraway had left together, Dundee
rose and addressed the district attorney:

"I'm going out to the Selim house now, to look for that
secret hiding place where Roger Crain kept his securities,
and which Judge Marshall evidently displayed to Nita, as
one of the charms of the house when she 'rented' it."

"Why not simply telephone Judge Marshall and ask
him where and what it is?" Sanderson asked reasonably.

"Do you think he'd tell?" Dundee retorted. "The old
boy's no fool. Even if he didn't kill Nita himself and hide
the gun there, my question would throw him into a panic
of fear lest one of his best friends had done just that....
No, I'll find it myself, if it's all right with you!"

But after a solid hour of hard and fruitless work,
Bonnie Dundee was forced to admit ruefully to himself
that his parting words to the district attorney might have
been the youthful and empty boast that Sanderson had
evidently considered them.

For nowhere in the house Roger Crain had built and
in which Nita Selim had been murdered could the
detective find anything remotely resembling a concealed
safe. The two plainclothesmen whom Strawn had detailed
to guard the house and to continue the search for the
missing gun and silencer looked on with unconcealed
amusement as Dundee tapped walls, floors and ceilings in

a house that seemed to be exceptionally free of architectural eccentricities.

Finally Dundee grew tired of their ribald comments and curtly ordered them to make a new and exhaustive search of the unused portions of the basement—those dark earth banks, with their overhead networks of water and drain pipes, heavily insulated cables of electric wires, cobwebby rafters and rough shelves holding empty fruit jars and liquor bottles—which contrasted sharply with the neatly ceiled and cement-floored space devoted to furnace, laundry and maid's room. Dundee himself had given those regions only a cursory inspection with his flashlight, for it was highly improbable that Nita Selim would have made use of a secret hiding place for her jewelry and valuable papers, if that hiding place was located in such dark, awesome surroundings.

No. The hiding place, if it really existed—and it must exist—had been within easy reach of Nita dressing and bedecking herself for a party, or Lydia Carr could not have been kept in complete ignorance of its location.

With that conviction in mind, Dundee returned to Nita's bedroom, to which he had already devoted at least half an hour. Nothing in the big clothes closet, where Flora Miles had been hiding while Nita was being murdered. No secret drawers in desk or dressing-table or bedside table. No false bottom in boudoir chair or chaise longue.... He had even taken every book out of the four-shelf bookcase which stood against the west wall near the north corner of the room, and had satisfied himself that no book was a leafless fake.

His minute inspection of the bathroom and back hall, upon which Nita's bedroom opened, had proved as fruitless, although he had removed every drawer from the big linen press which stood in the hall, and measured spaces to a fraction of an inch. As for the walls, they were, except for the doors, unbroken expanses of tinted plaster.

And yet—

He stepped into the clothes closet again, hammer in hand for a fresh tapping of the cedar-board walls. Nothing here.... And then he tapped again, his ear against the end wall of the closet—the wall farthest from the side porch....

Yes! There was a faintly hollow echo of the hammer strokes!

Excitement blazing high again, he took the tape measure with which he had provided himself on his way out, and calculated the length of the closet from end to end. Six feet....

Emerging from the closet he closed his eyes in an effort to recall in exact detail the architect's blueprint of the lower floor, which Coroner Price had submitted to his jury at the inquest that morning. Yes, that was right! The inner end wall of Nita's clothes closet was also the back of the guest closet in the little foyer that lay between Nita's bedroom and the main hall.

Within ten minutes, much laying-on of the tape measure had produced a startling result. Instead of having a wall in common, the guest closet and Nita's clothes closet were separated by exactly eleven inches! Why the waste space? The blueprint, bearing the imprint of the architects, Hammond & Hammond, showed no such walled-up cubbyhole!

Exultantly, Dundee again entered Nita's closet and went over every inch of the narrow, horizontal cedar boards, which formed the end wall. But he met with no reward. Not through this workmanlike, solidly constructed wall had an opening been made....

But in the foyer closet he read a different story. Its back wall had an amateurish look. This closet was not cedar-lined, as was Nita's, but was painted throughout in soft ivory. But it was the back wall of the closet in which Dundee was interested. Unlike the other walls, which were of plaster, the back was constructed of six-inch-wide boards—the cheapness of the lumber not concealed by its coat of ivory paint. No self-respecting builder had put in that wall of broad, horizontal boards....

And then, directly beneath the shelf which was set regulation height, just above the pole on which swung a dozen coat hangers, Dundee found what he was looking for.

A short length of the cheap board, a queer scrap to have been used even in so shoddy a job as that wall was.... Eight inches long. And set square in the center of the wall, just below the shelf and pole. If he had not been looking for something odd, however, Dundee acknowledged to himself, he would not have noticed it. Did anyone ever notice the back walls of closets?

Sure of the result, he pressed with his finger tips upon the lower end of that short piece of board. And slowly it swung inward, the top slanting outward.

He had found the secret hiding place. And Dundee silently agreed with Judge Marshall that it was "the simplest and most ingenious arrangement you ever saw," for it was nothing more nor less than a shelf set between the two closets, in those eleven inches of unaccounted for space!

"I take off my hat to Roger Crain!" Dundee reflected. "No burglar in the world would ever have thought of pressing upon a short piece of board in a foyer closet, in search of a safe.... But how did Judge Marshall know of its existence?"

The only answer Dundee could think of was that Crain, overseeing the building of his house, had suddenly conceived this brilliant and simple plan, and had tipped one of the carpenters to carry it out for him. Possibly, or probably, he had bragged to Clive or Ralph Hammond, his architects, of his clever invention. And the Hammond boys had passed on the information to Judge Marshall, when, after Crain's failure and flight, the house had become the property of the ex-judge.

These thoughts rushed through his mind as his flashlight explored the shelf through the tilted opening.

The gun and silencer *must* be here, since they could be no place else!... But the shelf was bare except for a small brass box, fastened only by a clasp. In his acute disappointment Dundee took little interest in the collection of pretty but inexpensive jewelry—Nita's trinkets, undoubtedly—which the brass box contained.... No wedding ring among them....

In spite of his chagrin at not finding the gun, Dundee studied the simple mechanism which Roger Crain's ingenuity had conceived. From the outside, the eight-inch length of board fitted smoothly, giving no indication whatever that it was otherwise than what it seemed— part of a cheaply built wall. But Dundee's flashlight played upon the beveled edges of both the short board and the two neighboring planks between which it was fitted. The pivoting arrangement was of the simplest, the small nickel-plated pieces being set into the short board and the other two planks with small screws which did not pierce the painted outside surface.

His curiosity satisfied, Dundee stepped out of the closet into the tiny foyer. He was about to leave when a terrific truth crashed through his mind and froze his feet to the floor.

Of course the gun and silencer were not there!

This was the *guest closet*! In it had hung the hat of every person who had been Nita's guest, either for bridge or cocktails, that fatal Saturday afternoon!

And to this closet, to retrieve hat, stick or—in the case of the women, summer coat and hat—had come every person who had been questioned and then searched by the police.

Dundee tried to recapture the picture of the stampede which had followed upon his permission for all guests to go to their homes. But it was useless. He had stayed in the living room with Strawn, had taken not the slightest interest in the scramble for hats, coats and sticks. For Strawn had previously assured him that the guest closet had been thoroughly searched.

So quickly that he felt slightly dizzy, Dundee's thoughts raced around the new discovery. This changed everything, of course. Any one of half a dozen persons could have arrived with the gun and silencer—not screwed together, of course, because of the ungainly length—and seized the opportunity presented by Nita's being alone in her bedroom to shoot her. What easier, then, than to hide the weapon on this secret shelf, the "door" of which yielded to the slightest pressure? And what easier than to retrieve the weapon after permission had been granted to all to return to their homes? Easy enough to manage to go alone to the closet for a hat, the extra minute of time unnoticed in the general excitement. It had been vitally necessary, too, to retrieve the weapon, since any innocent member of that party might have remembered later to mention the secret hiding place to the police—secret no longer since Judge Marshall had gossiped about it....

Then another thought boiled up and demanded attention. In the new theory, what place did the "bang or bump" have—that noise which Flora Miles, concealed in Nita's closet, had dimly heard? Dundee had been positive, when Lydia had discovered the shattered electric bulb in the big bronze lamp that its position in Nita's room indicated the progress of the flight of the murderer— flight diagonally across the room toward the back hall. But now—

A little dashed, Dundee returned to the bedroom. The big lamp was where he had first seen it—about a foot beyond the window nearest the porch, and at the head of the chaise longue which was set between the two west windows, where, according to Lydia, the lamp always stood. The too-long cord lay slackly along the floor near the west wall, and extended to the double outlet on the baseboard behind the bookcase.... *A slack cord!*

Down on his hands and knees Dundee went, to peer under the low bottom shelf of the bookcase.... Yes! The pronged plug of the lamp cord had been jerked almost out of the baseboard outlet! It was easy to visualize what had happened: The murderer, after firing the shot, had involuntarily taken a step or even several steps backward, until his foot had caught in the loop of electric cord, causing the big lamp to be thrown violently against the wall near which it stood.... But who?

Any one of half a dozen people! But—*who*?

CHAPTER NINETEEN

Having ticketed the big bronze lamp, which he had brought with him from the Selim house, and locked it away in the room devoted to "exhibits for the state," Bonnie Dundee hurried into Penny's office, primed with the news of his discovery of the secret hiding place and eager to lay his new theory before the district attorney.

"Bill's gone," Penny interrupted her swift typing to inform him. "To Chicago. He had only fifteen minutes to make the three o'clock train, after he received a wire saying his mother is not expected to live. He tried to reach you at the Selim house, but one of Captain Strawn's men said you had left."

"I stopped on my way in to get a bite to eat," Dundee explained mechanically. "I'd dashed off without my lunch, you know."

"Did you find the gun and silencer?" Penny asked.

"No. Whoever used it Saturday afternoon walked out of the house with it, in plain view of the police, and still has it.... Very convenient, too, in case another murder seems to be expedient—or amusing."

"Don't joke!" Penny shuddered. "But what in the world do you mean?"

Briefly Dundee told her, minimizing the hard work, the concentrated thinking, and the meticulous use of a tape measure which had resulted in the discovery of the shelf between Nita's bedroom closet and the guest closet in the little foyer.

"I see," Penny agreed, her husky voice slow and weighted with horror. She sat in dazed thought for a minute. "That rather brings it home to my crowd—doesn't

it?... To think that Dad—!... Probably everyone at the
party—except me—had heard all about Dad's 'simple and
ingenious' arrangement for hiding the securities he sent
on to New York before he ran away.... And no outsiders—
nobody but *us*—had a legitimate excuse for entering that
closet.... Not even Dexter Sprague. It's one of his
affectations not to wear a hat—"

"Is it?" Dundee pounced. "You're sure he wore no hat
that afternoon? Did you notice him when he left after I
had dismissed you all?"

"Yes," Penny acknowledged honestly. "I paid attention
to him, because I was hating him so. I believed then that
he was the murderer, and I was furious with you and
Captain Strawn for not arresting him.... He was the first
to leave—just walked straight out; wouldn't even stop to
talk with Janet Raymond, who was trying to get a word
with him. I saw him start toward Sheridan Road—
walking. He had no car, you know."

"Did you observe the others?" Dundee demanded
eagerly. "Do you know who went *alone* to the guest
closet?"

Penny shook her head. "Everybody was milling
around in the hall, and I paid no attention. Lois said she
would drive me home, and then I went in to ask you to let
me stay behind with you—"

"I remember.... Listen, Penny! I'm going to tell you
something else that nobody knows yet but Sanderson,
Lydia and me. I don't have to ask you not to tell any of
your friends. You know well enough that anything you
learn from either Sanderson or me is strictly
confidential."

Penny nodded, her face very white and her brown
eyes big with misery.

"I have every reason to believe that Nita Selim was a
blackmailer, that she came to Hamilton for the express
purpose of bleeding someone she had known before, or
someone on whom she had 'the goods' from some
underworld source or other.... At any rate, Nita banked

ten thousand mysterious dollars—$5,000 on April 28, and $5,000 on May 5. I talked to Drake last night, and I have his word for it that the money was in bills of varying denomination—none large—when Nita presented it for deposit. Therefore it seems clear to me that Nita got the money right here in Hamilton; otherwise it would have come to her in the form of checks or drafts or money orders. And it seems equally clear to me that she did not bring that large amount of cash from New York with her, or she would have deposited it in a lump sum in the bank immediately after her arrival."

"Yes," Penny agreed. "But why are you telling *me*?... Of course I'm interested—"

"Because I want you to tell me the financial status of each of your friends," Dundee said gently. "I know how hard it is for you—"

"You could find out from others, so I might as well tell you," Penny interrupted, with a weary shrug. "Judge Marshall is well-to-do, and Karen's father—her mother is dead—settled $100,000 on her when she married. She has complete control of her own money.... The Dunlaps are the richest people in Hamilton, and have been for two or three generations. Lois was 'first-family' but poor when she married Peter, but he's been giving her an allowance of $20,000 a year for several years—not for running the house, but for her personal use. Clothes, charities, hobbies, like the Little Theater she brought Nita here to organize—"

"I wouldn't say she spends a great deal of it on dress," Dundee interrupted with a grin.

"Lois doesn't give a hang how she looks or what anyone thinks of her—which is probably one reason she is the best-loved woman in our crowd," Penny retorted loyally. "The Miles' money is really Flora's, and she has the reputation of being one of the shrewdest business 'men' in town. When she married Tracey nearly eight years ago, he was just a salesman in her father's business—the biggest dairy in the state ... 'Cloverblossom'

butter, cream, milk and cheese, you know.... Well, when
Flora married Tracey, her father retired and let Tracey
run the business for Flora, and he's still managing it, but
Flora is the real head.... Now, let's see.... Oh, yes, the
Drakes!... Johnny is vice president of the Hamilton
National Bank, as you know, and owns a big block of the
stock. Carolyn has no money of her own, except what
Johnny gives her, and I rather think he isn't any too
generous—"

"They don't get along very well together, do they?"

"N-no!" Penny agreed reluctantly. "You see, Johnny
Drake was simply not cut out for love and marriage. He's
a born ascetic, would have been a monk two or three
centuries ago, but he cares as much for Carolyn as he
could for any woman.... The Hammond boys have some
inherited money, and Clive has made a big financial
success of architecture.... That leaves only Janet and
Polly, doesn't it?... Polly's an orphan and has barrels of
money, and will have barrels more when her aunt, with
whom she lives, dies and leaves her the fortune she has
always promised her."

"And Janet Raymond?"

"Janet's father is pretty rich—owns a big wire-fence
factory, but Janet has only a reasonable allowance,"
Penny answered. "As for me—I'm *very* rich: I get thirty-
five whole dollars a week, to support myself and Mother
on."

Dundee remained thoughtfully silent for a long
minute. Then: "All you girls are alumnae of Forsyte-on-
the-Hudson, and Nita Selim came here immediately after
she had directed a Forsyte play.... Tell me, Penny—was
any of the Hamilton girls ever in disgrace while in the
Forsyte School?"

Penny's face flamed. "I'm sorry to disappoint you, but
so far as I know there was never anything of the sort. Of
course we all graduated different years, except Karen and
I, and I might not have heard—But no!" she denied

vehemently. "There wasn't any scandal on a Hamilton girl ever! I'm sure of it!"

But her very vehemence convinced Bonnie Dundee that she was not at all sure....

He looked at his watch. Four o'clock.... By this time Nita Selim—tiny cold body, royal blue velvet dress, black curls piled high in an old-fashioned "French roll," bullet-torn heart—were nothing more than a little heap of grey ashes.... Would Lydia Carr have them put in a sealed urn and carry them about with her always?

"I'm going out now, Penny, and I shan't be back today," he told the girl who had returned to her furious typing. "I'll telephone in about an hour to see if anything has come up.... By the way, how do I get to the Dunlap house?"

"It's in the Brentwood section. You know—that cluster of hills around Mirror Lake. Most of the crowd live out there—the Drakes, the Mileses, the Beales, the Marshalls. The Dunlap house stands on the highest hill of all. It's grey stone, a little like a French chateau. We used to live out there, too, in a Colonial house my mother's father built, but Dad persuaded Mother to sell, when he went into that Primrose Meadows venture. The Raymonds bought it.... But why do you want to see Lois?"

"Thanks much, Penny. I don't know what I should do without you," Dundee said, without answering her question, and reached for his hat.

After ten minutes of driving, the last mile of which had circled a smooth silver coin of a lake, Dundee stopped his car and let his eyes rove appreciatively. He had made this trip the day before to question Lydia, already installed as nurse for the Miles children, but he had been in too great a hurry then to see much of this section consecrated to Hamilton's socially elect....

Georgian "cottage," Spanish hacienda, Italian villa, Tudor mansion—that was the Miles home; Colonial mansion where Penny had once lived; grey stone chateau.... Not one of them blatantly new or marked with the dollar sign. Dundee sighed a little enviously as he turned his car into the winding driveway that led up the highest hill to the Dunlap home.

Lois Dunlap betrayed no surprise when the butler led Dundee to the flag-stoned upper terrace overlooking Mirror Lake, where she was having tea with her three children and their governess. For a moment the detective had the illusion that he was in England again....

"How do you do, Mr. Dundee?... This is Miss Burden.... My three offspring—Peter the third, Eleanor, and Bobby.... Will you please take the children to the playroom now, Miss Burden?... Thank you!... Tea, Mr. Dundee? Or shall I order you a highball?"

"Nothing, thanks," Dundee answered, grateful for her friendliness but nonplussed by it. Not for the first time he felt a sick distaste for the profession he had chosen....

"It's all over," Lois Dunlap said in a low voice, as the butler retreated. "Lydia made her look very beautiful.... I thought it would be rather horrible, having to see her, as the poor child requested in her note to Lydia, but I'm glad now I did. She looked as sweet and young and innocent as she must have been when she first wore the royal blue velvet."

"I'm glad," Dundee said sincerely. Then he leaned toward her across the tea table. "Mrs. Dunlap, will you please tell me just how you persuaded Mrs. Selim to come to Hamilton—so far from Broadway?"

"Why certainly!" Lois Dunlap looked puzzled. "But it really did not take much persuasion after I showed her some group photographs we had made when we Forsyte girls put on 'The Beggar's Opera' here last October—a benefit performance for the Forsyte Alumnae Scholarship fund."

With difficulty Dundee controlled his excitement. "May I see those photographs, please?"

"I had to hunt quite a bit for them," his hostess apologized ten minutes later, as she spread the glossy prints of half a dozen photographs for Dundee's inspection. "Do you know 'The Beggar's Opera'?"

"John Gay—eighteenth century, isn't it?... As I remember it, it is quite—" and Dundee hesitated, grinning.

"Bawdy?" Lois laughed. "Oh, very! We couldn't have got away with it if it hadn't been a classic. As it was, we had to tone down some of the naughtiest passages and songs. But it was lots of fun, and the boys enjoyed it hugely because it gave them an opportunity to wear tight satin breeches and lace ruffles.... This is my husband, Peter. He adored being the highwayman, 'Robin of Bagshot'," and she pointed out a stocky, belligerent-looking man near the end of the long row of costumed players, in a photograph which showed the entire cast.

"You say that Mrs. Selim accepted your proposal *after* she saw these photographs?" Dundee asked. "Had she refused before?"

"Yes. I'd gone to New York for the annual Easter Play which the Forsyte School puts on, because I'm intensely interested in semi-professional theatricals," Lois explained. "Nita had done a splendid job with the play the year before, and I spoke to her, after this year's show was over, about coming to Hamilton. She was not at all interested, but polite and sweet about it, so I invited her to have lunch with me the next day, and showed her these photographs of our own play in the hope that they would make her take the idea more seriously. We had borrowed a Little Theater director from Chicago and I knew we had done a really good job of 'The Beggar's Opera.' The local reviews—"

"These 'stills' look extremely professional. I don't wonder that they interested Nita," Dundee cut in. "Will you tell me what she said?"

"She rather startled me," Lois Dunlap confessed. "I first showed her this picture of the whole cast, and as I was explaining the play a bit—she didn't know 'The Beggar's Opera'—she almost snatched the photograph out of my hands. As she studied it, her lovely black eyes grew perfectly enormous. I've never seen her so excited since—"

"What did she say?" Dundee interrupted tensely.

"Why, she said nothing just at first, then she began to laugh in the queerest way—almost hysterically. I asked her why she was laughing—I was a little huffy, I'm afraid—and she said the men looked so adorably conceited and funny. Then she began to ask the names of the players. I told her that 'Macheath'—he's the highwayman hero, you know—was played by Clive Hammond; that my Peter was 'Robin of Bagshot', that Johnny Drake was another highwayman, 'Mat of the Mint', that Tracey Miles played the jailor, 'Lockit'—"

"Did she show more interest in one name than another?"

"Yes. When I pointed out Judge Marshall as 'Peachum', the fence, she cried out suddenly: 'Why, I know him! I met him once on a party.... Is he really a *judge*?' and she laughed as if she knew something very funny about Hugo—as no doubt she did. He was an inveterate 'lady-killer' before his marriage, as you may have heard."

"Do you think her first excitement was over seeing Judge Marshall among the players?" Dundee asked.

"No," Lois answered, after considering a moment. "I'm sure she didn't notice him until I pointed him out. The face in this group that seemed to interest her most was Flora Miles'. Flora played the part of 'Lucy Lockit', the jailor's daughter, and Karen Marshall the other feminine lead, 'Polly Peachum', you know. But it was Flora's picture she lingered over, so I showed her this picture," and Lois Dunlap reached for the portrait of Flora Miles, unexpectedly beautiful in the eighteenth century costume—tight bodice and billowing skirts.

"She questioned you about Mrs. Miles?" Dundee asked.

"Yes. All sorts of questions—her name, and whether she was married and then who her husband was, and if she had had stage experience," Lois answered conscientiously. "She explained her interest by saying Flora looked more like a professional actress than any of the others, and that we should give her a real chance when we got our Little Theater going. I asked her if that meant she was going to accept my offer, and she said she might, but that she would have to talk it over with a friend first. Just before midnight she telephoned me at my hotel that she had decided to accept the job."

Dundee's heart leaped. It was very easy to guess who that "friend" was! But he controlled his excitement, asked his next question casually:

"Did she show particular interest in any other player?"

"Yes. She asked a number of questions about Polly Beale, and seemed incredulous when I told her that Polly and Clive were engaged. Polly played 'Mrs. Peachum', and was a riot in the part.... But Nita's intuition was correct. Flora carried off the acting honors.... Oh, yes, she also asked, quite naively, if all my friends were rich, too, and could help support a Little Theater. I reassured her on that point."

"And," Dundee reflected silently, "upon a point much more important to Nita Selim." Aloud he said: "I don't see *you* among the cast."

"Oh, I haven't a grain of talent," Lois Dunlap laughed. "I can't act for two cents—can I, Peter darling?... Here's the redoubtable 'Robin of Bagshot' in person, Mr. Dundee—my husband!"

The detective rose to shake hands with the man he had been too absorbed to see or hear approaching.

"You're the man from the district attorney's office?" Peter Dunlap scowled, his hand barely touching Dundee's. "I suppose you're trying to get at the bottom of the mystery of why my wife brought that Selim woman—"

"Don't call her 'that Selim woman', Peter!" Lois Dunlap interrupted with more sharpness than Dundee had ever seen her display. "You never liked the poor girl, were never just to her—"

"Well, it looks as if my hunch was correct, doesn't it?" the stocky, rugged-faced man retorted. "I told you at the beginning to pay her off and send her back to New York—"

"You knew I couldn't do that, even to please you, dear," Lois said. "But please don't let's quarrel about poor Nita again. She's dead now, and I want to do anything I can to help bring her murderer to justice."

"There's nothing you can do, Lois, and I hope Mr.— ah—Dundee will not find it necessary to quiz you again."

Dundee reached for his hat. "I hope so, too, Mr. Dunlap.... By the way, you are president of the Chamber of Commerce, aren't you?"

"Yes, I am! And we're having a meeting tonight, at which that Sprague man's bid on making a historical movie of Hamilton will be turned down—unanimously. Now that the Selim woman isn't here to vamp my fellow-members into doing anything she wants, I think I can safely promise you that Dexter Sprague will have no further business in Hamilton—unless it is police business!"

"Thanks for the tip, Mr. Dunlap," Dundee said evenly. "I hope you enjoyed your fishing trip. Where do you fish, sir?"

"A tactful way of asking for my alibi, eh?" Dunlap was heavily sarcastic. "I left Friday afternoon for my own camp in the mountains, up in the northwest part of the state. I drove my own car, went alone, spent the week-end alone, and got back this noon. I read of the murder in a paper I picked up in a village on my way home. I didn't like Nita Selim, and I don't give a damn about her being murdered, except that my wife's name is in all the papers.... Any questions?"

"None, thanks!" Dundee answered curtly, then turned to Lois Dunlap who was watching the two men with troubled, embarrassed eyes. "I am very grateful to you, Mrs. Dunlap, for your kindness."

The detective's angry resentment of Peter Dunlap's attitude lasted until he had circled Mirror Lake and was on the road into Hamilton. Then commonsense intervened. Dunlap was undoubtedly devoted to his wife. Penny had said that he had "never looked at another woman." It was rather more than natural that he should be in a futile, blustering rage at the outcome of Lois' friendship for the little Broadway dancer....

Free of anger, his mind reverted to the story Lois Dunlap had told him. For in it, he was sure, was hidden the key to the mystery of Nita Selim's murder. Not at all interested in the proposition to organize a Little Theater in Hamilton, Nita had been seized with a strange excitement as soon as she was shown photographs of a large group of Hamilton's richest and most prominent inhabitants.... But there was the rub! *A large group!* Would that group of possible suspects never narrow down to one? Of course there was Judge Marshall, but if Lois Dunlap's memory was to be trusted Nita had not noticed the elderly Beau Brummel's picture until *after* that strange, hysterical excitement had taken possession of her. And if it had been Judge Marshall whom she had come to Hamilton to blackmail would Nita not have guarded her tongue before Lois? The same was true about her extraordinary interest in Flora Miles....

Dundee tried to put himself in Nita's place, confronted suddenly with a group picture containing the likeness of a person—man or woman—against whom she knew something so dreadful and so secret that her silence would be worth thousands of dollars. Would *he* have chattered of that very person? No! Of anyone else but that particular person! It was easy to picture Nita, her head whirling with possibilities, hitting upon the most conspicuous player in the group—dark, tense, theatrical

Flora, already pointed out to her as one of the two female leads in the opera.... But of whom had she really been thinking?

Again a blank wall! For in that group photograph of the cast of "The Beggar's Opera" had appeared every man, woman and girl who had been Nita's guest on the day of her murder....

Dundee, paying more attention to his driving, now that he was in the business section of the city, saw ahead of him the second-rate hotel where Dexter Sprague had been living since Nita had wired him to join her in Hamilton. On a sudden impulse the detective parked his car in front of the hotel and five minutes later was knocking upon Sprague's door.

"Well, what do you want now?" the unshaven, pallid man demanded ungraciously.

Dundee stepped into the room and closed the door. "I want you to tell me the name of the man Nita Selim came here to blackmail, Sprague."

"Blackmail?" Sprague echoed, his pallid cheeks going more yellow. "You're crazy! Nita came here to take a job—"

"She came here to blackmail someone, and I am convinced that she sent for you to act as a partner in her scheme.... No, wait! I'm *convinced*, I tell you," Dundee assured him grimly. "But I'll make a trade with you, in behalf of the district attorney. Tell me the name of the person she blackmailed, and I will promise you immunity from prosecution as her accomplice."

"Get out of my room!" and Dexter Sprague's right forefinger trembled violently as it pointed toward the door in a melodramatic gesture.

"Very well, Sprague," Dundee said. "But let me give you a friendly warning. *Don't try to carry on the good work.* Nita got ten thousand dollars, but she also got a bullet through her heart. And the gun which fired that bullet is safely back in the hands of the killer.... You're not going to get that movie job, and I was just afraid you might be tempted!... Good afternoon!"

CHAPTER TWENTY

It was Wednesday evening, four whole days since Nita Leigh Selim, Broadway dancer, had been murdered while she was dummy at bridge. Plainclothesmen, in pairs, day and night shifts, still guarded the lonely house in Primrose Meadows, but Dundee had taken no interest in the actual scene of the crime since Carraway, fingerprint expert, had reported negatively upon the secret shelf between Nita's bedroom closet and the guest closet. So far as any tangible evidence went, only Dundee's fingers had pressed upon the pivoting panel and explored the narrow shelf.

The very lack of fingerprints had of course confirmed Dundee's belief that the murderer's hand had pressed upon that swinging panel, had quested in vain for the incriminating documents or letters which had been the basis of Nita's blackmail scheme, had deposited upon the shelf the gun and silencer with which the murder had been accomplished, and had later retrieved the weapon in perfect safety. A hand loosely wrapped in a handkerchief or protected by a glove.... The hand of a cunning, careful, cold-blooded murderer—or murderess.... But—who? *Who?*

Bonnie Dundee, brooding at his desk in the living room of his small apartment, reflected bitterly that he was no nearer the answer to that question than he had been an hour after Nita Selim's death.

"Well, 'my dear Watson'," he addressed his caged parrot finally. "What do you say?... Who killed Nita Selim?"

The parrot stirred on his perch, thrust out his hooked beak to nip his master's prodding finger, then disdainfully turned his back.

"I don't blame you, Cap'n," Dundee chuckled. "You must be as sick of that question as I am.... And what a pity it ever had to be asked! If the murderer had not been so hasty—or so pressed for time that he really could not wait to listen to Nita—he would have learned from Nita herself that she had decided to be a very good girl, and had burned the 'papers'—all because she was genuinely in love with Ralph Hammond.... One comfort we have, 'my dear Watson': the murderer still does not know that Nita burned the papers Friday night. Sooner or later, when he believes police vigilance has been relaxed, he'll go prowling about that house, and to Captain Strawn, who doesn't take the slightest stock in my theory, will go credit for the arrest.... Unless—"

Dundee reached for a telegraph form and again scanned the pencilled message. Only that afternoon had it occurred to him to ask the telegraph company for a copy of the wire by which Dexter Sprague, according to his own story, had been summoned to Hamilton by Nita Selim.

The manager had been obliging, had looked up the message and copied it with his own hand. It was a night letter, and had been filed in Hamilton April 24—the third day after Nita's arrival. Addressed to Dexter Sprague, at a hotel in the theatrical district, New York City, the message read:

"EVERYTHING JAKE SO FAR BUT WOULD FEEL SAFER YOU HERE CHAMBER OF COMMERCE PLANNING BOOSTER MOVIE FOUNDING AND DEVELOPMENT OF HAMILTON LOOKING GOOD DIRECTOR WHY NOT TRY FOR JOB AS GOOD EXCUSE ALL MY LOVE—NITA"

Dundee laid the paper on his desk, locked his hands behind his head, and addressed the parrot again. The habit of using the bird for an audience and as an excuse for puzzling and mulling aloud had grown on him during the year he had owned the doughty old Cap'n.

"As I was about to say, 'my dear Watson', Captain Strawn's boys out at the Selim house will have their chance to nab our man—or woman—unless Dexter Sprague ignores my warning, pretends to have the papers himself, and tries to carry on the blackmail scheme, which he undoubtedly knew all about and which, most probably, he encouraged Nita to undertake—the 'friend' she had to consult, you know, before she decided to accept Lois Dunlap's offer."

The parrot interrupted with a hoarse cackle.

"Have you gone over to the enemy, Cap'n?" Dundee reproved the bird. "You sound exactly like Strawn when he laughed at my interpretation of this message this afternoon. My late chief contends—and it is just possible, of course, that he is right—that Nita was afraid she couldn't swing the job of organizing and directing Lois' Little Theater, and wanted Sprague here, both as lover and unofficial assistant. But that's a pretty thin explanation, don't you think, 'my dear Watson'?... Oh, all right! Laugh, damn you! But I'd feel better if Strawn had taken my advice and set a dick to trail Sprague, to see that he keeps out of mischief.... All this, however, gets us no nearer to answering that eternal question—'Who?'"

With a deep sigh the troubled young special investigator reached for the "Time Table" he had drafted from his notes made during the grisly replaying of the "death hand at bridge," and scanned it again:

5:20—Flora Miles, dummy, Table No. 1, leaves living room to telephone.

5:22—Clive Hammond arrives and goes directly into solarium.

5:23—End of rubber at Table No. 1. Players: Polly Beale, Janet Raymond, Lois Dunlap, Flora Miles (dummy). Polly Beale leaves living room to join Clive Hammond in solarium.

5:24—Janet Raymond leaves room; says she went straight to front porch.

5:25—Tracey Miles parks car at curb; walks up to the house, hangs up hat in clothes closet and at (his estimate)

5:27—Miles enters living room, talks with Nita, who, as dummy, has just laid down her cards at Table No. 2. Players: Karen Marshall, Penny Crain, Carolyn Drake.

5:28—Nita leaves living room, goes to her bedroom to make up.

5:28-1/2—Lois Dunlap and Miles go into dining room, Miles to make cocktails.

5:31—Judge Marshall enters living room, interrupts bridge game.

5:33—John C. Drake enters living room, having walked from Country Club, which he says he left at 5:10, and which is only three-quarters of a mile from the Selim house.

5:36—Karen finishes playing of hand, and Dexter Sprague and Janet Raymond enter from front porch, proceeding into dining room.

5:37—Penny Crain finishes scoring, and Karen leaves room to tell Nita the score.

5:38—Karen screams upon discovering the dead body at the dressing-table.

Dundee laid aside the typed sheet and reached for another, the typing of which was perfect, since Penny's efficient fingers had manipulated the keys.

When he had telephoned to the office just before five o'clock Monday afternoon to see if anything had come up, Dundee had learned from Penny that Peter Dunlap had issued an informal call to "the crowd" for a meeting at his home that evening.

"You're going, of course?" Dundee had asked. "Then, during the discussion of the case, I wish you'd try to get the answers to some questions which need clearing up—if you can do so without getting yourself 'in Dutch' with your friends.... Fine! Got a pencil?... Here goes!"

And now he was re-reading the "report" she had conscientiously written and left on his desk Tuesday morning:

"Peter, declaring he wanted to get at the bottom of this case, presided almost like a judge on the bench, and asked nearly every question you wanted the answer to. Everyone in the crowd adores gruff old Peter and no one dreamed of resenting his barrage of questions. What a detective *he* would make!

"First: Janet admitted that she did not go directly to the front porch when she left the living room after her table finished the last rubber. Went first to the hall lavatory to comb her hair and renew her make-up. Said she was there alone about five minutes, then went to the front porch. (Revised her story after Tracey had said he did not see her on the porch when he arrived.)

"Second: Judge Marshall said he glanced into the living room when he arrived, saw Karen, Carolyn and me absorbed in our game, and went on down the hall, to hang up his hat and stick. Proceeded immediately to the living room.

"Third: John Drake told Peter he entered the front hall and passed on to the lavatory to wash up. Felt sticky after his walk from the Country Club. Hung up hat in the guest closet. Went to living room within three minutes after reaching the house.

"Fourth: Polly and Clive told Peter they stayed together in the solarium the whole time, stationed at a front window, watching for Ralph. When Peter asked them if they could confirm Judge Marshall's story and Johnny Drake's story, they said they had seen them both arrive, but had paid no attention to them after they were in the house. It occurred to Peter, too, to wonder if either Polly or Clive went to Nita's room to warn her that Ralph knew about Sprague's having slept the night before in the upstairs bedroom. They both denied emphatically that they had done so.

"Fifth: Judge Marshall—the pompous old darling— still smarting under the insinuations you made about him and Nita right after the murder, volunteered the information to Peter that Nita had *not* paid her rent, on the plea that she was short of funds, and that he had told her to let it go until it was quite convenient.

"Sixth: The word 'blackmail' was not mentioned, and Johnny Drake, because of professional ethics, I suppose, did not tell about Nita's two deposits of $5,000 each in his bank.

"Seventh: The secret shelf in the foyer closet was not mentioned.

"Peter's verdict, after he got through with us, was that only Sprague could have done it—using the gun and silencer which Nita herself had stolen from Hugo. I couldn't tell him that you are convinced that Lydia's alibi for him is a genuine one, for apparently Lydia hasn't told either Flora or Tracey that she was able to furnish Sprague an alibi.

"And that's all, except that Peter asked me to convey to you his apologies for his rudeness Monday afternoon.... Penelope Crain."

With a deep sigh Dundee laid Penny's report aside.

"And that does seem to be all, 'my dear Watson'," he told the parrot. "Exactly half a dozen possible suspects, and not an atom of actual evidence against one of them— except that Judge Marshall owned the gun. Six—count 'em: Judge Marshall, John Drake, Flora Miles, Clive Hammond, Polly Beale, Janet Raymond.... Every single one of them a possible victim of blackmail, since the girls all attended the Forsyte School, where Nita directed the Easter play for two years, and since the men make several trips a year to New York.... Six people, all of whom probably knew of the existence of the secret shelf.... Six people who knew Nita was in her bedroom, either from having seen her go or from hearing her powder box tinkling its damnable tune!... Yes, Penny! You're right! That's all—so far as Hamilton is concerned! If Sanderson won't let me go to New York—which is where this damned business started—I'll resign and go on my own, without wasting another day here!"

But Dundee did not go to New York the next morning. He was far too busy in Hamilton....

CHAPTER TWENTY ONE

"Hello, Penny!" Dundee greeted the district attorney's private secretary Thursday morning at five minutes after nine. "Any news from Sanderson?"

"Yes," Penny Crain answered listlessly. "A night letter. He says his mother is still very low and that we're to wire him at the Good Samaritan Hospital in Chicago if anything turns up."

"Then I suppose I can reach him there by long distance," and Dundee lifted the telephone from Penny's desk to put in the call.

"What's happened?" Penny demanded, her brown eyes wide and startled.

"And hurry it up, will you, please?" Dundee urged the long distance operator before hanging up the receiver and answering Penny's question. "That's just the trouble—nothing's happened, and nothing is very likely to happen here. I'm determined to go to New York and work on this pesky case from that end—"

"Then you've come around to Captain Strawn's theory that it was a New York gunman?" Penny asked hopefully.

"Not by a jugful!... But what's the matter with you this morning, young woman? You're looking less like a new penny and more like one that has been too much in circulation."

"Thanks!" Penny retorted sarcastically; then she grinned wryly. "You are right, as a matter of fact. I was up too late last night—bridge at the Mileses'."

"*Bridge!*" Dundee ejaculated incredulously. "So the bridge party *did* take place, in spite of the society editor's discreet announcement yesterday that 'owing to the

tragic death of Mrs. Selim, the regular every-other-
Wednesday dinner-bridge of the Forsyte Alumnae
Association will not be held this evening at the home of
Mr. and Mrs. Tracey Miles, as scheduled'."

"It wasn't a 'dinner-bridge' and it really wasn't
intended to be a party," Penny corrected him. "It just sort
of happened, and of all the ghastly evenings—"

"Tell me about it," Dundee suggested. "Knowing this
town's telephone service as I do, I'll have plenty of time to
listen, and you don't know how all-agog I am for inside
gossip on Hamilton's upper crust."

"Idiot!" Penny flung at him scornfully. "You know
society would bore you to death, but I don't think you
would have been exactly bored last night, knowing, as I
do, your opinion of Dexter Sprague."

"Sprague? Good Lord! Was he there?... This does
promise to be interesting! Tell me all!"

"Give me time!" Penny snapped. "I might as well talk,
since there's almost no work for me to do, with Bill
away.... Ralph called me up last night at dinner time, and
asked me if I felt equal to playing bridge again. He said
that he, Clive, Tracey and Johnny Drake had lunched
together yesterday—as they frequently do—at the
Athletic Club, and that Judge Marshall, who had been
lunching at another table with his friend, Attorney
Sampson, stopped at their table and suggested a bridge
game at his home for last night. Hugo said he wanted to
coax Karen into playing again, so she would get over her
hysterical aversion to the game since she had to replay
that awful 'death hand'.... You see," Penny explained
parenthetically, "Hugo is a regular bridge fiend, and
naturally he doesn't want to be kept out of his game."

"Brute!" Dundee cried disgustedly. "Why couldn't he
give the poor girl a few days more?"

"That's what I thought," Penny acknowledged. "But *I*
didn't get an inhibition against bridge, and the idea
rather appealed to me personally. The last few days
haven't been particularly cheerful ones, so I told Ralph I'd

be glad to go. Tracey had suggested his house, instead of
Hugo's, because Betty wasn't well yesterday and Flora
wouldn't want to leave her for a whole evening. Well,
Ralph and I—"

"Are you going to marry Ralph Hammond, Penny?"
Dundee interrupted, as if prompted by casual interest.

Penny's pale face flushed vividly. "No. I'm not in love
with him, and I'm sure he realizes I'm not and won't ask
me again. But I *had* to say yes Sunday! I simply couldn't
let you walk in on us, after I'd permitted you to eavesdrop
while he was talking, without first saying the one thing
that would convince him that I believed in his innocence
and hadn't set a trap for him."

"I see!" Dundee acknowledged soberly, but his blue
eyes shone with sudden joy. "Oh! There's long distance!
Just a minute, darling!... Hello! Hello!... Yes, this is
Dundee.... Oh! All right! Try again in fifteen minutes, will
you?" He hung up the receiver and explained to Penny:
"Sanderson hasn't reached the hospital yet, but is
expected soon.... Go on with your story.... Who all played
bridge at the Mileses'? You don't mean to say Dexter
Sprague was invited, too!"

Penny's face was still a brilliant pink as she
answered: "I refuse to have my climax spoiled!... When
Ralph and I got there at eight, we found that Peter and
Lois had dined with Tracey and Flora and that they were
delighted at the prospect of bridge, as a relief from
endless discussions of the murder. We'd hardly got there
when the Marshalls came, poor little Karen not
suspecting that she was going to have to play. Then came
Johnny Drake alone, with the news that Carolyn was in
bed and very miserable with a summer cold. Polly walked
over from her house, which is on the next hill to the right,
you know. She said Clive had decided to work late at the
office, and had promised to call for her about eleven, to
take her home."

"What about Janet Raymond? Was she left out?"
Dundee asked.

"I told you it wasn't a planned affair," Penny reminded him. "But Flora did telephone her, and she said she didn't feel like coming. She's been moping about like a sick cat since Nita's death. We all knew she was idiotically in love with Dexter Sprague, and it must have been an awful blow to her to hear you read aloud that note Nita received from Sprague."

"So I noticed," Dundee nodded, recalling the deathly pallor of the girl's face as Sprague had glibly explained away that damning note and all its implications.

"Well," Penny continued, "Tracey suggested bridge, and at first Karen flatly refused to play, but Hugo finally persuaded her.... Karen would do absolutely *anything* for that ridiculous old husband of hers! I simply can't understand it—how she can be in love with him, I mean!"

"I thought you liked Judge Marshall," Dundee laughed.

"Oh, I do—in a way.... But fancy a young girl like Karen being in love with him!... Well, anyway, we all went out to the east porch, which is kept in readiness for bridge all summer. Iron bridge tables, covered with oilcloth, and with oilcloth pouches for the cards and score pads, so there's never any bother about scurrying in with things on account of rain. It's a roofed, stone-floored porch, right outside the living-room, and under it are the garages, so it's high and cool, with a grand view of Mirror Lake down below, and of the city in the distance." She sighed, and Dundee knew that she was thinking of her own lost home in Brentwood—the fine old Colonial mansion which had been sacrificed to her father's disastrous Primrose Meadows venture. Then she went on: "I don't know why I am telling you all this, except that the setting was so pleasant that we should have had a much better time than we did."

"You're an artful minx, Penny!" Dundee chuckled. "You're working up suspense for the entrance of the villain!"

"Then let me do it justice," Penny retorted. "Lois and Peter, Ralph and I, made up one table for bridge; Tracey and Polly, Judge Marshall and Karen the other. Flora said she didn't want to play, because she wanted to be free to keep an eye on Betty, although she protested she had perfect faith in Lydia, who, Flora says, is proving to be a marvel with the children. And Johnny Drake asked her to play anagrams with him, in between trips to the nursery. Johnny has a perfect pash for anagrams, and is a wow at 'em. So Tracey got the box of anagrams out of the trophy room—"

"The trophy room?" Dundee repeated, amused.

"That's what Tracey calls it," Penny explained impatiently, "because he has a couple of golf cups and Flora has an immense silver atrocity which testifies to the fact that she was the 'lady's tennis champion' of the state for one year. There are also some mounted fish and some deer heads with incredible antlers, but the room is really used as a catch-all for all the sports things— racquets, golf clubs, skis, ping-pong table, etc.... Anyway, Tracey brought out the box of anagrams, and we were all having a pretty good time when, at half past eight, the butler announced '*Mr. Dexter Sprague*'!"

"Your tone makes me wish I'd been there," Dundee acknowledged. "What happened?"

"You know how slap-em-on-the-back Tracey always is?" Penny asked, grinning. "Well, you should have seen him and heard him as he dismissed poor Whitson—the butler—as if he were giving him notice, instead of letting him off for the night! And the icy dignity with which he greeted poor Sprague—"

"*Poor* Sprague?" Dundee echoed.

"Well, after all, Sprague *had* been received by all the crowd before Nita's death," Penny retorted. "I think it was rather natural for him to think he'd still be welcome. He began to apologize for his uninvited presence, saying he had felt lonesome and depressed and had just 'jumped into a taxi' and come along, hoping to find the Mileses in.

Flora tried to act the lady hostess, but Peter got up from his bridge table and said in tones even icier than Tracey's: 'Will you excuse me, Flora? And will you take my place, Drake?... I'm going into the library. I don't enjoy the society of murderers!'"

"Good Lord!" Dundee ejaculated, shocked but admiring. "Did Sprague make a quick exit?"

"Not just then," Penny said mysteriously. "Of course everyone was simply stunned, but Sprague retorted cheerfully, 'Neither do I, Dunlap!' Peter stalked on into the living room on his way to the library, Johnny took his place at the bridge table, and Tracey, at an urgent signal from Flora, offered his seat at the other table to Sprague, as if he were making way for a leper. Poor Polly had to be Sprague's partner. Flora, as if she were terrified at what might happen—you know how frightfully tense and nervous she is—made an excuse to run upstairs for a look at Betty."

"And something terrible did happen," Dundee guessed. "You're looking positively ghoulish. Out with it!"

"After about half an hour of playing without pivoting," Penny went on imperturbably, "Hugo bid three spades, Karen raised him—in a trembling voice—to five spades, Hugo of course went to a little slam, and Dexter Sprague, if you can believe me, said: 'Better not leave the table, Karen. *A little slam-bid in spades has been known to be fatal to the dummy!*'"

"*No!*" Dundee was genuinely shocked, but before he could say more the telephone rang. "Sanderson at last.... Hello! Chicago?... Oh, hello, Captain Strawn!... *What's that?*... Oh, my God!... Where did you say the body is?"

He listened for a long minute, then, with a dazed "Thanks! I'll be over," he hung up the receiver.

"Sprague—murdered!" he answered the horrified question in Penny's eyes. "Body discovered this morning about nine by one of the Miles' maids, in what you described just now as the 'trophy room'.... Shot—just below the breastbone, Captain Strawn says."

"The trophy room!" Penny cried. "Then—*that's* where he was all the time after he disappeared so strangely last night—"

"Whoa, Penny!" Dundee commanded. "Get hold of yourself! You're shaking all over.... I want to know everything *you* know—as quickly and as accurately as you can tell it. Go right on—"

"Poor Dexter!" Penny groaned, covering her convulsed face with her hands. "To think that he was *dead* when we were saying such horrid things about him—"

"Don't waste sympathy on him, honey!" Dundee cut in, his voice very gentle but urgent. "If he had heeded my warning Monday he wouldn't be dead now."

"What do you mean?" Penny gasped, but she was already calmer. "Your warning—?"

"I had a strong suspicion that he was mixed up with Nita in her blackmail scheme and I took the trouble to warn him not to try to carry on with it. Yesterday afternoon I begged Strawn to have him shadowed to see that he kept out of mischief. I was afraid the temptation would be too strong for him, but Strawn wouldn't listen to me—still clinging to his theory of a New York gunman.... Feeling better now, honey? Can you go on? I want to get out to the Miles house as soon as I can."

"You're getting very—affectionate, aren't you?" Penny gave him a wobbly smile in which, however, there was no reproof. "I think I can go on now—. Where was I?"

"Good girl!" Dundee applauded, but his heart was beating hard with something more than excitement over Sprague's murder. "You'd just told me about Sprague's warning Karen not to leave the table when she became dummy after Judge Marshall's little slam bid in spades."

"I remember," Penny said, pressing her fingers into her temples. "But Karen *did* leave the table. When Sprague said that awful thing, poor Karen burst into tears and ran from the porch into the living room, Hugo started to follow her, but Sprague halted him by apologizing very humbly, and then by adding: 'I'd really like to see you play this hand, sir. I believe I've got the cards to set you with....' Of course he could not have said anything better calculated to hold Hugo, who, as I said, is a regular fiend when it comes to bridge.... Well, Hugo played the hand and made his little slam, and then he again started to go look for Karen, but Polly, who was Sprague's partner, you know, told him in that brusque way of hers to go on with the game and give Karen a chance to have her little weep in peace. Probably Hugo would have gone to look for her anyway, but just then Flora came back. She said Betty was asleep at last and that her temperature was normal, and when she heard about Karen, she offered to take her hand until Karen felt like coming back."

"What did Drake do then? He'd been playing anagrams with Mrs. Miles, you said," Dundee interrupted.

"Don't you remember?—I told you Johnny had taken Peter's place at our table after Peter refused to breathe the same air as Dexter Sprague," Penny reminded him. "Ralph and I, Lois and Johnny were playing together, and just at the time I became dummy, Sprague became dummy at the other table. He rose, saying he had to go telephone for a taxi, and passed from the porch into the living room—"

"Where is the telephone?"

"The one the guests use is on a table in the hall closet, where we put our things," Penny explained. "You can shut the door and hold a perfectly private conversation.... Well, *we never saw Dexter Sprague again!*"

"Good Lord! Another bridge dummy murdered!" Dundee groaned. "At least the newspapers will be happy!... Didn't anyone go to look for him after the hand was played?"

"Not straight off," Penny answered, with an obvious effort to remember clearly every detail. "Let's see—Oh, yes! That hand was played out before Ralph had finished playing his, at our table, so I was free to pay attention to the other table. Flora said that since they couldn't play another hand until Dexter came back, she thought she'd better hunt up Karen, who hadn't come back yet."

"How long was Mrs. Miles away from the porch?" Dundee asked quickly.

"Oh, I don't know—ten minutes, maybe. She came back alone, saying she had found Karen in her bedroom— Flora's room, of course—crying inconsolably. Flora told Hugo he'd better go up to her himself, since she evidently had her feelings hurt because he hadn't followed her in the first place. Tracey, who wasn't playing bridge, you remember, because he had given up his place to Sprague, asked Flora if she'd seen Sprague, and Flora said, in a surprised voice, 'No! I wonder where he is all this time,' and Polly said that probably he'd gone to the lavatory, which opens into the main hall and is next to the library.... Well, pretty soon Judge Marshall and Karen came back—"

"Pretty soon?—Just how long was Judge Marshall gone?" Dundee pressed her, his pencil, which had been flying to take down her every word, poised over the notebook he had snatched from her desk.

"I can't say exactly!" Penny protested thornily. "I was playing again at the other table. I suppose it was about ten minutes, for Ralph and I had made another rubber, I remember.... Anyway, Karen was smiling like a baby that has had a lot of petting, but she said Hugo had promised her she wouldn't have to play bridge any more that evening, so Flora remained at that table, playing opposite Hugo, while Tracey played with Polly. As soon as Tracey became dummy, Flora suggested he go look for Sprague."

"And how long was *he* gone from the porch?" Dundee asked.

"Less than no time," Penny assured him. "He was back before Polly had finished playing the hand. He said he'd gone to the hall closet, where Whitson, the butler, would have put Sprague's hat and stick, and that he had found they were gone.... Well—and you needn't put down 'well' every time I say it!" Penny interrupted herself tartly. "Tracey said he supposed Sprague had ordered his taxi and had decided to walk down the hill to meet it, and he added that that was exactly the kind of courtesy you could expect from a cad and a bounder like Sprague— walking in uninvited, making Karen cry, then walking out, without a word, leaving the game while he was dummy. Flora spoke up then and said it was no wonder Dexter had left without saying good-by, considering how he'd been treated. Then Tracey said something ugly and sarcastic about Flora's being disappointed because Sprague had decided not to spend the whole evening—"

"A first-class row, eh?" Dundee interrupted, with keen interest.

"Rather! Flora almost cried, said Tracey knew good and well that she had only been playing-up to Sprague before Nita's death, in the hope of getting the lead in the Hamilton movie, if Sprague got the job of directing it, and Tracey said, 'So you call it playing-up, do you? It looked like high-powered flirting to me—or maybe it was more than a flirtation!...' Then Flora told him he hadn't acted jealous at the time, and that he *knew* he'd have been glad if she'd got the lead.... Well, just then along came Janet—"

"*Janet Raymond?*" Dundee ejaculated. "I thought you said she had refused the invitation when Mrs. Miles phoned her."

"So she had, but she said she changed her mind, had been blue all evening, and needed cheering up."

"How did she get in?"

"She walked over from her house, which isn't very far from the Mileses', and simply came up the path to the porch," Penny explained. "Tracey asked her if she had seen Sprague on the road—it's the same road Dexter would have had to take going down the hill to the main road—and she acted awfully queer—"

"How?" Dundee demanded.

"Exactly as she would act, since she was in love with him," Penny retorted. "She turned very red, and asked if Sprague had inquired for her, and Flora quite sharply told her he hadn't. Then Janet said she was very much surprised that Sprague had been there, and that she couldn't understand why he had behaved so strangely. Then Lois said she might as well go fetch Peter from the library, since Sprague was no longer there to contaminate the atmosphere. She came back—"

"After how long a time?"

"Oh, about five minutes, I suppose," Penny answered wearily. "She came in, her arm linked with Peter's, and laughing. Said she had found him reading a 'Deadwood Dick' thriller.... One of Tracey's hobbies—" she broke off to explain, "—is collecting old-fashioned thrillers, like the Nick Carter, Diamond King Brady, Buffalo Bill and Deadwood Dick paper-bound books. Of course he didn't take up that hobby until a lot of other rich men had done it first. There was never anybody less original than poor Tracey.... Well, Flora gave up her place to Janet, and again played anagrams with Johnny, Peter taking his original place at our table. Suddenly Polly threw down her cards—she'd been having rotten luck and seemed out of sorts—and said she didn't want to play bridge any more. So poor Flora again had to be the perfect hostess, and switch from anagrams to bridge."

"And Polly played anagrams with Drake?" Dundee prompted.

"No. She said she thought anagrams were silly, and wandered off the porch and down the path, calling over her shoulder that she was going to take a walk. Tracey asked Johnny if he'd mind mixing the highballs and bringing out the sandwiches. Said Whitson had left a thermos bucket of ice cubes on the sideboard, some bottles of ginger ale, and a tray of glasses and sandwiches. Told him he'd find decanters of Scotch and rye, and to bring out both."

"So Drake left the room, too," Dundee mused. "Oh, Lord. I *knew* I'd find that every last one of the six had a chance to kill Sprague, as well as Nita!... How long was Polly Beale gone on this walk of hers?"

"She came in with a pink water lily—said she'd been down to the lily ponds, and that Flora had enough to spare her one," Penny answered. "She couldn't have been away more than ten minutes, because Johnny was just mixing the highballs, according to our preference for Scotch or rye—or plain ginger ale, which both Ralph and I chose. After we'd had our drinks and the sandwiches, we went on with bridge. Polly and Johnny just wandered about the porch or watched the game at the two tables. And about five minutes after eleven Clive Hammond arrived, coming up the path to the porch, just as Janet had. After he came, there was no more bridge, but we sat around on the porch and talked until midnight. Clive said he was too tired to play bridge—that he'd been struggling all evening with a knotty problem."

"I can sympathize with him!" Dundee said grimly, as he rose. "I've got my own knotty problem awaiting me.... When that call comes through from Chicago, tell Sanderson the bad news, and say I'll telephone him later."

CHAPTER TWENTY TWO

The Miles home, still known in Hamilton as the Hackett place, since it had been built more than thirty years before by Flora's father, old Silas Hackett, dead these seven years, dominated one of the most beautiful of the wooded hills which encircled Mirror Lake in the Brentwood section. Of modified Tudor architecture, its deep red, mellowed bricks had achieved in three decades almost the same aged dignity and impressiveness as characterized the three-century-old mansion in England which Silas Hackett's architect had used as an inspiration.

The big house faced the lake, a long series of landscaped terraces leading down to the water's edge, but the driveway wound from the state road up a side of the hill, to the main entrance at the rear of the house.

Once before—on Sunday, the day after Nita Selim's murder, when he had come to interview Lydia Carr and had secured the alibi which had eliminated Dexter Sprague as a suspect—Dundee had driven his car up this hill between the tall yew hedges. But then he had taken the fork which led to the hooded doorway over the kitchen; had descended the kitchen stairs with Lydia, to the servants' sitting room in the basement. Now he continued along the main driveway to the more impressive entrance, whose flanking, slim turrets frowned down upon a line of police cars and motorcycles.

His approach must have been expected and observed, for it was the master of the house who opened the great, iron-studded doors and invited the detective into the broad main hall, at the end of which, down three steps, lay the immense living room. The detective's first glance took in stately armchairs of the Cromwell period, thick, mellow-toned rugs, and, in the living room beyond, splendid examples of Jacobean furniture.

"A horrible thing to happen in a man's home, Dundee," Miles was saying, his plump, rosy face blighted with horror. "I can't realize yet that we actually slept as usual with a corpse lying down here all night! And I have only myself to blame—"

"What do you mean?" Dundee asked.

"Why, that the—the body wasn't discovered sooner," Miles explained. "If it had occurred to me that Whitson hadn't closed the trophy room windows, I should have gone in to close and lock them when I made the rounds of living room, dining room and library, after our guests were gone last night."

A pale-faced, bald-headed butler had materialized while his master was speaking. "Beg pardon, sir, but I did not close the trophy room windows because I thought you might be using the room again.... You see, sir," and Whitson turned to Dundee, "Mr. Miles and Mr. Dunlap played ping-pong in the trophy room after dinner until the other guests began to arrive, and I did not want them to find the room stuffy—it was a warm night—if any of the guests—"

"I see," Dundee interrupted. "Who, to your knowledge, was the last person to enter the trophy room last night, Mr. Miles?"

"I was, except Sprague, of course, and I had no idea he'd gone there. Drake wanted to play anagrams, and before the bridge game started, I went to the trophy room to get the box," Miles explained. "I turned off the light when I left, and there was no light burning in there this morning when Celia, the parlor maid, went there to put the anagram box back in the cabinet, and found the body.... Flora—Mrs. Miles—had brought the anagrams in from the porch and left them on a table in the living room, as our guests were getting ready to leave. There was nothing else to bring in, in case of rain. The bridge tables are of iron, covered with oilcloth, and fitted with oilcloth bags for the cards, score pads, and pencils—"

"Yes, I know," Dundee interrupted. "Miss Crain has already told me all about that, and a good many details of the party itself.... By the way, where is Mrs. Miles now?"

"In bed. The doctor is with her. She is prostrated from the shock."

"Where is this room you call the trophy room?" Dundee asked. "No, don't bother to come with me. Just point it out. It's on this floor, I understand."

Miles pointed past the great circular staircase that wound upward from the main hall. "You can't see the door from here, but it's behind the staircase. Celia found the door closed this morning, and no light on, as I said—"

Dundee cut him short by marching toward the door which was again closed. He entered so noiselessly that Captain Strawn, Dr. Price and the fingerprint expert, Carraway, did not hear him. For a moment he stood just inside the door and let his eyes wander about the room which Penny Crain had already described. It was not a large room—twelve by fourteen feet, possibly—but it looked even smaller, crowded as it was with the long ping-pong table, bags of golf clubs, fishing tackle, tennis racquets, skis and sleds. There were two windows in the north wall of the room, looking out upon the yew-hedged driveway, and between them stood a cabinet of numerous big and little drawers.

Not until he had taken in the general aspect of the room did Dundee look at the thing over which Captain Strawn and the coroner were bending—the body of Dexter Sprague.

The alien from New York had fallen about four feet from the window nearer the east wall of the trophy room. He lay on his side, his left cheek against the floor, the fingers of his left hand still clutching the powder-burned bosom of his soft shirt, now stiff with dried blood, a pool of which had formed and then half congealed upon the rug. The right hand, the fingers curled but not touching each other, lay palm-upward on the floor at the end of the rigid, outstretched arm. The one visible eye was half open, but on the sallow, thin face, which had been strikingly handsome in an obvious sort of way, was a peace and dignity which Dundee had never seen upon Sprague's face when the man was alive. The left leg was drawn upward so that the knee almost touched the bullet-pierced stomach.

"How long has he been dead, doctor?" Dundee asked quietly.

"Hello, boy!" Dr. Price greeted him placidly. "Always the same question! I've been here only a few minutes, and I've already told Strawn that I shall probably be unable to fix the hour of death with any degree of accuracy."

"Took your time, didn't you, Bonnie?" Captain Strawn greeted his former subordinate on the Homicide Squad. "Doc says he's been dead between ten and twelve hours. Since it's nearly ten now, that means Sprague was killed some time between nine and eleven o'clock last night."

"Better say between nine o'clock and midnight last night," Dr. Price suggested. "He may have lived an hour or more—unconscious, of course. For the indications are that he did not die instantly, but staggered a few steps, clutching at the wound. But of course I shall have to perform an autopsy first——"

Dundee crossed the room, stepping over the dead man's stick—a swank affair of dark, polished wood, with a heavy knob of carved onyx, which lay about a foot beyond the reach of the curled fingers of the stiff right hand.

"Sprague's hat?" he asked, pointing to a brightly banded straw which lay upon the top of the cabinet.

"Yes," Strawn answered. "And did you notice the window screen?"

He pointed to the window in front of which the body lay. The sash of leaded panes was raised as high as it would go, and beneath it was a screen of the roller-curtain type, raised about six inches from the window sill.

A pair of curved, nickel-plated catches in the center of the inch-wide metal band on the bottom of the coppernet curtain showed how the screen was raised or lowered.

Dundee nodded, frowning, and Strawn began eagerly:

"You'll have to admit I was right now, boy. You've sneered at my gunman theory and tried to pin Nita's murder on one of Hamilton's finest bunch of people, but you'll have to admit now that every detail of this set-up bears me out."

"Yes?"

"Sure. This is the way I figure it out: Sprague has good reason to be afraid he's next on the program. He's nervous. He hops a taxi at his hotel and comes here— can't stick to his room any longer. Wants a little human companionship. This crowd here—and I have Miles' word for it—ain't any too glad to see him, and shows it. He phones for a taxi to go back to his hotel—about 9:15, that was, Miles says—but decides to walk down the hill to meet it. Don't want to go back out on the porch and lie about having had a good time, when he hasn't.... Well, he opens the front door, or what would be the front door if this was any ordinary house, but before he steps out he sees or hears something—probably a rustling in the hedge across the driveway, or maybe he even sees a face, in the light from the lanterns on each side of the door. He feels sure Nita's murderer has trailed him and is lying in wait for him. In a panic he darts into this room, and don't turn on the light for fear he'll be seen from the windows, but he can see well enough to make out how the screens work, and he was familiar with the house anyway. I'll bet you anything you like Sprague stayed in this room for an hour or two, till he thought the coast was clear, then eased up this screen, intending to climb out of the window and drop to the ground.... Not much of a drop at that. You can see that the tall hedge on this side of the driveway comes pretty near up to these windows.... Well, I figure he laid his hat on this cabinet, intending to reach in for it when he was outside, but that he had already made some little noise which the gunman was listening for, and that when he got the screen up this high, the gunman, crouching under the window, let go with the same gun and silencer that he used to bump off Nita.... I've got Miles' word for it that neither he nor anybody else heard a shot.... Of course, nobody knew Sprague was in here, and since his hat and stick was both missing from the hall closet, they took it for granted he'd beat it.... Any objections to that theory, boy?"

"Just a few—one in particular," Dundee said. "But I grant it's a good one, provided Dr. Price's autopsy bears you out as to the course of the bullet, and that Carraway finds Sprague's fingerprints on that contrivance for raising the screen. Even then——"

But Dundee was not allowed to finish his sentence, for Strawn was summoned to the telephone, by Whitson. When he returned there was a slightly bewildered look on his heavy old face.

"That's funny.... Collins—the lad I sent to check up on the taxi companies—says he's located the driver that answered Sprague's call last night. The driver says he was called about 9:15, told to come immediately, and to wait for Sprague at the foot of the hill, on the main road. He says he waited there until half past ten, then went on back to town, sore'n a boiled owl."

"It doesn't look exactly as if Sprague were afraid of anyone *outside of this house* last night, does it?" Dundee asked. "By the way, I suppose you've sent for everyone who was here?"

"Sure!" But again Captain Strawn looked uncomfortable. "But we haven't been able to locate the Beale girl and Clive Hammond."

CHAPTER TWENTY THREE

"I'd give a good deal to know which of those two suggested that it would be a good idea to get married the first thing this morning," Dundee mused aloud, as he put down the second extra which *The Hamilton Morning News* had had occasion to issue that Thursday.

It was two o'clock, and the district attorney's "special investigator" sat across the desk from Captain Strawn, in his former chief's office at Police Headquarters.

The first extra had screamed in its biggest head type: SECOND BRIDGE DUMMY MURDER! and had carried, in detail, Captain Strawn's comforting theory that Dexter Sprague's erstwhile friends had again been made the victims of a New York gunman's fiendish cleverness in committing his murders under circumstances which would inevitably involve Hamilton's most highly respected and socially prominent citizens in the police investigation.

But the second extra had a more romantic streamer headline:

HAMMOND WEDDING DELAYS MURDER QUIZ.

The story beneath a series of smaller headlines began:

"At the very moment—9:05 o'clock this morning— when Celia Hunt, maid in the Tracey Miles home in the Brentwood district of Hamilton, was screaming the news of her discovery of the dead body of Dexter Sprague, New York motion picture director, in what is known as the 'trophy room,' Miss Polly Beale and Mr. Clive Hammond were applying for a marriage license in the Municipal Building.

"At 9:30, when Miss Beale and Mr. Hammond were exchanging their vows in the rectory of St. Paul's Episcopal Church, of which both bride and groom have been members since childhood, Captain John Strawn of the Homicide Squad was listening to Tracey Miles' account of the strange disappearance of Dexter Sprague last night from an impromptu bridge game, after he had announced his intention of taking advantage of the fact that he was 'dummy' to telephone for a taxi.

"And at 10 o'clock, when the new Mrs. Hammond called her home to break the news of her marriage to her aunt, Mrs. Amelia Beale, the bride was in turn acquainted with the news of Sprague's murder and the fact that both she and her husband were wanted at the Miles home for questioning by the police, since both had been guests of Mr. and Mrs. Miles last night, although Mr. Hammond did not arrive until about 11 o'clock."

There followed a revision of the murder story as it had appeared in the first extra, with additional details supplied by Strawn, and with a line drawing of the scene of the crime—the trophy room itself and the forked driveway with its tall yew hedges. A dotted line illustrated Strawn's theory of Sprague's plan to elude the murderer who had followed him to the Miles home. Because of the curved sweep of the driveway toward the main entrance of the house, the tall hedge was less than two feet from the window with the partly opened screen.

"Captain Strawn's theory," read the text below the large drawing, "is that Sprague had good cause to fear he was being followed on his way to the Miles home; that he telephoned for a taxi to wait for him at the foot of the hill, and that he planned to leave the Miles house by way of the trophy room window, so that his lurking pursuer might have no knowledge of his departure. The drawing shows that his proposed flight would have been protected by hedges until he reached the wooded slope of the hill, provided his Nemesis was lurking in the opposite hedge across the driveway, where he could observe every departure from the Miles home."

"You've sure got a single-track mind, boy," Strawn chuckled. "So you think those two got married in such a hurry this morning because the law says a husband or a wife can't be made to testify against the other?"

"Possibly." Dundee grinned, unruffled. "But there is another possibility—which is why I should like to know who suggested this sudden wedding. I mean that we can't overlook the possibility that these two murders made either the bride or the groom feel perfectly safe in going on with the marriage. Polly Beale and Clive Hammond had been engaged for more than a year, you know, with no apparent reason for a long engagement.... As for my having a single-track mind, Captain, what about you? I have six possible suspects, all of whose names I know, and you have only one—whose name you do not know, and whose motive you can only guess at, while *I* have a perfectly good motive that might fit any one of my six— blackmail!"

"Is that so?" Strawn growled. "I'm not telling the papers everything, and if they are satisfied to call these murders '*crimes passionnels*,' it's all right with me. But I'm not forgetting that Nita Selim banked ten thousand dollars cash after she got to Hamilton. My real theory now that Sprague has been killed is that Nita and Sprague had cooked up some sort of racket between them, and that when Nita got the chance to come to Hamilton with Mrs. Dunlap, she jumped at it, and she and Sprague sprung their racket, whatever it was, either just before or just after Nita left New York. Probably it was Nita's tip-off and Sprague did the actual dirty work himself, which explains that telegram that Nita sent him April 24, just three days after she got to Hamilton. Let's see again just what it says," and Strawn reached for a copy of the night letter which Dundee himself had unearthed the day before. "See: '*Everything Jake so far, but would feel safer you here—*'"

"Yes, I remember the wording quite well," Dundee interrupted. "But you did not take it so seriously when I showed it to you yesterday. If you had—"

"All right! Rub it in!" Strawn snapped, flushing darkly. "If I had assigned a man to 'tail' Sprague, as you suggested, he wouldn't have been murdered—"

"He probably would have been murdered just the same," Dundee comforted the older man, "but we might have been lucky enough to have had an eye-witness."

"Oh, you and your theory!" Strawn growled. "But let me go on.... Nita meant she would feel safer about Sprague if he was here in Hamilton, too. But the guy they double-crossed in New York, or worked the badger game on, or something like that, got on their trail. But it took him weeks to do it, and Sprague followed Nita's advice. He got here on Sunday April 27, and on Monday the 28th Nita banked the first $5,000! Don't you see it, boy? Sprague brought with him the dough they'd got for their stunt, and thought it was safer for Nita to bank it in her name, since it wasn't the name she was known by in New York anyway. We've checked up on Sprague pretty thoroughly. He didn't have a bank book, either on his body or in his room, and every bank in town denies he had an account with them."

"If that theory is correct, it makes Nita Selim a pretty low character," Dundee mused aloud. "Not only did she kick him out as a lover, but she double-crossed him as her partner in crime, by willing the whole wad to Lydia Carr. Sprague must have received quite a shock when he heard Nita's will read at the inquest."

"Yeah," Strawn agreed. "It looks like Mrs. Dunlap picked a sweet specimen to make a friend out of.... Well, that's my theory, and I think it explains everything. Their victim in New York simply hired a gunman, or come down here himself, when he got on their tracks. Of course it was a good stunt to make it look like a local crime— figured he'd fool *me* just as he fooled *you*! So the murderer simply trailed Nita around, and saw that whole bunch of society people shooting at a target at Judge Marshall's place, with a gun equipped with a Maxim silencer. Too good an opportunity to be missed, so he bides his chance to swipe the gun and silencer. To make sure it will look like a local crime, he pops off Nita when that same bunch is at her house, but it takes a few days longer before he has the same opportunity to get Sprague. But it come last night and he grabbed it."

"A very plausible theory, and one which, in general, the whole city of Hamilton has been familiar with since the night Nita was murdered," Dundee remarked significantly.

"What do you mean?" Strawn demanded. "It's waterproof, ain't it? Doc Price says the bullet—and a .32 caliber one at that—entered Sprague's body just below the breastbone and traveled an upward course till it struck the extreme right side of the heart. The bullet entered exactly where it would have to, if the murderer was crouching under that window while Sprague was raising the screen. And we have Carraway's report that it was Sprague's fingerprints on those nickleplated things you have to press together to make the screen roll up or down. Furthermore, I haven't a doubt in the world that the ballistics expert in Chicago will report that the bullet was fired from the same gun that killed Nita Selim."

"Neither have I," Dundee agreed. "But what I meant was that you had obligingly furnished the murderer who fits *my* theory with a theory he—or she—would not have upset for the world!... Listen!" and he bent forward very earnestly: "I'm willing to grant that Sprague was shot from the outside, through the window, when Sprague raised the screen. But there our theories part company. I believe that the murderer was a guest in the Selim home last night, that he or she had made an appointment to meet Sprague there, on the promise of paying the hush money he had demanded, in spite of my warning to him not to carry on with the blackmail scheme. Naturally he or she—and I'll say 'he' from now on, for the sake of convenience—had no intention of being seen entering that room. The bridge game was suggested by Judge Marshall at noon. There was plenty of time for the rendezvous to be made with Sprague. As I see it, the murderer told Sprague to excuse himself from the game when he became dummy, and to go to the trophy room and wait there until the murderer had a chance to slip away and appear beneath the window. Sprague had been promised that, when he raised the screen at a tap or a whispered request, a roll of bills would be handed to him, but—he received a bullet instead."

"And which one of your six suspects have you picked on?" Strawn asked sarcastically.

"That's just the trouble. There are still six," Dundee acknowledged with a wry grin. "After Sprague's disappearance, every one of the six was absent from the porch at one time or another.... No, by George! There are *seven* suspects now! I was about to forget Peter Dunlap, who admits he was alone on a fishing trip when Nita was murdered and who left the porch last night to go to the library, as soon as Sprague arrived!... As for the movements of the original six after Sprague disappeared: Polly Beale took a walk about the grounds; Flora Miles went upstairs to hunt for Karen Marshall, and was gone more than ten minutes; Drake went to the dining room to get the refreshments, and no one can say exactly how long he was gone; Judge Marshall went up to get his wife, and had time to make a little trip on the side; Janet Raymond walked over from her home, and passed that very window, arriving after Sprague had disappeared; and, finally, Clive Hammond arrived alone in his car, which he parked within a few feet of that window. This morning he gets married——"

"A telegram, sir!" interrupted a plainclothesman, who had entered without knocking.

Strawn snatched at it, read it, then exulted: "Read this, boy! I guess *this* settles the business!"

The telegram had been filed half an hour before and was from the city editor of *The New York Evening Press*:

"WORKING ON YOUR THEORY OF NEW YORK GUNMAN RESPONSIBLE MURDERS OF JUANITA LEIGH SELIM AND DEXTER SPRAGUE THIS PAPER HAS DISCOVERED THAT SELIM WOMAN WAS SEEN AT NIGHT CLUBS SEVERAL TIMES DURING JANUARY FEBRUARY WITH QUOTE SWALLOW TAIL SAMMY END QUOTE UNDERWORLD NAME FOR SAM SAVELLI STOP SAVELLI TAKEN FOR RIDE TUESDAY APRIL TWENTY SECOND TWO DAYS AFTER SELIM WOMAN LEFT NEW YORK STOP POLICE HERE WORKING ON THEORY SAVELLI SLAIN BY OWN GANG AFTER THEY WERE TIPPED OFF SAVELLI WAS DOUBLE CROSSING THEM STOP IN EXCHANGE FOR THIS TIP CAN YOU GIVE US ANY SUPPRESSED INFORMATION YOUR POSSESSION STOP SAVELLI HAD BROTHER WHO IS KNOWN TO US TO HAVE PROMISED REVENGE SWALLOW TAIL SAMMYS MURDER STOP BE A SPORT CAPTAIN."

"Well, that puts the lid on it, don't it?" Strawn crowed. "I'll send Sergeant Turner to New York on the five o'clock train.... Pretty decent of that city editor to wire me this tip, I'll say!"

"And are you going to reciprocate by wiring him about the $10,000 Nita banked here?" Dundee asked.

"Sure! Why not? There's no use that I can see to keep it back any longer, now that no one can have any excuse to think as you've been doing—that it was blackmail paid by a Hamiltonian."

"Then," Dundee began very slowly, "if you really think your case is solved, I'll make one suggestion: take charge of Lydia Carr and put her in a very safe place."

"Why?" Strawn looked puzzled.

"Because, when you publish the fact that Nita and Sprague got $10,000 for tipping off Savelli's gang that he was double-crossing them, and that Nita willed the money to Lydia, the avenger's next and last job would be to 'get' Lydia, since his natural conclusion would be that Lydia had been in on the scheme from the beginning," Dundee explained.

"God, boy! You're right!" Strawn exclaimed, and his heavy old face was very pale as he reached for the telephone, and called the number of the Miles residence. "I'm going to put it up to her that it will be best for her to be locked up as a material witness, for her own protection."

Five minutes later Strawn restored the receiver to the hook with a bang. "Says she won't budge!" he explained unnecessarily. "Says she ain't afraid and the Miles kids need her.... Well, it's her own funeral! But I guess *you* are convinced at last?"

Dundee slowly shook his head. "Almost—but not quite, chief!"

"Lord, but you're stubborn! Here's a water-tight case——"

"A very pretty and a very satisfactory case, but not exactly water-tight," Dundee interrupted. "There's just one little thing——"

"What do you mean?" Strawn demanded irritably.

"Have you forgotten the secret shelf behind the guest closet in the Selim house?" Dundee asked.

"I can afford to forget it, since it hasn't got a thing to do with the case!" Strawn retorted angrily. "There's not a scrap of evidence——"

"Of course it does not fit into *your* theory," Dundee agreed, "for 'Swallow-tail Sammy's' avenging brother could not have known of its existence, but there is one thing about that secret shelf and its pivot door which I don't believe you can afford to forget, Captain!"

"Yeah?" Strawn snarled.

"Yeah!... I refer, of course, to the complete absence of fingerprints on the door and on the shelf itself! Carraway didn't even find Nita Selim's fingerprints. Since Nita would have had no earthly reason for carefully wiping off her fingerprints after she removed the papers she burned on Friday night, it's a dead sure fact that someone else who had no legitimate business to do so, touched that pivoting panel and the shelf, and carefully removed all traces that he had done so!... And—" he continued grimly, "until I find out who that someone is, I, for one, won't consider the case solved!"

Fifteen minutes later Dundee was sitting at Penny Crain's desk in her office of the district attorney's suite, replacing the receiver upon the telephone hook, after having put in a call for Sanderson, who was still in Chicago, keeping vigil at the bedside of his dying mother.

"Did you find out anything new when you questioned the crowd this morning?" Penny asked. "Besides the fact that Polly and Clive got married this morning, I mean.... I wasn't surprised when I read about the wedding in the extra. It was exactly like Polly to make up her mind suddenly, after putting Clive off for a year——"

"So it was Polly who held back," Dundee said to himself. Aloud: "No, I didn't learn much new, Penny. You're a most excellent and accurate reporter.... But there were one or two things that came out. For instance, I got Drake to admit to me, in private, that Nita did give him an explanation as to where she got the $10,000."

"Yes?" Penny prompted eagerly.

"Drake says," Dundee answered dryly, "that Nita told him it was 'back alimony' which she had succeeded in collecting from her former husband. Unfortunately, she did not say who or where the mysterious husband is."

"Pooh!" scoffed Penny. "Don't you see? She just said that to satisfy Johnny's curiosity. After all, it was the most plausible explanation of how a divorcee got hold of a lot of money."

"So plausible that Drake may have thought of it himself," Dundee reflected silently. Aloud, he continued his report to the girl who had been of so much help to him: "Among other minor things that came out this morning, and which the papers did not report, was the fact that Janet Raymond tried to commit suicide this morning by drinking shoe polish. Fortunately her father discovered what she had done almost as soon as she had swallowed the stuff, and made her take ipecac and then sent for the doctor."

"Oh, poor Janet!" Penny groaned. "She must have been terribly in love with Dexter Sprague, though what she saw in him——"

Dundee made no comment, but continued with his information: "Another minor development was that Tracey Miles admitted that he and Flora had quarreled over Sprague after all of you left, and that Flora took two sleeping tablets to make sure of a night's rest."

"She's been awfully unstrung ever since Nita's murder," Penny defended her friend. "She told us all Monday night at Peter's that the doctor had prescribed sleeping medicine.... Now, you look here, Bonnie Dundee!" she cried out sharply, answering an enigmatic smile on the detective's face, "if you think Flora Miles killed Nita Selim and Dexter Sprague, because she was in love with Dexter and learned he was Nita's lover from that silly note——"

"Whoa, Penny!" Dundee checked her. "I'm not linking exactly that. But I've just remembered something that had seemed of no importance to me before."

"And what's that, Mr. Smart Aleck?" Penny demanded furiously.

"Before I answer that question, will you let me do a little theorizing?" Dundee suggested gently. "Let us suppose that Flora Miles was *not* in love with Sprague, but that she was being blackmailed by Nita for some scandal Nita had heard gossiped about at the Forsyte School.... No, wait!... Let us suppose further that Nita recognized Flora's picture in the group Lois Dunlap showed her, as the portrait of the girl whose story she had heard; that she was able, somehow, to secure incriminating evidence of some sort—letters, let us say. Nita tells Sprague about it, and Sprague advises her to blackmail Flora, who, Lois has told Nita, is very rich. So Nita comes to Hamilton and bleeds Flora of $10,000. Not satisfied, Nita makes another demand, the money to be paid to her the day of the bridge luncheon——"

"Silly!" Penny scoffed furiously. "The only evidence you have against poor Flora is that she stole the note Dexter had written to Nita!"

"That's the crux of the matter, Penny darling!" Dundee assured her in a maddeningly soothing voice, at which Penny clinched her hands in impotent rage. "Flora, seeing Nita receive a letter written on her husband's business stationery, jumps to the conclusion that Nita had carried out her threat to tell Tracey, or that Nita has at least given Tracey a hint of the truth and that Tracey's special-messenger note is, let us say, a confirmation of an appointment suggested by Nita.... Very well! Flora goes to Nita's bedroom at the first opportunity, knowing that Nita will come there to make up for the men's arrival. Let's suppose Flora had brought the gun and silencer with her, intending to frighten Nita, rather than kill her. But having had proof, as she believes, that Nita means business, Flora waits in the closet until Nita comes in and sits down at her dressing-table, then steps out and shoots her. Then she recoils step by step, until her foot catches in the slack cord of the bronze lamp, causing the very 'bang or bump' which Flora herself describes later, for fear someone else has heard it. Her first concern, of course, is to hide the gun and silencer. She remembers Judge Marshall's tale of the secret shelf in the guest closet, and not only hides the gun there but seeks in vain for the incriminating evidence Nita has against her. But she also remembers the note she believes Tracey has written to Nita, and which, if found after Nita's death, may give her away. So she goes to the closet in Nita's bedroom, finds the note, and faints with horror at her perhaps needless crime when she realizes that the note was written by Sprague, and not Tracey. Of course she is too ill and panic-stricken to leave the closet until the murder is discovered——"

"But you think she was not too panic-stricken to have the presence of mind to retrieve the gun and silencer and walk out with them, under the very eyes of the police," Penny scoffed.

"*No! I think she was!*" Dundee amazed her by admitting. "And that is where my sudden recollection of something I had considered unimportant comes in! Let us suppose that Flora, half-suspected by Tracey, confesses to him in their car as they are going to the Country Club for their long-delayed dinner, as were the rest of you. Tracey, loyal to her, decides to help her. He tells her to suggest, at dinner, that Lydia come to them as nurse, so that he can go back to the house and get the gun and silencer from the guest-closet hiding place, if an opportunity presents itself—as it did, since I left Tracey Miles alone in the hall while I went into Nita's bedroom to talk with Lydia before I permitted her to go with Tracey."

"You're crazy!" Penny told him fiercely, when he had finished. "I suppose you are going to ask me to believe that Tracey was a big enough fool to leave the gun and silencer where Flora could get hold of it and kill Sprague last night."

"Why not let us suppose that Tracey himself killed Sprague to protect his wife, not only from scandal, but from a charge of murder?" Dundee countered. "Tell me honestly: do you think Tracey Miles loves Flora enough to do that for her?"

Suddenly, inexplicably, Penny began to laugh—not hysterically, but with genuine mirth.

CHAPTER TWENTY FOUR

"What are you laughing at?" Dundee demanded indignantly, but the sustained ringing of the telephone bell checked Penny Crain's mirthful laughter. "My Chicago call!... Hello!... Yes, this is Dundee.... All right, but make it snappy, won't you?... Hello, Mr. Sanderson! How is your mother?... That's fine! I certainly hope—Yes, the inquest is slated for tomorrow morning, but there's no use your leaving your mother to come back for it.... Yes, sir, one important new development. Can you hear me plainly?... Then hold the line a moment, please!"

With the receiver still at his ear, Dundee fumbled in his pocket for a folded sheet of paper. "No, operator! We're not through! Please keep off the line.... Listen, chief!" he addressed the district attorney at the other end of the long distance wire. "This is a telegram Captain Strawn received this afternoon from the city editor of The New York Evening Press.... Can you hear me?... All right!" and he read slowly, repeating when necessary.

When he had finished reading the telegram, he listened for a long minute, but not with so much concentration that he could not grin at Penny's wide-eyed amazement and joy. "That's what I think, sir!" he cried jubilantly. "I'd like to take the five o'clock train for New York and work on the case from that end till we actually get our teeth into something.... Thanks a lot, and my best wishes for your mother!"

"Why didn't you tell me about this 'Swallow-tail Sammy'?" Penny demanded indignantly. "Tormenting me with your silly theory about poor Flora and Tracey, when all the time you knew the case was practically solved—"

"I'm afraid I gave the district attorney a slightly false impression," Dundee interrupted, but there was no remorse in his shining blue eyes. "But just so I get to New York—By the way, young woman, what *were* you laughing at so heartily? I didn't know I had made an amusing remark when I asked you if you thought Tracey Miles loved his wife well enough to commit murder for her."

Penny laughed again, white teeth and brown eyes gleaming. "I was laughing at something else. It suddenly occurred to me, while you were spinning your foolish theory, how *flattered* Tracey would have been if Flora had confessed to him Saturday night that she had killed Nita because she was jealous!"

"Which was *not* my theory, if you remember!" Dundee retorted. "But why is the idea so amusing? Deep in his heart, I suppose any man would really be a bit flattered if his wife loved him enough to be that jealous."

"You don't know Tracey Miles as well as I do," Penny assured him, her eyes still mirthful. "He's really a dear, in spite of being a dreadful bore most of the time, but the truth is, Tracey hasn't an atom of sex appeal, and he *must* realize it.... Of course we girls have all pampered his poor little ego by pretending to be crazy about him and terribly envious that it was Flora who got him—"

"But Flora Hackett *did* marry him," Dundee interrupted. "She must have been a beautiful girl, and she was certainly rich enough to get any man she wanted—"

"You would think so, wouldn't you?" Penny agreed, her tongue loosened by relief. "I was only twelve years old when Flora Hackett made her debut, but a twelve-year-old has big ears and keen eyes. It is true that Flora was beautiful and rich, but—well, there was something queer about her. She was simply crazy to get married, and if a man danced with her as many as three times in an evening she literally seized upon him and tried to drag him to the altar.... Her eagerness and her intensity repelled every man who was in the least attracted to her, and I think she was beginning to be frightened to death that she wouldn't get married at all, when she happened to meet Tracey, who had just got a job as salesman in her father's business. She began to rush him—there's no other word for it—and none of the other girls minded a bit, because, without Flora, Tracey would have been the perfect male wallflower. They became engaged almost right away, and were married six months or so later. All the girls freely prophesied that even Tracey, flattered by her passion for him as he so evidently was, would get tired of it, but he didn't, and there were three marriages in 'the crowd' that June."

"Three?" Dundee repeated absently, for his interest was waning.

"Yes.... Lois Morrow and Peter Dunlap; Johnny Drake and Carolyn Swann; and Tracey and Flora," Penny answered. "Although I was thirteen then and really too old for the role, I had the fun of being flower girl for Lois and Flora both."

"Do you think Flora was really in love with Tracey?" Dundee asked curiously.

"Oh, yes! But she'd have been in love with anyone who wanted to marry her, and the funny thing is that, with the exception of Peter and Lois, they are the happiest married couple I have ever known.... You see, Tracey has never got over being flattered that so pretty and passionate a girl as Flora Hackett wanted *him*!... And that's why I laughed!... Tracey, with that deep-rooted sexual inferiority complex of his, would have been so flattered if Flora had told him she killed Nita out of jealousy that he would have forgiven her on the spot. On the other hand," she went on, "if Flora had told him that Nita had documentary proofs of some frightful scandal against her, can't you see how violently Tracey would have reacted against her?... Oh, no! Tracey would not have taken the trouble to murder Sprague, when Sprague popped up for more blackmail!"

"Perhaps he might have, if the scandal dated back to before the marriage," Dundee argued. "Let's suppose

Sprague did pop up, and Flora turned him over to Tracey. When Sprague appeared apparently uninvited last night, Flora must have been on pins and needles, trying to make Tracey treat him decently and hoping against hope that Tracey would simply pay the scoundrel all the blackmail he was demanding——"

"Which is exactly what Tracey would have done, instead of taking the awful risk of murdering him in his own home," Penny cut in spiritedly. "Besides, Tracey wasn't gone from the porch long enough to go outside, signal to Sprague in the trophy room, shoot him when Sprague raised the screen, and then hide the gun. I told you Tracey was gone only about a minute when he went to see if Sprague's hat and stick were gone from the closet."

"Did Tracey and Flora both step outside to see their guests into their cars?" Dundee asked suddenly.

"Tracey did," Penny answered. "Flora told us all good night in the living room, then ran upstairs to see if Betty was still asleep.... But remember we didn't leave until midnight, and Dr. Price says Sprague was killed between nine and eleven last night."

"Dr. Price would be the first to grant a leeway of an hour, one way or another," Dundee told her. "Of course, if Tracey did kill him, he let Flora believe that he had given Sprague the blackmail money he was demanding. For it is inconceivable that a woman of Flora Miles' hysterical temperament could have slept—even with two sleeping tablets—knowing that a corpse was in the house."

"Oh, I'm sick of your silly theorizing!" Penny told him with vehement scorn. "Listen here, Bonnie Dundee! You probably laugh at 'woman's intuition', but take it from me—*you're on the wrong track!*"

"Oh, I'm not so wedded to that particular theory!" Dundee laughed. "I can spin you exactly six more just as convincing—"

"And I shan't listen! You'd better dash home and pack your bag if you want to catch the five o'clock train for New York."

"It's already packed and in my office," Dundee assured her lazily. "Got lots of time.... Hullo! Here's the home edition of *The Evening Sun*," he interrupted himself, as a small boy, making his rounds of the courthouse, flung the paper into the office. He reached for it, and read the streamer headline aloud: "ITALIAN GANGSTER SOUGHT IN BRIDGE MURDERS ... I wager a good many heads will lie easier on their pillows tonight."

"Let me see!" Penny commanded, and snatched the paper unceremoniously. "Oh! Did you see this?" and she pointed to a boxed story in the middle of the front page. "'Bridge Parties Cancelled'," she read aloud. "'The society editor of *The Evening Sun* was kept busy at her telephone today, receiving notices of cancellations of bridge parties scheduled for the remainder of the week. Eight frantic hostesses, terrified by Hamilton's second murder at bridge——' Oh, that's simply a *crime*! The newspapers deliberately work up mob hysteria and then——"

"I'd rather not play bridge for a while myself!" Dundee laughed, as he rose and started for his own office. "And don't *you* dare leave the room when you become dummy, if you have the nerve to play again! Remember, that gun and silencer are still missing!"

"What do you mean?.... You don't think there'll be more——?"

Dundee became instantly contrite before her terror. "I didn't mean it, honey," he said gently. "I think it is more than likely that the gun is at the bottom of Mirror Lake. But do take care of yourself, and by that I mean don't work yourself to death.... Any messages for anyone in New York?"

Penny's pale face quivered. "If you—happen to run across my father, which of course you won't, tell him that—Mother would like him to come home."

At intervals during the sixteen-hour run to New York, Penny's faltering words returned to haunt the district attorney's special investigator, although he would have preferred to devote his entire attention to mapping out the program he intended to follow when he reached the city which, he fully believed, had been the scene of the first act of the tragic drama he was bent upon bringing to an equally tragic conclusion.

As soon as he had registered at a hotel near the Pennsylvania Station, and had shaved and breakfasted, he took from his bag a large envelope containing the photographs Carraway had made of Penny alive and of Nita dead, both clad in the royal blue velvet dress. In the envelope also was the white satin, gold-lettered label which the dress had so proudly borne: "Pierre Model. Copied by Simonson's. New York City."

Half an hour later he was showing the photographs and the label to a woman buyer, in the French Salon of Simonson's, one of New York's most "exclusive" department stores.

"Can you tell me when the original Pierre model was bought, and when this copy was made and sold?" he asked.

The white-haired, smartly dressed buyer accepted the sheaf of photographs Bonnie Dundee was offering. "I'll do my best, of course," she began briskly, then paled and uttered a sharp exclamation as her eyes took in the topmost picture. "This is Juanita Leigh, isn't it?... But—" she shuddered, "how odd she looks—as if—"

"Yes," Dundee agreed gravely. "She was dead when that picture was taken. Did you know Mrs. Selim?"

"No," the woman breathed, her eyes still bulging with horror. "But I've seen so many pictures of her in the papers.... To think that it was one of *our* dresses she chose for her shroud! But you want to know when the dress was sold to her, don't you?" she asked, brisk again. "I can find out. We keep a record of all our French originals and of the number of copies made of each.... Let me think! I've been going to Paris myself for the firm for the last fifteen years, but I can't remember buying this Pierre model.... Oh, of course! I didn't go over during 1917 and 1918, on account of the war, you know, but the big Paris designers managed to send us a limited number of very good models, and this must have been one of them. Otherwise, I'd remember buying it.... If you'll excuse me a moment——"

When she returned about ten minutes later, Miss Thomas brought him a pencilled memorandum. "This Pierre model was imported in the summer of 1917, several months in advance of the winter season, of course. Only five copies were made—in different colors and materials, naturally, since we make a point of exclusiveness. The royal blue velvet copy was sold to Juanita Leigh in January, 1918. I am sorry I cannot give you the exact day of the month, but our records show the month only. I took the liberty of showing a picture of the dress to the only saleswoman in the department who has been with us that long, but she cannot remember the sale. Twelve years is a long time, you know."

"Indeed it is," Dundee agreed regretfully. "You have been immensely helpful, however, Miss Thomas, and I thank you with all my heart."

"If you could just tell *me*—confidentially, of course," Miss Thomas whispered, "what sort of clue this dress is— "

"I don't know, myself!" the detective admitted. "But," he added to himself, after he had escaped the buyer's natural curiosity, "I intend to find out!"

Before he could take any further steps along that particular path, however, Dundee had an appointment to keep. Upon arriving at his hotel that morning he had made two telephone calls. He smiled now as he recalled the surprise and glee of one of his former Yale classmates, now a discouraged young bond salesman, with whom he had kept in touch.

"You want to borrow my name and my kid sister?" Jimmy Randolph had chortled. "Hop to it, old sport! But you might tell me what you want with such intimate belongings of mine."

"You may not know it," Dundee had retorted, "but young Mr. James Wadley Randolph, Jr., scion of the famous old Boston family, is going to visit that equally famous school, Forsyte-on-the-Hudson, to see whether it is the ideal finishing school for his beloved young sister, Barbara.... She's about fifteen now, isn't she, Jimmy?"

"Going on sixteen, and one of Satan's prize hellions," Jimmy Randolph had answered. "The family would be eternally grateful if you could get Forsyte to take her, but make them promise not to have any more chorus girls who plan to get murdered, as directors of their amateur theatricals. Bab would be sure to be mixed up in the mess.... I suppose that's the job you're on, you flat-footed dick, you!"

The second telephone call had secured an appointment at the Forsyte School for "Mr. James Wadley Randolph, Jr., of Boston," and Dundee, rather relishing his first need for such professional tactics, relaxed to enjoy the ten-mile drive along the Hudson.

It was a quarter to twelve when his taxi swept up the drive toward the big grey-stone, turreted building, sedately lonely in the midst of its valuable acres.

"Miss Earle says to come to the office," a colored maid told him, when he had given his borrowed name, and led him from the vast hall to a fairly large room, whose windows looked upon a tennis court, and whose walls were almost covered with group pictures of graduating classes, photographs of amateur theatrical performances, and portrait studies of alumnae.

A very thin, sharp-faced woman of about forty, with red-rimmed eyes which peered nearsightedly, rose from an old-fashioned roll-top desk and came forward to greet him.

"I am Miss Earle, Miss Pendleton's private secretary," she told him, as he shook her bony, clammy hand. "I should have told you when you telephoned this morning that both Miss Pendleton and Miss Macon sailed for Europe yesterday. We always have our commencement the last Tuesday in May, you know.... But if there is anything I can do for you——"

"I should like to know something at first hand of the history of the school, its—well, prestige, special advantages, curriculum, and so on," Dundee began deprecatingly.

"I should certainly be able to answer any question you may wish to ask, Mr. Randolph, since I have been with the school for fifteen years," Miss Earle interrupted tartly.

"Then Forsyte must take younger pupils than I had been led to believe, Miss Earle," Dundee said, with his most winning smile.

"I was never a pupil here," the secretary corrected him, but she thawed visibly. "Of course, I was a mere child when I finished business school, but I *have* been here fifteen years—fifteen years of watching rich society girls dawdle away four or five years, just because they've got to be *somewhere* before they make their debut.... But I mustn't talk like that, or I'll give you a wrong impression, Mr. Randolph. Of its kind, it is really a very fine school— very exclusive; riding masters, dancing masters, a golf 'pro' and our own golf course, native teachers for French, Italian, German and Spanish.... Oh, the *school* is all right, and will probably not suffer any loss of prestige on account of that dreadful murder out in the Middle West— —"

"Murder?" Dundee echoed, as if he had no idea what she was talking about.

"Haven't you been reading the papers?" Miss Earle rallied him, with a coquettish smile. "But I don't suppose Boston bothers with such sordid things," she added, her thin-lipped mouth tightening. "Miss Pendleton was all cut up about it, because Mrs. Selim, or Juanita Leigh, as she was known on Broadway, had directed our Easter play the last two years, and the reporters simply hounded us the first two days after she was murdered out in Hamilton, where a number of our richest girls have come from——"

"By Jove!" Dundee exclaimed. "Was the Selim woman connected with this school, really?... I only read the headlines—never pay much attention to murders in the papers—"

"I wish," Miss Earle interrupted tartly, fresh tears reddening her eyes, "that people wouldn't persist in referring to her as 'that Selim woman'.... When I think how sweet and friendly she was, how—how *kind*!" and to Dundee's surprise she choked on tears before she could go on: "Of course I know it's dreadful for the school, and I ought not to talk about it, when you've come to see about putting your sister into the school, but Nita was *my friend*, and it simply makes me *wild*——"

"You admired and liked her very much?" Dundee asked, forgetting his role for the moment.

"Yes, I did! And Miss Pendleton liked her, too. And you can imagine how clever and popular she was, when a wonderful woman like Mrs. Peter Dunlap, who was Lois Morrow when she was in school here, admired her so much she took her to Hamilton with her to direct plays for a Little Theater.... Why, I never met anyone I was so congenial with!" the secretary went on passionately. "The girls here snub me and make silly jokes about me behind my back and call me nicknames, but Nita was just as sweet to me as she was to anyone—even Miss Pendleton herself!"

"Were you with her much?" Dundee dared ask.

"*With her much?*... I should say I was!" she asserted proudly. "I have a room here, live here the year 'round, and both years Nita shared my room, so she would not have to make the long trip back to New York every night during the last week of rehearsals. We used to talk until two or three o'clock in the morning—Say!" she broke off, in sudden terror. "You aren't a reporter, are you?"

"A reporter? Good Lord, no!" Dundee denied, in all sincerity. Then he made up his mind swiftly. This woman hated the school and all connected with it, had grown more and more sour and envy-bitten every year of the fifteen she had served here—and she liked Nita Leigh Selim better than anyone she had ever met. The opportunity for direct questioning was too miraculous to be ignored. So he changed his tone suddenly and said very earnestly: "No, I am not a reporter, Miss Earle. But I am *not* James Wadley Randolph, Jr. I am James F. Dundee, special investigator attached to the office of the district attorney of Hamilton, and I want you to help me solve the mystery of Mrs. Selim's murder."

It took nearly ten precious minutes for Dundee to nurse the terrified but obviously thrilled woman over the shock, and to get her into the mood to answer him freely.

"But I shan't and *can't* tell you anything bad about Nita!" she protested vehemently, wiping her red-rimmed eyes. "The papers are all saying now that she got $10,000 for double-crossing some awful racketeer named 'Swallow-tail Sammy', but I *know* she didn't get the money that way! She was too good——"

"From Nita's confidences to you, do you have any idea how she did get the money?" Dundee asked.

Miss Earle shook her head. "I don't know, but she got it honorably. I know that!... Maybe she found her husband and made him pay alimony——"

Dundee controlled his excitement with difficulty. "Did she tell you all about her marriage and divorce?"

Again Miss Earle shook her head. "The only time she ever spoke of it was last year—the first year she directed our play, you know. I asked her why she didn't get married again, and she said she couldn't—she wasn't divorced, because she didn't know where her husband was, and it was too expensive to go to Reno.... Of course she may have found him or something—and got a divorce some time this last year, and this money she got was a settlement——"

"She must have got a divorce, since she was planning to be married again to a young man in Hamilton," Dundee assured her soothingly.

"The way everybody puts the very worst interpretation on everything, when a person gets murdered!" Miss Earle stormed. "If poor Nita had belonged to a rich family, like the girls here, they would have spent a million if necessary to hush up any scandal on her!... I've seen it done!" she added, darkly and venomously.

CHAPTER TWENTY FIVE

Bonnie Dundee's heart leaped, but he forced himself to go softly. "I suppose," he said casually, "a fashionable school like this has plenty of carefully hushed-up scandals——"

"I'll say it has!" Miss Earle retorted inelegantly, and with ghoulish satisfaction. "*Money* can do anything! It makes my blood simply boil when I think of how those Forsyte girls in Hamilton—so smug and snobbish in their hick town 'society'—must be running poor Nita down, now that she's dead and can't defend herself!... If the truth were only known about some of *them*——"

Dundee could almost have embraced the homely, life-soured spinster—she was making his task so easy for him.

"I've met them all, of course, since Mrs. Selim was murdered," he said deprecatingly, "and I must say they seem to be remarkably fine women and girls——"

"Oh *are* they?" Miss Earle snorted. "Flora Hackett—Mrs. Tracey Miles she is now—didn't happen to tell you the nice little fuss *she* kicked up when she was here, did she? Oh, no! I guess not!"

"She looks," Dundee agreed, "like a girl who would have made things lively."

"I'll say so! Miss Pendleton nearly had nervous prostration!" Miss Earle plunged on, then fear blanched her face for a moment. "You know you've promised you'll never tell Miss Pendleton or Miss Macon that you talked to me!"

"You can depend on it that I will protect you," Dundee assured her. "When did Flora Hackett kick up her little fuss?"

"Let's see.... Flora graduated in June, 1920," Miss Earle obliged willingly. "So it must have been in 1919— yes, because she had one more year here. Of course they let her come back!... *Money!*... She took the lead in our annual Easter play in 1919, and just because Serena Hart complimented her and told her she was almost as good as a professional—"

"*Serena Hart!*" Dundee wonderingly repeated the name of one of America's most popular and beloved stage stars.

"Yes—Serena Hart," Miss Earle repeated proudly. "She was a Forsyte girl, too, and of course she *did* go into the chorus herself, after she graduated in—let's see— 1917, because it was the second year after I'd come to work here—and Miss Pendleton nearly died, because she was afraid Forsyte's precious prestige would be lowered, but when Serena became a star everything was grand, of course, and Forsyte was proud to claim her.... Anyway, Serena comes to the Easter play every year she can, if she isn't in a Broadway play herself, of course, and so she saw Flora acting in the Easter play in 1919, and told her she was awfully good. She was, too, but not half the actress that little Penny Crain was, when she had the lead in the play four or five years ago."

Dundee's heart begged him to ask for more details of Penny's triumph, but his job demanded that he keep the now too-voluble Miss Earle to the business in hand.

"And Flora Hackett——?" he prompted.

"Well, the next day after the play the Easter vacation began, you know, and Flora *forged* a letter from her father, giving her permission to spend the ten-days' Easter holiday with one of the girls who lived in Atlanta," Miss Earle continued, with great relish. "Well, sir, right in the middle of the holidays, here came her father and mother—they were both alive then—and asked for Flora! They wired the girl in Atlanta, and Flora wasn't there, and the Hacketts were nearly crazy. But as luck would have it, Mr. Hackett ran into a friend of theirs on

Broadway, and this friend began to tease Mr. Hackett about his daughter's being a chorus girl!"

"A chorus girl!" Dundee echoed, taking care not to show his disappointment.

"Of course they nabbed her right out of the show, but that wasn't the worst of it!" Miss Earle went on dramatically and mysteriously. "They tried to hush it up, of course, but the word went through the school like wildfire that Flora wasn't only in the chorus, but that she was *living with an actor* she'd been writing fan letters to long before the Easter play went on!"

"Did you hear his name?" Dundee asked.

"No," Miss Earle acknowledged regretfully. "But I'll bet anything it was the truth!... Why, Flora Hackett was so man-crazy she flirted scandalously with every male teacher in the school. The golf 'pro' we had then got so scared of her he quit his job!"

"I suppose," Dundee prompted craftily, "she wasn't any worse than some of the other Hamilton girls."

"We-ell," Miss Earle admitted reluctantly, "nothing ever *came out* on any of the others, but it looked mighty funny to me when Janet Raymond's mother took her out of school right in the middle of a term and hauled her off to Europe *for a whole year*!... I guess,"—she suggested, with raised eyebrows, "you know what it *usually* means when a girl has to spend a whole year abroad, and her mother says she's taking her away for her health—and Janet looking as healthy as any other girl in the school, except that she was crying half the time, and smuggling special delivery letters in and out by one of the maids—"

"Did you tell Nita these stories and point out the pictures of the girls?" Dundee had to risk asking.

Miss Earle froze instantly. "Naturally she was interested in the school, and once when she said it always made her mad the way chorus girls were run down, I told her that in my opinion society girls were worse than actresses, and—well, of course I gave her some examples, a lot of them worse than anything I've told you about

Flora Hackett and Janet Raymond.... I hope," she added viciously, "that Nita dropped a hint or two if Flora or Janet had the nerve to high-hat her when she was in Hamilton!"

"Perhaps she did," Dundee agreed softly. "By the way, how did Nita happen to get the job here of directing the Easter plays?"

"That's what the reporters wanted to know," Miss Earle smiled. "But Miss Pendleton wouldn't tell them, for fear Serena wouldn't like it, and maybe be drawn into the scandal, when everybody knows she's as straight as a string——"

"Did Serena Hart get her the job?" Dundee was amazed.

"Yes.... Wait, I'll show you the letter of recommendation she wrote for Nita to Miss Pendleton," Miss Earle offered eagerly. "Remember, now, you're not to tell on me!"

She went to a tall walnut filing cabinet, and quickly returned with a note, which she thrust into Dundee's willing hands. He read:

"Dear Miss Pendleton: The bearer, Juanita Leigh, is rather badly in need of a job, and I have suggested that she apply to you for a chance to direct the Easter play. I have known Miss Leigh personally for ten years, and have the highest regard, both for her character and for her ability. Since you usually stage musical comedies, I think Miss Leigh, who has been a specialty dancer as well as an actress in musical comedy for about twelve years, would be admirably suited for the work. Knowing my love for Forsyte as you do, I do not have to assure you that I would suggest nothing which would be detrimental to the school's best interests.... Fondly yours, Serena Hart."

"She was wrong there, but I know it wasn't Nita's fault," Miss Earle, who had been looking over his shoulder, commented upon the last sentence of the letter.

"Is Miss Hart appearing in a play now?" Dundee asked.

"No, but she's rehearsing in one—'Temptation'—which will open at the Warburton Theater next Monday night," the secretary answered. "At commencement Tuesday night, Serena told Miss Pendleton how awfully sorry she was about Nita, and gave me tickets for the opening.... You go to see her, but don't tell her *I* told you anything.... I know she's rehearsing at the theater this afternoon, because she said she would be all week, and couldn't go to the boat to see Miss Pendleton and Miss Macon off for Europe."

"I will!" Dundee accepted the suggestion gratefully, as if it had not occurred to him. "But first I want you to come out to lunch with me. I'm sure you know of some nice tearoom or roadhouse in the neighborhood."

During the luncheon, which Miss Earle devoured avidly, without its interfering with her flow of reminiscences concerning the girls she hated, Dundee was able to learn nothing more to the detriment of Forsyte's Hamilton alumnae, but he did add considerably to his knowledge and pity of female human nature.

It was nearly three o'clock when he presented his card, with a message pencilled upon its back, to the aged doorkeeper who drowsed in the alley which led to the stage entrance of the Warburton Theater, just off Broadway near Times Square, and fifteen minutes later he was being received in the star's dressing-room by Serena Hart herself.

"You're working on poor Nita's murder?" she began without preamble, as she seated herself at her dressing-table and indicated a decrepit chair for the detective. "I was wondering how much longer I could keep out of it.... Of course you've been pumping that poor, foolish virgin— Gladys Earle.... Why girls who look like that are always called *Gladys*—God! I'm tired! We've been at it since ten this morning, but thank the Lord we're through now for the day."

Dundee studied her with keen interest, and decided that, almost plain though she was, she was even more magnetic than when seen from the footlights.... Rather carelessly dressed, long brown hair rather tousled, her face very pale and haggard without the make-up which would give it radiance on Monday night, Serena Hart was nevertheless one of the most attractive women Dundee had ever met—and one of the kindest, he felt suddenly sure....

"When did I first meet Nita Leigh?" she repeated his question. "Let me think—Oh, yes! The first year after I went on the stage—1917. We were in the chorus together in 'Teasing Tilly'—a rotten show, by the way. The other girls of the chorus were awfully snooty to me, because I was that anathema, a 'society girl', but Nita was a darling. She showed me the ropes, and we became quite intimate—around the theater only, however, since my parents kept an awfully strict eye on me. The show was a great hit—ran on into 1918, till February or March, I believe."

"Then do you know, Miss Hart, whether Nita got married during the winter?" Dundee asked.

"Why, yes, she did!" Serena Hart answered, her brow clearing after a frown of concentration. "I can't remember exactly when, but it was before the show closed—certainly a few weeks before, because the poor child was a deserted bride days before the closing notice was posted."

"Deserted!" Dundee exclaimed. "Did you meet her husband, Miss Hart?"

"No," Serena Hart replied. "As a matter of fact, she told me extraordinarily little about him, and did not discuss her marriage with the other girls of the chorus at all. I got the impression that Mr. Selim—Mat, she called him—wanted it kept secret for a while, but I don't know why.... This was early in 1918, as I've told you, though I have no way of fixing even the approximate date, and New York was full of soldiers. I remember I jumped to the conclusion that Nita had succumbed to a war romance, but I don't think she said anything to confirm my suspicion."

"When did she tell you of her marriage—that is, when—in relation to the date of the wedding itself?" Dundee asked.

"The very day she was married," Serena Hart answered. "She was late for the matinee. Our dressing-tables were side by side, and as she slipped out of her dress——"

"This dress?" Dundee asked, and handed her the photograph of dead Nita in the royal blue velvet dress she had kept for twelve years.

"Yes," and Serena Hart shuddered. "And her hair was dressed like that, too, although she had been wearing it in long curls, and had to take it down before she would go on for the opening number. She whispered to me that she had been married that day, that she was terribly happy, very much in love, and that her husband had asked her to dress her hair in the French roll, a favorite hair-dress with him. Between numbers she whispered to me again, telling me that her husband was 'so different', 'such a lamb'—totally unlike any man she had met on Broadway, poor child.... For she was a child still—only twenty, but she had been in the 'show business' since she was a motherless, fatherless little drifter of sixteen.... No, she did not tell me how old he was, where he came from, his business, or what he looked like, and I did not inquire. As the days passed—weeks, probably, she became more and more silent and reserved, though once or twice she protested she was still 'terribly happy.' Then came a day when she did not show up for the performance at all. The next night she told me—in just a few words, that her husband had left her, after a quarrel, and had not returned. It seems that she had innocently told him how she had 'vamped' Benny Steinfeld, the big revue producer, you know, into giving her a 'spot' in his summer show, and that her 'Mat' had flown into a rage, accusing her of having been untrue to him. She never mentioned his desertion to me again, but——"

"Yes?" Dundee prompted.

"Well," Serena Hart went on, uncomfortably, "I'm afraid I rather forgot poor Nita after 'Teasing Tilly' closed, for my next work was in stock in Des Moines. After a year of stock I got my chance in a legitimate show on Broadway, and one day I met her on the street. Not having much to talk with her about, I asked her if she and her husband were reconciled. She said no, that she had never seen him again. Then, in a burst of confidence, she told me that she had hired a private detective out of her meager earnings to investigate him in his home town, or rather the city he had told her he came from. The detective had reported that no such person as Mat or Matthew Selim had ever lived there, so far as he could find out. I asked her if she was going to get a divorce and she said she was not—that being already married was a protection against getting married in haste again. After that, I rather lost sight of Nita, and practically forgot her, our paths being so very divergent."

"And you never saw her again?" Dundee asked, very much disappointed.

"Oh, yes, two or three times—at openings, or on the street, but we never held any significant conversation," Serena Hart answered, reaching for her plain, rather dowdy little hat. "Wait! I was about to forget! I had quite a shock in connection with Nita. One afternoon—let's see, that was when I opened in 'Hullabaloo,' in which I made my first real success, you know—I bought *The New York Evening Star*, which devotes considerable space to theatrical doings, to see what sort of review the show had got, and on the first page I saw a picture of Nita, beneath a headline which said, 'Famous Model Commits Suicide'——"

"What!" Dundee exclaimed, astounded.

"Oh, it wasn't Nita Leigh," Serena Hart reassured him. "There was a correction the next day. You see, an artists' model named Anita Lee—spelled L-e-e, instead of Le-i-g-h—had committed suicide, and, as the *Star* explained it the next day, the similarity of both the first name and the last had caused the error in getting a photograph from the 'morgue' to accompany the story. There was a picture of Nita Leigh, with Nita's statement that 'the report of my death has been exaggerated,' and a picture of the real Anita Lee."

"When did the mistake occur?" Dundee asked, in great excitement.

"Let me think!" Serena Hart frowned. "'Hullabaloo' opened in—yes, about the first of May, 1922.... Just a little more than eight years ago."

Dundee reached for his own hat, in a fever to be gone, but to his surprise the actress stopped him, a faint color in her pale cheeks.

"Since you're from Hamilton, and are investigating the murder, you have undoubtedly met little Penelope Crain?"

"I know her very well. It happens that she is private secretary to the district attorney, under whom I work.... Why?"

"I saw her play the lead in the Easter show at Forsyte four or five years ago," Miss Hart explained, her face turned from the detective as she dusted it with powder, "and I was impressed with her talent. In fact, I advised her father, who had come from Hamilton to witness the performance, as proud parents are likely to do, to let her go on the stage."

"So you met Roger Crain?" Dundee paused to ask.

"Oh, yes.... A charming man, with even more personality than his daughter," the actress answered carelessly, so carelessly that Dundee had a sudden hunch.

"Have you seen Mr. Crain recently?... He deserted his family and fled Hamilton, under rather unsavory circumstances."

"What do you mean?" Miss Hart asked sharply.

"Oh, there was nothing actually criminal, I suppose, but he is believed to have withheld some securities which would have helped satisfy his creditors, when bankruptcy was imminent," Dundee explained. "Have you seen him since then—January it was, I believe?"

"January?" Miss Hart appeared to need time for reflection. "Oh, yes! He sent in his card on the 'first night' of my show that opened in January.... It was a flop— lasted only five weeks.... We chatted of the Forsyte girls who are now in Hamilton, most of whom I went to school with or have met at the Easter plays."

"Do you know where Mr. Crain is now?" Dundee asked. "I have a message for him from Penny—if you should happen to see him again——"

"Why *should* I see him again?" Miss Hart shrugged. "And I haven't the least idea where he is living or what he is doing now.... Of course, if he should come to see me backstage after 'Temptation' opens—What is the message from Penny?"

"That her mother wants him to come home," Dundee answered. "And I am very sure Penny wants him back, too.... The mother is one of the sweetest, gentlest, most tragic women I have ever met—and you have seen Penny for yourself.... The disgrace has been very hard on them. It would be splendid if Roger Crain would come back and redeem himself."

Half an hour later Bonnie Dundee, in the file room of *The New York Evening Star*, was in possession of the bound volume of that newspaper for the month of May, 1922. On the front page of the issue of May 3, under the caption which Serena Hart had quoted so accurately, was a picture of a young, laughing Nita Leigh, her curls bobbed short, a rose between her gleaming teeth. And in the issue of May 4 appeared two pictures side by side—

exotic, straight-haired, slant-eyed Anita Lee, who had found life so insupportable that she had ended it, and the same photograph of living, vital Nita Leigh.

When he returned the files he asked the girl in charge:

"Does this copyright line beneath this picture—" and he pointed to the photograph of Nita which had appeared erroneously, "—mean that the picture was syndicated?"

The girl bent her head to see. "'Copyright by Metropolitan Picture Service'," she read aloud. "Yes, that's what it means. When *The Evening Star* was owned by Mr. Magnus, he formed a separate company called the Metropolitan Picture Service, which supplied papers all over the country with a daily picture service, in mat form. But the picture syndicate was discontinued about five years ago when the paper was sold to its present owners."

"Are their files available?" Dundee asked.

"If they are, I don't know anything about it," the girl told him, and turned to another seeker after bound volumes of the paper.

"It doesn't matter," Dundee assured her, and asked for a sheet of blank paper, on which he quickly composed the following telegram, addressed to Penny Crain:

"PLEASE SEARCH FILES ALL THREE HAMILTON PAPERS WEEK OF MAY FOURTH TO ELEVENTH YEAR OF NINETEEN TWENTY TWO FOR STORY AND PICTURES ON SUICIDE ANITA LEE ARTISTS MODEL STOP SAY NOTHING TO ANYONE NOT EVEN SANDERSON IF HE IS THERE STOP WIRE RESULT"

In his hotel, while impatiently awaiting an answer from Penny, Dundee passed the time by scanning all the New York papers of Thursday and Friday, on the chance of meeting with significant revelations concerning the private life of Dexter Sprague or Juanita Leigh Selim united by death—in the press, at least. There was much space devoted to the theory involving the two New Yorkers with the murder of the racketeer and gambler, "Swallow-tail Sammy" Savelli, but only two pieces of information held Dundee's interest.

The first was a reminder to the public that certain theatrical columns of Sunday, February 9, had carried the rumor of Dexter Sprague's engagement to Dolly Martin, popular "baby" star of Altamont Pictures, and that the same columns of Tuesday, February 11, had carried Sprague's own denial of the engagement—Dolly having "nothing to say."

"So that is why Nita tried to commit suicide on February 9—and her attempted suicide, with its tragic consequences for Lydia Carr, is probably the reason Sprague gave up his movie star," Dundee mused. "Did Nita let him persuade her to go into the blackmail business, in order to hold his wandering, mercenary affections?... Lord! The men some women love!"

The second bit of information which the papers supplied him was winnowed by Dundee himself, from a news summary of Nita Leigh's last year of life as chorus girl, specialty dancer, "double" in pictures, and director of the Easter play at Forsyte-on-the-Hudson.

"If Nita got a divorce or even a legal separation from her husband after her talk with Gladys Earle a year ago, she got it in New York and so secretly that no New York paper has been able to dig it up," Dundee concluded. "*And yet she had promised to marry Ralph Hammond!*"

A bellboy with a telegram interrupted the startling new train of thought which that conclusion had started.

CHAPTER TWENTY SIX

With a sharp exclamation of excitement and triumph, Dundee read Penny's telegram:

"HAMILTON EVENING SUN DATE OF MAY FIFTH NINETEEN TWENTY TWO PUBLISHED STORY OF SUICIDE ANITA LEE ARTISTS MODEL BUT PICTURE ACCOMPANYING WAS UNDOUBTEDLY NITA LEIGH SELIM'S STOP NO CORRECTION FOLLOWED STOP WHAT DOES IT MEAN"

"What does it mean?" Dundee repeated exultantly to himself. "It means, my darling little Penny, that *anyone in Hamilton who had any interest in the matter believed Nita Leigh Selim was dead, and thought the spelling of her name was wrong, not the picture itself!*... The question is *who* read that story and gazed on that picture with exquisite relief?"

Two hours before he had dismissed as impossible or highly impractical his impulse to investigate the eleven-year-old scandal on Flora Hackett, who was now Flora Miles, as told him by Gladys Earle of the Forsyte School. Even more difficult would it be to find out why Janet Raymond's mother had taken her abroad for a year. Of course—he had ruefully told himself—Nita Leigh might have been lucky—or unlucky enough to run across documentary proof of one of the scandals of which Gladys Earle had told her, or had dared to blackmail her victim by dark hints, as Miss Earle had unconsciously suggested to her.

But this new development could not be ignored. A picture of Nita Leigh as a suicide had appeared eight years ago in a Hamilton paper, and the paper had either remained unaware of the error or had thought it not worth the space for a correction.... *Eight years ago!...*

Eight years ago in June three weddings had occurred in Hamilton! The Dunlap, the Miles, the Drake wedding. And within the last year and a half Judge Marshall, after proposing season after season to the most popular debutante, had married lovely little Karen Plummer. Suddenly a sentence from Ralph Hammond's story of his engagement to Nita Leigh Selim popped up in Dundee's memory: "And once I got cold-sick because I thought she might still be married, but she said her husband had married again, and I wasn't to ask questions or worry about him."

If Ralph Hammond had reported Nita accurately she had not said she was *divorced*. She had merely said her husband was *married again*! Why was Ralph to ask no questions? Divorced wives were not usually so reticent....

Had Nita planned to commit the crime of bigamy? If not, when and where and how had she secured a divorce?

To Serena Hart, years before, she had denied any intention of getting a divorce, for two reasons—*because she did not know where her husband was*, and because, being married although husbandless, was a protection against matrimonial temptations.

To Gladys Earle, a year ago in April, she had confided that she could not marry again, because she was not divorced and because she did not know the whereabouts of her husband.

And so far as New York reporters had been able to find out, Nita Leigh had done nothing to alter her status as a married woman during the past year. Moreover, if Nita had secured either a divorce or a legal separation, her "faithful and beloved maid," Lydia Carr, would certainly have known of it. And Lydia had vehemently protested more than once to Bonnie Dundee that she knew nothing of Nita's husband, although she had worked for the musical comedy dancer for five years. Surely if Nita, loving and trusting Lydia as she did, had entered into negotiations of any kind with or concerning her husband during the last year, her maid would have been the first to know of them. And yet——

Suddenly Dundee jumped to his feet and began to pace the floor of his hotel bedroom. He was remembering the belated confidence that John C. Drake, banker, had made to him the morning before—after the discovery of Dexter Sprague's murder. He recalled Drake's reluctant statement almost word for word:

"About that $10,000 which Nita deposited with our bank, Dundee.... When she made the first deposit of $5,000 on April 28, she explained it with an embarrassed laugh as 'back alimony', an instalment of which she had succeeded in collecting from her former husband. And, naturally, when she made the second deposit on May 5, I presumed the same explanation covered that sum, too, though I confess I was puzzled by the fact that both big deposits had been made in cash."

In cash!

Had Nita, by any chance, been telling a near-truth? Had she been blackmailing her own husband—a husband who had dared marry again, believing his deserted wife to be dead—and justifying herself by calling it "back alimony?"

But—wasn't it, in reality, no matter what coercion Nita had used in getting the money, exactly that?... *Back alimony! And the price of her silence before the world and the wife who was not really a wife....*

In a new light, Bonnie Dundee studied the character of the woman who had been murdered—possibly to make her silence eternal.

Lois Dunlap had liked, even loved her. The other women and girls of "the crowd"—that exclusive, self-centered clique of Hamilton's most socially prominent women—must have liked her fairly well and found her congenial, in spite of their jealousy of her popularity with the men of the crowd, or they would not have tolerated her, regardless of Lois Dunlap's championship of her protegee.

Gladys Earle had found her "the sweetest, kindest, most generous person I ever met"—Gladys Earle, who envied and hated all girls who were more fortunate than she.

Serena Hart, former member of New York's Junior League and still listed in the Social Register, had found her the only congenial member of the chorus she had invaded as the first step toward stardom. And Serena Hart had the reputation of being a woman of character and judgment, a kind and wise and great woman....

Finally, Ralph Hammond had loved Nita and wanted to marry her.

Was it possible that Nita Selim's only crime, into which she had been led by her infatuation for Dexter Sprague, had been to demand, secretly, financial compensation from a husband who had married and deserted her, a husband who, believing her dead, had married again?

But who was the man whose picture—to spin a new theory—Nita had recognized as that of her husband among the male members of the cast of "The Beggar's Opera," when Lois Dunlap had proudly exhibited the "stills" of that amateur performance?

With excitement hammering at his pulses, Dundee took the bunch of photographs which Lois Dunlap had willingly given him, and studied the picture that contained the entire cast—the picture which had first attracted Nita's attention. And again despair overwhelmed him, for every one of his possible male suspects was in that group....

But he could not keep his thoughts from racing on.... Men who stepped out of their class and went on parties with chorus girls frequently did so under assumed names, he reflected. Serena Hart was authority for the information that Nita's had been a sudden marriage. Was it not entirely possible that the man who married Nita in

1918 had done so half-drunk, both on liquor and infatuation, and that he had not troubled to explain to Nita his motives for having used an assumed name or to write in his real name on the application for a marriage license? Had Nita's private detective journeyed out to *Hamilton* years ago in a fruitless attempt to locate "Matthew Selim?"

Bonnie Dundee lay awake for hours Friday night turning these and a hundred other questions over and over in his too-active mind, and slept at last, only to awake Saturday with a plan of procedure which he was sensible enough to realize promised small chance of success.

And he was right. Not in Manhattan, or in any of the other boroughs of New York City, did he find any record of a marriage license issued to Juanita Leigh and Matthew Selim. Not only was it entirely probable that Juanita Leigh was a stage name and that Nita had married conscientiously under her real name, but it was equally possible that the license had been secured in New Jersey or Connecticut.

When he gave up his quest at noon Saturday and returned to his hotel, Dundee bought at the newsstand a paper whose headline convinced him that Sergeant Turner was, at that moment, even more discouraged than himself. For the big type told the world:

JOE SAVELLI "GETS" BROTHER'S SLAYER

And smaller headlines informed the sensation-loving public:

"SWALLOW-TAIL SAMMY" SAVELLI'S DEATH AVENGED BY BROTHER WHO SURRENDERS TO POLICE; "SLICK" THOMPSON, ALLEGED MEMBER OF SAMMY'S GANG, SHOT TO DEATH ON SIXTH AVENUE.

Still smaller head-type acknowledged that Joe Savelli, after giving himself up, with a revolver in his hand, had disclaimed any knowledge of or connection with the murders of Juanita Leigh Selim and Dexter Sprague.

Two hours later, Dundee received a long telegram from District Attorney Sanderson:

"INFORMED BY EVENING SUN SAVELLI ANGLE COMPLETE WASHOUT STOP HAVE YOU MADE ANY PROGRESS ALONG OTHER LINES STOP HAVE INFORMED REPORTERS YOU WORKING INDEPENDENTLY WITH STRONG CHANCE OF SOLVING BOTH CASES STOP WOULD LIKE YOU HERE FOR ADJOURNED INQUESTS ON BOTH MURDERS MONDAY STOP MOTHER IMPROVED AM ON JOB AGAIN"

Since Dundee felt that there was little chance of following through either on the scandals which Gladys Earle had hinted at, or on Nita's strangely secret marriage of twelve years before, he immediately dispatched a wire to Sanderson, assuring him that vital progress had been made and that he would leave New York on the four o'clock train west, arriving in Hamilton Sunday morning at 8:50. The concluding sentence of the wire was:

"SUGGEST YOU PACIFY PRESS WITH ONLY VAGUEST OF HINTS."

Sanderson's wire, with its confession of an interview on Dundee's trip to New York, had upset him and left him with a cold, sick feeling of fear that, stumbling half in darkness, the district attorney had unwittingly warned the murderer of Nita Selim and Dexter Sprague that his special investigator was on the right track. But he consoled himself with the hope that the final sentence of his answering telegram would prevent any further damage.

But he was wrong. An hour before he reached his destination on Sunday morning he went into the dining car and found a copy of *The Hamilton Morning News* beside his plate. And on the front page was a photograph of dead Nita, her black hair in a French roll, her slim, recumbent body clad in the royal blue velvet dress. Beneath the picture was the caption:

"What part does the outmoded royal blue velvet dress which Nita Selim chose as a shroud play in the solution of her murder?... That is the question which Special Investigator Dundee, attached to the district attorney's office, who is due home this morning from fruitful detective work in New York, is undoubtedly prepared to answer."

Dundee was still seething with futile rage when he climbed the stairs to his apartment. On the floor just inside his living room door he found an envelope— unstamped and bearing his name in typing.

The note inside, on paper as plain as the envelope, was typed and unsigned.

"If Detective Dundee will consult page 410 of the latest WHO'S WHO IN AMERICA, he will find a tip which should aid him materially in solving the two murder cases which seem to be proving too difficult for his inexperience."

A wry grin at his anonymous correspondent's unfriendly gibe was just twisting his lips when a double knock sounded on the living room door, which he had not completely closed.

"Come in, Belle!"

A morose, slack-mouthed mulatto girl in ancient felt slippers sidled into the room.

"Howdy, Mistah Dundee," Belle greeted him listlessly. "You got back, lak de papers said you would, didn' yuh? An' I ain't sayin' I ain't glad! Dat parrot o' yoahs sho is Gawd's own nuisance—nippin' at mah fingahs an'

screechin' his fool head off.... 'Cose I ain't sayin' it's *his*
fault—keepin' dat young gemman on de secon' flo' awake
las' night.... But lak I say to Mistah Wilson, when he
lights into me dis mawnin', runnin' off at de mouf 'cause I
fo'got to put Cap'n's covah on his cage las' night, I ain't de
onliest one what fo'gits in dis hyar house.... Comin' home
Gawd knows when, leavin' de front do' unlocked de res' o'
de night, so's bugglers and murderers and Gawd knows
who could walk right in hyar——"

Dundee, itching to consult his own copy of "Who's
Who", flung a glance at the parrot's cage, intending to
pacify the mournful mulatto by scolding his "Watson"
roundly. But he changed his mind and consoled the
chambermaid instead:

"Just tell Mr. Wilson that for once he's wrong. You did
not forget to cover Cap'n's cage, Belle. Look!"

The girl's dull eyes bulged as they took in the cage,
completely swathed in a square of black silk.

"Gawd's sake, Mistah Dundee!" she ejaculated. "*I*
didn't put dat covah on dat bird's cage! An' neithah did
Mis' Bowen, 'cause she been laid up with rheumatiz eveh
since you lef, an' eveh las' endurin' thing in dis ol' house
has been lef fo' me to do!"

"Then I suppose the indignant Mr. Wilson came up
and covered Cap'n himself," Dundee suggested, crossing
the room to the bookcase which stood within reaching
distance of his big leather-covered armchair.

"Him?" Belle snorted. "How he gonna get in hyer
widout no key? 'Sides, he'd a-tol' me if'n——"

"Belle, how many times must I ask you not to
misplace my things?" Dundee cut in irritably, for he was
tired of the discussion, and angry that his copy of "Who's
Who" was missing from its customary place in the
bookcase.

"Me?... I ain't teched none o' yoah things, 'cep'n to dus'
'em and lay 'em down whar I foun' 'em," Belle retorted,
mournfulness submerged in anger.

Dundee looked about the room, then his eyes alighted upon the missing book, lying upon a shelf that extended across the top of an old-fashioned hot-air register, set high in the wall between the two windows. The thick red volume lay close against the wall, its gold-lettered "rib" facing the room.

"Belle, tell me the truth, and I shall not be angry: did you put that red book on that shelf?" Dundee asked, his voice steady and kindly in spite of his excitement.

"Nossuh! I ain't teched it!"

"And you did not put the cover over my parrot's cage, although I had tipped you well to feed Cap'n and cover him at night," Dundee said severely.

"I gotta heap o' wuk to do——"

"And you say that Mr. Wilson, one of the two young men on the second floor, left the front door unlocked when he came in last night?" Dundee asked. "Does he admit it?"

"Yassuh," Belle told him sulkily. "He say he was tiahed when he got home 'long 'bout midnight, an' he clean fo'got to turn de key in de do' an' shoot de bolt."

"Thanks, Belle. That will be all now," and Dundee did a great deal to dispel the chambermaid's gloom by presenting her with a dollar bill.

When she had gone, the detective read the note again, then looked at it and its envelope more closely. They had a strangely familiar look.... Suddenly he jerked open a drawer of his desk, on which his new noiseless typewriter stood, selected a sheet of plain white bond, and rolled it into the machine. Quickly he tapped out a copy of the strange, taunting message.

Yes! The left-hand margin was identical, the typing and its degree of blackness were identical, and the paper on which he had made the copy was exactly the same as that on which the original had been written.

The truth flashed into his mind. It was no coincidence that he had a copy of the very book to which his unknown correspondent referred him. For the note had been written in this very room, on stationery conveniently at hand, on the noiseless typewriter which had been far more considerate about not betraying the intruder than had the parrot whose slumbers had been disturbed.

"But why did my unknown friend risk arrest as a burglar if he wanted to give me an honest tip?" Dundee remarked aloud to the parrot, who croaked an irrelevant answer:

"Bad Penny! Bad Penny!"

"I'm afraid, 'my dear Watson,' that those words will not be so helpful in this case as they were when your mistress was murdered," Dundee assured his parrot absently, for he was studying the peculiar situation from every angle. "Another question, Cap'n—why did the unknown bother to take my 'Who's Who' out of the bookcase, where I should normally have looked for it, and put it on that particular shelf?"

Warily, for his scalp was prickling with a premonition of danger, Dundee crossed the room to the shelf, but his hand did not reach out for the red book, which might have been expected to solve one problem, at least. "*Why the shelf?*" he asked himself again. Why not the desk top, or the mantelpiece, or the smoking table beside the big armchair?

The shelf, with its drapery of rather fine old silk tapestry, offered no answer in itself, for it held nothing except the red book, a Chinese bowl, and a humidor of tobacco. And beneath the shelf was nothing but the old-fashioned register, the opening covered with a screwed-on metal screen which was a mass of big holes to permit the escape of hot air when the furnace was going in the winter....

Suddenly Dundee stooped and stared with eyes that were widened with excitement and a certain amount of horror. Then he rose, and, standing far to one side, picked up the fat volume which lay on the shelf. As he had expected, a bullet whizzed noiselessly across the room and buried itself in the plaster of the wall opposite—a bullet which would have ploughed through his own heart if he had obeyed his first impulse and gone directly to the shelf to obey the instructions in the note.

But more had happened than the whizzing flight of a bullet through one of the holes of the hot-air register. The "Who's Who" had been jerked almost out of Dundee's hand before he had lifted the heavy volume many inches from the shelf. Coincidental with the disappearance of a bit of white string which had been pinned to a thin page of the book was a metallic clatter, followed swiftly by the faint sound of a bump far below.

Dropping "Who's Who" to the floor, Dundee flung open his living room door and raced down three flights of stairs. He brought up, panting, at the door of the basement. It was not locked and in another minute he was standing before the big hot-air furnace. Above the fire box was a big metal compartment—the reservoir for the heated air. And set into the reservoir, to conduct the heat to the regions above, were three huge pipes.

With strength augmented by excitement, Dundee tugged and tore at one of the pipes until he had dislodged it. Then thrusting his hand into the heat reservoir, he groped until he had found what he had known must be there—*Judge Marshall's automatic, with the Maxim silencer screwed upon the end of its short nose.*

At last he held in his hands the weapon with which Nita Leigh Selim and Dexter Sprague had been murdered.

The ingeniousness of his own attempted murder moved him to such profound admiration that he could scarcely feel resentment. If, in the excitement of hunting for a promised clue, he had gone directly to the shelf, standing in front of the hole in the register into which the end of the silencer had been jammed, so that it showed scarcely at all, even to eyes looking for it, he would now have been dead. And the gun and silencer, after hurtling down the big hot-air pipe behind the register, could have lain hidden for months, even years, in the heat reservoir of the furnace.

With the weapon carefully wrapped in his handkerchief, Dundee went up the stairs almost as swiftly as he had gone down them, meeting no one on the way to his rooms on the top floor.

"My most heartfelt thanks to you, Cap'n!" he greeted his parrot. "If you had not squawked last night and so frightened the murderer that he made the vital error of covering your cage, I should never have annoyed you again with my Sherlock ruminations on cases which do not interest you in the slightest."

The parrot cackled hoarsely, but Dundee paid him scant attention. He picked up the now harmless "Who's Who" and turned to page 410, a corner of which had disappeared with the string that was still fastened to the hair-trigger hammer of the Colt's .32. Very clever and very simple! The murderer of two people and the would-be murderer of a third had had only to unscrew the metal covering of the register, wedge the end of the silencer into one of the many holes, replace the screws, and paste the end of the string, drawn through another hole hidden by the tapestry, to a page of the book he had selected as the one most likely to appeal to a detective as a clue source....

No, wait! He had had to do more! Dundee bent and examined the metal cover of the register. The circumference of the hole the murderer had chosen as the one which would be directly in front of Dundee's heart gleamed brightly. It had been necessary to enlarge it considerably. *The murderer had left a trace after all!*

But the book was open in Dundee's hands and his eyes rapidly scanned page 410. And he found what the murderer had not expected him to live to read, but which he had counted on as an explanation of the note which the police would have puzzled over, if all had gone well with his scheme....

CHAPTER TWENTY SEVEN

Dundee laughed, the parrot which had saved his life echoing his mirth raucously, as his eyes hit upon the following lines of fine print halfway down the third column of page 410 of "Who's Who in America":

BURNS, William John, detective; b. Baltimore, Oct. 19, 1861—

"A taunt and a joke which turned sour, 'my dear Watson'!" he exulted to the parrot. "A joke I was not intended to live to laugh over!"

He closed the book and replaced it in the bookcase, careless of fingerprints, for he was sure the murderer had been too clever to leave any behind him in that room—or upon the gun and silencer either, for that matter.

Interestedly, Dundee surveyed the scene of his attempted murder. If he had unsuspectingly gone up to the high shelf to reach for the book he would have stood so close to the register that there would have been powder burns on his shirt front—just as there had been on Dexter Sprague's. And he would have been shot so near an open window—no chance for fingerprints there, either, since he had not closed the windows on his departure for New York, not wishing to return to a stuffy apartment—that the police would have been justified in thinking he had been shot from outside. It was an old-fashioned house in more ways than in the manner of its heating. Outside of one of his two unscreened windows there was an iron grating—the topmost landing of a fire escape. Dundee could imagine Captain Strawn's positiveness in placing the murderer there—crouching in wait for his victim....

Yes, damned ingenious, this attempted murder! Undoubtedly Strawn would have dismissed the note as the work of a crank, not hitting upon the fact that it had been written in that very room, on Dundee's own typewriter and stationery. Strawn might even have got a mournful sort of amusement out of the fact that Dundee had been advised to call upon a greater detective than himself for assistance!... Yes, ingenious indeed! And so amazingly simple——

Suddenly the young detective snatched for his hat. If the murderer was so ingenious in this case, might he not have been equally clever in planning and executing the murder of Nita Leigh Selim?

Twenty minutes later he parked his car in the rutty road before the Selim house in Primrose Meadows, and honked his horn loudly to attract the attention of the plainclothesmen Captain Strawn had detailed immediately after the murder to guard the premises during the day. There was no answer. And a violent ringing of the doorbell also brought no response. The guard had been withdrawn, probably to join the small army of plainclothesmen and patrolmen who had been foolishly and futilely searching for the New York gunman—the keystone of Captain Strawn's exploded theory.

With an oath, Dundee used his skeleton key to release the Yale lock with which the front door was equipped. Straight down the main hall he went and into the little foyer between the hall and Nita's bedroom. He snatched up the telephone and to his relief it was not dead. He gave the number of Captain Strawn's home, and had the pleasure of learning that he had interrupted his former chief at a late Sunday breakfast.

"When did you withdraw the guard from the Selim house?" he asked abruptly, cutting short Strawn's cordial welcome-home.

"Late Thursday afternoon," the Chief of the Homicide Squad answered belligerently. "I needed all my men, and the Selim house had been gone over with a fine tooth comb half a dozen times.... Why?"

"Oh, nothing!" Dundee retorted wearily, and hung up the receiver after assuring his old friend that he would call on him later in the day.

No use to explain now to Strawn that the murderer had been given every chance to remove any betraying traces of his crime. Besides, his first excited hunch, after his own attempted murder, might very well be a wild, groundless one. In his—Dundee's case—the impossibility of the murder's being delayed or arranged so that the detective might be slain when the whole "crowd" was assembled was obvious. The murderer had read in a late Saturday afternoon extra—a copy of which was now in Dundee's pocket—District Attorney Sanderson's boast to the press that his office had been working on an entirely different theory than that which connected the two murders with "Swallow-tail Sammy," that Special Investigator Dundee, *expected back in Hamilton early Sunday morning*, had been investigating Nita Leigh's past life in New York. And despite Dundee's telegraphed warning, he had hinted sensational revelations connected with the twelve-year-old royal blue velvet dress which Nita had chosen to be her shroud. And in his desire to reassure the public through the press, Sanderson had mysteriously promised even more specific revelations than Dundee had actually brought home with him. Prodded by reporters, Sanderson had admitted that he did not himself know the nature of those revelations.

The exasperated young detective could picture the murderer reading those sensational hints and promises, could imagine his panic, the need for immediate action, so that Special Investigator Dundee should not live to tell the tale of his New York discoveries to the district attorney or anyone else.

But whether he was right or wrong, Dundee determined to give his hunch a chance. He went into the over-ornate bedroom in which Nita Leigh Selim had been murdered—shot through the back as she sat at her dressing-table powdering her face. If her murder had been accomplished by mechanical means, how had it been done? There was no hot-air register here....

From the dressing-table Dundee walked to the window, upon whose pale-green frame there was still the tiny pencil mark which Dr. Price had drawn, to indicate the end of the path along which the bullet had traveled, provided it had traveled so far. Nothing *here* to aid in a mechanical murder—

But in a flash Dundee changed his mind. For just slightly above the pencil mark there was a small dent in the soft painted pine of the window frame.

And before his mind could frame words and sentences he thought he saw how Nita Leigh had been murdered.

Nothing here?... *Not now, because he himself had taken the lamp to the courthouse for safe-keeping.*

He saw it clearly in imagination—that bronze floor-lamp which Lydia Carr had given to Nita Leigh, its big round bowl studded with great jewels of colored glass. And in recalling every detail of the lamp he saw what he had dismissed as of no importance at the time, in the excitement of finding that the lamp's bulb had been shattered by the "bang or bump" which Flora Miles had described. *One of the big glass jewels had been missing, leaving an unsightly hole.*

No wonder there had been a "bang or bump" hard enough to dent the frame of the window! For if his hunch was correct, the gun, wedged into the big bowl, with the silencer slightly protruding from the jewel-hole, had "kicked," just as it had kicked an hour before, when it had dislodged itself from the hole in the hot-air register and clattered down the big pipe to the heat reservoir of the furnace.

That the big lamp, when he, following Strawn, had first examined the scene of Nita's murder, had not stood in front of the window frame, did not dampen Dundee's excitement in the least. After Karen Marshall's scream that room had been filled with excited people, who had rushed about, looking out of the window for the murderer and doing all the other things which terror-stricken people do in such a crisis. No, the murderer—or murderess—had found no difficulty in shifting the big lamp one foot nearer the chaise longue, to the place it had always occupied before.

But—*how* had the gun been fired from the lamp? Electrically? Another picture flashed into Dundee's mind. He saw himself stooping, on Monday afternoon, to see if the plug of the lamp's cord had been pulled from the socket, saw it again as it was then—nearly out, so that no current could pass from the baseboard outlet under the bookcase into the bronze lamp. How far from the truth his conclusion that Monday had been!

But what was the *real* truth?

Suddenly Dundee flung back the moss-green Wilton rug which almost entirely covered the bedroom floor and revealed the bell which Dexter Sprague had rigged up so that Nita might summon Lydia from her basement room, in case of dire need—a precaution with which the murderer was probably familiar, since Lois Dunlap might innocently have spread the news of its existence.

There was a half-inch hole in the hardwood floor, and out of it issued a length of green electric cord, connected with two small, flat metal plates, one upon the other, so that when stepped upon a bell would ring in Lydia's basement room.

But there was something odd about the wire. Although it was obviously new, a section of it near the two metal plates was wrapped with black adhesive tape. Another memory knocked for attention upon Dundee's mind. *The long cord of the bronze lamp had been mended with exactly the same sort of tape—about a foot from where it ended in the contact plug.*

Within another two minutes, Dundee, with a flashlight he had found in the kitchen, was exploring the dark, earthy portion of the basement which lay directly to the east of Lydia Carr's basement room. And he found what he was looking for—adhesive tape wrapped about the wire which had been dropped through the floor of Nita's room before it had been carried, by means of another hole, into Lydia's room.

He was too late—thanks to Captain Strawn. The bell which Sprague had rigged up was in working order again. But as he was passing out of the basement he glanced at the ceiling of the large room devoted to furnace, hot-water heater and laundry tubs. And in the ceiling he saw a hole....

The murderer had left a trace he could not obliterate!

*   *   *   *   *

At three o'clock that Sunday afternoon Bonnie Dundee, fatigued after a strenuous day, and suffering, to his own somewhat disgusted amusement, from reaction— even a detective feels some shock at having narrowly escaped death—permitted himself the luxury of a call upon Penny Crain.

He found the girl and her mother playing anagrams. After greeting him, Mrs. Crain rose, to surrender her place to the visitor.

"*You* play with this girl of mine, Mr. Dundee. She's too clever for me! She's beaten me every game so far, and when I plead for two-handed bridge as a chance to get even, she shudders at the very word."

"Why did you drag poor Ralph away from his dinner here today?" Penny demanded, scrambling the little wooden blocks until they made a weird pattern of letters.

"Because I wanted to find out exactly *how* Nita Selim was killed—and I did," Dundee answered. "I wish I knew as well *who* murdered her!"

Mute before Penny's excited questions, the detective idly selected letters from the mass of face-up blocks on the table, and spelled out, in a long row, the names of all the guests at Nita's fatal bridge party. Suddenly, and with a cry that startled Penny, Dundee made a new name with the little wooden letters....

Now he knew the answers to both "*How?*" and "*Who?*"

CHAPTER TWENTY EIGHT

"I fail to see any necessity for all this secrecy and hocus-pocus," District Attorney Sanderson protested irritably. "Why the devil don't you come clean and give us the low-down—if you have it!—on this miserable business, instead, of high-handedly summoning Captain Strawn to my office, so that you can give orders to us both?"

Before Dundee could answer, Captain Strawn came to his assistance.

"I worked with this boy for pretty near a year, Bill, and never yet did he fail to make good when he said he had a pot on to boil. If he says it will boil over this evening, provided we help him, boil over it will, or I don't know Bonnie Dundee!"

Sanderson scowled but capitulated. "All right! What do you want?"

"Thanks, chief! And thanks, Captain!" Dundee cried, with heartfelt gratitude. "First, I want to be excused from attending the adjourned inquests into the two murders, scheduled for three o'clock today."

"O.K." Sanderson agreed shortly.

"Second, after about an hour of routine stuff, I wish you'd ask for another adjournment until tomorrow, on the plea that important developments are expected today."

"O.K. again!"

"Third, I'd like you personally to request the appearance of every person connected in any way with each of the murders, in your office this afternoon at four o'clock—so the whole bunch will be kept together and have no chance to go to their homes or anywhere else until I am ready for them. You can say that, owing to the illness of your mother during the investigations, you want to question everyone personally."

"Do you want all the servants brought here, too?" Sanderson asked.

"None but Lydia Carr," Dundee answered. "After about an hour's innocuous questioning, please invite them to accompany you to the Selim house. For that—" and he grinned, "—is where the pot is scheduled to boil over. I'd like everybody to be there by 5:15."

"Where do I come in?" Captain Strawn demanded, almost jealously.

"Now that you are no longer looking for a New York gunman, I suppose you have plenty of plainclothesmen at your disposal?" Dundee asked, and was instantly sorry he had reminded his former chief of the collapse of his cherished and satisfying theory.

"Plenty," Strawn answered gruffly. "How many will you need?"

"Enough to keep every person on Mr. Sanderson's invitation list under strictest observation until—the pot boils over," Dundee replied.

"When do you want them to get on the job?"

"As soon as they can do so, after you get back to your office."

"Are they to follow the whole gang clear out to the Selim house?"

"Most decidedly! After the unwilling guests are safely within the house, your boys must guard the premises so that *no one* leaves without permission."

"That's all as good as done," Strawn assured him. "Now—about them inquiries you asked me to make yesterday of the secretary of the American Legion." He drew a scrap of paper from his breast pocket. "I find that John Drake, Peter Dunlap and Clive Hammond were all in service, in the ——th Division, which was held up late in January, 1918, for nearly two weeks, in Hoboken, before the War Department could get transports to send 'em to France. Miles, who enlisted the day war was declared, was wounded and shipped home late in 1917. He was discharged as unfit for further service—spinal operation—from a New Jersey base hospital on January 12, 1918. Furthermore, Judge Marshall was in New York the whole winter of 1917-'18, attached to the Red Cross in some legal capacity. He donated his services and—"

"All that doesn't matter now, Captain, but thanks just the same," Dundee interrupted. "Now if you will both excuse me, I've got a lot of work to do before five o'clock today!"

Dundee had not exaggerated. That Monday was one of the busiest days he had ever spent in all the twenty-seven years of his life. He began, rather strangely, by visiting half a dozen of Hamilton's hardware stores, exhibiting a peculiar instrument and making annoying inquiries as to when and to whom it had been sold. But at his sixth port of call success so completely rewarded his efforts that he was jubilant when he bade the mystified proprietor good day, a signed statement reposing in his wallet.

Two other calls—both in office buildings—took up only an hour of his time, and a taxicab delivered him at Police Headquarters just as the factory whistles were sirening the news that it was twelve o'clock.

He was lucky enough to find the fingerprint expert, Carraway, in his cubbyhole of an office, his desk almost crowded out by immense filing cabinets.

Five minutes later Dundee sat at that desk, photographs of Dexter Sprague's dead body, just as it had been discovered on the floor of the trophy room in the Miles home, and a labelled set of fingerprints spread out before him.

"You're sure there can have been no mistake?" he asked. "No chance that these fingerprint photographs were *reversed* when the prints were made?"

"Not a chance—with my system!" Carraway retorted positively.

"Fine!" Dundee cried. "May I take these photographs?... You have copies, I presume?"

It was half past two o'clock when Dundee, after a much needed lunch, parked his car in the driveway of one of the most splendid houses overlooking Mirror Lake—a home whose master and mistress were now attending an inquest into two murders....

Half an hour later he climbed into his roadster again, his head spinning. "Did I say *ingenious*?" he marvelled....

He drove directly to the Selim house, for he had much to do before the arrival of Sanderson's compulsory guests at 5:15.

His first visit there was to a small room in the basement—a dark cubbyhole next to the coal room. He had locked it carefully after exploring it the day before, for he had taken no chance on leaving unguarded—as he had found it—treasure worth more to him than its weight in gold.

And queer treasure it was that he extracted now—a coiled length of electric wire, which he and Ralph Hammond had measured the day before, with triumphant excitement; a box of thumb tacks, many of them surprisingly bent at the point; an augur with a set of bits of varying sizes, a step-ladder, and a hammer. If Dexter Sprague had not overestimated the amount of electric wire needed for the job of installing an alarm bell between Nita's bedroom and Lydia's.... Dundee was about to close the tool chest when his eyes fell upon a piece of hardware he had not expected ever to find, although he had known of its existence for more than an hour.

At 5:15 he was entirely ready for D. A. Sanderson, Captain Strawn and their party of indignant and unwilling guests....

"Oh, Mr. Dundee!" Carolyn Drake squealed. "You're not going to make us play that awful 'death hand' again, are you?"

They were all crowding about him—the men and women who had been Nita Selim's guests at her last bridge and cocktail party....

"Not only are the bridge tables exactly where they were at this time on the evening of May 24," Dundee answered *so* significantly that all stopped chattering to listen, "*but everything else in the house is precisely as it was then.* Fortunately, not even the *electricity* has been cut off! But to make sure I have forgotten nothing, I wish you would all follow me into Mrs. Selim's bedroom and look for yourselves."

Like sheep, they crowded into the little foyer and on into the bedroom. There stood the big bronze lamp, set squarely in front of the window frame and in a direct line with the musical powder box on dead Nita's dressing table.

At 5:25, Penny Crain, Karen Marshall, Carolyn Drake, and Flora Miles, who had been requisitioned by Dundee to play the part of the murdered woman, were seated at table No. 2, and behind Karen's chair stood Lois Dunlap. Clive Hammond and his new wife were again together in the solarium. But there Dundee's restaging of the original scene in the tragic drama ended. Everyone else, including Lydia Carr and Peter Dunlap, were huddled together in a far corner of the living room.

"Now, Mr. Miles!" Dundee called. "Your cue! Never mind the comedy about 'How's tricks?' Simply go into the dining room, with Mrs. Dunlap, to mix cocktails. You'll find all the ingredients still on the sideboard, exactly as there were when Mrs. Selim sent you to mix drinks on May 24.... And Mrs. Miles, will you, pretending that you are Nita Selim, go to powder your face at Mrs. Selim's dressing-table?"

Her face white and drawn, Flora Miles stumbled from the room, just as her husband, dumb for once with rage, entered the dining room with Lois Dunlap.

Dundee was about to follow the latter two when an interruption occurred. Followed by a plainclothesman, a middle-aged man entered the living room. Tall, broad-shouldered, determined, he strode to the bridge table, his handsome head upflung, his brown eyes fixed upon the widened brown eyes of Penny Crain.

*   *   *   *   *

"Dad!" the girl breathed; then, joyously: "Oh, Dad! You've come home!"

But Dundee halted the reconciliation with a stern word of command. "Please join the group in the corner, Mr. Crain!"

Regardless of the ensuing hubbub Dundee strode into the dining room, where Tracey Miles stood at the sideboard, pouring whiskey from an almost empty decanter into a small glass.

"May I drink the Scotch Tracey has poured for me, Mr. Dundee?" Mrs. Dunlap asked shakily, leaning against the big round table.

"Yes, but—Silence, please!" he cried, as there came the first faint, tinkling notes of *Juanita*, from Nita's musical powder box, penetrating the thin wall between the bedroom and dining room.

"As I have said," the detective spoke loudly and clearly above the tinkle of music, "*everything is now exactly as it was when Nita Selim was murdered!* Permit me to show you all how that murder was accomplished!"

A chair at the bridge table was overturned. Lois Dunlap almost choked on her drink of Scotch. Women screamed. In a few seconds every person in the living room, including the district attorney and Strawn, was huddled in the wide opening into the dining room, their eyes fixed in horror upon Bonnie Dundee.

He spoke again, his voice very clear, but slow and weighted with a dreadful significance:

"Mrs. Dunlap, step on the bell beneath the dining table!"

Lois Dunlap dropped the empty whiskey glass, her face suddenly wiped of all expression.

"Step on that bell, Mrs. Dunlap—*just as you did before!*"

As if hypnotized, Lois Dunlap began to grope with the toe of her right pump for the slight bulge under the rug which indicated the position of the bell used for summoning the maid from the kitchen.

With a strangled cry Tracey Miles lunged across the few feet which separated the woman and himself, seized her arm and whirled her violently away from the table.

"*Do you want to kill my wife, too?*" he panted, his usually florid face the color of putty. "You—*you*—!"

CHAPTER TWENTY NINE

"That would be impossible, Miles," Dundee said deliberately. *"For your wife is already dead!"* Then his clear words rang out like the knell of doom:

"Tracey Arthur Miles, I arrest you for the murder of your wife, known as Juanita Leigh Selim, and for the murder of Dexter Sprague. And it is my duty to warn you that anything you say may be used against you."

Tracey Miles lifted his ashen face and stared at the detective blankly, as though he had gone deaf and blind. "All—over—isn't it? May I—have a—drink?" he managed to articulate at last.

"Poor devil! He needs it," the too-soft-hearted young detective told himself, as Miles poured a drink from the almost empty whiskey decanter and raised the little glass to his lips.

"I have—nothing—to say!" the murderer gasped thickly, then fell heavily to the floor.

*   *   *   *   *

It was three-quarters of an hour later. District Attorney Sanderson, Captain Strawn and Dundee were alone in the house where Nita "Selim" had been murdered and where her husband had confessed his crimes by committing suicide. The morgue ambulance had come and gone....

"I should have known," Dundee admitted ruefully, as the three men entered Nita's bedroom, "that so ingenious a criminal as Tracey Miles would not have failed to provide against the possibility of discovery. He must have seized an opportunity to spill cyanide of potassium into the decanter when my eyes were off him for a moment—and upon Lois Dunlap."

"I'm glad he did," Sanderson said curtly. "But it was ghastly that poor Lois had to know that it was she, in all innocence, who fired the shot that killed her friend."

"It was," Dundee sighed. "But I believed that the only way I could make Miles confess was to frighten him into thinking Flora would be killed in the same manner.... Well, it worked!"

"Captain Strawn and I are still in the dark as to exactly how Miles managed his wife's murder," Sanderson reminded him. "This morning you chose to tell us nothing more than that a Hamilton man had married Nita Leigh in New York in January, 1918, and that eight years ago, when he saw her picture in *The Hamilton Evening Sun*, along with the story that 'Anita Lee' had committed suicide, he felt free to marry again.... You said then you knew who the man was but you would not even tell us how you knew—"

"Because I had very little actual proof then," Dundee answered. "As to who he was, the salient clue had been staring me in the face the whole time, but it was not until I was fooling with a set of anagrams last night, idly spelling out the names of all the men who *might* have married her and then murdered her, that I saw it—"

"Saw *what*?" Strawn demanded irritably.

"That Selim is simply Miles spelled backwards," Dundee explained. "Possibly because he considered it the sophisticated thing to do, Miles used an assumed name at the party at which he met Nita Leigh—and married her under that name shortly afterward. Even the first name, 'Mat', by which she knew him, was only his initials reversed."

"Simple—but clever," Sanderson commented.

"Just as were all of Miles' schemes after Nita, egged on by Sprague, turned up in Hamilton to demand 'back alimony' as the price of her silence.... But let me show you how he killed his wife."

He strode to the big bronze lamp. "It took me less than an hour today to reconstruct the death machine so that it would be almost exactly as it was when Miles finished his work just before 2:30 on Saturday, May 24— and as it remained until he had an opportunity to come back here and dismantle it. Trust him to find out that the guard was removed from the house Thursday!"

As he spoke, he was unscrewing the big, jewel-studded bowl of the bronze lamp. Wedged, at a down-slanting angle inside the bowl, which was twelve inches in diameter, was Judge Marshall's snub-nosed automatic, the attached Maxim silencer projecting slightly from the hole whose jewel was missing.

"Lydia told me last night over the telephone—and very much surprised she was, too, when I swore her to secrecy—that the jewel had been lost when the lamp was shipped from New York," Dundee explained. "There's a blank cartridge in the gun now, of course, but Miles, in his panic, took my words literally.... See the electro-magnet strapped to the gun butt? He got it from the bell Sprague had installed in Lydia's bedroom, and he returned it when he was 'cleaning up', so that the bell would ring again. The magnet he connected with the electric wire in one of the two lamp sockets, as you see it now, and the long cord of the lamp was connected with the wire of the bell in the dining room—so connected that when anyone stepped on the two little metal plates under the dining room rug, the kitchen bell would ring and the gun would be fired simultaneously. But if you will examine the jewel hole," he suggested, "you will see that Miles had to enlarge it considerably, using a reamer, which I found in the tool chest in the basement, along with all the apparatus Sprague had bought for installing Nita's alarm bell. I could see no reason for Sprague's having needed a reamer for his little job, however, and this morning I was lucky enough to get proof that Miles himself had purchased it at a hardware store on the Tuesday before Nita's murder."

"How did he connect the lamp cord with the dining room bell?" Strawn puzzled. "These modern houses don't have exposed wiring—"

"You forget Sprague's wiring for the alarm bell from here to Lydia's room!" and Dundee threw back the rug, showing them the hole in the floor, out of which came a short length of electric wire, ending in two small metal plates. But attached now to the wire was the cord from the bronze lamp.

"The plug of the lamp cord is nearly out of the baseboard outlet behind the bookcase, just as Miles left it, so that there is no contact with electricity there. And the rug, which almost entirely covers the floor, hides, as you have seen, the joining of the two wires. An inexplicable wrapping of adhesive tape both on the lamp cord and on the wire of Nita's alarm bell here gave me the clue.... In installing the alarm bell, Sprague copied the arrangement under the dining table, of course. And Miles simply had to drop a bit, fastened to the augur Sprague had bought and used for his own job, down the four inches which separate the dining room floor from the basement ceiling, boring a hole through the ceiling. It was that fresh-bored hole in the ceiling that I could not understand, and which Ralph Hammond assured me was not there Saturday morning before Nita was killed.... Miles joined a piece of electric wire to the dining room bell wires, and pushed it down through the hole he had bored into the basement ceiling. Now if you'll come down with me—"

When the three men stood staring upward at the basement ceiling, Dundee continued:

"See this long wire running along the ceiling from the hole beneath the dining room bell? The tacks Miles used to secure it were also returned to the tool chest, but he could not get rid of either the augur hole or the tiny holes showing the course of the wire.... Let's follow it."

He led them across the basement to a door leading into a dank, unfinished portion of the cellar, directly east of Lydia's bedroom and beneath Nita's. The wire whose course they were following led under the top frame of the door, and, with a flashlight in his hand, Dundee showed how it continued along a rafter until it reached the place where it was joined, by adhesive tape, to the wire Sprague had dropped from Nita's bedroom floor above.

"Miles simply cut the wire here where it enters another hole through Lydia's bedroom wall, and attached the new wire," Dundee explained. "The connection between the dining room bell and the electro-magnet in the lamp upstairs was then complete.... Sprague had bought yards too much of the wire—fortunately for Miles' scheme."

"But what a chance Miles took on the bullet's not hitting her in a fatal spot!" Sanderson commented in an awed voice.

"Not much of a chance!" Dundee denied. "He would fire the gun only when he knew Nita was seated before her dressing-table. Experienced marksman that he was, he could calculate the path of the bullet to a nicety. Of course the machine had to be used that very day. As you know Nita herself gave him his chance. Miles, standing at the sideboard, which was separated from Nita's dressing table only by a thin wall, listened until the first faint notes of *Juanita* told him that Nita was powdering her face. He could be almost positive that Nita was sitting down to her task.... The poor girl saw nothing to alarm her, but the gun kicked when the shot was fired by Lois' innocent stepping upon the dining room bell, and the big lamp was rocked so that it banged against the window frame, shattering the one bulb Miles had left in it. Of course he moved the lamp a foot or so, in the resulting excitement. And if Nita had been wounded only, living to tell how the shot was fired, Miles would have committed suicide then and there."

"What if Nita had not asked him to mix cocktails or had not gone to powder her face?" Strawn asked.

"The whole party was going to dine and dance at the Country Club. Miles would have escorted her home, as he had done on Monday night, when Nita had probably made her last demand. He could have counted on Nita's going into her bedroom to powder her face, even if he had had to tell her that her nose was shiny, and would himself then have gone to the dining room, on the excuse that he needed a drink before discussing 'business'.... But I must tell you that on Saturday morning, according to the telephone operator in Miles' office, into whom I put the fear of the Lord and the law when I interviewed her this morning, Nita rang Miles to say she must see him as soon as possible, her unexpressed intention being to tell him that she was not going to make him come across again. Miles—the telephone operator confessed to having listened-in on the Whole conversation—told her he would be right out, but Nita said she and Lydia were going into Hamilton and would not be back until 2:30—the time the bridge game was scheduled to begin. That was the opportunity Miles had been praying for, and he came on out, having previously stolen the gun and silencer and having studied this house—"

"How had he got in?" Sanderson wanted to know.

"Judge Marshall had lent him a key in February, when Miles wanted to show the house to an engaged young man in his offices, and Miles had neglected to return it.... Well, when he arrived, he found Ralph Hammond here, and had to leave, waiting at a safe distance, probably, until the coast was clear about one o'clock. Even so, he had more than an hour to do his carefully planned job.... *Nita had to die!* Miles could not continue to pay her large sums of money, since he was really only an employee of Flora's. Everything he held dear in the world was threatened. He loved Flora, he adored his children, and he could not give up the luxury and social position which his bigamous marriage with Flora——"

"Why didn't he make a clean breast of the whole mess to Flora, since he had not married her until he believed Nita Leigh was dead?" Sanderson interrupted.

"You must remember that Flora was carrying on a violent flirtation with Sprague—'vamping' him to get the lead in the Hamilton movie, if Sprague got the job of directing it," Dundee reminded him. "Miles, victim of a deep-rooted sexual inferiority complex, must have felt sure that Flora, on discovering she was not legally married, would snatch at the chance to marry Sprague— which was of course what Sprague had planned in case Nita published the truth."

"But you were wrong about the secret shelf! The gun was never there!" Strawn gloated.

"No. But it was the absence of fingerprints on the pivoting panel and shelf which kept me on the right track. Miles had searched the shelf for the marriage certificate which he could not know Nita had already burned. Probably, too, he had written her a few letters during their short courtship——"

"How was Sprague killed?" Sanderson interrupted impatiently.

Dundee led the way across the basement to a cubbyhole next to the coal room, entered and came out with a narrow, deep drawer of ebony inlaid with mother-of-pearl....

"First I must tell you that Miles got the gun out of the lamp that Saturday night, parking his car at a distance and sneaking into the house while I was talking with Lydia in the basement. We can guess that he stowed gun, silencer and electro-magnet in a pocket of his car. At any rate, he came back noisily enough a little later, to offer Lydia a job as nurse in his home. Doubtless he assured himself that she knew nothing, or poor Lydia would have gone the way of her mistress and Sprague."

"Was Sprague——?" Strawn began.

"Despite my warning," Dundee went on, refusing to be hurried, "Sprague made a demand for blackmail money

upon Miles. It is possible that Sprague, also sneaking into
the house that Saturday night to get his bag, saw Miles
retrieve the gun. At any rate, Sprague knew that Miles
was the only person among all the company who had a
real motive for killing Nita Selim, and he undoubtedly
blackmailed Miles as a murderer as well as a bigamist.
Perhaps Miles put him off for a day or two, but on
Wednesday Judge Marshall begged for a bridge game,
and Miles seized the opportunity of again having the
original crowd present—a sort of wall of integrity
surrounding and including him. For I don't think he
really wanted to involve his best friends as suspects. I
believe he merely wanted to hide among them—
apparently as above suspicion as they were. And there is
safety in numbers, you know.... At any rate, Miles made
an appointment Wednesday afternoon with Sprague,
telling him that, if he would come to his home that
evening, and manage to leave the bridge game while he
was dummy, he would find the money he was
demanding—*in a drawer of the cabinet that stood between
the two windows in the trophy room!*"

Dundee exhibited the drawer he had taken from the
basement tool room. "This drawer! I took it away from the
Miles home this afternoon while everyone but a
chambermaid was at the inquest. Miles did not have time
to go home before going to your office, Mr. Sanderson,
with the rest of the crowd you had summoned for
questioning. If he had, he would have killed himself as
soon as he found the incriminating drawer was missing
from the cabinet."

"But—*how*——?" Sanderson began, frowning with
bewilderment.

"Very simple!" Dundee answered. "When Sprague
pulled open this drawer, which was set in the cabinet at
just the height of his stomach, he received a bullet in his
heart.... See these four little holes?... A vise was screwed
into the bottom of the drawer so that it gripped the gun
with its silencer, at an upward angle. A piece of string

was tied to the trigger and fastened somehow to the underside of the drawer, so that when Sprague pulled the drawer open the string was drawn taut and the trigger pulled. Practically the same mechanism by which he tried to murder me.... The kick of the gun jerked the drawer shut. All Miles had to do when he was pretending to look for Sprague was to turn off the trophy room light by a button—one of a series on the outside wall of the hall closet. Probably it had been agreed between them that Sprague would not return to the bridge game, hence Sprague's telephoning for a taxi to wait for him at the foot of the hill, and his taking his hat and stick into the trophy room with him."

"Then Miles had from midnight till dawn to remove the gun!"

"Yes. Some time during the night, after Flora was asleep with a sedative, which she badly needed because of the quarrel—a genuine one—which she and Tracey had had over Sprague—Miles slipped down to the trophy room and removed the gun and vise. But he could not remove the holes the screws had made, although he did cover the bottom of the usually empty drawer with old pamphlets on the care and feeding of dogs.... By the way, the chambermaid told me that her master spent about half an hour before dinner that Thursday night in the trophy room, 'going over his fishing tackle'.... His next concern was to make the murder jibe completely with Captain Strawn's theory of a gunman who had trailed his quarry to the Miles home and shot him through the window. The window was already open, but the screen had to be raised, too, and Sprague's fingerprints had to be on the nickel catches by which the screen curtain is raised or lowered. Of course Sprague had not touched the screen——"

"Do you mean to say he lugged the corpse to the window and lifted it up so that he could press the stiff fingers upon the nickel catches?" Sanderson asked with a shudder. "What a fiend——"

"No," Dundee assured him. "That was unnecessary. He simply removed the curtain screen, which is so designed that it can be taken down and put up as easily as a window shade. He carried the screen—his own hands protected by gloves, I suppose—to where Sprague's right hand lay *palm upward*, on the floor, and pressed the thumb and forefinger against the catches, making fingerprints all right, but they were reversed—as I discovered when it occurred to me to examine the photographs of Sprague's fingerprints in Carraway's office today. Miles could not turn the stiff hand over without bruising the dead flesh; consequently the print of the forefinger was on the catch where the thumb would normally have left its mark—and vice versa.... Before I forget it, I should also tell you that I found a master key hanging on the keyboard in the butler's pantry. Big houses, with their many locks, are usually provided with a master key, and Miles undoubtedly used that one to gain entrance into my room after midnight Saturday morning."

"Where did you find the vise?" Strawn asked.

"In the tool chest right here, where he had also placed the reamer he had bought. The vise probably belonged to Miles originally, but he was taking no chances on anything's being found in his possession, provided we tumbled to *how* the two crimes were committed.... The reamer he must have brought out here after he used it to enlarge the hole in my hot-air register after midnight Sunday morning. It is possible he did his cleaning up job here at the same time. It was safe enough to have lights on, since the house is so isolated and there had been no guard here since Thursday."

"Well—" Sanderson drew a deep breath. "He was a far cleverer man than any of us suspected. The mechanical arrangements were absurdly easy to rig up, in all three cases, but the *thinking* of them——. It is a pity Nita did not fear him as she feared Sprague's vengeance——"

"You're right," Dundee answered. "Nita did not fear Miles, not even when she was making him pay and pay.... No woman could look at Miles and believe him capable of murder. But a conviction of sexual inferiority leads to strange things, as psychologists can tell you.... I believe Miles married the only two women who ever fell in love with him, and there can be no doubt that Nita really loved him, for she kept her wedding dress for more than twelve years and chose it to be her shroud. It is possible she was still fond of him, although she was infatuated with Sprague when she came down here and was later sincerely in love with Ralph Hammond. Another reason she did not fear Miles when she made her will was that she counted on being able to tell him Saturday night at the latest that she would never ask him for money again, if he would trade silence for silence. How she hoped to secure Sprague's silence we can only guess at. Probably she meant to buy it with the remainder of the $10,000 she had already got from Miles—provided Sprague did not kill her for ditching him as a lover. We know she foresaw that possibility, since she willed the money to Lydia. Of course if Sprague had proved tractable, Nita as Ralph's wife would have been able to compensate Lydia handsomely for the injury she had done her."

"Poor Nita—and poor Flora!" Sanderson sighed, as he led the way up the basement stairs. "Hello! Someone's calling you, Bonnie——"

Dundee ran through the kitchen and dining room and into the living room, for he had recognized Penny Crain's sweet, husky contralto.

"What are *you* doing back here, young woman?" he demanded. "You were told to go home and forget all this ugly business——"

"Dad wants a private word with you," Penny explained, her brown eyes luminous with happiness. "He's on the front porch.... And you ought to see Mother! She looks like a twenty-year-old bride!"

When Dundee joined him on the porch, Roger Crain flushed painfully but there was happiness in his eyes, too....

"Serena asked me to thank you for giving her Penny's message to pass on to me," Crain began in a low voice. "I'm sure you've guessed a lot, but what you probably don't know is that Serena used the securities I had sent her for safe keeping, to play the market with. When she knew what I had done here, she wouldn't let me touch a penny of the money until she had turned it into enough to clear up all my debts in Hamilton.... Then," and he sighed slightly, "she sent me home.... Not that I'm sorry. I'm going to try to make Margaret and Penny happy, make them and the town forget that I disgraced them——"

"Through?" Penny called from the doorway, and Bonnie Dundee forgot Tracey Miles and all his ingenious schemes.

THE END

The Black Pigeon

There were plenty of reasons for "Handsome Harry" Borden to be murdered. After all, he had cost numerous investors their life savings with questionable securities. And he had left his wife for a string of actresses and dancers, only to shed each in turn for a new flame. And the office boy that he had bullied. Not to mention the jealous boyfriend of his secretary to whom he had made unwanted advances. So there were plenty of suspects when was found dead of a gunshot wound in his office. The question is, which of them actually committed the crime?

One Drop of Blood

When Dr. Koenig, head of Mayfield Sanitarium is murdered, the District Attorney's Special Investigator, "Bonnie" Dundee must go undercover to find the killer. Were any of the inmates of the asylum insane enough to have committed the crime? Or, was it one of the staff, motivated by jealousy? And what was is the secret in the murdered man's past. Find the answer in . . . **One Drop of Blood**

AVAILABLE FROM RESURRECTED PRESS!

THE EDWARDIAN DETECTIVES
LITERARY SLEUTHS OF THE EDWARDIAN ERA

The exploits of the great Victorian Detectives, Poe's C. Auguste Dupin, Gaboriau's Lecoq, and most famously, Arthur Conan Doyle's Sherlock Holmes, are well known. But what of those fictional detectives that came after, those of the Edwardian Age? The period between the death of Queen Victoria and the First World War had been called the Golden Age of the detective short story, but how familiar is the modern reader with the sleuths of this era? And such an extraordinary group they were, including in their numbers an unassuming English priest, a blind man, a master of disguises, a lecturer in medical jurisprudence, a noble woman working for Scotland Yard, and a savant so brilliant he was known as "The Thinking Machine."

To introduce readers to these detectives, Resurrected Press has assembled a collection of stories featuring these and other remarkable sleuths in The Edwardian Detectives.

- The Case of Laker, Absconded by Arthur Morrison
- The Fenchurch Street Mystery by Baroness Orczy
- The Crime of the French Café by Nick Carter
- The Man with Nailed Shoes by R Austin Freeman
- The Blue Cross by G. K. Chesterton
- The Case of the Pocket Diary Found in the Snow by Augusta Groner
- The Ninescore Mystery by Baroness Orczy
- The Riddle of the Ninth Finger by Thomas W. Hanshew
- The Knight's Cross Signal Problem by Ernest Bramah

- The Problem of Cell 13 by Jacques Futrelle
- The Conundrum of the Golf Links by Percy James Brebner
- The Silkworms of Florence by Clifford Ashdown
- The Gateway of the Monster by William Hope Hodgson
- The Affair at the Semiramis Hotel by A. E. W. Mason
- The Affair of the Avalanche Bicycle & Tyre Co., LTD by Arthur Morrison

RESURRECTED PRESS CLASSIC MYSTERY CATALOGUE

Journeys into Mystery
Travel and Mystery in a More Elegant Time

The Edwardian Detectives
Literary Sleuths of the Edwardian Era

Gems of Mystery
Lost Jewels from a More Elegant Age

E. C. Bentley
Trent's Last Case: The Woman in Black

Ernest Bramah
Max Carrados Resurrected:
The Detective Stories of Max Carrados

Agatha Christie
The Secret Adversary
The Mysterious Affair at Styles

Octavus Roy Cohen
Midnight

Freeman Wills Croft
The Ponson Case
The Pit Prop Syndicate

J. S. Fletcher
The Herapath Property
The Rayner-Slade Amalgamation
The Chestermarke Instinct
The Paradise Mystery
Dead Men's Money

Fergus Hume
The Mystery of a Hansom Cab
The Green Mummy
The Silent House
The Secret Passage

Edgar Jepson
The Loudwater Mystery

A. E. W. Mason
At the Villa Rose

A. A. Milne
The Red House Mystery
Baroness Emma Orczy
The Old Man in the Corner

Edgar Allan Poe
The Detective Stories of Edgar Allan Poe

Arthur J. Rees
The Hampstead Mystery
The Shrieking Pit
The Hand In The Dark
The Moon Rock
The Mystery of the Downs

Mary Roberts Rinehart
Sight Unseen and The Confession

Dorothy L. Sayers
Whose Body?

Sir William Magnay
The Hunt Ball Mystery

Mabel and Paul Thorne
The Sheridan Road Mystery

Louis Tracy
The Strange Case of Mortimer Fenley
The Albert Gate Mystery
The Bartlett Mystery
The Postmaster's Daughter
The House of Peril
The Sandling Case: What Would You Have Done?
Charles Edmonds Walk
The Paternoster Ruby

John R. Watson
The Mystery of the Downs
The Hampstead Mystery

Edgar Wallace
The Daffodil Mystery
The Crimson Circle

Carolyn Wells
Vicky Van
The Man Who Fell Through the Earth
In the Onyx Lobby
Raspberry Jam
The Clue
The Room with the Tassels
The Vanishing of Betty Varian
The Mystery Girl
The White Alley
The Curved Blades
Anybody but Anne
The Bride of a Moment
Faulkner's Folly
The Diamond Pin
The Gold Bag
The Mystery of the Sycamore
The Come Backy

Raoul Whitfield
Death in a Bowl

And much more!
Visit ResurrectedPress.com
for our complete catalogue

About Resurrected Press

A division of Intrepid Ink, LLC, Resurrected Press is dedicated to bringing high quality, vintage books back into publication. See our entire catalogue and find out more at www.ResurrectedPress.com.

About Intrepid Ink, LLC

Intrepid Ink, LLC provides full publishing services to authors of fiction and non-fiction books, eBooks and websites. From editing to formatting, from publishing to marketing, Intrepid Ink gets your creative works into the hands of the people who want to read them. Find out more at www.IntrepidInk.com.

www.ingramcontent.com/pod-product-compliance
Lightning Source LLC
Chambersburg PA
CBHW071101250626
47159CB00002B/555